P9-DGB-554

# The Bubble Reputation

Also by Cathie Pelletier

*Widow's Walk* (Poems)

*The Funeral Makers*

*Once Upon a Time on the Banks*

*The Weight of Winter*

# The Bubble Reputation

*A Novel*

CATHIE PELLETIER

*Crown Publishers, Inc.*
*New York*

Grateful acknowledgment is made to EMI Music Publishing for permission to reprint from "In the Winter" by Janis Ian. © 1975 by Mine Music Ltd. Rights assigned to Toshiba-EMI Music Pub. Co. Ltd. All rights for the United States and Canada controlled and administered by EMI April Music Inc. All rights reserved. International copyright secured.



Published by Crown Publishers, Inc., 201 East 50th Street, New York, New York 10022. Member of the Crown Publishing Group
Random House, Inc., New York, Toronto, London, Sydney, Auckland
CROWN is a trademark of Crown Publishers, Inc.

Manufactured in the United States of America

Library of Congress Cataloging-in-Publication Data

Pelletier, Cathie.
The bubble reputation : a novel / Cathie Pelletier.
I. Title.
PS3566.F42B8 1993
813′.54—dc20 92-25447
CIP

ISBN 0-517-59311-4

10 9 8 7 6 5 4 3 2 1
First Edition

*For my sister* JOAN ST. AMANT
*who insisted that I remove a fictional possum*
*from this northern Maine setting.*
*(Audubon says that possums, at least the kinder, gentler ones, only*
*venture as far north as Kennebunkport.)*

*and for* JIM GLASER
*who has read this book, actually my second novel, in so many stages*
*over the years.*

*And who abides the stray animals,*
*and who loves the moths, the spiders, the trees,*
*the flowers, the snakes, the very stars*
*that hover over our oak-hickory forest.*

*And, as usual, for my parents:*
*Louis Allan Pelletier*
*and*
*Ethel Tressa O'Leary Pelletier*

**Acknowledgements and Special Thanks to:**

Patti Kelly, Beena Kamlani, Rhoda Weyr, Betty Prashker, and Irene Prokop.

Rosemary Kingsland, now at her Old Vicarage in Wales, who read this novel several years go, while living in the Tennessee yurt, and for whom I named Rosemary O'Neal.

Dr. Perry Harmon (who is nothing like the vet described in this story) for supplying needed information.

Dr. Diana K. Pelletier, who is (at last!) a full-fledged vet at Goodlettsville Animal Hospital.

Shawna Cathie O'Neal (and her daddy, Steve) for Rosemary's last name.

Paul, Sue, and Ashley Norris Gauvin, in memory of the migrating monarch butterflies.

Janis Ian, for helping me secure permission to quote from her wonderful song.

And to all the novelists and songwriters who accompany Jim Glaser and me each year on the now infamous Robert Altman Tour of Nashville.

In memory of Clubby, Winston, and Grady, old pets, old compadres, whose stories are partially told in this book.

To my friends and readers in northern Maine,* who continue to support me, and welcome me home.

Thanks to Carl Hileman, for painting *The Chinese Horse* for me.

Thanks to Benoit Michaud, all those college years ago, for planting the seeds of wild grasses on Winston's grave, and adding to the weight of this story.

And it's time, indeed, to pay attention to the memory of Harry Kimball, who was a superb dog.

*For those who may not know, northern Maine is not Bangor. It's not even Millinocket. Look for *Allagash* on the map. If it's not there, find *Fort Kent*. See what I mean? Now I won't have to explain anymore.

*Jealous in honour, sudden and quick in quarrel,*
*Seeking the bubble reputation,*
*Even in the cannon's mouth.*

—William Shakespeare,
"The Seven Ages of Man"

# The Cannon's Mouth

FOR THREE MONTHS after the funeral she refused to go back into the mainstream of laughing, talking, loving, hating people. She began to think of the world out there as a large department store where many mannequins interwove themselves. The mornings began with Mr. Coffee, and filling the feeders with seeds for the birds that were silhouetted in the hedges and along the dark tops of the trees. Even on the dull, overcast morning of the funeral she had made her sister, Miriam, her brother, Robbie, and her uncle, Bishop, wait in the car until all five feeders were loaded with sunflower seeds, millet, cracked corn, and hemp; and the long tubular feeder was filled with tiny black niger for when the delicate goldfinches finally arrived. "Because the birds are still alive," she said to Miriam, when asked about it. Even on the day of William's one and only funeral, she had not forgotten to feed the birds.

There was no easy way to settle into the big house alone. The immensity of it, all the extra, empty space was a cruel reminder of her singleness, the way a prisoner feels when he suddenly finds himself back on the outside. William *had* been gone a month before the telephone's ringing had broken through her sleep and brought her awake enough to hear the words, via satellite, from England, from William's good friend Michael. A sharp, sirenlike song in the black of night, the alarm sounded by a cornered bird, or a mourning mate sitting alone on a telephone wire. "Rosemary? I have some bad news about William."

He *had* been gone a month, but he was coming back. It was only what he called one of his *artistic binges,* a madcap dash across Europe to gaze longingly at Rembrandt, Van Gogh, Manet. All of them. Any of them. "He's off on another independent study," Rosemary told anyone who asked. That was one of the reasons William had never looked for a stable job. He needed the freedom that came with tending a neighborhood bar, driving a milk truck, painting someone's house, mowing the occasional lawn. He needed freedom because he loved the intimacy of setting up an easel before the likes of El Greco's *The Annunciation* and repainting it, as students do. Because it was his for the moment. Because he was sharing with El Greco, stroke by stroke, the painter's genius.

Postcards came often from the cities that claimed the paintings he loved. From Amsterdam came Van Gogh's self-portrait and Rembrandt's *Nightwatch.* From Madrid, *The Garden of Delights.* From Paris, Titians and Raphaels. Once, a card arrived from Spain of shadowy mountains and pastel blue skies. "I dreamed of Goya last night," it said, "and how he lay on his back in the Sierra Morena to fix the axle on the duchess of Alba's carriage." This was the secret of William's passion. He was not so much in love with *art* as he was with the frantic lives of its creators. The last postcard came bent at one corner, with curious stamps from Belgium, and was a reproduction of Brueghel's *The Fall of Icarus,* bearing the words *Today Brussels. Tomorrow?* It was an ironic ending to an erratic trail across centuries, down through painting styles, and visions, and visionaries.

But he *was* coming back to the big old house and the birds and the cats and Rosemary. They had given eight years to each other, with an annual hiatus for William's ramblings. She was almost certain he would be back. *Almost.* The truth was that his last departure had left her shaken. There was a kind of finality in the way he said good-bye, in his reluctance to let her hand slip away from his. And there were things he took along that were impractical: heavy art books, a Civil War bayonet belonging to a great-grandfather, a tiny photo album of the two of them during the happiest occasions. But he'd gone off again with his old college friend Michael, who sometimes went along on these artistic rages. Had she touched upon some foreknowledge of his impending death? Was that the prophetic aura of doom that seemed to hang over this last sojourn of his? Or had he simply made a decision to stay away?

In the month that he was gone, and he rarely stayed away longer, Rosemary read the numerous postcards that fluttered like colorful birds across the Atlantic, pinpointed their origins on her big, round globe, then left them to pile up on her desk. There was no need to worry about it. She would simply wait out an answer. William would face her with whatever had gone wrong between them when he was ready, if something *had* gone wrong. So she went on discussing Coleridge and Wordsworth and Keats and Shelley with her high school students. She went about trying to get teenagers to understand melancholy and despair, to grasp hold of sudden hope and inspiration in an age of neon clothing, street gangs, and cocaine lunches. That William would die and take his answers to her questions with him had caught her completely unawares. It had happened quickly, a sharp, cutting sound in the night. It was Michael, crying: "He's committed suicide, Rosemary."

And now there was no more William upon the planet. No more combination of brain cells, and tissue, and muscle, and bone that made up William the man. Michael? She had only met Michael twice, and briefly, when he passed through and had needed one of their extra bedrooms for the night. He was quiet, intelligent, an art student with William at the University of Maine. But Michael, unlike William, had given up dreams of finding his own canvases hanging on the walls of world museums. He worked, instead, for his father in one of those small but successful family businesses. The day might come when she would have to go to Michael for the answers about William's last emotional leanings. In case he knew. In the meantime, she went quietly to pieces, alone, in the house of many rooms and long, quiet hallways. "The Spruce Goose," William had called it.

The family rained in on her at first with solemn faces, words of hope, and far too many casseroles. She let them have their way for a few days, let the funeral come and go. William's body came back from England to *New* England, across the ocean his ancestors had sailed centuries before, to Maine, "Vacationland," the land of colors and shadows and shapes that William never grew to love. "Maine just doesn't do it for me," he had said a thousand times. "The tourists can have it."

Throughout the funeral she let the family coddle and protect and force themselves upon her in the form of company she didn't want. But once it was over, she emphatically informed them that she was leaving her teaching job, was going to squander her nest egg, was backpacking into the caverns of the big house as though it were a cave. She would nurse herself. She would heal her own wounds. She would begin a quiet rearranging of life's notions.

For two weeks she cried endlessly. The sight of almost every *thing* in the house, however loosely connected to William, would set her off. Once, when she went on a mad cleaning binge and was vacuuming behind a trunk in an upstairs room, the nozzle made a clinking sound. When she pushed the trunk aside, she found a Papermate pen. But it wasn't the pen that upset her. It was the glitter of a tiny, garnet earring, half-hidden in the dust balls, an earring with her birthstone on it, given to her by William several years before. It would have been swallowed up by the vacuum and forgotten had it not been for the pen. Rosemary dropped to her knees by the trunk, the earring clutched in her hand so tightly it left red marks when she opened her palm to look at it. The tiny red garnet had sparkled, pulsating as though it were the beating heart of some delicate creature. She wondered where the mate to it was at that very moment. Hadn't she lost it on some picnic? Or a school outing that involved a softball game? It had been ages ago, was all she could remember, and that she had grieved at losing it. William had thought so long and hard on what to get her that year before he'd decided on fragile little gold earrings, with garnet stones, for Rosemary, who wore no jewelry. Sweet, thoughtful, *impractical* William, the kind of person who bought cat food only if he himself liked the flavor. "No, Seafood Buffet just isn't what I feel like tonight," he would say to Rosemary as he put the can back on the shelf. Rosemary knew he picked the earrings out because of the artist in him, because they suddenly burst onto his corneas as little red berries. Chiseled angles. Precise shapes. She had turned the single earring over and over in her hand. After a long cry in the large room facing the road, the one William chose most frequently as the room in which to paint, the room that was most William, she went downstairs and put the earring on a can in the kitchen. And for nights after, when she dreamed of him, she saw him standing near the sink, next to the little earring she had left on the top of a coffee can filled with wheat-back pennies.

Nights were the hardest. During the day she kept busy by grooming the cats, studying her bird guidebooks, trying out an occasional new birdseed from her catalog. She ordered many things through the mail. It became her main source of contact with the world out there. She joined numerous book clubs and received, once, for joining, a set of Gibbon's *Decline and Fall of the Roman Empire* for $29.95. The first volume stayed on the coffee table for three weeks until she dusted it off and slid it onto the shelf with the other six. She ordered flower bulbs and magazines and kitchen gadgets. She bought a Japanese bonsai tree in a small glass bowl, then forgot about it in one of the upstairs windows. She clipped dozens of coupons out of magazines for pennies off on paper towels, egg rolls, tea bags, and a variety of other products she rarely used. *In case she fell on hard times.* She ordered her groceries from Laker's Food Store because they delivered for a small fee. She left an occasional note in the mailbox with a five-dollar bill, so that the postman would leave her a book of stamps. Her car collected dust in the garage.

It occurred to her she might never need the external world again. She ate simple meals, a cream-of-something soup, cheese, a lettuce-and-tomato sandwich, a handful of pecans or walnuts, seasonal fruit, and fixed a small pot of tea inside a cozy, a slice of lemon on her saucer. Simple, quiet affairs, most unlike the boisterous lunches with William, who rarely sat still at the table for more than a minute.

Her physical appearance changed little. She had always maintained a minimum of fashion, usually wore jeans, flannel shirts, tennis shoes, sweaters, unless the occasion demanded something a bit more formal, and avoided occasions that demanded something *very* formal. Makeup involved a $4.50 tube of dark brown mascara and a $3.89 tube of wine-colored lipstick, if she wore any makeup at all. The shoulder-length brown hair hadn't changed since her college days, except for three or four strands of grayish white coming to the bangs. It hung freely in its natural wave, or went up into a ponytail if she was busy working with her hands. "You're one of those women who will be even more attractive at forty and fifty," William once told her, but now he would never find out if that was true. She lost ten pounds but had always considered herself a bit overweight, so she didn't mind when the scales turned up one day with new numbers. Some dark circles developed under her eyes from a lack of proper sleep but, all in all, her appearance changed little.

All through the long evenings she sat out on the swing with one or both of the cats asleep at her feet, or sniffing about the corners of the porch. She watched the birds feed until they drifted off to their night roosts, until just the cardinals, and one or two house sparrows, or the white-throated sparrow, were left behind. Then, just she and the cardinals and the cats, until those birds were gone, too, off into the hedges and trees and fields for the night. She usually brought a glass of wine out to the swing after dinner, around eight or nine o'clock, and sat sipping it and staring at the craters on the moon with her binoculars. The next major purchase she made, she decided, would be a powerful telescope, and she would buy one of those books called *Astronomy Made Simple.*

The first two months there had been a river of wine. Only Robbie, who'd been asked to deliver it for her by the case, knew just how much wine. But even at those times he was not invited inside. He stood, uncomfortable on her front porch, a hand holding open the screen door until he finally hugged her, let the door slam behind him, and went off, back into the world, back into the swirl of the marketplace. But after drinking herself to sleep for two months, she began to taper off on the wine, except for those especially cruel nights that still crept in on her. Except for those incredibly long nights when she could even smell the sweet smell of William among the extra blankets, among his shirts still in the closet. Those nights when she'd come wide awake with his name half-formed between tongue and teeth; except for *those* nights, a glass of wine after dinner and one before bedtime would pull her through. She'd sip the wine slowly, her knees cradling an opened book, in the big cherry-wood bed William had found at an auction in Canada for $18.95. "See how it's fit together by grooves?" he bragged the day he came home with it piled in the back of Uncle Bishop's pickup. He had rubbed the wood with linseed oil until it gleamed. "It's worth hundreds. They don't make these anymore." But now she knew that there were lots of things they didn't make anymore, as she sat in the antique bed with her knees pulled up, with one of her old college books, and relearned many of the things she had paid a tuition to learn, but had forgotten. And she relearned herself, whom she thought she knew, but didn't. She'd had a jolt to the nervous system. Like a patient who undergoes shock treatment and sits up on the table alone to ask, "Where am I? Who am I?" she came awake one day and didn't know Rosemary O'Neal, aged thirty-three, teacher, lover of cats *and* birds, single, childless, and, except for a mother gone insane, an orphan.

At first she had kept the family at bay by lying to them. Each time the phone rang during her three months of re-collecting herself, Rosemary turned the typewriter on, held the receiver down to the keys, and then punched a few at random. "I'll phone you back," she told the caller. "I'm in the middle of writing a letter." Then she hung up the phone, turned the typewriter off, and went back to the pair of binoculars that brought the rufous-sided towhee up so close she could see its delicate, frantic breathing. "Nobody, not even Dear Abby, writes that many letters!" Uncle Bishop finally shouted after weeks of never being phoned back. "You're lying to us!" So the family gathered together in a huddle and decided her time was up.

Uncle Bishop appeared first, in his little blue Datsun. Rosemary watched him from behind the curtains until he tired of knocking and disappeared back down Old Airport Road. Miriam was second up at bat, turning up on the porch one day with a chocolate cake, catching Rosemary by surprise. "There will be, hard as it is to believe, another man in your life," said Miriam, divorced three times, restless with a fourth husband, eyeing the possibility of a fifth. Miriam had seen three husbands disappear into the world as neatly as if into coffins. Miriam, giving advice. And then came Robbie, soft, creative, malleable Robbie. "I miss William, too," Robbie said one evening, when Rosemary finally let him inside the door.

They went out to the backyard swing to watch the last of the late feeders peck about the dried grass. The blaring, male-red cardinal with its conical beak, perfect for cracking seeds, was in its head-forward display, wings fluttering to drive off the female. "Any day now, during courtship, he'll give her seeds from his beak," Rosemary had said. "It's called mate feeding." And she wondered why the male cardinal couldn't, by nature, treat his mate as if it were always spring. Why couldn't he bring himself, in the bluish cold of January, to thrust a frozen little seed from his beak into hers?

"I miss him, too," Robbie said. The evening had gathered in around them as they watched the fat cats climb up and down the rick of firewood stacked along the back fence. "But it's time you came back to us." And so she pulled down most of what she had put up. It was as easy as that, after three long, hard months.

"The birds are still alive," Rosemary said, as she had on the day of William's funeral. With Robbie's smooth hand in hers she rubbed it until the fine gold hairs stood up about his knuckles. "*We're* still alive." And it was the first time she realized it herself, that for whatever reason, no matter how just or unjust, there was a small round organ inside her, receiving blood from the veins and pumping it through the arteries. Dilating and contracting. And there was a mass of nerve tissue in her cranium receiving sensory impulses and transmitting motor impulses. She was alive. Robbie was alive. So they went, an arm around the other's waist, into her big rambling house with the wide, airy rooms and full windows that took in all the light. "Levels of consciousness," William had said of that light. Robbie and Rosemary went up the back steps where the bowls of food and water had been set out for the cats. They went inside and left the last of the dusk feeders moving quietly among the scattered seeds and doughnut scraps.

There would be a dinner the very next evening. It would represent her *coming out* and back into the society of the family. She would be a debutante, stripping away her black mourning clothes to discover that gossamer wings had sprouted beneath. Robbie would inform the family. He would tell Uncle

Bishop, the family's sense of humor. He would escort Mother, their insanity rolled into one person. He would alert Miriam, all the blunders a family could possibly make. Robbie, the baby of the family, would let them know that there would be a spaghetti-and-wine dinner the next evening in Rosemary's big old mushroom of a house. And Rosemary, the family's glue, the old adhesive Rosemary, would officiate. She would abandon her plans to grow old alone while feeding countless stray cats and wild birds, while letting the gray come rapidly into her hair, and then letting the hair itself go wild. She would not, after all, become a *crazy* old woman, wearing five or six dresses at a time, chanting remedies and searching for herbs along the crags and barren hedges. She would not become a *dangerous* woman, full of secrets, full of early reasons for her craziness. Rosemary would put aside the image of William lying dead in a rented room in London, a suicide among the paints and canvases, his blood spread out on the floor as though it were a new color he was experimenting with. There would be a family dinner and Rosemary, she promised, would put all these pictures and questions neatly away in order to make the salad.

# The Children's Hour

WHEN SHE HEARD Uncle Bishop's familiar thrumping on the door, Rosemary flicked on the porch light. From his stance on the front steps, Uncle Bishop was shouting out into the rainy night at Miriam, who had, he was informing her, bummed her last ride from him. Rosemary opened the screen door and waited.

"Get yourself a bicycle!" Uncle Bishop shouted from the porch. Miriam was still in the pickup, searching in her purse for a rain scarf. "Get a goddamn horse, as the kids say!"

"I see some things haven't changed," said Rosemary. Uncle Bishop glowered as he shook rain from his umbrella. He hung it from the coatrack and then stretched a big arm out to circle her neck. "What are you two fighting about now?"

"Medusa wanted to get under my umbrella," Uncle Bishop explained. "She's afraid of getting her snakes wet. But there was just room enough for me and *this.*" He nodded to the pot of homemade spaghetti sauce in the crook of his arm.

"I've missed that sauce of yours," said Rosemary, and held the door open as he stomped past her and into the foyer.

"It's good to see you like this again," Uncle Bishop said. In among the strands of his thinning hair, rain sparkled in little drops. He had worn his usual drawstring pants, tied tightly about his heavy belly, and an *extra-large* sweatshirt, which was still too small. As he pulled off his galoshes Rosemary saw that all he was wearing inside them were some thick, woolly socks, which were supposed to be white, but were more a yellowish gray.

"Don't ask where his shoes are," said Miriam, scaling the top step of the porch, her red hair flattened beneath a plastic scarf. She eased past Rosemary and then kicked her shoes off on the inside rug. "It's a long and overly sordid story, even for him." She dramatically checked her cigarettes and, assured that they were still dry, gave Rosemary her coat.

"You might start by saying hello," Rosemary said.

"I can't believe you finally asked us over," said Miriam. "Bishop has been referring to this place as the Gulag Archipelago. Weren't you, Bishop?" Uncle Bishop—Miriam never referred to him as *Uncle*—ignored her as she tapped a cigarette out of its pack, popped it into her mouth, and then rummaged one hand in her purse.

"Robbie and Mother are already here," Rosemary told them. "Robbie's building us a nice fire."

"I know I've got matches in here somewhere," Miriam declared. She quit rummaging.

"I'll get you some from the kitchen," Rosemary offered, and Miriam followed her out into the hall. Uncle Bishop disappeared into the den.

"He's getting worse," Miriam whispered. "You should see the little boyfriend he's got now. They have shoe fights. That's why he's not wearing any. He's thrown them all." Then, for Uncle Bishop's benefit, she said loudly, "It *is* good to see you looking so well."

"I *heard* that, Miriam," Uncle Bishop shouted from the den. Rosemary smiled. Uncle Bishop knew from experience, as they all did, that when Miriam raised her voice unnaturally to say something bouncy, it was because she had previously lowered it to say something scandalous.

"She reminds me of a dolphin when she raises that voice of hers," Rosemary heard Uncle Bishop telling Robbie. "She's not as *smart* as a dolphin. She just sounds like one."

"Homosexual shoe fights," Miriam whispered. She accepted a book of matches from Rosemary. "What will he do next?"

It had been a long time since Rosemary had seen so many people in her house. William had been present for the last family gathering and now he was conspicuously absent. Only Mother wouldn't notice.

"Doesn't she look good?" Rosemary asked, patting Mother's little hand. Robbie had driven Mother over from Aunt Rachel's and now she sat in her rocker and rocked back and forth in a dazed frenzy, all the little blond curls on her head bobbing up and down like daffodils. The rocker had made the trip in the backseat of the car; Mother would rock in no other chair but her own.

"She can't tell night from day," Miriam said, a neat halo of smoke now above her head. She was watching Mother in earnest. "How the hell does she know which is her rocker?"

"She knows," said Rosemary. Mother rocked serenely.

"And why doesn't Aunt Rachel just hide her makeup?" Miriam asked. "She's even got lipstick on her *teeth.*" Mother stopped rocking to eye Miriam with a vague curiosity. Her cheeks were red circles of rouge, and under a layer of thick lipstick her mouth appeared rubbery.

"You'll wonder where the yellow went," Mother promised, "when you brush your teeth with Pepsodent."

"If you ask me," Miriam continued, "Aunt Rachel is almost as batty." Rosemary encouraged Mother's rocker to begin again, slowly, its steady rock. Rocking calmed her greatly.

"We've been lucky to have Aunt Rachel," said Rosemary. It was true. Aunt Rachel had never married, and after a long career at Bixley's hospital as a nurse she had retired early to look after Mother. By that time, Mother's illness had progressed to stages where nonprofessionals were helpless. So Aunt Rachel moved Mother into her home, the old family homestead, and was taking excellent care of her.

"You didn't forget my box of chocolates, did you?" Mother asked Robbie. She no longer knew their names. Like the dolls she had once owned and loved and named in childhood, Mother had forgotten her children. The rocking chair stopped abruptly until Robbie assured her that there would soon be chocolates. Then Mother went back to her automatic rocking.

"Good!" she said, scolding. "I like soft chocolates with my cup of tea."

"Talk about soft," whispered Uncle Bishop. "If brains were marshmallow."

"Now, if *I* said that," Miriam suggested to Rosemary, "you'd have a conniption. But it's okay for Bishop to say what he likes."

"I'm her little brother," said Bishop. And so he was, the

little brother by fourteen years. "I'm the baby of the family, and let me tell you this. If ever a sad cabal deserved to weep on 'Donahue,' it's the babies of nuclear families. We're automatic members of the petite bourgeoisie."

"Babies," scoffed Miriam. "He's forty-eight years old, weighs three hundred pounds, and he still thinks of himself as a *baby*. That's just too sick."

Rosemary watched as Mother canted forward, suspended, rocked backward, and then canted again. The family had grown into Mother's illness the way one grows into all of life's surprises, at first with denial, and then with bleak acceptance. Only Miriam still found the gaping hole between Mother and reality an unfathomable one. Sometimes, Rosemary almost envied Mother's neat little world, where dimensions were bent to one's own specifications, where laws of nature were changed at a whim.

Mother rocked on. Uncle Bishop tugged at Robbie's earlobe and said, "You get better looking every day, kiddo." Robbie went into a mock boxing stance, fists up to cover his face. He battered Uncle Bishop about the stomach and temples with pretend lefts and rights and uppercuts.

"I'll have none of that in my house!" Mother shouted. She bounded up out of her chair, the daffodil curls twitching dramatically.

"There," said Rosemary, her hand lightly on Mother's shoulder, easing her back into the rocker. "They're only playing." Miriam opened a new pack of cigarettes.

"I need another book of matches," she said. "The one you gave me had only two in it."

"We were hoping you'd smoke only two cigarettes," Uncle Bishop said. "Instead of two packs."

Rosemary went up the narrow stairway, down the hall, and finally found a book of matches in the drawer of William's desk. She smiled when she read BAMBI'S DINE-IN OR TAKE-AWAY printed neatly on the cover. Leave it to William to find the tiniest, greasiest, out-of-the-way places. But after he'd dragged her down there to meet the proprietor—always with a name like Bambi or Prince or Miss Tootsie—it was usually Rosemary who kept going back. "I think you just like the newness of things and places," she had often told him. "I think you get to know people so that you can paint them, William. Once you have their soul on canvas, you no longer care. The art transcends the human being."

With the matches in her hand, with another sharp memory of William coursing through her, Rosemary stood outside the door to the den and listened. She hadn't been sure that she was ready to take the family on alone, without William there for balance. As a group, they were like some big wallowing mutt, an Old English sheepdog, its head and paws too large for a small room, uncontrollable in its leaps and bounds. Things could easily get broken. But William had loved her family, studied them, rejoiced in them, painted them. "Van Gogh would've adored those yellow ringlets," he had said of Mother's curls. "They look just like the stars in *Starry Night*. I've never met people so proud to be crazy."

"When is Father getting here?" Mother asked. Rosemary passed the book of matches to Miriam and found a seat on the sofa next to Uncle Bishop. Robbie flopped into the recliner and dangled a leg over the side. He had cut his short hair even shorter, and now the white of his scalp gleamed along the hairline. Good, clean-cut looks, back in style now. He was twenty-six, well muscled from the weights he lifted, a runner who logged thirty miles every five-day week. The new breed.

"I *said* when is Father getting here?" Mother pounded the arm of her rocker. No one answered her, hoping she would forget she had asked the question and eventually go on, into one of the other disheveled rooms of her mind. But Mother had stuck to the thought, had caught it by the wings as though it were a little bug, and held on. "By God, I want to know!" she thundered.

"In twenty minutes," said Rosemary. "He just called."

"That's more like it," Mother sniffed. She rubbed her nose, getting a little of the lipstick on her sweater sleeve.

"Doesn't she look like the cutest little doll?" Uncle Bishop asked lovingly. "What do you suppose she thinks of all day long?" He had propped both woolly feet up on Rosemary's coffee table and was staring at Mother the way one stares at an interesting pet.

"Why don't you bleach those socks, Bishop?" asked Miriam. She had not—she whispered to Rosemary—recovered from the hair-raising ride over in Uncle Bishop's little blue Datsun. "Even that pickup is deranged," Miriam had said, the day Uncle Bishop bought the Datsun and insisted on taking the entire family, one by one, for an unforgettable first ride. "It reminds me of one of those cars we used to see on 'The Twilight Zone.' He rarely bothers to steer."

"I don't bleach my socks, Miriam," said Uncle Bishop, "because I assume that all of the bleach in the free world has gone onto your hair."

"Please," said Rosemary. "Don't the two of you start." Years before, Miriam had developed a mental block about the true color of her hair.

"I do not bleach my hair!" Miriam screamed.

"You were a brunette at your high school graduation," Uncle Bishop noted, and then loosened the drawstring on his pants. Rosemary smiled. No matter how childish, how petty, how crazy the family was, it was wonderful to see them all again, all under one roof.

"I'm glad we're all together again," she said softly.

"I don't have the gums anymore for hard chocolates," Mother announced.

Uncle Bishop went off into the kitchen to put his sauce on to simmer. Rosemary had the dining room table ready with her best china and silver. All the linen napkins were fluffed in their rings. The tapered candles were a rose color, to match the roses in the centerpiece. Robbie had picked up the flowers at Bixley's only floral shop. Rosemary hated buying them. In less than a month, her backyard would be ablaze with blooms of all kinds.

Uncle Bishop stood in the kitchen doorway and banged a wooden spoon against the casing to rally the diners before him.

"And Julia Child has the audacity to call that slop she serves *food?* Come, children. Tomorrow the headlines will read: *Bishop Makes Julia Weep.*" Uncle Bishop loved sputtering about with a messy spoon, in some ghastly apron splattered with colorful blotches, some of which had nothing at all to do with food. Rosemary was thankful that the sauce had been prepared on his own stove and not hers. She imagined the little daisies on his kitchen wallpaper bespattered that very minute with tomato puree.

They gathered around the big rectangular table in the dining room, another auction treasure. It was the first time Rosemary had eaten in the huge room, upon the shiny oak table, since the news of William. It was just too immense. She felt as though she were Lily Tomlin in *The Incredible Shrinking Woman,* trying to pull a heavy chair up to a giant's table. On the wall hung a painting William had done a few years before. It was a work Rosemary dearly loved, a reproduction of *The Chinese Horse,* a cave painting found deep in the Lascaux caves in France. During dinners with William the candlelight had touched upon the delicate, simple horse, wavered across the canvas, causing those primitive muscles to ripple.

"I've said it before and I'll say it again," said Miriam, as the family took their places around the table. "That's the worst horse I've ever seen. A child could do better than that." Uncle Bishop spooned sauce over the plates of spaghetti, which Robbie placed before them.

"Miriam prefers paint-by-number things," he explained, as Rosemary brought the garlic bread to the table. "She understands composition better when dealing with clowns and the enlarged heads of cocker spaniels."

"At least I don't throw shoes at members of the same sex," said Miriam. She squashed her Virginia Slim into the ashtray and then handed it to Rosemary for disposal.

"Shoes?" asked Robbie. Rosemary gave him a fast little look.

"Has your wine breathed enough, Robbie?" she asked. He forgot about shoes and went out to the kitchen for the wine.

"If I know Robbie," said Uncle Bishop, "once his wine has breathed, it will want to eat."

"Where's Father?" Mother shouted. Like an unhappy prisoner, she banged her fork on the table.

"I can't believe she's back to Father," Rosemary said, taking the fork before any damage was done to the oak. "She's getting better and better at retaining a thought." She placed the fork in Mother's spaghetti, encouraged her to hold it, hoping something new would take possession of her mind, a different swarm of bugs. It worked. Mother smiled and said, "I'm very, very hungry."

"She's brilliant all right," said Miriam. "I wonder if Mondale is still looking for a female running mate." Robbie poured the wine. It was a French table wine, red, called Partager.

"It means *to share,*" said Robbie, and raised his glass for a toast. The others did the same, except for Mother. "Here's to our family." He put Mother's hand to her glass, helped her curl her little fingers around it.

"Here's to the family," said Rosemary.

"The family," said Uncle Bishop. Miriam drank along with the toasts, but did not propose one herself. The family was a society she rejoiced in only if she needed it. In the candlelight her hair gleamed as red as Mother's did yellow.

"They look like pansies, don't they?" Uncle Bishop leaned over and whispered to Rosemary.

"I just don't like hard chocolates with my tea," Mother stated honestly. She had guzzled her wine. "Too hard on the gums," she added, and then smiled her big red smile at Rosemary, a stranger to her.

Rosemary felt the little panic rising up again, that urge to wish Mother normal. She stared instead at *The Chinese Horse,* fought the panic off. If she didn't, when the panic went away it would leave remorse behind. Rosemary had lived through it all many times before. The problem with Mother began long ago. Nine years. Ten years. She'd been cleaning the outside kitchen window and had fallen from the stepladder. What was lost when she came to, days later, was her ability to retain new memory. And she remembered only hit-and-miss sketches of the past. All life became new to her, over and over again. New happiness. New loss. Perpetually. To tell her that Father, her husband, had died twenty-some years earlier was to no avail. She merely resuffered the pain and then, a short time later, could no longer remember he was dead. Miriam had much less patience with her than Rosemary, who tried to sidetrack her with candy, a television program, a magazine, until Mother at last forgot that she had even asked the question about Father.

This memory loss happened to many people, Rosemary was surprised to learn, and they had managed to go about life effectively, to hold jobs, raise a family, have hobbies. It was hard work for them, but it *could* be done. Yet Mother's problem was more than just the terrible brain malfunction. Her emotional instabilities had cropped up years earlier, before the fall. Rosemary remembered days of coming home from school to find Mother wrapped in a blanket, in the heat of June, sobbing in an upstairs room. "We're all going to die someday," was the only excuse Mother could offer. When Father finally did die, the year Rosemary turned ten, Mother experienced her first real wash of craziness. "His heart," she said of the organ that had killed her husband, "must have known what was best." But she never really pulled out of the low dive his death had thrust her in. She cried often, and was forgetful. Scatterbrained, at best. The family had learned to deal with it simply as Mother's ups and downs. But the woman who emerged from the hospital two years after Father's death, after the fall, could hardly be called *forgetful.* She had gone from scatterbrained to Mad Hatter. Robbie barely remembered her as anything but crazy. Miriam remembered nothing more than embarrassment in front of her teenaged friends. "Personally, I think she jumped," Miriam said often of the stepladder incident. Rosemary had been so caught up in losing Father that when she finally came around to ask questions, Mother was gone, too. In her place was a woman who wanted nothing more from her children than the courtesy one receives from strangers when meeting them on the street, when dining with them in the same restaurant, and plenty, plenty of soft chocolates.

In Rosemary's lovely dining room, upon the old oak table, the family ate dinner and mentioned everyone and everything but William. She was thankful. The suicide was not a subject she wanted brought up, something to be discussed as minutes of the meeting. She saw a great irony in the fact that William was the only person with whom she could discuss such a delicate issue.

"I'm a homicide away from doing something to Mrs. Abernathy," Uncle Bishop said, and passed the garlic bread to Rosemary, who took a buttered piece and passed it on to Robbie. "She's threatening to have Ralph shot if he comes near her bird feeder again."

"Can't you just keep him away?" asked Rosemary.

"But Ralphie's a tomcat," Uncle Bishop explained sadly. "He's already sprayed the daylights out of that tray feeder, and now he thinks it's his."

"I've never heard of anything so ridiculous," Miriam hooted.

"Miriam knows what spraying is, don't you, Miriam?" Uncle Bishop said. "I've seen your husbands dripping at the altar." He forked a large spool of spaghetti into his mouth. Miriam snatched her garlic bread away from Mother, who had reached a tiny hand out to steal it. "Personally, I think Ralphie is getting the raw end of this deal," Uncle Bishop continued. "He's even blamed for the dead birds Mrs. Abernathy sees along the road, miles from the house."

"Did I get a letter from Aunt Sophie?" Mother asked suddenly, her little clown face redder than ever beneath its yellow, hatlike hair. There was a short silence as Robbie, Rosemary, Miriam, and Uncle Bishop thought about her question. Robbie was the one to finally ask.

"Who in hell is Aunt Sophie?"

"You always do the dishes when we're at your house," Rosemary said to Uncle Bishop. "Just take Mother in by the fire and I'll cram everything into the dishwasher." Mother was absorbed in *The Chinese Horse.* She cocked her little yellow head to one side, like a goldfinch, and squinted her tiny eyes at the painting.

"Just what *did* happen to Mr. Ed?" Mother asked Uncle Bishop, gazing up at his face, a child looking up at an adult.

"He's trying to break into movies," said Uncle Bishop, and Mother seemed pleased to hear that an old friend was doing well. She let Uncle Bishop lead her down to the empty rocker in the den.

Miriam offered to help and followed Rosemary to the kitchen with water glasses and a handful of forks. Rosemary suspected something else. It had been three months since Miriam had griped to her about the family, about her own life's problems.

"I seriously think Bishop is trying to turn Robbie toward gaiety," said Miriam, rinsing the glasses.

"Gaiety?" asked Rosemary.

"You know," said Miriam. "Gayhood. Gaydom. Gayness. Whatever noun they use for that kind of lifestyle."

"Uncle Bish?" Rosemary shook her head at the nonsense. "Don't be silly. Uncle Bishop is a good leveling force on Robbie."

"Rosemary, he's in love with a man who *wears dresses*. You didn't know that, did you? Well, there's a lot that's happened during your little vacation." Rosemary looked evenly at her sister. *Little vacation*. In Miriam's mind, getting over William's death was as easy as sunning in the Bahamas. "He has to go out of state to find them," Miriam continued. "There aren't a lot of that kind in Maine, you know. At least not north of Bangor."

"Robbie's an intelligent adult," Rosemary said. She turned on the garbage disposal. "He knows what's best for himself."

"That's where you're wrong," said Miriam. Rosemary handed her a crystal water glass and Miriam feigned searching for a dish towel in one of the kitchen drawers. Miriam never *found* a dish towel because she chose to look in every drawer but the correct one. Miriam didn't *want* to find a dish towel. "I worry that those are the only role models Robbie has."

"Robbie is twenty-six years old," said Rosemary. "Not four. And try to remember that Mother has been one of his role models."

"All right then," Miriam said. She wrapped aluminum foil about the last of the bread. "Don't say I didn't warn you. If Robbie turns up one day in a skirt and a cashmere sweater, don't look at *me*."

"Is cashmere still in style?" Rosemary asked. She finished loading her wear-and-tear dishes into the washer, and then pushed the start button. Inside, the dishes clinked happily. The dishwasher had been a contribution to the household from William, evidence of a lucrative summer along the coast, near Mount Desert Island, selling quick sketches of Maine's ocean, lobster traps, and gnarled fishermen to tourists. Those lucrative summers, however, had been sparse. Rosemary had taken her summer salary in a lump sum that year and bought the clothes washer and dryer. But the noisy dishwasher had been William's gift to the big old house, and even the watery sound of it at work saddened her.

"Where does Bishop get his money, anyway?" Miriam went on. "That's what I'd like to know. He hasn't worked in years. In fact, I can't remember him ever working. Yet he has plenty of money. Where does he get it, Rosemary? Do you think he's involved in some sort of porno racket with homosexuals?"

"I *heard* that, Miriam," Uncle Bishop yelled from the den.

❧ ❧ ❧

In the living room Mother beckoned to Robbie for more wine. Then she held the glass tightly in her two little hands and rocked back and forth in her rocking chair. Miriam sat in the recliner, her plump legs crossed, and readjusted the thirty pounds she'd been threatening for years to lose.

"Where's Raymond?" asked Robbie.

"Looking at some land along the coast," Miriam answered. She and Raymond met at a "Get Rich Through Real Estate" seminar and had fallen head over heels into buying land at dirt-cheap prices, dividing it into plots, and then selling it to anyone who would give them money for it. "We're going to erect some condos," she added.

*"Condoms?"* Uncle Bishop inquired. "You say you're going to erect some condoms, Miriam? You should be good at that."

"Raymond thinks it'll develop nicely," Miriam said smugly.

"Miriam and Raymond are selling the state of Maine to New York City," Uncle Bishop warned the listeners. "Mark my words. We'll get up one morning and see a big arm sticking up in the air, holding a torch."

" ''Tis the last rose of summer,' " Mother sang out loudly, " 'left blooming alone.' " She curled one foot to still the rocker. "Where's Aunt Sophie's piano?" she asked. Rain hit against the big, churchlike windows of the house. Rosemary heard Mugs the cat scratching on the back door and went to let him in.

"It's really coming down out there," she told them, hoping to speed up the good-byes. She needed to take this reacquaintance thing slowly. Mother rubbed her little red cheeks and yawned loudly.

"I'd better drive her home," said Robbie. "Aunt Rachel will be waiting up." He touched Mother's arm lightly.

"Hey, mister," Mother said, gingerly, her little eyes locked on her son. "You got any money?"

"I'll catch a ride home with you, Robbie," said Miriam, who had refused to drive again after an accident she'd had ten years earlier. "The year I hit the ice cream truck was the year I turned thirty," she liked to note, as though that chronological fact were connected in some cosmic way to her bad driving.

"Miriam's mad because I won't let her smoke in my Datsun," said Uncle Bishop. "I don't know why she just doesn't quit. A cigarette is the dirtiest thing you can put in your mouth."

"And this from a *homosexual,*" said Miriam. "Go figure." She found her plastic rain hat in her purse and unfolded it. Mother was already at the door, peering out intently at the rainy night.

"That damn bus," Mother said, when she felt Rosemary put a warm hand on her tiny shoulder. "That damn bus is always late."

When the others had left, Rosemary poured herself another glass of wine, and Uncle Bishop another scotch. They sat before the last of the fire in the Schrader fireplace.

"What's this Miriam tells me about a new boyfriend?" she asked.

"Just what did Tokyo Rose say?" Uncle Bishop's eyes had narrowed at the mention of Miriam's name.

"Nothing, really. So you tell me."

"He has such a keen sense of fashion," Uncle Bishop said sadly. He twirled the scotch in his glass. "He was waiting tables when I met him. The man should have his name on asses all over the world, like Calvin Klein does, and instead he's shoveling cheese sticks to college students." Mugs had come to Rosemary's side and was rubbing back and forth against her arm, marking her well with his scents.

"Where are your shoes?" Rosemary asked cautiously. Uncle Bishop looked at her, studied her face for a bit.

"Miriam's mouth isn't shaped like a megaphone for nothing, is it?" he wanted to know.

"Well?" Rosemary prodded.

"Some people throw knives," Uncle Bishop pointed out. "And a shoe is really a very friendly missile."

"Unless it has a heel," Rosemary noted.

"Heels can sting," Uncle Bishop conceded. He looked at Rosemary. "So he has a thing for shoes," he said. "Some people collect dead insects. Miriam collects husbands. Forget what Miss Rona Barrett told you. Someone needs to muzzle that woman before she sinks all our ships. Come over some night and have dinner. Meet Jason for yourself."

"Jason?" asked Rosemary. "You know, I *can* see that on the asses of the world." Uncle Bishop beamed at her.

"Jason," he said musically. Rosemary walked him to the door, and then opened it. They stood in the casement and listened to the rain beat upon the roof, then drip down from the eaves.

"Pants by Jason," Rosemary added, and Uncle Bishop smiled again. He squeezed her tightly. "Oh, Uncle Bish," said Rosemary, and all the words she wanted to say caught up in her throat. He patted her hand and twirled her ponytail.

"It's okay, baby doll," Uncle Bishop said softly. "It's gonna be okay." He put an arm around her, hugging her up to his big chest. Rosemary saw spaghetti sauce spots on the gray sweatshirt.

"I miss William so much," she whispered.

"You always will," said Uncle Bishop. He held her to him and she sank into the fleshiness of his body, a huge soft mattress. She let him cradle her. Uncle Bishop had, after all, been father and mother to her, and to Robbie. So what if he loved a man with a passion for shoes, and who occasionally threw them at him?

Rosemary watched Uncle Bishop drive off into the wet night in his baby-blue truck, with the plastic Paul Bunyan dangling from the rearview mirror. Then she went back to check on the fireplace, Mugs trailing behind. With a strip of shimmering rain still running down his back, Mugs looked like a fluorescent skunk. Rosemary gave him a quick pat before she took the screen off the fireplace and closed the heavy doors. The last thing she needed was for sparks to pop out during the night.

As Rosemary was fixing a late snack the phone rang, startling her. She looked at the clock. It was almost one. She was now more suspicious than ever of phones ringing late at night.

"Oh no," she said, remembering just who it would be. " 'The Children's Hour.' " She picked up the receiver and heard that booming, familiar voice.

"It's the worst thing you can imagine," Uncle Bishop said. He never waited for her to say hello. Even when William was there, he knew *she'd* pick up the phone for his late-night panic calls. "It's to the point where I may never sleep again."

"Tell me about it," Rosemary said.

"The accumulation of ice at the North Pole?" he asked. He seemed to be gone for a couple of seconds, and then was back, full voice in her ear. Rosemary knew he'd taken the time to pour another scotch. "The Children's Hour" was not, contrary to what Longfellow thought, between the dark and the daylight, but between midnight and a bottle of scotch.

"Yes," said Rosemary, "the accumulation." She knew very well that it was an accumulation of ice in Uncle Bishop's scotch glass that had brought on the current panic.

"It's been going on for a long, long time," said Uncle Bishop sadly. "Up there at the North Pole. Up at old Santa's place. And when that baby tips we're gonna go ass-end. They'll find washing machines from Detroit out in Santa Monica." He dropped something. Rosemary heard a thump. It was the receiver, but soon he was back.

"Is there anything we can do to save ourselves?" Rosemary asked. The rain had stopped. Large beads of water clung to the window, yellow with light from the yard.

"Thanks to gravitational force," Uncle Bishop said, slurring, "there's four safe spots on the earth. But only the Freemasons know where they are."

"How much time do we have?" Rosemary asked, suppressing a yawn. She would never let Uncle Bishop think that these panics, which occurred each time he sat down with a new book from his Strange But True Book Club and a bottle of Glenlivet, were trifles.

"Until May fifth, in the year 2000," Uncle Bishop told her. He was trying to sound most clinical. "That's when all the planets in the solar system line up. It's all recorded in the Great Pyramid, Rosie. And then kaput. No more earth as we know it. No more people. Except for four goddamn gaggles of Freemasons. I never trusted those smug little bastards, with their rings and their secrets."

"Try to get some sleep," Rosemary said soothingly. "Try not to think about it. Okay?"

"Okay."

"Good night then."

"Wait!" Uncle Bishop shouted.

"What now?"

"For Chrissakes, don't say a word about those four safe spots to Miriam. She'll be down there erecting condos and throwing an Ice Accumulation Party."

"I won't say a word," said Rosemary.

"She's selling the state of Maine, you know," Uncle Bishop warned.

Before going up to bed, Rosemary went down to the den to check the fireplace one more time. The room was intensely quiet, the fire died away, the rain done outside. She could see Winston, the outdoor cat, lounging on the patio. Inside, on the shelves, hundreds of books stared down at her quietly, books she and William had collected from bookstore sales, garage sales, and the countless times they broke down and paid full price. Shelves of books. Millions of words. Things people wanted to say. Things they *had* to say. She reached for the worn copy of Shakespeare's collected works, one of William's prized books from college, and opened it.

" 'All the world's a stage,' " Rosemary read, " 'And all the men and women merely players: they have their exits and their entrances, and one man in his time plays many parts.' " Her part, now, seemed to be nothing more than dealing with William's *exit.* She stepped back so that she could look at all the book covers, tried to guess the titles from the colors of the spines. It was a room full of books. And spring was coming to the land around the house of words. Rebirth was coming to Bixley, Maine, population 23,160. The warm rain would take away the last remnants of snow along the edge of the woods. It had been a long winter and now it was over. The slush would soon let the fields and roads and driveways turn dry again. During the day she had heard the far-off murmur of softball teams being organized at the ballpark. April was turning into May, and soon there would be buds everywhere, and shoots coming up out of the ground with the promise of new green grass, and silky petals. And the migrant birds would return, their heads full of broken images of faraway places most of Rosemary's neighbors had never been. Places *she* had never been. The birds had been there and back, to cities and towns in the South where the magnolia and dogwood had burst into flowers weeks before. Now it was Maine's turn. And spring *was* coming. Rosemary could sense it lying in wait for her. And she could sense something else waiting, too. She could feel change rising up inside her like an old, smoldering flame. She had some questions she needed answered, not just about William, but questions about herself. She had a skin to shed, and that would not be easy.

# The Disturbed Pairs

JUNE FOLLOWED MAY into Bixley, Maine, bringing with it the last of the shoots, and buds, and a card that came in the afternoon mail. Rosemary had gone outside to check on the new plants, which already had tiny flowers on them. The afternoon was perfectly June. The land had finally dried from the aftermath of winter. A few birds fluttered about the feeder that hung in the front yard. The cats lounged in furry balls on the steps, jingling the tags on their collars when they stretched, and keeping an occasional lazy eye on the birds. When she remembered the mail, she left her gardening gloves on the front steps, and went on down to the box. It was a small card, the kind that comes ten to a packet, with seashells on the front.

It was postmarked Portland and Rosemary smiled, knowing it was from Elizabeth, her best old college chum, whom she hadn't seen in years.

As Rosemary closed the door to the mailbox, she heard a faint buzzing, as if a distant lawn mower was cutting someone's grass farther down Old Airport Road. Her house sat one mile out on this road. Most traffic used New Airport Road, which came into the tiny airport on its other side. A few families lived along Rosemary's road, and some folks still used it to get out to the airport. But the business done there was conducted on a small scale, with five or six Cessnas and Piper Cubs a day scheduled for flights to Bangor, Portland, and Boston. The occasional takeoff of a small plane over Rosemary's house was certainly no sound pollution, no window-shaking, Congress-petitioning noise. The planes were already up fairly high and merely purring by the time they passed overhead. But this droning sound was different.

Rosemary looked above the row of birches and pines and sugar maples that lined the small field beyond the house, in the direction of the airport, and saw a strange, birdlike creature skirting the tops of the trees, buzzing faintly. Caught by surprise, she felt a sudden jolt of fear. Her mind raced for a word of description.

"Pterodactyl," she said aloud. It was all she could think of until the apparatus swerved into a graceful arc and came back toward her, casting an earthbound shadow on her field.

"Pterodactyl," Rosemary said again, as the man in the ultralight soared over her head, close enough that she could see his goggles, and the red glove of his hand as he waved down to her. Then he was gone, over the tops of the trees, and down the slope of the hill, back to the airport. Maybe into extinction, never to be seen again. He had waved. And she had waved back. There had been an interaction between strangers, as though they were in a busy New York airport, and not the sparsely populated town of Bixley where the horizon, like some uncharted graveyard, had risen up to swallow him. A flying man, in a red-and-yellow suit, birdlike, in and out of her life almost as quickly as William. "What is eight years when pitted against the course of time?" William had asked her, one night just before he left for London, and she only supposed he was right. That time made no difference. Time was more coincidence than importance. Rosemary remembered William's Time Chart, a huge, long thing he had ordered from the History Book Club. It began by charting those murky eons after the earth's crust formed, when the chemical soup of the oceans held only the seaweeds and the soft little creatures without backbones. "Rosie, did you know that after the earth cooled down and formed its crust, it rained for sixty thousand years?" William had asked. This had been just a year ago, a summer's night when they stood with their arms around each other's waist and watched a shower of light rain beat its way up Old Airport Road. "The clouds were high-banked and the rain was a continual downpour. Three thousand million years ago, it finally stopped. This little drizzle is nothing, Rosie, nothing at all." And he had taken her by the hand, over to the massive Time Chart, the history of the ages, encapsulated. He ran a finger past the coming of the reptiles and mammals, the Old Stone Age, the introduction of farming, the Metal Age. He scuttled past Mesopotamia and Egypt and Greece. He skipped over Byzantium and Russia and China. The Aztecs and the Mayans. He crept to the Western Civilizations and followed his finger up through the ages, to the Atomic Age, and Man on the Moon. Then he wrote in gentle, artistic strokes, in thin, wiry letters: *William Meets Rosemary, 1983 A.D. Love at First Sight.* What had happened to that chart? She should find it and unroll its full length. She should put it up in the den. There were some truths, there, to be learned. "This little drizzle, Rosemary, this little time, is nothing at all. There's no downpour nowadays. Nowadays, even the gods are lazy."

With the birdman surely gone, Rosemary brought the mail into the big airy kitchen. She had raised the window earlier to put a portable screen beneath it and now a puff of breeze came through to ruffle the curtains. She filled her copper water kettle and put it on the stove to heat, then got the pot ready, measured some Earl Grey leaves into her tea-leaf holder, and waited for the water to boil.

While the tea was steeping, Rosemary stepped in and out of the shower quickly, then came back to the kitchen wrapped in a fuzzy blue bathrobe to pour herself a cup of tea. She sat at the table and sipped, the little card before her. The tea and the shower had been a means of savoring the anticipation before the unveiling. She always did this with personal mail since it was so rare. Without William's occasional cards now, it was, in fact, nearly phenomenal. The most personal mail she'd received in months, since the last prophetic postcard from Brussels, was from a book club that had referred to her as *Miss O'Neal* instead of the usual *Dear Member*. Rosemary hoped Elizabeth's card was not just a quick note but full of the news of her life. Aside from a couple of phone calls a year, the friendship was not maintaining the constancy they swore, at their college graduation, that it would. Lizzie usually filled her in on family news each December, when her Christmas card included a sheet of holiday stationery, like a cheerful bibliography, their lives decked out with holly and enhanced by small snowmen holding shovels. But to hear from Lizzie in June was most unusual.

The message was brief and not at all what Rosemary had expected. Lizzie was dropping the kids off at a camp downstate for the summer. She needed a few days to get shed of a husband, and a cute little puppy that was now a large dog and still not housebroken. She was driving on up to Bixley. Would arrive Saturday afternoon. Please forgive her the short notice. *Saturday afternoon!*

"Day after tomorrow," Rosemary thought, and wished she had more time to get things in order. But then it was, after all, Lizzie. Lizzie wouldn't notice if there were cobwebs in every corner, or dust mice the size of baseballs beneath the bed. Lizzie, who had once been her college roomie at the University of Maine at Fort Kent, had come seven hours north from Portland to go to school. "I want to find out what it's like to live among you Eskimos up here in northern Maine," she had told Rosemary, at their first meeting. Lizzie, who brushed her teeth while in the shower because her mother had always hated for any of the children to waste water. Lizzie, who had taken motherhood and done wonderful things with it, who had turned marriage into what appeared to be an extended honeymoon. Lizzie with her long lazy legs, and movements, and lilting voice, had married Charles Vanier, another college classmate, and had settled down peacefully with him, with their two children, back in Portland, Maine.

Rosemary watched the evening inch in, heard some threatening thunder clapping away in the distance. She would need to gather the towels from her little clothesline. On balmy summer days she couldn't bring herself to start up the clothes dryer. There was something in the smell of a towel that has flapped all afternoon in the outdoors. There was something in the sound of a sheet snapping sweetly that she was addicted to. These were the smells and sounds of childhood, wrapped up with the memory of Mother, only flirtatiously crazy, pushing a plastic basket of wet clothes across the ground with her foot, one clothespin at a time in her mouth, as she moved down the line. Then in the mornings, if there were screens beneath the windows to let in the breeze, noises came in, too, and Rosemary would waken to what sounded like the flapping of giant, prehistoric wings, a flock, perhaps, of ultralights. One meager clothesline was all that she had strung in the backyard, from the corner of the house to the fence. But it was at least *something* attached to the past, connecting her to the old way.

"The screens," she told Mugs, as she heard the first thunder again. "I need to take out all the screens before the rain hits." But she sat instead and drank another cup of warm tea before it grew cold, and smiled at the little card with the brownish seashells on the front. Elizabeth was coming to the big house, Elizabeth of the college-girl world of young, foolish dreams. Rosemary would need to ready the guest room with the wide pumpkin-pine boards and delicate rose wallpaper. She would need to take the handmade quilt, a treasure from her grandmother O'Leary, out of its plastic protector and let it sprawl and breathe again. She would let all the designs burst forth, designs made of clothing scraps, articles that had belonged to Grandmother and her family. The pink was from a dress that Mother wore one Easter, a dress saved all year round and ordered out of the Almighty Catalog, the seams let out each year until there was nothing more to give. The quilt's blue was from Grandfather's wedding suit. The green had been from an old tablecloth belonging to some ancestor back in Ireland, before the famine, when there was still need for a tablecloth. It had been a treasure to Grandmother, this patch of green, as though it were the blessed field of shamrocks her own grandmother had longed to dally in once again before she died. Now the green was quietly in the quilt, little Irish hills here and there among the memories. It upset Rosemary, this notion of one's most precious belongings in a lifetime falling into such disrepair, falling *behind* new fashions to become a kind of museum. A shrine to the old days. Sleeping beneath the quilt at night, she felt pressed down, smothered with forgotten, heavy wishes. The very *earth* of the old country, burying her alive. Elizabeth, however, would go hog wild over the quilt.

After the light rain came and went, Rosemary did the stretching exercises that Robbie had taught her. He had finally talked her into running, if not for the exercise, at least for a release of tension. Now she had, in two months, built up to a two-mile run, which took her down to Bixley, around its circumference, and home again. Jiggedy-jog. "You'll be in a marathon before long," Robbie had teased her.

"I'm already in one," Rosemary reminded him. "It's called life, and it's hell on the home stretch." But running did calm her.

At Uncle Bishop's, Rosemary spotted the baby-blue Datsun, which was driven furiously up to the front steps. Its little face was pinched and angry. "It does look like one of those cars in 'The Twilight Zone,' " she decided, as she ran past the yard. She heard angry voices rise up from inside the beige house with brown shutters, the house that was home to Uncle Bishop and the elusive Jason, whom Rosemary still had not met. She kept her stride and passed the house. Next door Mrs. Abernathy, who wrote a column about birds for the local paper, was in her front yard inspecting one of her purple martin houses.

"They fight constantly now!" she shouted to Rosemary. "The town should do something about them!" When Rosemary saw Mr. Cobb in his own front yard, listening hard to hear what Mrs. Abernathy had said, she felt suddenly like a relay runner, carrying gossip instead of a baton. Perhaps she should shout to Mr. Cobb, "They're at it again!" and let him run to the next yard and pass on the juicy news. But Rosemary quickened her pace and left the flowering faces in all the yards behind her to depend upon the modern conveniences of the mail and the telephone to glean news of their most unusual street-mates.

Back at the house, she soaked in a hot bath and read sections from the latest *Newsweek*. Then she crawled into a fresh pair of sweat pants and a T-shirt and poured a little wine for herself. She settled into the big armchair in the den and dialed the numbers that would cause the phone to ring at Uncle Bishop's house. It rang four times before he picked it up and shouted, "What?" into the receiver. Miss Manners would blanche. In the background a man was screaming hysterically.

"Uncle Bishop, is this a bad time for me to call?" Rosemary asked. She heard the sound of glass shattering.

"No, no," Uncle Bishop insisted. "It's just Ralph. He's refusing to eat his cat food again." There was a loud crescendo of what sounded like drum cymbals. Uncle Bishop was suddenly no longer on the phone. Rosemary waited.

"*Ralph* is making that noise?" she asked, when he finally returned.

"You haven't seen him lately, Rosie." Uncle Bishop was winded. "He's really grown." Rosemary said good-bye, knowing Uncle Bishop would call back when he felt the time was right to air his large and dirty laundry.

It was early evening when Rosemary backed her bicycle out of the garage and dusted off the seat. Running had preoccupied most of her exercise time, but now she would bicycle innocently past Uncle Bishop's house to see if all had quieted down behind the chocolate shutters. As she turned down Uncle Bishop's street, things seemed peaceful enough. Even the Datsun appeared more relaxed. It had given up its snarl and was sighing instead. Rosemary swerved her bike into a graceful arc, as the man in the ultralight had done earlier in the sky, and was about to pedal back down College Street when she spotted Mrs.

Abernathy, still busily moving about her front yard, dusting and polishing, as if the yard were an extension of her living room. Mrs. Abernathy's front lawn was a carpet of fake grass that she had had Gauvin's Landscaping install for her the very year Mr. Abernathy died. "To discourage insects and their ilk," Mrs. Abernathy had told Rosemary. "The backyard I leave to my birds so they can find their juicy little snacks. But the front yard is mine." Uncle Bishop was not so charitable about her reasoning. "She vacuums her goddamn grass," he told Rosemary, after a particular afternoon of fighting with Mrs. Abernathy. "She hooks a big orange extension cord to her rickety old Hoover."

Mrs. Abernathy waved a silhouetted hand, so there was little Rosemary could do but clasp the hand brake and walk her bike into Mrs. Abernathy's driveway.

"You've missed my morning glories closing up," Mrs. Abernathy yelled, loudly enough to *waken* all those sleepy-headed flowers. Rosemary imagined them lifting their puzzled heads, like confused children who have heard their mother shout, unreasonably, in the middle of the night.

"How have your birds been?" Rosemary asked, and leaned the bicycle on its kickstand.

"They put in a hard winter," Mrs. Abernathy answered. "There's an eighty percent mortality rate, you know. But the ones who have survived are really enjoying this mild weather." She waved an ancient hand about her head, emphasizing.

"I've read about those mortality rates in one of my books," said Rosemary. "They're awfully high." She sat on Mrs. Abernathy's steps, where she could stretch her legs. She felt a bit of a shinsplint coming on in the right one.

"Do you still have the stray kitten?" Mrs. Abernathy asked, and Rosemary remembered in a flash the rainy morning of the lost kitten, covered with fleas and starving. How soft it was after food and a thorough cleaning. How soft William's skin was, that thunderous morning when she had crawled back into the warm bed beside him, with the kitten rejuvenated and running its padded feet up and down William's back. "A stray?" he'd rubbed his eyes and asked. And the little yellow-eyed kitten had curled into a safe ball, as though it were a huge caterpillar, next to William's pillow.

"It's a big cat now," Rosemary said, thinking of how quickly Mugs had grown, remembering in bits and clips that morning of the big summer storm, when she and William made love early, Rosemary having been awakened by the scratching at the back door, by the tiny, desperate meows.

"That's nice," Mrs. Abernathy said. "Cats are okay if they're well behaved." As she hovered over her morning glories, inspecting each blossom, Rosemary realized how birdlike the old woman had become. Her little white head dipped and bobbed as she spoke. The eyes seemed to see at all angles. There was something almost feathery in the fine hairs that grew above her lip. She was tiny, nervous as a bird, flitting almost, as she arranged flower pots near the steps, tugged at the sweater resting on her shoulders.

"Your flowers are very pretty," said Rosemary. Mrs. Abernathy's toes seemed to curl in their sandals, perhaps in search of a round fat twig on which to perch. In search, perhaps, of the careless earthworm.

"They are lovely, aren't they?" Mrs. Abernathy agreed, straightening a potted geranium. A door slammed sharply, over in Uncle Bishop's yard, and Rosemary glanced up to see a small man on the front steps. He plunked a suitcase down on the porch, and then disappeared back inside the house.

"Jason," thought Rosemary. Mrs. Abernathy looked up, too, and then frowned. With Uncle Bishop and Jason living in the beige house with chocolate shutters, it wasn't exactly Mr. Rogers's Neighborhood.

"The noise is sometimes deafening," said Mrs. Abernathy. "I've never known a *normal* couple to fight that much. Mr. Abernathy would be up in arms, I tell you, if he were still with us."

Lightning bugs came and went above the fake grass, probably confused, maybe even embarrassed, until they found the real grass beyond the trees, beyond the so-many-dollars-a-foot turf. Mrs. Abernathy's seashell chimes clinked and clanked from where they hung near the door, bragging of an ocean they'd never see again. Two neighborhood boys biked by, rearing their bicycles up in the air as if they rode wild horses. One swerved precariously close to the other, nearly causing a spill.

"Bailey, you fucker! Watch where you're goin'!"

"Get your ass out of my way," Bailey warned.

"These children nowadays," said Mrs. Abernathy sadly. "I didn't know anyone in my generation who would speak like that. Even the wild ones were polite." The chimes sang again, agreeing.

"They get to me, too," said Rosemary, "and not long ago, I had a whole classroom of them."

A mourning dove was singing far off in the tangles of a thicket. Mrs. Abernathy cocked her head, as though interpreting.

"He's been mate-singing all day long," she said to Rosemary. "He'll sing until he finds one. It pains me to hear him."

"He'll find a mate," Rosemary assured her, and wondered if maybe *she* should perch atop a TV antenna and sing all day. The simple truth was that even if she were ready to find a *nice* man, just a man to eat dinner with, see an occasional movie, there was no one in Bixley like William, with his head full of wonderful notions and swirling brainstorms. At least no one she had met.

Suddenly a clamor started up on the front porch of Uncle Bishop's little house. Rosemary saw that Jason was back with a large box in his arms, Uncle Bishop at his heels.

"I know what's in that box, Jason!" Uncle Bishop shouted. He grabbed at the box as Jason jerked it away. Uncle Bishop pursued it, with Jason turning from him, spinning round and round as Uncle Bishop followed. Baryshnikov and Kirkland.

"That vase belonged to my mother, and my grandmother before her!" Uncle Bishop screamed. "I know you've got it buried in there!"

"You never *had* a mother!" the little man who was Jason shouted back. He stopped suddenly, too dizzy to pirouette any longer. "They found you floating in the reeds in a basket," he said feebly. "A very sizable basket, may I add." He put the box down.

"You can steal what you want, but not Grandmother's vase!" Uncle Bishop lashed out. He went to work rummaging through the box of clothing, which appeared to be feminine, until a mass of apparel lay scattered about the steps and on the lawn. It looked very much like the aftermath of a large, angry yard sale.

"Are you satisfied, you big barn?" Jason asked, picking up his things and folding them gently in an effort to repack the box.

"You gave it to *her,* didn't you?" Uncle Bishop demanded. Rosemary could tell that he was not just angry. He was in a state of emotional pain, a genre she knew well. She'd just never brought herself to unpack boxes and strew clothing about her front lawn. The lover's pain.

"You broke that vase in a drunken stupor," Jason sputtered. "This jealousy of yours is what has finally ended this relationship." He twirled on his heel and disappeared back into the house. Uncle Bishop threw what looked like a splendid black pump out across the lawn. It bounced off his mailbox and skipped across the road like a flat stone on water. Then he stomped back into the house behind Jason and slammed the door.

"Two men ranting about a vase," Mrs. Abernathy gasped from her front steps, where she had slumped when the action grew fierce. "This world expects us senior citizens to take every abnormality it hurls at us with a grain of salt. Without so much as a howdy-do." Rosemary had not realized that the relationship between Uncle Bishop and his latest lover was such a boiling one. She sympathized with Mrs. Abernathy, but there was really nothing she could do. If Uncle Bishop's neighbors decided to report him to the police, so be it. She would try to raise bail money, as a good niece should.

"Good night, Mrs. Abernathy," Rosemary said, and patted her arm. "Don't worry about the dove. He'll be fine. And I'll be looking forward to your column this Sunday." Mrs. Abernathy brightened. She churned inside her sweater, dabbing at the arms of it, as though it were something most rare and valuable, something she could moisten and twist and bend into a nest for herself. To avoid the mortality rate. Eighty percent a year. Such horribly dim odds.

"The cedar waxwing," Mrs. Abernathy fairly chirped. "And his fondness for mountain ash berries. Be sure you read it."

"I wouldn't miss it," said Rosemary.

Out on the road she stopped to toss the black pump back into Uncle Bishop's yard. It was a large shoe, compared to the size she herself wore, but it was small for a man, and slightly scratched from wear. A delicate blue bow was attached to the side, insectlike, a butterfly just arrived for its first brood. Rosemary turned the shoe over and over in her hand, expecting the bow to fly off at any minute, and thought about its mate. It was like the one remaining garnet earring she had in her jewelry box, that little gift from William. There was a sadness in seeing what was really just *part of a whole,* something nonfunctioning alone. The rejoining of such a pair of shoes had whisked Cinderella out of the ashes and into the castle. But *one* shoe? What good was it? Rosemary imagined Uncle Bishop desperately trying to fit it on pinkish male feet all over Bixley, seeking out his prince, years after Jason had gone, growing pale and old, until the shoe itself lost its string, like a rotten tooth, and fell apart.

"We've been taught to think in pairs," Rosemary thought, as she stood on the black road in front of Uncle Bishop's house. "We've been taught that we're no good alone." She tossed the black leather pump back across the yard, watched the blue butterfly settle happily, right side up, by the front steps where Jason would surely discover it. Now the shoe was back as close to its mate as possible. Rosemary had done her part, if only symbolically, to help reunite that most unusual prince and princess who lived, once upon a time, unhappily, behind shutters as chocolate as any witch could whip up for enticement, in the beige, gingerbready house on the edge of Mrs. Abernathy's fairy-tale green, enchanted grass.

"It's Noah who's responsible for all this pair shit," Rosemary thought.

She pedaled home slowly, away from the serenade of the mourning dove, the poor bird's *coo coo cooah,* rolling in from some unseen shrubbery. The night was alive with tapping sounds, the tiny beat of June bugs hitting their drum bodies against the windows with lights in them. Rosemary went home to turn down her grandmother's quilt of memories, to make ready the room that would soon have Elizabeth's blouses and belts scattered to and fro, and used Kleenex with makeup on them lolling about like dusty snowballs.

At one-thirty, an hour into a troubling sleep about canvases, and oils spilling about on Grandmother's quilt, the phone rang sharply with its discordant urgency. It rang the way it had a few months earlier, to bring the news about William, and Rosemary had so casually answered it, thinking it surely another "Children's Hour." *Ask not for whom the phone rings.* She finally collected herself enough to let William and his canvases and colors sink back into her subconscious. The situation was finally clear to her. She had even suspected earlier that unless Uncle Bishop and Jason made up, he would call. It wasn't just a strange-but-true book that precipitated "The Children's Hour." She reached out and caught the phone in the middle of its sixth barrage. He would never give up. The apparatus would still be ringing at dawn.

"He's gone," Uncle Bishop said sadly, and there was a trembling behind his words, and a stillness in the house around him. A large difference from the noisy clanging and banging, shaking and breaking. Rosemary knew such stillness. "He's gone for good," Uncle Bishop said, prophesying.

"Ralph?" asked Rosemary, but Uncle Bishop didn't laugh.

"Don't be a smartass," he said.

Then, suddenly, Uncle Bishop was gone, too, off in the house somewhere, and the line lay quiet until he did whatever he did at those times: go to the bathroom, pour more scotch, feed Ralph, start an ant farm, take up karate. Rosemary had learned that if he wasn't back in ten minutes to hang up. He'd forgotten. But she knew he felt better just knowing the line was open. "That telephone line is like an umbilical cord to him," Miriam had said once, in Uncle Bishop's presence. "What's this?" Uncle Bishop had asked incredulously. "Miriam stumbles upon a metaphor? Did it hurt, Miriam?" But he was back in a minute. Jason's leaving was too sharp an ache, this "Children's Hour" more painful than Alger Hiss being framed by Nixon's lying pumpkin, or Bruno Hauptmann's innocence. This blast was closer to home than UFO landing pads in Vermont.

"Where did he go, Uncle Bish?" Rosemary asked. The moon was shining brightly outside. No more rain. Maybe there would even be sun for Lizzie's arrival. Rosemary flicked on the bedside lamp and the pale moonlight disappeared in the hundred-watt flash. She could never tell Uncle Bishop *another time* even though there were nights when she'd like to. He was the one who had come to the school plays, who paid for the prom dresses, who encouraged her in calculus, even studied for exams with her.

"Back to his ex-wife," Uncle Bishop all but sobbed. "She knows he's a transvestite and she's taking him back anyway. Have you ever heard of anything so sick?"

Rosemary smiled. "It'll be okay," she said.

"This is a typical case of denial," Uncle Bishop whined. "This is just another fags-to-bitches story."

"I see," said Rosemary. What else could she say?

"I just needed to hear someone's voice."

"I know."

"You're an ace," Uncle Bishop said.

"And this from a *queen?*" Rosemary asked, and put the receiver back on its cradle.

She slept late, unable to curl into a deep sleep after the panicky phone call from Uncle Bishop, and mostly because of the unsettling montage of broken dreams about William. When she finally opened her eyes at eleven-thirty, she heard Lizzie blaring away on the horn of her car. It was the same incessant bleat as back in college, when Lizzie came home with sacks of groceries, or baskets of laundry, and needed Rosemary's help in dragging it all up the stairs and into their apartment. Rosemary lifted a curtain panel and looked down the slope of the veranda to where Lizzie's car squatted in the drive. She half expected to see the same old college campus off in the distance, the Saint John River traipsing among the birches, Mr. Nadeau's tiny grocery, and Lizzie's orange Rabbit parked on the street below. She half wished she could reel the years in, as though they were trout straight out of that same old river, leave them flopping on the banks beneath those magnificent birches.

"Only in Hollywood," Rosemary sighed, when she saw the long, glaring New Yorker, and Lizzie's dark head bobbing out from behind the wheel.

# The Colored Nightmares

LIZZIE HAD BEEN in Bixley for a week before she told Rosemary the truth about her visit. They had spent the nights drinking wine, retelling the old college stories, playing records from Rosemary's towering stack of forty-fives, records that skipped so much a spool of thread had to be tied to the arm so that the needle couldn't possibly jump. This would have made William cringe, this haywire job on the needle. But, because of it, Joan Baez sang "George Jackson" over and over. Steppenwolf told potheads they were *born to be wild.* The Doors, with handsome Jim Morrison, dead in his bones, invited groupies everywhere to light his fire. And Creedence Clearwater Revival, good ole CCR, could still see that bad, bad moon, forever rising.

They were on the front porch with cold glasses of cheap champagne, toasting each other, toasting the weary memories, when Lizzie leveled with her about the sudden visit.

"It's all come crashing down," she said, and Rosemary looked at her friend's face, knowing how easy it was to read Lizzie. But her face was older than the storytelling face of the coed and, veiled, it said nothing.

"London Bridge?" Rosemary asked, and looked away from Lizzie's hushed-up face and off into the wild apple trees in the field across the road. The trees were no longer a burst of flowery dots as they had been that spring, but now held a scattering of tiny, sour apples, still growing.

"I wish it were," said Lizzie. "However, it's my marriage."

"In a million years I wouldn't have guessed," said Rosemary. "I thought you and Charles were indecently happy."

"Some of us who are unhappy become masters of the fake smile." Lizzie unloosed her long brown legs, which seemed to shoot out of her cutoff jeans. She pushed her bangs back. Her mouth was small as ever, pouty, and the oval eyes were still large and green. She picked up the bottle of champagne and refilled her glass. "We get so good at pretense," Lizzie added, "we start to believe the myth ourselves."

Rosemary listened to the muffled noises of the frogs camouflaged among the grasses of the little creek that ran through its culvert under the road in front of her house. She waited for Lizzie's confession to unfold. A car roared down Old Airport Road. Jan Ferguson, the driver, tooted and waved. Rosemary waved back. Lizzie drank more champagne; her eyes were suddenly red and watery.

"Charles has found himself a little diversion," she said,

and took a pink tissue out of her sweater pocket, blew her nose.

"Jesus, I'm sorry to hear that," Rosemary said, and put a hand on Lizzie's arm, patted it gently.

"A goddamn doctor. What would you do about that? He cheated me out of my script. Can you hear me shouting, 'What? You're leaving me for a lowly neurosurgeon?' "

Rosemary nodded sympathetically. "How did he meet her?" she asked.

"She's actually a dermatologist," said Lizzie. "He developed a little thing on his lip, and then a bigger thing for her. I believe she was successful, however, in removing the mole. And you know what else, Rosie?"

"Oh God, there's a *what else?*"

"I've found someone, too." Rosemary filled her own glass back up with champagne. You just couldn't count on anything anymore. Lizzie and Charles, the immortal wedding couple, the perpetually happy pair, unraveling like old socks.

"And I've got another *what else,*" Lizzie went on. "I was the first one to fall by the wayside. Charles taking up with his skin doctor—and don't you love that, *skin* doctor—was just his reaction to having no one. Would you have guessed that? That it was me who pulled the first nail out? Now there's no nails left. I don't know what's held us together for the past year."

"A year?" Rosemary was shocked. "This has been going on for a full year and you never told me?" She thought of all the mistletoed, seasonal lies that had appeared on the Christmas stationery, of all the fickle snowmen cheering Lizzie on.

"I didn't want to destroy your illusions," Lizzie laughed, and slapped Rosemary's ponytail. She pulled her long legs in again, brought them up in a graceful arch, and rested her chin on her knees. "I think I was just trying to get Charles's attention is why I did it in the first place."

"It amazes me, Lizzie. I just had no idea."

"You've always thought of Charles and me as so happily married," Lizzie said. "Yet all that time I was thinking that *you* were the blissful one. Your letters about life with William were so exciting. I was reading Dr. Spock, and Charles was honing his executive skills at General Motors."

Rosemary hadn't spoken of William yet. She hadn't decided if her old college friend was someone she could pour it all out to, sort over the mess. Robbie had phoned Lizzie with the awful news and she had wanted to come to the funeral. But Rosemary convinced her over the phone that it would be more burdensome than helpful. "The next time I see your face, I want to be back together again as a human being," she had told her. "Because right now, Lizzie, I'm all loose ends. I want it to be happiness that brings us together again, and not this." So sadness had brought them together after all.

"It isn't out of misery that I've come," said Lizzie, with her old talent for reading Rosemary's thoughts. "If that were the case, I would have roared into your yard a year ago. I'm all over the teary-pillow stage. I just need to think about what I should do. I didn't even plan on bringing any of this up. The truth is, I've missed you. And I know how you must miss William."

Rosemary smoothed her hair back, twirled the ponytail around her finger. *William.* How just the mention of his name could elicit such a quiet panic in her, could start a soft trembling, a tiny emotional earthquake with sharp tremors.

"Do you want to talk about him?" asked the telepathic Lizzie. Rosemary shook her head.

"Not just yet," she said. The orange sun was dipping down

behind the apple trees, about to disappear in a golden swirl of clouds and horizon. A red-winged blackbird, its epaulets flashing a blood red, flew away from the cattails growing across the road. Orange. Gold. Red. The green leaves of the apple trees. Even colors pained her now, knowing how William understood them, broke them down into components, admired them. Above the sinking sun was the lonely trace where a jet had been and gone, a puffy trail of white, ghostlike, a mere memory, as William's life was now becoming. And even her memory of William was shaken. It had occurred to her, during her three-month hiatus in the old house, that perhaps she didn't know him very well at all. Why hadn't he confided in her, if his pain had grown to proportions large enough for him to commit suicide? This was the terrible knowledge nagging at her, trailing her about. After eight fleeting years, *she did not know him well at all.* She had had no inkling of the catastrophe ahead, she who was closest to him. And so his wrists had opened up in a flowering red, his veins cut like telephone lines. "No communication anymore with the people around him," Michael had said, when he phoned with the news, and Rosemary had shouted, "Why?" over the phone, via the busy satellite, slow enough to miss a word or two in his answer, which was no answer at all. No communication. All the lines cut. Severed. "The vena amora," William had said to her once, "leads directly to the heart. The Greeks believed that, anyway. That's why we put a ring on the third finger of the left hand when we marry." But William had cut all his veins. William had done away nicely with the vein of love.

Rosemary looked at the mailbox, fading into the shadows by the edge of the road, and tried to think of other things than William and paints and suicide. She was afraid she might cry.

"Speaking of destroying someone's illusions," she said, "does your mother know about you and Charles?"

"Are you absolutely unwound in the brain?" Lizzie asked in astonishment. "I might be an adulteress, but I'm not stupid."

"I guessed she'd be the last person to know."

"Did I ever tell you how she studied my freckles when I was a child?"

"A thousand times, Lizzie, you've told me."

"She called them *pigmentary disturbances,*" Lizzie said sadly.

"And she made you brush your teeth in the shower to save water," Rosemary added.

"Oh, well, that's just good common sense," Lizzie said. "My kids do that, too."

"Poor little children," said Rosemary, imagining them as tiny waterlogged raisins.

Night was emerging now, out of the trees, out of the meadows, casting dark shapes upon the road.

"Do you remember last night?" Lizzie asked quietly. "The nightmare?" Rosemary sighed, wishing Lizzie had forgotten it herself. It wasn't a nightmare, really, but just another of the William dreams she'd been having since his death. She'd gone down to clean the basement, a task she'd dreaded and delayed for months, and there, among the forgotten junk and bottled cranberries, she'd found William dead in a delicate puddle of scarlet blood. And then the bottles of cranberries dropped one by one from the shelf, crashed to the cement below, each one hitting with a deadening *splat!* They were as loud as guns going off. *Splat! Splat! Splat!* Each bottle spilled its contents out across the floor in bloody spurts, the last of the wild cranberries she and William had picked the summer before and bottled for winter. Foolish work, she realized now. You can never prepare for a winter. "They'll cry to get out," William had teased her, the day they set about canning up the berries. "They'll burst the jars, these poor things. Don't you see them as little wild creatures?" And then Lizzie was shaking her, cradling her and saying, "There, there, sweetie, it's all right." Rosemary had come wide awake in the big hand-crafted, lovely, cherry bed. Dear Lizzie. How many times had she done this for her children? The dream, as they all seemed to be since the suicide, was pure color, all deep, billowing, cranberry red. Blood red and basement gray. Colors William would love.

"It's all canned nowadays, Lizzie," Rosemary had whispered in the darkness. "The memories. Even the laughter. All bottled up."

Lizzie had held her closer. "I know, sweetie," she had whispered, when she really hadn't the slightest idea what Rosemary meant, hadn't journeyed into the horrible dream, into the dark notions that had been swirling around in Rosemary's head while she slept.

"Yes, I remember it," said Rosemary. It seemed silly to her now, as nightmares can the day following their terror.

"You were crying," Lizzie said.

"Was I?" Rosemary asked. The evening grew darker around them but Rosemary made no move to get up and flick the porch light on. That would be an extended invitation to every early summer bug within a mile. More cars passed on the road but no one waved or tooted their horn because they couldn't see the two women sitting on the steps with silence between them. Finally, Lizzie spoke. She was emptying the last of the champagne into their glasses, dividing it up between them.

"I was thinking earlier, you know," Lizzie said, "when we were talking about my marriage, and a little about William, how funny it is."

"What is?"

"Well, it's just that after years of not seeing each other,

here we are still talking about boys like the old days. I'll grant you the talk has become much more serious, but nonetheless we're talking about boy troubles."

"Let's go in," said Rosemary. "I'm tired of talking about boys."

In the den, they sprawled on each end of the sofa, as though it were the flowered eyesore in the University of Maine lounge. Lizzie hadn't mentioned a day she'd be leaving, and Rosemary didn't ask for one. It was such a pleasure to have some company again in the monstrous house, to have a spare room cluttered with suitcases, tennis shoes, and paperback novels—Lizzie's large, inanimate entourage had not changed much since college.

At ten-thirty the phone rang and a man asked to speak, please, to Elizabeth Vanier.

"It certainly isn't Charles," Rosemary told her.

"In that case," Lizzie said, and winked, "I'll take it upstairs."

While Lizzie was on the phone, Rosemary refilled her champagne glass and flopped down on the sofa. She opened *Harrowsmith* magazine to an article she'd begun earlier, advice on how to turn a small acreage into a habitat for wildlife. She liked the idea of animals roaming freely about the fields and woods behind her house. But after reading the same paragraph over and over again, she closed the magazine. The dream was still haunting her with its muted noises and fuzzy images. William, it seemed, had become even more elusive in death than he had been while he lived and loved and painted in the big house, a house with an abundance of light beating in through all the windows.

"Can you still be trusted with secrets?" Lizzie asked, peeking around the den's door. Rosemary tossed the magazine aside and sat up.

"Try me," she said, as Lizzie danced into the den and executed a shaky pirouette.

"Philip is coming to Bixley!" she shouted, and then did a quick cheerleader's jump into the air. "Can he stay here, Rosemary?"

"So, he's a Philip, is he?" Rosemary asked. The idea of more company than Lizzie was not appealing to her. She wasn't ready for strangers. "He doesn't throw shoes, does he?" Lizzie widened her eyes at this, but Rosemary waved the comment away with a flick of her hand.

"Listen," Lizzie said, and kissed the top of Rosemary's head. "I'll tell you all about this tomorrow. Right now I'm going upstairs to curl up in bed and think about Philip and practice kissing the back of my hand." Rosemary smiled. Maybe Philip would decide not to come after all. "Actually," Lizzie added. She was picking at a red lump just above her knee that looked like a mosquito bite. "I need to go up to bed, turn out the light, and think about how I'm going to handle this mess."

"Sweet dreams," Rosemary told her, and hoped that when she herself fell asleep, her own dreams would be a bit sweeter.

# The June Christmas

A WEEK AND a half into her visit, Lizzie still said nothing about when she planned to leave. She kept in touch with her children at camp and, occasionally, her mother in Portland. But Rosemary noticed that there were no outgoing or incoming calls to or from Charles. Lizzie did announce, much to Rosemary's displeasure, that Philip Sheppard would be arriving in two days, on Friday.

"Then maybe we should visit my family before Philip gets here," Rosemary suggested. "He already has enough problems. There's no need to complicate things for him." Lizzie, on the other hand, had met the family many times when she and Rosemary piled their things into the orange

Rabbit, and left the university campus behind them as they headed home to Bixley, forty miles away, for a weekend of Uncle Bishop's home-cooked meals and warped philosophies.

"Maybe I shouldn't tell you this," Lizzie said, "but when I first met your family I used to think of you as that girl on 'The Munsters.' Remember the one who was out of place because she looked and acted normal?"

When Lizzie and Rosemary arrived at Uncle Bishop's the rest of the family were already there and in the midst of a rather loud argument. But they quickly abandoned their squabbling at the sight of Lizzie. Uncle Bishop hugged her hardest and longest, finally letting her go only when Rosemary insisted he do so. He had bowls of pretzels everywhere, pretzels of every possible shape. Some were circles, some long sticks, some medium-length sticks, some short sticks, some shaped like a baby's teething ring. There were assorted cheeses, candies, chips, and a dip that looked a bit too violet to be taken seriously. All this extra hostessing was because of Lizzie. Uncle Bishop was very fond of Lizzie, and had even called her several times during Rosemary's sojourn from society to keep her apprised of the goings-on.

"Now, look here," Mother said to Lizzie, pulling her down by the arm to get a closer look. "I don't think you should put geese in that pond. They'll freeze to death."

"Those curls are as yellow as ever, Mrs. O'Neal," Lizzie said. Mother forgot all about the perils of her geese and beamed up at this visitor.

"You tell Aunt Sophie to write," Mother cautioned.

"I can't believe how you've grown!" Lizzie said to Robbie, who had stopped by to say hello before he rushed off to some important date. "You were only seventeen the last time I saw you."

"He's got a degree in biology now," Rosemary said proudly.

Miriam had never been happy with any attractive woman, and she was less than pleased with Lizzie's precise features and thick auburn hair. And it didn't serve Raymond well to stare at Lizzie with wild abandon, but he did just that, and with such obvious admiration that Miriam finally said, "This is my husband, Raymond." Raymond eagerly put a hand out.

"Oh, yes, I've met your husband before," Lizzie said, and shook the sweaty hand that had just that afternoon closed a real estate deal.

"No you haven't," said Uncle Bishop. "This is a new one strutting and fretting his hour upon the stage."

Mother rocked in her rocker, bouncing back and forth in quick jerks. Uncle Bishop had driven the chair over from Aunt Rachel's in the back of his Datsun, nearly losing it—according to Miriam's account—on the sharp turn by the Bixley IGA.

"He was going at least ninety," Miriam announced. She opened a fresh pack of Virginia Slims. "We looked just like the Clampetts." Raymond had come directly from a proposed site of future condos, and would have had to go miles out of his way to pick up Miriam.

"And just why am I stuck with being your chauffeur?" asked Uncle Bishop, his voice wavering with anger.

"You know I haven't been able to drive since the accident," Miriam said. "My psychologist says it's a classic trauma."

"Well, I got news for your psychologist," Uncle Bishop said. "The man you hit, that poor man driving the ice cream truck, has more reason to be traumatized than you do. *He's* the one I should be driving around."

"He was very childish about it all," Miriam told Lizzie. "Just because he had to pick up all those Popsicles."

"Listen," Uncle Bishop advised. "You either drive yourself next time, or take one of your so-called *business* cab rides. The IRS and I are going to sit down one of these days for a cup of coffee and a very long talk."

"Do you honestly think the IRS would believe a man who has a subscription to *Doll House World?*" asked Miriam, filing the rough edge of a nail with an emery board while her cigarette smoked in the ashtray.

"And put out that burning log," Uncle Bishop snarled, the veins bulging in his temples. He appeared ready to grab Miriam. His hands rose up together and formed a circle perfect for a small neck. It reminded Rosemary of what Anne Boleyn had said of her executioner. *I heard say the executor is very good, and I have a little neck.* But Uncle Bishop saw that Lizzie had turned away from her good-bye to Robbie and was listening, so he quickly let the issue be. The hands dropped back to his side. Miriam had been luckier than the small-necked Anne.

Telling Robbie to be careful, Uncle Bishop spun on his large heel to beam at Lizzie and Rosemary.

"Well, well. My two little college girls," he said again.

"When is Father getting here?" Mother asked.

"Still?" Lizzie looked at Rosemary with surprise.

"Still," said Rosemary. "I guess there are some men you can't forget." She smiled. The childhood ache was back, suddenly, that old longing for her father. William wasn't the only disappearing act.

"Father's dead," said Miriam. She'd been staring at Lizzie's long, tanned legs with open envy. Raymond had been staring, too.

"Oh, my Lord!" Mother cried, and clutched her little chest with one hand. "Dead? Father? Father dead?" Now Mother was in tears, and only Rosemary's constant reassurance that

Father was merely late, a flat tire, a stopping off for chocolates perhaps, could loosen the obituary lodged in Mother's mind and send it floating like driftwood down the uncharted rivers of her brain.

"He'd better not forget my chocolates, then," Mother warned, and wiped her tiny red eyes.

"You never fail to amaze me," Rosemary said angrily to her sister. Several times a year, Miriam told Mother the truth about the fragile people who had come and gone through her life, leaving Mother to clutch at her heart and whisper, "Dead? Uncle Perry? Uncle Perry dead?" This time it was Raymond's ogling of Lizzie's legs that had prompted Miriam to cross her own short, plump ones and deliver the news of Father's demise.

"What has the face that's launched a thousand real estate deals done now?" asked Uncle Bishop, returning from the kitchen with even more pretzels.

"You really are something, do you know that?" Rosemary asked Miriam, who appeared unfazed at the muddle she'd caused in Mother's emotions.

"Well, look at her," said Miriam. "She's rocking away and waiting for her chocolates. He never brought her any goddamn chocolates when he was alive." Miriam pulled with her teeth at a piece of fingernail. "Besides, it was only in fun."

"You've got a warped sense of humor," Rosemary said.

"Don't let Miriam spoil our fun," Uncle Bishop pleaded. "Miriam gets a sugar high when she spoils someone's fun." To complement his sandwiches, he had brewed one of his special pots of coffee. He poured those persons interested a steaming cup.

"It's delicious, Uncle Bishop," Lizzie said. "Is this your own recipe?" Uncle Bishop was swept away with pride. And he loved for Lizzie to call him *uncle*. He hovered by her side with the pot, keeping her cup up to the brim at all times, sometimes above it, which had Lizzie mopping the saucer dry with her napkin.

"It's a *secret* recipe," Uncle Bishop whispered loudly to Lizzie. "The major part of the secret is in how you mix your beans. I like South American beans." Rosemary's entire family, and this was something William had pointed out, loved to whisper loudly enough to be heard around the room. "I think that the sole responsibility of secrets frightens them," William had said.

Miriam was now glaring at Raymond, who was still manhandling Lizzie with his eyes. She was obviously taking notes for the fight they would most assuredly have later. And poor Raymond seemed to have no idea that, as the evening wore on, the evidence against him was piling up like garbage.

Uncle Bishop wanted to see pictures of Lizzie's children, so she passed the latest school photo of each around the room to the general approval of the audience.

"Looks just like you, Lizzie," they all said of little Diana, now seven years old, and, "Just like his father," they agreed about nine-year-old Charlie, the baby Lizzie had been pregnant with for her college graduation. "My graduation present from Charles," she had said of the occasion.

"We'd better go," Rosemary suggested to Lizzie.

"Why don't you two little college girls just kick off your shoes and relax?" Uncle Bishop suggested. "Put your feet up."

"Don't kick off any shoes in *this* house," Miriam warned. "Not if you care to see them again. Where is the wo-*man* of the house, by the way?" She looked around dramatically. Rosemary frowned. Apparently, Miriam hadn't heard the news that Jason was gone. Uncle Bishop regarded Miriam thoughtfully.

"Do you know what would be lovely, Miriam?" Uncle

Bishop asked evenly. He was still held in check by Lizzie's presence. "A postal card informing me to take note of your change of address, and a zip code in that new address that I couldn't possibly recognize because it's so far away. Maybe even one with *letters* in it, such as Canada or England has." Jason was still a sore spot, and Uncle Bishop's voice had a soft tremble in it.

"I see that lots of things haven't changed," Lizzie whispered to Rosemary, who only nodded, and thought about the letters in English zip codes, of London, the last place to see William alive.

"Let's go," Rosemary said. An hour was time enough to visit, especially when Miriam and Uncle Bishop were verbally circling each other, like talkative sumo wrestlers. She picked up her purse from where it leaned against Uncle Bishop's fat armchair, home, no doubt, of many "Children's Hours" of the past. A good chair in which to drink and think and panic. She kissed Mother's little powdered face. "Who puts that makeup on her?" she once asked Aunt Rachel. "She does it herself," Aunt Rachel had answered, "with the same wickedness little girls have when they discover their mommy's lipstick."

"I'll see you next week," Rosemary said to Mother. Mother was coming to stay with her while Aunt Rachel went on her summer vacation. Last year it had been Uncle Bishop, this year it would be Rosemary who baby-sat. Miriam refused to take turns, insisting that Mother frightened her pet chihuahua, Oddkins Bodkins.

"I'd take her home with *me,*" Miriam was now telling no one in particular, "but even my plants die when she visits."

"I wouldn't feel safe leaving her with Miriam and that animated rat anyway," Uncle Bishop whispered to Rosemary. "It looks just like one of those monkeys sitting in a teacup in comic books."

"Good night, love," Rosemary said to Mother, who stopped rocking long enough to gently button the top button of Rosemary's shirt.

"That was sweet," said Lizzie, who saw.

"Sometimes," Rosemary said sadly, "when she does something like this, it's as if she *almost* remembers."

"Don't forget to unplug the Christmas tree," Mother said suddenly, then sank back down in her rocker, drifted into some old memory of a smashing Christmas tree ablaze with color. Across the room, outside of the pleasant holiday going on in Mother's head, Uncle Bishop loudly told Miriam where she could stick her Virginia Slims and reminded her that there would be ample room there.

"Even in the heat of June," Rosemary said, as they opened the front door and quietly closed it behind them, leaving the skirmish inside to burn itself out.

"What?" asked Lizzie.

"A Christmas tree," said Rosemary. "Mother has a wonderful Christmas tree even in June. I miss her, but it must be wonderful to live in the mind, where unhappy facts can be changed into pleasant ones. I wish someone would tell me that William has had a flat tire, that he's on his way home with chocolates."

As they stood on the front steps of Uncle Bishop's little beige house—where just a short time ago he had thrown a delicate black pump at his mailbox—Ralph the cat came slinking out from under Lizzie's New Yorker and peed, doglike, on one of the back tires.

"Jesus, was that a *cat?*" Lizzie asked, and squinted her eyes.

"That's Ralph," said Rosemary. "He has an identity problem. Miriam says it's because he lives with Uncle Bishop."

Rosemary looked next door, over the thick expanse of

Mrs. Abernathy's startlingly green grass, and saw a small light coming from the old woman's living room. A tiny light, almost too weak in wattage to be seen. Mrs. Abernathy's little head and shoulders formed a shadowy silhouette through the window, sitting motionless. The *outline* of a woman alone, without a mate, with night coming on again, with summer passing and fall descending with the threat of winter, winter with its high mortality rates. It was the outline of an old woman growing older, growing dependent on the birds for company, on Ralph the cat for some naughty excitement. Rosemary looked through this sad window at the vignette of Mrs. Abernathy's evening at home. She remembered Mr. Abernathy, a jovial man who liked to tease little girls about their freckles and knobby knees. A *nice* man. And Mrs. Abernathy was nice then, too. Or *nicer,* when she still had Mr. Abernathy. What must it be like for her now, with nothing but her tiny column in the *Bixley Times,* the long, sloping evenings, and her precious, year-worn memories? Rosemary hated to ponder those consequences. The mortality rates were high for humans, too, and summers were sometimes cruel as winters.

"Let's stop at BJ's Tavern for a couple beers," she suggested to Lizzie.

"No, I don't think so," Lizzie said. "You'd better go alone. If we start drinking beer, we might end up getting an apartment together and signing up for English one-oh-one."

BJ's Tavern was bustling for a Wednesday night in Bixley, Maine. All the blinking signs hanging over the bar were happily announcing their beer companies. The crowd was a mixture of lumberjacks still in their work clothes and boots, college students lingering around the fireplace that would be blazing again, come October, and the local business types who filled the tables in the center of the room. The college students were keeping the jukebox busy with quarters from the bar owner, who was apologetic that his singer-guitarist had quit just that morning in a squabble over money.

Rosemary sat at the bar. It had been late in January, two weeks before William's death, when she had last been to BJ's. The bartender was still Robert, whose wife worked as one of the waitresses. He smiled when he saw Rosemary, popped open a Miller Lite, and brought it over to her.

"You haven't changed your drinking habits, have you?" he asked, as he put the beer down. Rosemary laughed.

"Just my drinking *habitats,*" she answered. "I do it at home these days, with wine."

She sat for two hours, sipping beer, listening to the jukebox crank out the latest rage and, once in a while, some older song that reminded her of William. The bar was beginning to empty itself. Most of the people who had come in alone were now leaving with a partner. Going out in *pairs.* Rosemary imagined a large ark, bobbing in the parking lot at BJ's Tavern, and a steady stream of drunks heading out the door and up the creaking plank in shaky, staggering twos.

It was then that she noticed an attractive man, early thirties, dark eyes, dark hair, sitting across the bar and almost hidden behind a hanging Boston fern. She hadn't seen him because of the plant *and* the coagulation of lumberjacks obstructing her view. She was surprised to find herself staring, but there was something about this man, some clue about his demeanor, that brought her to believe she'd met him before. But where? He was the type that Rosemary had always found attractive, the Heathcliff sort, dark, brooding. But she couldn't quite remember when or where she might have made his acquaintance. Could she have taught a younger brother who looked like him? She caught his quick glance, and he smiled, a crooked kind of smile. Then he went back to staring ahead at the Budweiser lamp of circling Clydesdales. Maybe he was someone she knew but had forgotten, some substitute teacher who had come and gone at the high school. Wondering just what constituted a tasteful move these days, Rosemary was imagining herself sending him a drink when someone tapped her on the shoulder. It was Marvin Casey, who worked at the Bixley post office, a friend to Rosemary the summer she'd filled in part-time for a woman employee who needed a few weeks off to have a baby. They exchanged the usual conversation between acquaintances in bars, the "how are you, how are things going?" kind of chat.

"Its good to see you again," Marvin said, and squeezed her hand. "You take care."

"You too, Marv." It *was* good to see him, but Rosemary was glad he had said his particulars and moved on. She wanted to meet the man on the other side of the bar before the god-almighty lights were turned up full blast. But when she spun back around on her stool he was gone. Robert was just picking up his empty glass and dunking it into the bin of dishwater behind the bar. Rosemary looked quickly to the door and saw his back as he was leaving, his jacket a bright red and yellow, made of what looked like a nonflammable material.

"Pterodactyl," she said softly. It had been the unusual red and yellow of the jacket that had triggered familiarity to her. So colorful that he was like a large, escaped parrot, cavorting about the Maine countryside in his buzzing little ultralight. *He would fly through the air, with the greatest of ease, this daring young man on the flying trapeze.*

The door had already closed, but he was probably still unlocking his car in the parking lot. She could leave the money for her tab on the bar. If she went out into the parking lot *now* he would surely see her out there and attempt to say hello. He had left the bar, hadn't he, because it looked like she and

Marvin were pairing up. She really had intended to leave in a minute or two, anyway. It wasn't as if she was running after him.

"I can sneak you one more beer before we pick them up," Robert leaned over the bar and offered. "If you're interested."

"That sounds good," Rosemary told him, and settled back onto her barstool. It wasn't as if they were strangers. He had waved to her, and she had waved back. There was an interaction. An introduction. They were now acquaintances.

"Who was that guy at the end of the bar?" she asked, and pointed to the empty stool.

"The one in the Superman suit?" Robert wanted to know, and Rosemary nodded. "I've never seen him in here before. And he didn't say much."

"Brooders never do," Rosemary mumbled.

On the drive home she hummed along with a song on the radio, but as she pulled out of the congested part of Bixley and turned up Old Airport Road, she clicked the radio button off and began to sing, softly, with the same lilting voice her mother used to have. And Rosemary remembered, suddenly, those Sunday mornings with Mother cooking breakfast, and Father sitting at the kitchen table, waiting, teasing. Father, before the other woman. Mother, before the insanity. Rosemary, before the age of six or seven. Miriam would still be in bed, a late sleeper even as a youngster, and not there to spoil the magical effect. Robbie not yet born. And Mother's voice would fill the big airy kitchen as though it were an opera house, would echo through all the rooms, mix with the sounds of eggs snapping in the frying pan, and coffee perking like a little percussionist to Mother's beat. Father, untying Mother's apron strings. "She's only got a few strings tied now, Rosemary," Miriam had said. "She's almost completely crazy. You might as well admit it." Rosemary remembered Mother twirling her apron strings in the kitchen, around and around, with Father laughing his gutsy laugh, with Rosemary clapping her hands. "She was always a little bit crazy," said Uncle Bishop, when Rosemary had asked him. "Even as a girl. But it was rather charming then." Rosemary remembered Mother pirouetting like a tiny doll across the shiny kitchen floor, all her dreams attached to the main boat, all her anchors still keeping her steadily afloat. "I guess she's just a little ding-y," Robbie had said, because he could remember her no other way. And Rosemary saw Mother again, spinning across the floor, out the door. "Crazy as a loon," a school friend once commented, and Rosemary had decked her for it. "A little ding-y." And so Mother was, a thing adrift, all her anchors up, all the lines to the big boat cut, all her loved ones standing on shore, waving. People disappearing.

On the black drive up Old Airport Road, Rosemary tried her best to remember the childhood house, the way it had been in those early years, with Mother singing at the stove, Father at the kitchen table. But she could not pull up a single image of it. Hadn't it been white, with black shutters? Beige? It was gone, she realized sadly, from her mind. It had burned to the ground before her very eyes and yet she could not remember it. Not even Aunt Rachel had a photo of it. All the memories had curled up and disappeared in smoke.

On the drive up Old Airport Road, Rosemary sang Mother's old kitchen song, and cried the beery tears that sometimes fell when she allowed the past to creep back and find her. *His movements were graceful, all the girls he could please, and my love he purloined away.*

# The Butterscotch Universe

AT ELEVEN-FIFTEEN ROSEMARY and Lizzie sat at the kitchen table, drinking coffee that Lizzie had made.

"It's awfully strong," Rosemary told her.

"I dumped what *looked* like the right amount of grounds into the strainer," Lizzie defended herself.

"Where is Uncle Bishop's coffee when I really need it?" Rosemary asked. She had taken three aspirins and a vitamin C at Lizzie's suggestion.

"Beer drinkers pee away all their vitamin C," Lizzie said. Rosemary ignored her. She was trying, through her headache, to watch the activity at the bird feeders. Several evening grosbeaks were in a frenzy over the sunflower seeds. Rosemary saw

Mugs and Winston, paws curled under them, watching the birds from their perches atop the rick of firewood. They had long since given in to the burden of the bells they had worn around their necks, had ceased to take part in the hunt, thanks to the jingling intervention of mankind. Rosemary took the bells off two years ago, worried that if the cats became lost the ringing would be their downfall in the wilds. The habit had already set in, she was thankful to learn. They sat atop the firewood and surveyed the birds as though they still wore their cumbersome collars.

"I've got to go to the library this afternoon," Rosemary said finally. She had opened her briefcase and was searching through it. "Can I use your car? Mine is really low on gas."

"Why the library?" asked Lizzie.

"There are some things I want to look up," Rosemary told her. She unwrapped a stick of Trident gum that she found hiding inside the little pocket that was meant to house the briefcase key. It was rock-hard. Probably a tie-over from her old teaching days, a little something for her to look forward to in the teacher's room. Rosemary gave Lizzie a quick hug and moved past her to take the keys to the New Yorker off the wooden key holder near the back door.

"What am I supposed to do while you're gone?" Lizzie whined.

"Why don't you finish reading that novel you brought with you two weeks ago," Rosemary suggested. "It's still opened to the first page on the back of the commode, where you left it."

"I put it there in case we run out of toilet paper," Lizzie said.

At the library Mrs. Waddell smiled and exposed her old gums to Rosemary. They were orange in color. As a child, Rosemary had believed what Sarah Prescott told her about Mrs. Waddell's teeth, that they had been ordered from the Sears and Roebuck catalog for $9.95. Her gums were orange way back then, the creamy color of butterscotch pudding.

Mrs. Waddell dragged books, lovingly, down from shelves, unlocked others from their prisons away from natural light and the sweaty hands of careless readers. Then she suggested a dozen or more once Rosemary was finished with the mountain that towered on the table. The table was the same one from childhood that Rosemary had always selected, in the north corner overlooking the loping Bixley River, where the tiny park lay. It was here she first discovered *The Wizard of Oz, Kim,* and *Little Women.*

"We lived in a house on Norris Road," Rosemary had told Mrs. Waddell, when she first arrived at the library. "We lived there until I was eleven years old, until it burned down, and now I have no pictures of it. No one in the family has a picture of it. It's the house my father lived in until he died. Do you think books on the early architecture of Bixley would have a picture? It was an old house when we moved in." Mrs. Waddell was excited with the mission. Her withered ears pursed forward like pansies in need of nourishment. She had waited among the dusty spines and yellowing library cards a lifetime for this, for someone to come into her little cubicle of books and old newspapers, seeking the knowledge she'd been safeguarding. She smiled a large, wide smile, the way a book might smile if you imagined its covers as lips and its compressed pages teeth. The gums were more butterscotchy than Rosemary remembered, and the man-made teeth seemed ready to pop their artificial roots and scatter about on the floor. But then, that would be *noisy.* Mrs. Waddell, Bixley's head librarian, had never been such.

"Fire doesn't just destroy the older homes," Mrs. Waddell

whispered, as though it were a major secret. "It destroys so many important documents, too. If I were you, I'd look through some of the family histories compiled by the Bixley Historical Society. You find wonderful photos in those, things you never knew existed." And so she began dragging books out of their hiding places for Rosemary to peruse.

"After the big fire of 1929," Mrs. Waddell whispered, "the architecture of Bixley changed drastically. I was just a little girl but, my oh my, I can still see those flames." She *had,* really, waited a lifetime, kept an eye glued to the street, listened for the right footfalls, the best ears, the proper moment, when her little floodgate of memories could open. *I knew you would come,* the books whispered as Rosemary opened them. *We've been waiting for you,* all the strange faces lost to time said with their eyes.

"At five-thirty I take my supper break, Rosemary," Mrs. Waddell said. "I'll tell you about the big fire of 1929." And for the rest of the afternoon, when Rosemary looked up from her books and notes, she caught Mrs. Waddell keeping an even watch on her. *We mustn't let this one go,* the rows of books whispered. *Keep her. Keep her,* said all the names, long forgotten, in the rusty cabinets full of old library cards in the basement. People who have disappeared.

At seven o'clock Rosemary loaded her briefcase into Lizzie's car. She had checked out only one book, hating to be responsible for other people's books, as well as hating to give a book back once it had been inside her house and seemed a member of her library. But *A Pictorial History of Bixley* had come home with her. She wanted to study the old buildings a bit longer, the early architecture of the town her mother and father had grown up in, had fallen in love in, buildings they knew well in an age that had come and gone without Rosemary being aware that it had ever existed. "What is eight years," William had asked her, just before he left for good, "when pitted against the course of time?" But she knew now that it was much worse than that. William's Time Chart proved it. It wasn't just a matter of eight little years. It was a matter of *all time.* "What is a trifling twenty thousand years?" she could now ask William, if he were there to answer her, because it had been that long ago when man began his silly quest to create art, on the walls of dark underground caves. It had been that long, at least, that man had wanted to do more than make love and eat and find protection from the blustery winds and roving packs of animals. For some unexplained reason, he wanted to do more than live just to *die.* And then came his need to write words down, when the Sumerians began scratching cuneiform things on clay tablets. And what had it all been for? Now she saw the larger truth. What is the human race, William—that's what she'd say to him now—when it's pitted against the wash of time? She was beginning to understand his abrupt departure. What he left behind was only a meaningless swirl of activities, none more important than the rest. This was mankind's sojourn upon the planet.

"From outer space the oceans look like pudding," Uncle Bishop told her once, during an especially hectic "Children's Hour." It was *Chariots of the Gods* he'd been reading. It was too much Glenlivet he'd been drinking. "In the Bible Ezekiel described the waters of the earth beneath him as looking like porridge," Uncle Bishop had wailed. "And he could only know it looked that way if he had been taken up in a spaceship. Even a scientist at NASA says Ezekiel is the first recorded extraterrestrial ride." Rosemary thought of poor Ezekiel, one minute minding his business on the dusty plains of the Old Testament, the next being whizzed through the cosmos like the unwilling tail of a comet, caught up mindlessly in some extraterrestrial experiment. A little joke on the planet Earth and the terrified earthling. Rosemary could imagine a whole spacecraft of large-headed, brainy kidnappers guffawing as they disappeared among the glittery stars at the speed of light. At the edge of time. Maybe some people did have the answers to the whole earthly experiment. She had read about a woman, Spaceship Sally, who had grown brown and withered as a berry on some wild hilltop in California, out among the night stars and meteorites, windblown and crazy, waiting for a spacecraft to come out of the galaxies of time and take her home. "When I grow old, I want to grow crazy as well," Rosemary once told William. "I want to be so obsessed with some one thing that I don't notice the wrinkles. I won't even notice time anymore, so that after a while it all becomes like one long, stretched-out, lazy day that is passing, instead of my life."

As Rosemary drove through Bixley, on her way back to Old Airport Road, she thought of the universe as being nothing more than an endless cloud of butterscotch pudding, the color of Mrs. Waddell's gums. She drove slowly. She wanted to get a *new* look at Main Street, to acknowledge where all those old buildings in the library pictures had once stood so proudly, promised to stand *forever.* And she wanted to imagine the streets full of the faces that she had pored over all day, faces of another time, another generation, a sea of people who had quietly vanished from the wooden sidewalks of town. She wanted to find the Bixley her parents had known and loved, in their youth. It was the best she could do, especially since she and Mrs. Waddell had come to the conclusion that there were no longer any pictures of the childhood home on Norris Road. Only in Rosemary's mind was a blurred picture still hanging, placed there by an eleven-year-old child.

After her three-mile run, Rosemary perused the library book until two o'clock before she finally went up to bed. That night there were more troublesome dreams. There were Gregor Samsa dreams that night. This time the predominant figure in her nighttime drama was not William. Instead, Mrs. Waddell soared up and down the library aisles in a bright red-and-yellow ultralight, lovingly dusting each book, the tiny sound of her engine as smooth and quiet as Mugs's rhythmic purring. But when she spotted Rosemary over in her corner window, Mrs. Waddell bore down like the Red Baron. She focused her sights on Rosemary, who had no option but to run. And there was the terror of the dream: Rosemary tripping through a graying maze of old buildings she didn't recognize at first, ancient residences and stores and theaters she had seen in the library book, so real to her now that she felt she had grown up in that very era of Bixley. "What is a life when pitted against the rivers of time?" And yet she lost her way. Sidewalks ran out. Streets shifted beneath her. Signs turned their faces away as she tried to read their names. And all the while Mrs. Waddell, a cackling red-and-yellow dragonfly, was closing in on her, was beating the tiny wings of her ultralight, laughing her spinsterish, butterscotchy, old-woman laugh.

# The Fifteen Steps

WHEN ROSEMARY AWOKE at eleven the next morning there were voices from the front yard seeping in through the screen under her window. And so was the approaching noon heat of a summery day. She thumped her leg beneath the sheet covering. Her left shin was a bit sore. She had pushed too hard on her run the night before. A panicky kind of running. Once, she thought she'd heard the voices of a milling crowd behind her as she left the town limits of Bixley to begin the run back up Old Airport Road, and home. But she knew what distant, echoey sounds were creeping up on her. They were the voices of the dead, Bixley's old guard, wafting faintly from around the ghostly architecture.

The living voices were now in the kitchen, Lizzie's excited and hovering above the other, a quiet, manly bass. No doubt Philip had arrived. Rosemary chose to lie in bed and watch the cluster of white-throated sparrows that had gathered in the top of the maple tree. Something had disturbed them on the ground, perhaps Winston, the outdoor cat, who occasionally crawled up into the waist-high tray feeder and fell asleep.

She wished she had a cup of tea without having to go down to the kitchen for it. She was not ready to meet Lizzie's new paramour. Another car sped down Old Airport Road, much too fast. Rosemary could see the wake of dust as a thin, brownish cloud rose up to her window, and then drifted off over the fields. Maybe she could find a sign that said RADAR CHECK! and pound it into the earth near the CAT CROSSING sign. The latter had been Rosemary's idea, but William had painted the perfect letters on it. It stood by the road, near the culvert, where Mugs occasionally crossed over to get to the wide open fields.

Rosemary heard Lizzie on the long steep stairs, with Philip, the bang of luggage as it caught each step, and shopping sacks crinkling. The rustling and whispering went on down the hall to the spare bedroom across from Lizzie's room. There were five bedrooms, counting Rosemary's, in the big upstairs. Only her room and two others were fully furnished, with antiques and odds and ends that William was forever finding at auctions. The last two bedrooms had only beds, which Rosemary kept neatly made, although she never expected to entertain that much company at once. William's having no family, other than a sister who lived downstate, precluded an onslaught of relatives arriving from his side of the genetic tree. Because Rosemary's family lived nearby in their own homes, it was only on special occasions or if Uncle Bishop had too much to drink that they slept over in one of the more furnished bedrooms.

Rosemary assumed Lizzie was putting Philip in his own room for appearances only.

The phone rang but she ignored it. On the third bleat it stopped.

"Hey!" Lizzie said, and rapped on the bedroom door. "You awake?" Rosemary said nothing. Instead, she watched a robin bounce along the top branch of the maple, causing an uprising of discouragement from the sparrows. "Uncle Bishop wants to know if you'll go swimming with him," Lizzie added, her voice full of the excitement of Philip's arrival. "He's on the phone, waiting for an answer." Rosemary thought about this. *The primordial sea.* That's what Uncle Bishop called the Bixley swimming pool, insisting that it held beneath its murky waters angry crustaceans, and all sorts of slithering missing links.

"She must still be asleep," Rosemary heard Lizzie, whispering now, outside the door. Footfalls crept softly down the hallway, and then disappeared downstairs. Rosemary thought of Uncle Bishop's huge, white belly cascading like bread dough down over his purple-and-yellow swimming trunks, which said PRINCE EDWARD ISLAND LOBSTER CARNIVAL, an artsy-craftsy eyesore. Small children at the Bixley Pool considered him the bogeyman.

"Uncle Bishop says this is your last chance," Lizzie announced. She was back at the bedroom door. "I told him you were still asleep, but he says he knows better. He says you're lying in bed, wide awake, watching the birds." Rosemary said nothing. She kicked her toes beneath the sheet and waited for Lizzie's footfalls to disappear again. But the heat of the day was bombarding the house, with its high old-fashioned ceilings, was rising up to the bedrooms and prompting her to consider a swim, not at the Bixley Pool but at the Bixley River, a half mile from her house, where it teetered in little pools above a buildup of immense boulders, where the little crayfish and inch-long trout darted into shadows and behind rocks.

Rosemary flicked on the yellow aluminum fan that sat near her bed on the floor. She turned its face upward, as though it were a huge, beaming sunflower, and felt the cool spray of breeze spiral over her. She heard the mailman's car pull away from the box outside in a flurry of little pebbles, warm from lying in the sun. The flag on the mailbox would now be down, her letter to Michael, William's friend, would now be gone, on its way to Portland on such a hot June day. Rosemary had some questions for him, finally, about those last days in London. She heard a small whine coming up Old Airport Road and thought about her ultralight man.

"Pterodactyl," she said aloud. Primitive bird-watching. But the whine turned into an automobile as it got closer, and finally, the sound of pebbles once more against tires, it pulled noisily into Rosemary's yard. Uncle Bishop, no doubt about it. He'd had just enough time, ten minutes, to drive over. She heard a door slam and wondered what expression the Datsun had on its face. Sighing, she pulled on her jeans and then found her favorite denim shirt, worn thin by many washings. She tied the tail ends up in a large knot, a sturdy blue rose. Mugs waited patiently at the bedroom door for it to open, and then bounded down the fifteen steps and out into the kitchen. Rosemary knew this was the exact number of steps because one quiet autumn evening, when the fireplace was bursting and snapping with seasoned hardwood, and a cold rain was fingering its way across the big church windows, she had suddenly turned to William, who lay next to her, his head sharing her pillow in front of the fire, and she had asked him. For no reason. "How many steps are there going upstairs, William?" And he had answered easily. "Fifteen." As far as Rosemary knew there could've been forty. Or six. She paid no attention to the obvious. "How many steps, William?" It was so like him to know the correct answer. "I counted them, once, so I'd know, Rosie, how many to expect when I get up at night and come downstairs without turning on a light. I'm never afraid of falling that way."

Fear of falling was Rosemary's fear. She was always terrified of tumbling down the steep stairs at night, its hardwood, shiny steps little terraces of ice. Dangerous. And she was afraid of falling out of an airplane. Perhaps a stewardess, fixing a false eyelash, would lean unknowingly on the big handle to the emergency door and it would burst open, sucking up all the passengers close enough to be caught in its vorticose mouth. A rainy autumn night, earthbound, with an orange fire and a fiery wine, and William, and a fear of falling. Where? Down to China?

"Do you think Icarus was afraid?" Rosemary had asked William. There was a print of Brueghel's *The Fall of Icarus* hanging in a do-it-yourself frame on the wall. A print among dozens of prints. Their favorite paintings. "Was Icarus afraid when he fell? Did he cry out?" And William, as he began to undo the buttons on her flannel shirt so he could slip a hand inside to hold her warm braless breast, had said, "Icarus knew his limitations. He knew he could only go so high. He chose his own death, Rosemary, and that's what is so wonderful about it. Like a mountain climber. No one forces him to climb. He goes of his own free will. He knows one day the rope might saw across a sharp rock. Or his footing will be just a fraction off. And then the fall, with plenty of time to think about his life. And of how his body will look at the bottom, spread-eagle and bloody on the rocks. No, Rosie, Icarus wasn't afraid. He was enchanted by the blue swirl of the sea beneath him and the warm yellow of the sun above. It was all color, and then it was over."

Fifteen steps. Every night since William had died and she'd gotten up in the dark to let Mugs in or out, she had counted them. *One, two, three.* If she fell and died, how long would it be before they found her? How long before all the plants turned sere and brown in the windows, and the birds abandoned the empty, weathered feeders? How long before the cat, wan and weak, could no longer jump upon the sill and press his thin face against the glass? *Four, five, six.* Nights when she'd had too much wine, she made sure she was counting accurately by counting slowly. *Seven, eight.* Had William flown too high? What was it that threw him out of the sky and onto the bespattered floor of his London flat? "Icarus chose his own fate, Rosie, and that's what was so wonderful about it." *Nine, ten, eleven.*

That night, with William in front of the fire, Rosemary had thought *about fire,* that gift given to man by the sky, by the heavens, by the gods who let a frenzied finger of lightning bolt down four hundred thousand years ago, so that a frightened, then delighted Peking Man could take it with him, back into his icy cave. William had put his glass of wine aside and rolled over onto his stomach beside her, a hand undoing the zipper on her jeans while Rosemary stared at the painting on the wall. Icarus's visual obituary. His death, framed. "I think Icarus was framed," Rosemary had said, and laughed silently at her joke. And the rain had beat steadily against the house, run like rivers out of the roof gutters and downspouts, and lightning had lit up the backyard, illuminated all the ghostly feeders full of swollen millet and bloated corn. "Was Icarus afraid, William?" she asked again, as she stared at the print of Icarus trying to marry the cosmos. Icarus's wedding picture. "Did he cry out?" as William eased her jeans down over her hips and pulled them off. *Twelve, thirteen, fourteen.* "I think

Icarus was framed, William." And the big old house had rattled as if a mythical storm was passing overhead, a parade of centaurs and gorgons, griffins and minotaurs, in a frenzy of wings and snorts and bellows, while far below in the black, labyrinthine house William and Rosemary made love, in front of the ancient notion of fire, in front of Icarus, frightened and plummeting into the sea, in front of Mugs, who licked his paws and watched the goings-on with casual, detached amusement. *Fifteen.* At the bottom of the stairs Rosemary came face-to-face with a dark-haired, pleasant-looking man.

"There's a large gentleman sitting out on your swing," Philip said, extending his hand in greeting. "He's wearing very unusual shorts, and he seems to be crying."

As Lizzie and Philip drove off to do some minor shopping in Bixley, Rosemary brought two glasses of cabernet out to the backyard and handed one to Uncle Bishop. She noticed the dirty, sky-blue Datsun pulled sadly up to the porch steps. It looked as if it were about to weep. She sat next to Uncle Bishop on the wooden swing and they pushed off a few times with their feet to set them in motion. He had stopped crying, but his eyes were reddish, puffy. To top off his PRINCE EDWARD ISLAND LOBSTER CARNIVAL swimming trunks, he was wearing an extra-large, navy sweatshirt, sans arms and torn a bit about the neck. It reminded Rosemary of the foolish fad that had followed the movie *Flashdance,* when hordes of young American women scampered about in tattered, torn clothing they had paid top dollar to own. How confusing that style must have been to Third World countries, whose largest dreams were to cast aside their ragged clothing for the milk-and-honey fashions of America.

"So you didn't go swimming at the Bixley Pool," she said, and sipped her wine. On Uncle Bishop's feet were brown sandals with red toenails painted onto the ends, beneath Uncle Bishop's own pale-pink toenails. Where did he find such things?

"Pee sea," said Uncle Bishop. "Twenty-five percent chlorine and seventy-five percent kid urine." He drank at his own wine. Rosemary watched as two baby robins, the spots on their chests like brown freckles, flapped away in the birdbath she'd put under the wild cherry. The silvery grasses, growing back at the edges of the yard, rippled in a soft little breeze that crept up Old Airport Road. She waited. Sometimes Uncle Bishop wanted to talk. Sometimes he wanted to rant. It was anybody's guess.

"I hate the Bixley Pool," Uncle Bishop said. "No one under thirty should be allowed in it. It's just like Loch Ness anyway. A few inches down is all you can see. And it's choppy as hell. It should be condemned." He picked at a mosquito bite. It was a ranting kind of day, no doubt about it. Between the posts of the arbor, Rosemary saw the remains of a spider's web, an orb weaver's web, the strands now torn and dangling softly, the art destroyed. Rosemary had read about spiders. One in twenty, five percent, tend to be geniuses, working out problems about the web, remodifying, bettering, excelling. Many late evenings, she had watched the orb weaver at his job, and had wondered if it was the work of a genius unfolding before her eyes. Funny, but in the sharp light of day the web was nothing more than broken strings, no longer a dangerous shimmering trap for the helpless fly, the fluttering moth. "Levels of consciousness depend upon the light," William had always said. That must apply to spider webs as well.

"Do you think we got the idea for lace and doilies and stuff like that from spiders?" Rosemary asked Uncle Bishop, who simply stared at her with his puffy little eyes.

"I'm sitting here with my heart on my sleeve," Uncle

Bishop said, incredulous, "and you're talking about doilies. Does the word *suicidal* strike any maternal chord in you at all?"

"You *have* no sleeves," Rosemary reminded him.

"All right, I'm sitting here with my heart on my *arm,*" he snapped. "And you want to talk about spiders."

"Well, you weren't talking about your heart," said Rosemary. "You were ranting about the Bixley Pool."

"I don't *rant,*" Uncle Bishop protested. "Miriam rants."

"You both rant," Rosemary said. Uncle Bishop pushed them off again on the swing and they swayed nicely. Rosemary hoped the chains would hold. It was like swinging with Orson Welles. Someone would mutter "Rosebud" and they would crash to the patio below.

"Do you know that Mrs. Abernathy puts cookies in her birdfeeders?" Uncle Bishop asked. The swing creaked as he shifted his weight, lifted the right leg up and crossed it heavily over the left one. "And yesterday she put *ice cream* out there. If those goddamn birds had teeth they would've fallen out by now."

"It's all in how you perceive the birds," said Rosemary. "Mrs. Abernathy tends to be a little too anthropomorphic."

"I don't *rant,*" Uncle Bishop said again.

"You rant," said Rosemary. "How's the dollhouse coming?" She shooed away a large bumblebee that came suddenly out of the giant zinnias. "Did you get any further along?" Uncle Bishop appeared to be gazing at a tiny chickadee with sheer hatred while he sucked at the rim of his wineglass.

"I've wired the dining room and now there's lights in there, thank God," he said.

The dollhouse pattern had come from one of his magazines on the subject, but he had thrown the blueprint away and designed his own house. He had even built all the midget furniture. This was the second house he was on now. The other one was sitting silently in his basement workshop, black-windowed, covered with a plastic sheet, waiting for some imaginary family to take up residence. "I wouldn't want a family with children to move in," Uncle Bishop had said, thoughtfully, as he proudly displayed the first dollhouse to Rosemary and William the minute he finished it. "Kids would just ruin that white rug in the master bedroom." Rosemary had been astounded at the minute workmanship that Uncle Bishop's fat, sausagelike fingers were capable of. They hardly seemed adept at opening beer cans, yet here was consummate work in the tiny brick fireplace, the brassy doorknobs, the cushiony divan. Work small enough to be done by spiders, yet Uncle Bishop's large, mannish hands had accomplished it, there in his basement, beneath the earth, cavelike perhaps, like the early artists. Miriam had seen it all differently. "A fat homosexual hanging little drapes in all those tiny windows," Miriam had *ranted.* "He's even got itty-bitty towels in the bathroom and toothbrushes a quarter of an inch long. And he says he's only going to let an imaginary *gay* couple move in. Is that or is that not reason to move to Hong Kong?"

It was true that Uncle Bishop had all those things in the dollhouse. He even had a tiny plastic cat—one that looked uncannily like Ralph—curled on a braided rug in front of the hearth. And there was a cat's bowl by the kitchen door, small clothes on little hangers in the closets, pictures on the walls, dishes in the cupboard, a china cabinet full of wonderful treasures. "I wish I lived in this house," Rosemary had said, that night with William, in the basement workshop, as Uncle Bishop straightened a wishlike afghan on a Louis XV chair in the itsy parlor. "I'd let *you* move in, Rosie," he'd said. And then he had sadly closed the door to the dollhouse, straightened the plastic potted plants on the steps outside, turned off the miniature porch light that lit up the brick walk like a light-years-away, twinkling star.

"I need to lay the linoleum in the kitchen," Uncle Bishop said now. He was thinking of the work that needed doing in the new dollhouse. He and Rosemary sipped more wine and sunned themselves on the swing. "What you must realize about the people who build dollhouses," William had told Rosemary, that same night as they lay in bed talking about Uncle Bishop's wonderful hobby, "is that, after a while, they live in them."

"I hung a beautiful little Renoir print on the wall going upstairs," Uncle Bishop said. "But I've just been sitting here thinking about it. Even if I let someone move in who has no kids they might still have a party. People going up and down the stairs to the bathroom might knock it down."

As they swung quietly Rosemary imagined a boisterous crowd, perhaps at Christmastime, partying it up in the dollhouse, which would be sheathed in spruce boughs and pine cones and spicy red candles. And the little kitchen would be bulging with plates of hors d'oeuvres, canapés and caviars, shrimp cocktails, pâtés, plum puddings. And the guests, elegant and mysterious beneath the mistletoe, would, sometime after midnight, become loud and happy, clinking their fluted glasses of champagne, their martini glasses ringing out like brief songs from the baby grand in the parlor. And the blazing Christmas tree, with its thimble-sized packages, would cast blue, red, and green reflections out across the feathery drive, where the potted plants sat dreaming beneath the artificial snow. Would it be just past the stroke of midnight, on this synthetic Christmas Eve, that a man, resplendent in a black tuxedo with satin lapels, dark trousers, and bow tie, a martini glistening in his hand beneath the chandelier, would corner a young woman on the stairs? And would this young woman, demure in floor-length red satin, regal in white pearls about the neck and wrist, who had caught his eye among the festive crowd all evening, would she gush girlishly, leaning back against the wall to steady her heart, to steady her champagne notions? Would it be then that her pearl-white shoulder would wrench the painting from its hook to send it crashing down the stairs, the frame twisting, then breaking, causing all the partygoers to gather at the foot around the broken Renoir? Framed. "I think Icarus was framed, William." And there above the guests would be the lovers, blushing and embarrassed, a married man and his ripe little berry of a mistress, caught in the act, a Christmas party ruined.

"Flagrante delicto," Rosemary said, aloud. "Caught red-handed." And the red would be a *satin* red. "Caught with his hands full of red satin," said Rosemary.

"What?" asked Uncle Bishop. His wineglass was empty and he twirled it idly about his plump fingers as though it were a baton. "You sit here and talk about doilies and satin for no apparent reason and yet you say that *I* rant."

"You rant," said Rosemary.

"Miriam rants," Uncle Bishop said.

"Which Renoir is it that you have hanging on the stairway wall?" Rosemary asked, not wanting him to know she had peopled his dollhouse with revelers, had thrown a party the minute his back was turned. What must the house look like now? Were the rugs spotted with alcohol? All the little dishes sticky with food? Were the ashtrays bulging with imported cigarette stubs? Were all the presents opened and the tree lightless? Was the cat confused and hungry by the empty bowl near the kitchen door? "People who build dollhouses eventually live in them," William had said. And for nights after he died, nights when Rosemary could not find sleep, she had imagined herself sitting up in one of Uncle Bishop's dainty

Louis XV beds, beneath the Barbie-doll spread he had so lovingly crocheted for that purpose.

"*Girl with a Watering Can,*" said Uncle Bishop. "I think I'm going to move it upstairs somewhere, where it'll be safe. The Japanese pay top dollar for that stuff these days, you know."

"Do you want another glass of wine?" Rosemary asked him, and took the big hands so capable of tiny work up into her own. They were cold, clammy. He shook his head. No more wine. "Do you want to talk about Jason?" Again he shook his head.

"I'd better be going," he said. "It makes me nervous to think about that Renoir hanging there on the stairway. That was really stupid of me. Do you think my homeowner's insurance will cover it?" He lifted himself from the swing. Rosemary knew that if he didn't want to talk, there was no use to pry. Uncle Bishop was like Mrs. Abernathy's telepathic morning glories. He would unfold when the time was right.

She walked with him over to the Datsun, which still seemed on the verge of tears. She was about to mention that perhaps he should give the poor beast a bath when she heard the unmistakable whine, as if a motor scooter were coming up Old Airport Road. Nearly tripping over a startled Mugs, she raced around the Datsun and out into the front yard just in time to see, disappearing, the red-and-yellow flash of the ultralight man, with his insect motor and goggle-eye glasses, soft as a dream over the treetops, and then gone. He'd been blazing all kinds of trails in the sky over Bixley. Had he been going back to BJ's? Should she go back and look for him? Now the sky was empty. There was nothing left to prove he had even been there. There were no pinkish puffs of clouds left, like bread crumbs, to mark his trail. Men disappearing.

“So that’s the ultralight man Miriam says you’re obsessed with,” Uncle Bishop noted. “I’d be suspicious of anyone who can’t do a snap roll.”

“I’m not obsessed,” said Rosemary. “I just told her that if she’s ever at BJ’s, and sees a man in a red-and-yellow suit, to call me.” She was now embarrassed to think about this. She had asked *Miriam.*

“Miriam’s into real estate, Rosie,” Uncle Bishop said. “I wouldn’t be surprised but what all her male friends wear red-and-yellow suits.”

“You’re ranting,” said Rosemary. She hugged him goodbye. In her arms he felt soft and movable as jelly. She watched him drive off down the dusty road until he was out of sight. Men disappearing.

At ten-thirty she was already asleep. The dreams were back again and vivid in color: Renoir’s little girl, with her blue, satiny dress and shiny watering can, watering all the plastic flowers in Uncle Bishop’s dollhouse until, with the can empty and discarded, she pressed her sad face with its tiny eyes against the huge, churchlike windows of the house, ignored the cries of the starving cat, ignored the guests who came and went, waited, the blond in her hair turning to brown, then gray. Like an old plant in the window, orphaned, dead at the roots, she was trapped in the house, forever.

# The Moon-Pulled Women

PHILIP SHEPPARD WAS quiet, as houseguests go. The few times that he and Lizzie crossed paths with Rosemary, he was always polite, well mannered. And Rosemary had yet to see him in jeans and a casual shirt. Instead, he wore Versace jackets, slacks, and a colored array of Italian shoes. This was in complete opposition to Lizzie's disarray. She usually had her long blackish hair pinned up in a scarf that matched a pink or pale-blue sweatshirt, and Levi Strauss or Wrangler jeans. Seeing Lizzie and Philip together was a statement of their situation: they looked like they belonged with other people, Lizzie with Charles, Philip with someone else.

"Will Philip be here this weekend when Mother arrives?"

Rosemary asked Lizzie, when Philip went out to his car for a parcel he had forgotten to bring in.

"I think so. That's if you don't mind." Lizzie was looking tired these days. She'd been in Bixley for two weeks and instead of being rested and peaceful without Charles, the children, or the untrained dog, she appeared haggard. Rosemary was making tomato, cucumber, and lettuce sandwiches for the three of them. Lizzie took potato salad out of the refrigerator and sniffed it.

"Sniffing is not really a scientific test for salmonella," said Rosemary. She and Lizzie had had this argument many times before, in college. Lizzie put the salad on the table. It had obviously passed.

"It's test enough for me," she said.

"How will Philip react to Mother?" Rosemary asked. Mugs rubbed against her leg, then reached up a paw to touch her. "You don't like cucumber, Mugs," Rosemary said.

"Philip's a lawyer, remember," Lizzie said. "He's seen much worse than your mother. Did I ever tell you about the man from Portland who fell in love with a Shetland pony and sued Portland Riding Stables for visitation rights?"

"Don't," said Rosemary.

"Besides," Lizzie continued. "It's not your mother's fault she fell off that ladder and hit her head."

"I think the whole family agrees on one thing," said Rosemary. "That Mother's problem was only enhanced by the fall." It had always bothered her, this visual image of Mother tumbling from the ladder and onto her head. It was the comic notion of insanity. *Did someone give you a whack on the head? You must have been dropped on your head as a child.* When Rosemary received the phone call from Aunt Rachel that Mother had taken a wicked fall, and that it was most serious, maybe even fatal, she had thought suddenly of the Great Wallenda, falling from his tightrope. Aunt Rachel was giving her details, and instead of listening all Rosemary could think of was Carl Wallenda falling down, down, with plenty of time to think. The Great Wallenda. The *late* Wallenda, watching the little film of his life being rerun beneath his lids, while on the street below the pulsing crowd pushed forward like a giant mouth, waiting to swallow him up. "Take the mountain climber, Rosemary," William had said, that rainy night in front of the fire. "No one forces him to climb. He knows one day the rope . . . his footing . . . and then it's over."

Philip came into the kitchen and scooped Mugs up in an armful of black-and-white fur and round yellow eyes.

"If Philip is no problem for *you,*" Lizzie whispered in Rosemary's ear, "Mother is no problem for *us.*"

"Secrets?" Philip asked. His clothes, Rosemary noticed, never seemed to wrinkle, even after sitting about all day.

"We were just talking girl talk," said Lizzie. "That's all."

"I see." Philip nodded. "You told her about the pony fucker."

It was early in the evening, on Friday, when Aunt Rachel drove up Rosemary's drive with Mother bouncing in the front seat. The air was warm and thick, like the air after a house fire, an ashy, cinder-filled air. Lightning bugs came and went like busy shoppers among the fields of hay across the road, and crickets rubbed their tireless legs. Mother brought with her a little suitcase that looked more like a picnic basket. Rosemary imagined good things to *eat* inside, rather than to wear.

"I'm visiting friends in Old Orchard Beach," Aunt Rachel said, when Rosemary inquired about the vacation week. "A few walks on the beach, a few seashells, a few good chats, that sort of thing." Her face was a grayish pale, her cheekbones more prominent than ever. The family had learned, just weeks before, that Aunt Rachel was battling cancer. Rosemary and Uncle Bishop had insisted again on taking turns housing and caring for Mother, but Aunt Rachel would hear nothing of it. "It takes a professional," was all she'd say. "And what would I do alone in that big old house? Your mother is good company. We have an order to our lives." So Uncle Bishop and Rosemary continued to handle the financial burden, Uncle Bishop with the lion's share. Even Robbie, who was now out of college and working in construction until he decided his future, pitched in. Only Miriam never contributed. Instead, she wanted to know how Uncle Bishop was able to do so, and so generously. Two hundred dollars a week. "Where does he get his money?" Miriam ranted. "He's got to be involved in some homo-porno ring."

Mother didn't want to stay. She clung to Aunt Rachel's arm, crying a bit, mumbling. But Aunt Rachel talked to her gently, soothed her flouncing blond curls, and assured her there were worse things on the planet than spending a week with this *stranger*. Uncle Bishop had brought Mother's rocker over earlier in the day, so Rosemary took her by the hand and led her into the den. When Mother saw the rocker she quickly grabbed at it, the way a drowning man grabs at a piece of driftwood.

"My chair!" Mother gushed. "Mr. Talbot fixed it!" Robbie, Miriam, Uncle Bishop, Rosemary, all strangers to her. Yet Mr. Talbot—who was formerly of Talbot Hardware in Bixley and had moved away when Rosemary was in her early teens—still surfaced now and then in the theater of Mother's mind. And she never forgot her rocking chair. She still refused to sit in any other. Aunt Rachel was the one person Mother never failed to recognize. There was a most unusual umbilical cord stretching between the two sisters that Rosemary had never understood. They didn't seem to have a lot in common.

Aunt Rachel enjoyed classical music, sitting sometimes in the dark and listening to the melancholy notes of Mozart. Mother was all lights and the popular, raucous tunes of her girlhood. A little something by Sinatra or the Harry James Orchestra, yes, but never *The Magic Flute.* Aunt Rachel was a good bottle of wine. Mother had been gin-and-tonic in her day and, now, anything with an alcohol base. Aunt Rachel was always dressed primly in button-down blouses and sensible skirts. A serious dress. Rosemary had seen the old pictures of Mother in elegant Hollywood hairdos copied from magazines, and sweeping patterns she'd made by hand. She remembered Mother in velvet dresses, and silk skirts that washed about her hips like water. Even on washdays Mother wore makeup, a bluish tint to the upper lids, a trace of pinkish red to the lips, combs in her hair, a perfumy, musky smell about her bosom and neck. Aunt Rachel would never dance around the kitchen singing about daring young men who swing from woman to woman as though they were trapezes. Yet, even suffering from recurring cancer, Aunt Rachel refused to let anyone take Mother away.

Rosemary brought Mother a cup of tea and a slice of banana bread. Mother ate in little bites, breaking the pieces away with her fingers. Rosemary found the crocheted slippers that Aunt Rachel had said were in the suitcase, and she put them on Mother's feet.

"Thank you, dearie," said Mother, and sipped her tea. Rosemary turned the television set on but Mother paid no attention to the vicissitudes taking place on the screen. Entertaining her was akin to baby-sitting. She couldn't be left alone for very long. And she was a tiny stranger in Rosemary's huge house.

Rosemary unpacked a few of the things Aunt Rachel had sent, a magic slate, a tiny toy xylophone, a Cabbage Patch doll. The latter had upset Miriam greatly. "Aunt Rachel spoils her," Miriam had said. "Our mother owns a Cabbage Patch Kid called Betsy Kathleen. Is that or is that not reason to move to Siberia?" Seeing her unpacked, Mother grabbed for Betsy Kathleen. Except for the braids, the doll looked startlingly like Andy Rooney. As Rosemary watched, Mother undressed it and then changed its diaper. It unnerved Rosemary to see this. How many times had Mother performed this self-same task on her? On Miriam and Robbie? Somewhere in her mind, was Mother raising her family all over again? Rosemary stared at the doll as it was dressed again in its denim jumpsuit. Its hair was the brownish wheat color of her own. Its eyes were as blue as Rosemary's. Mother patted Betsy Kathleen's bottom to say *good girl,* and then wrapped her in a soft baby blanket to keep her warm. Rosemary felt short of breath, too warm, suddenly, as if a blanket were smothering her, as if Mother were clutching her too tightly. Perspiration formed on her forehead.

Rosemary left Mother alone with her new baby, her fourth child if anyone was counting, and went outside where the swing hung empty. She could see Mother through the glass door, could keep an eye on her antics. But Mother went on holding her child, her curls yellow as the sun, her hands turning old around the doll's lifeless body. Mother with her doll. Uncle Bishop with his dollhouse. Rosemary thought suddenly of her father, dead for twenty-two years, a ghost to her, almost. His memory was kept alive and tied to her by the sense of smell: his Old Spice after-shave and his white cotton T-shirt that had been all day on the clothesline, in the river breeze. Before falling asleep, Rosemary would go into his room and crawl into bed beside him. He would be half-asleep, half-awake enough to unfold one of his massive arms and take her in close. And there, next to the soft heat of his body, with the Old Spice lingering amidst the cool river breeze of the T-shirt, she could almost see the blue Yankee clipper ship on the white bottle bob gently up and down, bob up and down on the white T-shirt, then sail away, taking her with it.

Mother was putting her sleeping baby to bed on the couch. She covered it, now her *only* child, with the same pastel blanket and then, as mysteriously as it had appeared, this mother concern was gone. Off Mother went, into some other room of the house, where Rosemary would need to check up on her in ten minutes. "She's forgotten us the way little girls grow up and forget the dolls of their childhood," Rosemary told Robbie one night. "The way animals forget their beloved litters." And it suddenly occurred to her that, earlier, she was feeling *jealousy*. It was almost laughably unimaginable, but it was true. *Jealous of a Cabbage Patch Kid!* What would Miriam say of this? But Rosemary knew that she had been cheated out of a ritual. She would never partake in the mother-daughter ceremony, in that little dance between two women on a stage that is bare, but charged with emotion. An electric stage, as daughters become their mothers.

There was a tickling breeze about, a cat's-paw breeze. The fuzzy lights from the little airport created a Milky Way sky overhead. But after ten o'clock even these lights would go out, leaving the sky over Old Airport Road dark as pitch. Leaving Rosemary alone below the constellations where she silently named each of them, remembered the mythologies behind them: The Big Dipper. Cassiopeia. Little Dipper. Cepheus. Draco. The circumpolar constellations. She would check again to see if the six-inch reflecting telescope she had finally broken down and ordered from the camera shop in Bixley had arrived. It would be an expensive hobby, crippling her nest egg but, quite frankly, she was tiring of life on earth, of finding no answers there. Maybe it was time to look into the sky, as the early ancestors themselves had done. Out there would be even earlier connections: man had been born of the stars. His flesh and bone had risen out of cosmic explosions and now the planet was loaded with millions of people, *twinkling* with them. Stellar sparks. Before she went in search of Mother, Rosemary sat on the swing, her eyes closed, and thought of all the little people on earth who threw on their porch lights for the astronauts, who blinked in starlike unison, lighting up the United States of America as though it were a huge pinball machine.

Mother was huddled on one side of the bed, in Rosemary's bedroom, looking perplexed, holding something tightly in her hand, as though it were gold. And that's because it was. Rosemary unfurled the hand to see that it was a wedding band that Mother held. Her own. Had she, for some reason, taken it off and now it confused her? It had no beginning and no end, a little infinity, unlike most weddings. It was more like the measureless universe. Mother played with the ring frantically until Rosemary took it from her and slipped it easily back onto the bony finger. Mother's hands had always been so slender, with long, piano-playing fingers. Back in place, the wedding band caught the light and Mother smiled at this. Had the doll baby downstairs reminded her that, once upon a time, there had been real babies, with a man who had given her that very ring? Twenty-two years had come and gone since the man who put it on her finger went back into the earth, or went out to dance among the life-giving stars, wherever the listless, uninterested dead go. Rosemary sat on the bed and put an arm around Mother's thin shoulders. A screen was beneath the window and the curtains lifted up in the breeze, reached out to touch the women.

"Someone who loved you very much gave you that ring," Rosemary said, and pushed a yellow ringlet from Mother's forehead. *When she was good, she was very very good. When she was bad, she was crazy.* She remembered the wedding picture, had stared as a child at the porcelain beauty with the honey blond waves of hair, the snowy dress, the baby's breath and wild violets looking fresh enough in the bouquet to last forever. Mother half shook her head as memories and impulses bumped into each other like bumper cars.

"Jonathan," Mother said quickly, more to him than to his daughter, her voice raspy as a whisper. Rosemary smiled. She hugged Mother's little ship of bones, that sad malfunctioning universe.

"Yes," said Rosemary. "His name was Jonathan O'Neal, and we both loved him very much." Mother looked at Rosemary with new interest, the way one looks at a pen pal one has been writing to for years and finally gets to meet.

"He'd better bring me some chocolates then," Mother said. Rosemary closed her eyes and imagined them both ageless, just two women in their prime, scouring the sands of a blazing beach, holding seashells to their ears, listening to the songs of the sirens, the beautiful music of womanhood, before the moon-pulled tides swept in to wash them both away.

# The Class Reunion

ROSEMARY SET HER alarm clock for seven-thirty, early for her, but late for Mother, who was usually, as Aunt Rachel warned, up at daylight. "She has an uncanny sense of time," Aunt Rachel said. "She comes every hour to stand in front of my cuckoo clock just a second or two before it sounds. Yet, she wears no watch." Miriam would have loved hearing this little timely tidbit about Mother. "She's totally cuckoo, Rosemary, you may as well admit it."

Mother was sitting in the den watching the birds suspiciously. Rosemary had locked all the doors the evening before, hoping this would at least deter an escape. She hated to think of Mother loose in Bixley.

"Did you sleep well, Mom?" Rosemary asked the indifferent birder. Mother looked at her, perplexed. "Please don't call her Mother or Mom," Aunt Rachel had pleaded. "It seems to only confuse and upset her. Try not to call her any name at all."

Mother's little yellow head bobbed first one way and then the other, canting as she watched the numerous early morning feeders. She was a strange little bird herself, looking much like some exotic escapee with her head of brilliant yellow feathers, the violet cotton housedress forming exquisite underparts, the pink pockets blazing like unheard-of wing bars.

"Cuckoo!" Mother suddenly crooned. Rosemary realized she must be associating these living birds with Aunt Rachel's clock. She was glad Miriam had missed this, too. Miriam wanted badly to put Mother in a nursing home, much to the protests of the other family members. But Rosemary thought of those places as giant nurseries full of unblinking, wildly staring dolls whose batteries have run down, whose arthritic joints have melded from nonbending, whose mouths are frozen open, oval as spoons in the withering faces. Mother belonged with her family, even if she no longer gave a damn who they were.

Rosemary noticed that Betsy Kathleen, her Cabbage Patch half sister, was wearing sweatpants, sweatshirt, and what resembled honest-to-God tennis shoes.

"She's looking more and more like me every day," she thought.

For lunch Rosemary unfolded the legs of her card table and set it up on the small cement patio with two of the matching chairs. She covered it with a linen tablecloth, a soft peach color, and arranged the table with linen and crystal, her best china and silver. She cut a handful of African daisies that had finally come to life in the large wooden boxes she kept near the back fence and now they sat on the table in a glass vase. She poured champagne into two hollow-stemmed glasses and then brought the platters she'd prepared in the kitchen out to the table. One held an arrangement of cheeses, rye bread, and nuts. The other platter was an array of fresh fruits: chunks of apple, honeydew melon, cantaloupe, kiwi. Mother was pleased with the little outdoor table and let Rosemary arrange her napkin on her lap and fill her plate with goodies. They sat like old friends who have finally made plans to meet far away from the bustle of the city, at some obscure inn, where the birds are plentiful, where the cats are peaceful and snoozing. Rosemary tossed an occasional piece of bread out toward the feeders and watched as house sparrows hopped courageously toward it in little half spirals.

The champagne was cold and delicious, bubbling. It reminded her of a natural spring she and her father had discovered once, in the woods behind her childhood home, the one that had disappeared in fire and smoke. Rosemary missed that house almost as much as she missed her father. And she could remember, easily, the day it went up in flames. She had been paying old Mr. Fletcher a dime for a cone of vanilla ice cream when the fire truck rushed screaming through town with a chicklike procession of cars following. And so she and a handful of other Bixley kids had pedaled the half mile out of town, toward the blankety cloud of smoke that rose into the October air like a misplaced tornado. Her heart had begun to pound when she saw where it was coming from, the house, the childhood womb. She had thought it would always be there, a place for Father's ghost to live, a marker for the frosty little spring. Now there was fire in her bedroom window. She could almost hear the teddy bears and dolls shrieking, all the toys dying. And then the stairs crumbled like dominoes. The walls turned to ashes. All the memories were loosed and floating, all her childhood, cinders. There was no place left for Father's spirit to hang around. That was the day, aged eleven, she knew he was really dead, the day of the house disappearing. But perhaps the little spring was still there, pumping life out of the earth. She remembered they had been following a Canada warbler on the day they discovered it. Father wanted her to hear its *chip, chupety, swee-ditchety.* They rushed, that sunlighty day of exploration, through the thickly rooted spruce, and pine, and shimmering elms, stepped on the tiny mushroom bombs that bloomed beneath the trees, did not wait to watch them explode soundlessly beneath their feet, like small Hiroshimas and Nagasakis, flowering, cascading down upon the disturbed little worlds below them. Instead of the Canada warbler, they stumbled upon the delicious little spring bubbling like champagne out of the earth, *where Alp the sacred river ran, in caverns measureless to man.* They had drunk from it like wild horses, their lips soft as petals on the surface, their nostrils flaring wildly from the run. The spring was proof that Father had indeed, once, been here, before his ghostly profession. "What does your father do?" children had asked her over the years. "He's dead," Rosemary would say. "He doesn't do anything."

Rosemary had brought the champagne bottle out to the patio in a brass ice bucket, and she poured from it until the two glasses were full again. Mother slugged the second glass of champagne down so easily it might have been a thimble full of water. Rosemary left her there amid the cheese and fruit to go back inside the house. She'd heard a noise and assumed Lizzie and Philip must be finished with their showers and dressing to go off for their usual lunch in Thomasville. Rosemary intended to ask Lizzie to stop by Laker's for the suet they saved for her, from around the kidneys, for her gourmet woodpeckers. The noise again. But it was not coming from inside the house. Someone was gently rapping on the front door. "A salesman," thought Rosemary, "tapping at my chamber door. Fuller Brush and nothing more." She had learned over the years to recognize the approaches her infrequent visitors used at her front door. Uncle Bishop pounded loudly as a carpenter. Robbie gave a *shave and a haircut, two bits* knock, seven medium-sized raps. Miriam never knocked unless the door was locked. She liked to creep in. "The door was unlocked so I let myself in," she'd say, hoping she might find Rosemary and William fastened like dogs in some embarrassing position. But before Rosemary could open the door Lizzie and Philip came down the stairs.

"Who's that?" Lizzie asked, as she tucked an army-green T-shirt inside khaki shorts. Lizzie would perpetually remind Rosemary of a Girl Scout off to sell cookies.

"I don't know," Rosemary said. "I'm not expecting anyone." She was anxious to get back out on the patio to keep watch on the bottle of champagne. If left alone, Mother would surely empty it. With a curious Lizzie behind her, Rosemary opened the door and looked into a face she hadn't seen in some time, a face that was still handsome but now had tiny lines edging the eyes, and a tired worldliness in the eyes themselves that had not been there in college, where he'd been her fiercest competition in the debate club. Lizzie's husband, and now *Philip's* competition: Charles Vanier, Sr.

All Rosemary could do, really, was hug him and then step back to let him in. He kept his hands in his pockets as he looked from Lizzie's shocked face to Philip's. No one said anything, for what seemed to Rosemary a painfully long time, and then the accusals began, with Charles and Lizzie pointing angry fingers at each other. Philip stepped back as if to survey the case at a distance. "Flagrante delicto," Rosemary thought, remembering the Christmas party she'd imagined in Uncle Bishop's dollhouse. "Caught with his hands full of red satin."

"I knew this person must have been up here when you never called once," Charles said. He was not shouting, but he was furious in a clenched-teeth sort of way. "You were supposed to give yourself some time away from us both, to think things out, or so you said, and look at the little nest I've stumbled upon."

"What little nest have you stumbled *out of* to come and visit my little nest?" Lizzie, on the other hand, *was* shouting, very unbefitting a Girl Scout. "I'm surprised you found the time to drive—no, *sneak*—up here."

"Don't you go casting aspersions," Charles said, and Lizzie snorted. It was her *I'm so incredibly above this that it pains me* snort. She'd perfected it in college, during the passage of a cross-country skiing course, which, to everyone's amazement, she flunked. Rosemary could still hear her, fifty feet behind the other skiers, cold, snowy, and snorting.

"Aspersions?" Lizzie hissed. "Aspersions?" Philip was inching away. Rosemary had moved back against the foyer wall and stood there helplessly watching, the way a referee might in a boxing match. Lizzie raised her arms to put her hands on her hips. Rosemary recognized the meaning. She'd seen birds raise their contour feathers during territorial encounters.

"Excuse me," said Philip, "but I believe this is personal." Lizzie stared, stupefied, at his back, as he disappeared up the stairs. His footfalls padded down the long hallway to the room where Lizzie had put his suitcases, for respectability. A door shut softly and then all was quiet.

"Abandonment," said Charles, smirking. "And he hasn't even met our dog, not to mention the children." Lizzie glowered.

"Listen, I need to get back to Mother," said Rosemary. "Charles, for what it's worth, it's good to see you again." She gave him another little hug.

"You too, Rosie," he said. He was still pleased at Philip's exit, at Lizzie's blushed face. Rosemary felt a twinge of remorseful memory suddenly. Had it been so many years ago that this was all *before* them, waiting to happen, these twisted mistakes they'd all make? She remembered Lizzie and Charles on their wedding day, so soon after graduating, Lizzie beginning to swell just slightly with Charles Vanier, Jr. And Rosemary in her chafing maid-of-honor gown, so sure Lizzie was making a mistake.

"The least you could have done was crawl out of bed long enough to visit your children each weekend," Charles said.

"You will not instill that sort of guilt in me," snapped Lizzie. She'd calmed down a bit now that Philip had quit the scene. His presence had probably caused her to overreact, and surprise was a vicious weapon. "I take excellent care of my children all year long. They're at camp enjoying themselves. A phone call every few days is sufficient. Besides, what do you do for your children besides tuck them into bed each night?"

Rosemary remembered, suddenly, a day she'd come into the old college library, stomping snow from her boots and looking for Lizzie. She had found her in among the rows of quiet shelves, locked in a wet kiss, with Charles, two innocent college students with their assumed smugness of life. And they were in the child psychology section. "The last place I thought to look for you two," she'd told them, that sunny day of the snow-filled campus, and the exhilarating promise of thaw after a long, white winter. When life was still all titillation. When futures were dangling ahead of everyone, shiny as icicles. Rosemary left Lizzie and Charles, as emotionally charged as that feverish day in the library among the shelves of books, and went back out to the patio to find Mother.

After lunch, Rosemary took Mother upstairs and helped her get comfortable for the little afternoon nap she was fond of taking. The idea suddenly appealed to Rosemary, too, so she went to her own room, kicked her Nikes off, and stretched out on the bed. It was a surprise to her when she awoke and saw by the clock that she'd been asleep for almost two hours. Rarely did her mind quit racing long enough to let her sleep soundly in the afternoon. Even at night, desperately tired, thoughts about William, questions about those last minutes, did acrobatic maneuvers in her head. And when she did fall, finally, asleep, those thoughts got all dressed up in symbolic costumes and paraded themselves before her as dreams.

Mother was still sleeping, her small shoulders heaving up and down, as though she were a doll being inflated, the mouth painted much too red by some overly zealous factory worker, the yellow hair glued haphazardly onto the scalp. Rosemary went back to her bedroom and looked out to see what birds would be arriving for the late feeding. Lizzie and Charles were walking slowly about the backyard, their hands gesticulating and circling, two hearing people engaged in sign language.

On an impulse, she tried Uncle Bishop's number but there was no answer, just loud long rings that must be echoing around the empty rooms of the beige-and-chocolate house, bouncing off all the walls. She hoped he was okay. He'd been riding a high emotional crest lately, what with Jason's leaving. Putting Uncle Bishop aside, she opened up her ancient college paperback copy of *The Scarlet Letter,* which she'd just begun to reread. A half hour passed with Hester and Arthur before she looked out to see if the goldfinches had yet discovered the new niger feeder she had hung from the small cherry tree. It was then that a movement caught her eyes, figures walking from left to right across the range of her vision, as if in a film, Lizzie and Philip. Lizzie was looking terribly diplomatic. It was obvious that a great summit meeting was taking place in Bixley.

Rosemary tried Uncle Bishop's number again, and again, no answer. With the peace talks still going on in the backyard, she walked her bicycle quietly out to the road and headed for Uncle Bishop's little beige-and-chocolate house. She saw the Datsun first, a snarl on its lip, backed ass end into the garage. A small commotion of some sort was going on in the backyard. Rosemary could hear Uncle Bishop's large voice, on the shrill edge of excitement. She parked the bike in the front yard, by Mrs. Abernathy's spreading lilac bush, and headed around the house. Uncle Bishop was kneeling by the porch steps, his huge white buttocks peeping, like rising loaves of bread, out of his gray sweatpants.

"Hey," Rosemary called out. "What've you been up to?" But Uncle Bishop had no time for cordials.

"Look," he said, pointing, "at what that old crone has done now." He was aiming a finger at Ralph the cat, who was flopped out flat on his side, his two ears flattened in displeasure. But other than this feline signal of disapproval, Rosemary could see no evidence of anything wrong. Ralph had always been *très weird* anyway.

"What's the matter with him?" Rosemary asked. She moved closer, bending over for a better look. Ralph lifted his lip, the way Elvis used to, showing off a couple of formidable-looking canines.

"This!" said Uncle Bishop, and held up a bell for Rosemary to see. It was dangling from a brown leather cat collar. "She belled Ralph, against my permission. This is now a full-scale war." Rosemary sighed. Poor Mrs. Abernathy, to be a bird columnist *and* the next-door neighbor of Uncle Bishop and Ralph. Uncle Bishop had hated birds ever since a college zoology professor had told him they would eventually inherit the earth.

"So, what's the big deal?" Rosemary asked, reaching out to stroke the enormous cat. Ralph did his Elvis impression again, and Rosemary decided to withhold the affection.

"A *cow* would collapse under the weight of this thing!" Uncle Bishop ranted, holding the bell and collar above his head. He turned to face Mrs. Abernathy's yard, so the words would drift in the right direction. "My cat has whiplash, you old biddy!" he shrieked. Ralph yawned dramatically and then rolled over on his other side. He looked fine. Better shape than Elvis was.

"Other than the birds making fun of him," said Rosemary, "there's no harm done."

"This bell is the size of a Ping-Pong ball, Rosie," Uncle Bishop persisted. Ralph was now calmly licking his paws, tossing a spitty one behind his ear now and then for a little cleaning back there.

"You keep that cat home," a tiny voice peeped from beyond the picket fence, and Rosemary saw Mrs. Abernathy's small white head bobbing about between the narrow cracks.

"You'll spend the rest of your days in the Bixley clink for this!" Uncle Bishop warned. "This cat's neck is so swollen he can't eat!" Rosemary was glad she had left *The Scarlet Letter* behind on her nightstand. Mrs. Abernathy going to prison for *belling* Ralph was far more interesting than Hester Prynne *balling* Arthur Dimmesdale. Mrs. Abernathy's backyard, full of delicate feathery birds, was far more exotic than the grim, muddy streets of Puritan Boston. Besides, Arthur Dimmesdale was such a classic wimp.

"He can't eat because he just came into my yard and ate

a ripe cardinal," the small voice added. Ralph made a noise that sounded uncannily like a burp.

"Poor, poor baby," Uncle Bishop cooed.

"He looks okay," Rosemary said. She suspected Uncle Bishop's lashing out was in part meant for Jason. And it was a pity that Ralph seemed to be, indeed, his old self. He really was a mean-spirited cat, bullying even the neighborhood dogs, not to mention his chronic assault upon the birds.

"It was so pathetic," Uncle Bishop was now saying. His eyes had watered sufficiently for the drama of the moment. "I could hear this ringing and ringing but I couldn't figure out where it was coming from. I thought the goddamned Avon lady was on my porch." Uncle Bishop couldn't go on. He paused theatrically, his eyes searching out some distant, Hollywood horizon.

"You're ranting again," Rosemary noted. Usually, Uncle Bishop preferred Bixley's small, quiet veterinary clinic to partake in his Greek tragedies, frightening the receptionists by insisting that Ralph was suffering from any assortment of diseases. Only after he and the massive cat had been laughed out of every animal clinic in northern Maine did Uncle Bishop finally admit that perhaps only dogs contracted heart worms. "I swear I hear them crawling around in there, chewing up muscle," he would tell the startled veterinarians, his ear pressed against Ralph's well-padded rib cage.

"If that cat comes back in this yard," the small voice announced through the cracks, "I'm going to give him a nice little plate of strychnine." Rosemary gasped. It was all Uncle Bishop needed to hear. The collar in one hand, its bell clanging loudly, he lunged at the five-foot-high fence.

"No, Uncle Bishop!" Rosemary shouted. She heard Mrs. Abernathy scream lustily from the other side. Uncle Bishop was trying to pull himself up, his meaty arms flailing over the top of the fence, his belly and bottom weight too heavy to hoist.

"I'm gonna bell *you,* you old bat!" Uncle Bishop yelled. "And I'm gonna get a handful of that blue hair while I'm at it!" Rosemary grabbed his ankles and held on as Mrs. Abernathy wailed. A red broom handle suddenly appeared over the fence and thwacked Uncle Bishop's arm.

"Ouch!" he moaned. "Stop that, goddamn it!" He pushed himself farther up. Rosemary pulled his ankles farther back. She heard something tear and hoped it wasn't cartilage. The broom handle was back again, like a long red pencil, *thwack thwack.* It caught Uncle Bishop on one of his meaty hands.

"Stop that!" he roared. Then, "Let go of me, Rosie!"

"You let go of the fence first," Rosemary panted. How could she be this winded? She was a runner, wasn't she? Where was Uncle Bishop getting his strength? She got a better grip on his ankles and pulled again.

"My arm!" Uncle Bishop cried. "I think I'm stuck on a nail!" Ralph had come to the edge of the yard and was watching the commotion with bored green eyes. The broom was back again, this time the big yellow straw part. Mrs. Abernathy decided to go for the head, a vulnerable area, what with the eyes and nose being stuck there. *Thwomp. Thwomp. Thwomp.* Material ripped loudly—a long dramatic tear.

"There goes the stomach muscle!" Uncle Bishop howled. "Did you hear it, Rosie?"

"Let go of the fence!" Rosemary insisted. She had, indeed, heard more tearing, but it was most definitely material. Flesh had a softer rip to it.

"Even if Ralph *could* eat," Uncle Bishop wept, "I'll be too crippled to open a can of cat food." Ralph gave one more large yawn and then disappeared into a hole beneath Mrs.

Abernathy's fence, most likely in time for the evening feeding. Uncle Bishop finally got an arm extended over the fence. He waved his sausage fingers frantically about.

"I'm gonna pull you right through the cracks, Mrs. Abernathy," he threatened. "Just let me get my hands on that pug."

"Rape!" Mrs. Abernathy's little voice rose up, most unlike the mourning dove as it calls for a mate. "Raaaaaaape!" Uncle Bishop stopped struggling. Skewered on the pointy top of Mrs. Abernathy's fence, he had time to think about this.

"Mrs. Abernathy," Uncle Bishop said serenely. He was cautiously eyeing the white bun on the other side of the fence. "Let's say, for the sake of argument, that you're sixteen years old and a virgin. I'm *still* a homosexual." Mrs. Abernathy had apparently changed her mind again as to which part of the broom packed a greater wallop. The wooden handle appeared once more. *Thwack. Thwack. Thwack. Thwack.* A blow for each of Uncle Bishop's fat red knuckles. Then she went inside her little house and slammed the door.

"I'll be darned," said Uncle Bishop. He was blowing warm breath onto each of his battered knuckles and surveying the neighborhood from his new elevation. Above Rosemary's head, his ass cheeks rose like snowy twin peaks. "When did Mr. Cobb put in a swimming pool?"

# The Temporal Art

IT WAS AFTER her run around Bixley that Rosemary found the baby robin beneath one of the wild apple trees across the road, near Mugs's cat crossing. Winston, the outdoor cat, disappeared guiltily into the hay as she approached. *Flagrante delicto. Caught with his mouth full of feathers.* Rosemary lifted the baby bird, gently. It seemed to be okay, but when her hand came away from its breast there was blood smeared lightly about it. The baby robin was in trouble. Rosemary knew that a cat's wounds may not be large and noticeable, but the claws go deep and are sharper than needles. She could see no tree with a nest that might have held the fledgling. And she couldn't leave the tiny bird on the ground, where Winston would surely find it later, a little dessert, light as meringue. To hell with natural selection. That was a fine notion on paper, but when one is staring the *weak* straight in the eye it's difficult to toss them back to the *fittest.* She carried the baby robin across the road and into the garage. The thing now was to put it in a dark, quiet, grass-filled box and hope that the shock wouldn't kill it.

At seven-thirty Mother rubbed her eyes, yawned widely, and was in bed asleep by nine. Rosemary still hadn't made face-to-face contact with Lizzie, Charles, or Philip. All three cars were jammed into the big front yard, side by side, but the drivers were in their respective corners, apparently waiting for the next round. Wondering what was up with the houseguests, she stretched her leg muscles, something she had not been able to do right after her run, and went out to check on the baby robin. It was surprisingly alert and hungry. She had mashed up a few tablespoons of Cat Chow into a paste to feed the bird. If it lived a day or two, she would see about getting some mealworms from the feed store where she bought her bird seed. She hated this idea, but it was the robin or the mealworms, and natural selection came easier with worms. The robin opened its beak quickly and ate a good bit of the paste from the dropper she dangled over its head. She also fed it several drops of water before it crouched down among the leaves and twigs and shut the one staring eye that looked out at her. She covered the box with an old tablecloth to provide a serene darkness. All she could do now was hope for the best.

In the kitchen, Rosemary washed her hands, then went in search of her houseguests. In the den, she found Philip and Charles, each with a cocktail, each staring at the other from opposite sides of the room, pugilists waiting for the bell. Rosemary assumed that these were not the first drinks.

"Gentlemen," she acknowledged them both, and fairly.

"Hello, Rosie," said Charles.

"Rosemary." Philip nodded. Then silence and more glaring.

"And how has the day been?" she asked casually. All she really wanted to know was if there'd been any new slandering and philandering. Maybe she was taking up William's old job, now that he'd abandoned it. She had cautioned him many times, hadn't she? "You get to know people, know their innermost thoughts, just so you can paint them. Once you have them on canvas, William, you leave them behind. Your art transcends the human being."

"It started off fine," said Philip. "That was before it turned into 'Three's Company.' " He was nervous, suddenly, sweaty about the temples, not the same cavalier lover of yesterday. All that traipsing about the backyard had apparently been for naught. Or was it the booze, that Dionysian leveler of even the most steadfast lover? Philip got up to pour another scotch from Rosemary's meager bar supply. The bar itself was small but the limited contents—suggested to beginners by *Playboy's Host and Bar Book*—could accommodate most uncomplicated drinks, especially if one didn't forget the bottle of sweet vermouth, and the bottle of dry vermouth. Rosemary always forgot one or the other. *As your spirit world expands,* the book warned, *you'll begin to think of diversifying this basic closet with a variety of other potables.* She had admitted long ago that her *spirit world* must be very staid and nonexpandable, because she had not once thought of diversifying since she set up the tiny, makeshift bar. Having a séance better fit her notion of spirit expansion.

"Any lawyer worth his salt would know the ramifications of this little love nest," Charles said suddenly. He still had the same booming resonance in his voice, and surefootedness in his words that had won him so many medals in the debate club. He had put on fifteen extra pounds during his executive years with General Motors, and now the threat of a middle-age bulge peeped above his belt. But he was still the good-looking Charles, with a few traces of gray sprouting along his temples. The light brown hair was still closely cropped, and the bluish gray eyes were still lined with those dark, almost girlish lashes.

"A lawyer worth *half* his salt would know about a certain female doctor back in Portland," Philip answered. Charles crossed his legs angrily but Rosemary had caught a quick flash of pain in his eyes. He knew now that Lizzie had told about the female doctor. Perhaps this telling, this *verbal* cheating, was more hurtful than the physical.

"She started first," Charles said helplessly.

"Do you have proof as to when the relationship between Lizzie and me started?" asked Philip. He paced the den as though he were in court. Charles squirmed in the beige armchair, which had suddenly become the witness stand.

"I prefer to think of it as an affair, not a relationship," he informed Philip.

"Do you have any evidence at all?" Philip continued. "A motel receipt, perhaps? A registered name? A witness, God forbid?" Philip was good. He was on fire with facts and legalese. He could quote cases. "Hester Prynne versus Arthur Dimmesdale!" Rosemary wished he would shout loudly. Charles looked hopefully at her, as if for an objection. She simply raised her eyebrows and then visited her modest bar. She poured herself a glass of wine.

"There's one thing you've forgotten, Barrister," Charles said, and he drew himself upward. Rosemary recognized this body talk from college. Charles had found what he considered the most excellent loophole. "Lizzie."

"And what do you mean by that?" Philip seemed quite tipsy. Lizzie had mentioned that he was a social drinker. Perhaps by *social* she did not mean the occasion of Philip drinking with her husband Charles. Speaking of Lizzie, when was she coming down? Rosemary knew this little scene might be draining for her now, but it was the kind of legendary event they would sit over beers, years away, and laugh about. She could hear her own voice saying, "They were like schoolboys, Lizzie."

"What about Lizzie?" Philip asked, and put a hand on the sofa's back to steady himself.

"It's quite simple," Charles said smugly. So, he *was* still smug. Some things, Rosemary knew, one never outgrows. "Lizzie won't lie."

"What?" Philip was unnerved. Rosemary remembered Lizzie's words, two weeks earlier. "I've got another *what else,*" Lizzie had sat on the front porch and said sadly, over champagne. "I was the first one to fall by the wayside." Charles was right. Lizzie wouldn't lie.

"What you don't understand, Solicitor, is that the only thing Elizabeth is dishonest about is her feelings for you," Charles went on. Barrister. Solicitor. Had General Motors just sent him to England? "And that's because she's out of touch with her emotions." Let Lizzie hear him say that. He'd see some emotions.

"I doubt she would've married you in the first place," said Philip, "if you hadn't knocked her up." Rosemary winced. *Impregnated* was a more civil word. Charles wouldn't have said *knocked up*. He was full of English terms nowadays, and in England that meant waking someone up. Different case altogether.

"Why, you S-O-B," said Charles, spelling as though he were protecting Philip from the brutality of the word. More verbal cheating by Lizzie, this pregnant-before-marriage fact.

"Gentlemen," Rosemary said for the second time that evening, but with much less conviction. "Please."

"Who's the S-O-B?" Philip slurred, also spelling. It had become more a heated spelling bee than a domestic problem.

"Who's the S-O-B?" Philip demanded again. Rosemary wished they would spell something new. "I asked you a question," said Philip, and pointed a lawyer's index finger at Charles. "Is it me? Am I the S-O-B? You meant me, didn't you?" *Your honor, he's leading the witness.* Rosemary put her glass of wine down and moved quietly toward the stairs.

"Sit down, for Chrissakes," Charles said to Philip. "You're irrational."

"I'm *irrational?*" screamed Philip. Rosemary paused at the foot of the stairs.

"Charles, please," she appealed to the more sober, more victorious man still in the witness chair. "This is childish and silly."

"Yes, you," Charles said to Philip. "You're totally irrational."

"A man who has a Freudian obsession with toy trains tells *me* that *I'm* irrational." Rosemary flinched. Lizzie must have spoken of her husband's favorite hobby: model trains. Wasn't anything sacred? Charles seemed ready to hyperventilate.

"I need to listen to this from an ambulance chaser?" he snarled at Philip. *He also represents men who have the hots for Shetland ponies,* Rosemary wanted to say. Philip immediately began rolling up his sleeves. This was the first time Rosemary had seen a wrinkle befall any of his shirts. Charles stepped down from the witness stand and put his drink on the coffee table. He began, calmly, to undo the buttons on his cuffs. Why did men do that? Do sleeves really get in the way?

"Holy shit!" said Rosemary, and raced up the fifteen steps and down the hall to Lizzie's door. Mother opened her own door as Rosemary shot past.

"No running in school!" Mother warned. She rubbed her sleepy eyes.

"Lizzie!" Rosemary banged on the door. The radio was

playing soft music inside. No wonder Lizzie was oblivious to the bullfight she had created. She was situated safely above the heads of the two angry men down below, like a goddess, listening to the cherubic music of Barry Manilow. "I Write the Songs" was playing, a braggadocio statement that hardly fitted the circumstances: The whole world was fighting, not singing.

"Goddamn it, Lizzie, open up!"

Lizzie flung the door open wide, and stood before Rosemary in a fuzzy maroon bathrobe. She'd been doing her nails and still held the polish brush in one hand.

"What's the matter?" she asked. Her little enamel wand was propped in midair.

"There's a territorial fight going on downstairs," Rosemary announced.

"You mean like dogs have?" Lizzie wanted to know. She blew on the wet nails. Rosemary nodded.

"If you think of yourself as a fire hydrant," she told Lizzie, "they're arguing over who peed on you first."

Down in the den, Rosemary and Lizzie found things quite in order. Charles was back in the witness stand and Philip was sitting, neatly collected, on the sofa. Mother was shaking one of her piano-loving fingers into Philip's blanched face. She was drenched from neck to toes in a dazzling blue nightgown of a silkish fabric that was wet with perspiration from her sleep. It clung to her thick hips, and allowed her breasts to expose themselves, flat as pancakes, from within each circle of the sleeve holes.

"And I mean that," Mother was saying, her yellow curls unfurling. "There will be no fighting in this schoolhouse!"

Rosemary took Mother back to bed. She was giddily happy and smiled at her daughter the entire time. She had just exerted, downstairs, the power of being crazy, and had been obeyed for it. The two men had blatantly ignored Rosemary's plea for them to stop. But nobody argues with a crazy person. People, at least civilized people, are supposed to know better. Charles and Philip had both cowered before this whirling dervish and now Mother was beaming. Power, no matter how attained, is a warm fire in the groin, a sweet pattering in the pit of the stomach.

Rosemary pushed some ringlets, tight with natural curling and perspiration, back behind Mother's ear. The wrinkles had long ago traveled from Mother's eyes, a brush fire spreading, and now they traced all the laugh lines around her mouth. *Here's what you get for laughing,* the lines said.

"Boys shouldn't fight," Mother whispered, then giggled happily. Rosemary had rarely seen her so pleased. It was the same girlishness that had swept her about the old-memory kitchen, singing "The Daring Young Man on the Flying Trapeze," while Father smiled and breakfast cooked. Flirtatious even, this insanity.

"Go back to sleep, love," she said, and kissed Mother's damp little forehead, snapped off the bedside lamp.

Out in the garage, Rosemary draped the towel back over the box that housed the injured robin. It had turned around in the nest of grass and twigs so that its other eye stared out, beaded and black. She then rolled her Free Spirit bike out to the backyard, and checked to make sure the headlight was still functioning. She might not use it on the quick ride down Old Airport Road to Bixley, but she would surely need it on the dark, gravelly ride home.

A speeding car roared down the road toward town, bouncing over the bumps, thoughtless of the animals and humans who lived there. Rosemary shook a fist and shouted, "Slow down!" but the automobile kept up its frantic speed and soon disappeared.

Out on the road, she flipped up the kickstand, then situated herself comfortably on the seat and pushed off. The subtle June breeze was soft as it hit her, full-faced, then caught her hair up in a swift rush of wind that caused the ponytail to bob. The evening shadows were already billowing in, taking away the last of the yellow tinge the sun had left behind. As she rounded the turn that brought her quickly upon the summit of Russell Hill, she braked and sat on the bike, steadying it with both feet as she gazed down on the spectacle of Bixley. It lay like a beached spaceship, tossed out of the ocean of time, wiggling its helpless lights as though they were little electric antennae stretched out in the darkness.

She pushed off again, her breath pulled up into her throat as she cascaded down from the peak of Russell Hill for the half-mile glide into town. Reaching the field that stretched across her end of Bixley, she cut off into the clover and hay to follow the shortcut that bicycling kids still liked to take. Maybe it *was* true that some things never change. At least while the planet was still in one piece and functioning, at least while the old field held on to its own real estate, there would be a shortcut there. But Bixley was growing, thanks to the Miriams on the planet whose calling was to gobble up the disappearing land for money. Greedy Pac Men. Rosemary knew the day would come when she would recognize little of her old hometown. She had seen, in the library book, how much the place had changed in fifty years, and now there was a new technology to speed up change. She imagined herself, one day, wandering aimlessly up and down mysterious streets, past the unfamiliar stores and businesses, trying to stumble upon one little clue in a burgeoning city of strangers. What had she promised herself about growing old? "I'll let my hair go wild and gray. I'll be a crazy old woman, wearing five or six dresses at a time." There was a power in being crazy. That was a little secret that Mother already knew. Maybe Mother was waiting, in one of those bizarre rooms in her mind, wearing her flouncing skirts of old, singing about lithe young men who fly through the air, dusting everything off for her daughter.

The fireflies parted and shooed like tiny sparks as Rosemary careened through the hay, past Indian paintbrushes that were now colorless outlines in the dusk, out of the hay and onto the hot blacktop that brought her pedaling easily down Library Street. She whizzed to the end, circled the small cul-de-sac, and coasted back up to the front of Mrs. Abernathy's house. There was always a light burning late at Mrs. Abernathy's house, now that Mr. Abernathy had passed away. "I'm staying up later and later now that he's gone," Mrs. Abernathy had once admitted. Rosemary walked the bike down the concrete drive. It followed like an obedient deer being led by its antlers. Mrs. Abernathy answered on the third ring. She undid the chain and opened the door only after she was certain that it was not Rosemary's uncle Bishop lurking out on the steps, but the niece herself.

Rosemary was struck with how Mrs. Abernathy was aging daily. Her skin was cindery, almost to the point where it might be covered with a gray makeup. But this pallor was the work of nature and not Max Factor. Mrs. Abernathy's cheeks had fallen in as if perhaps, during one restless night, the bones had finally collapsed with the weight of the skin, the way a barn dies when it's left to the wind and snow. Prehistoric art. She remembered William telling her about *The Chinese Horse,* and the artists in primitive caves. "They may have created art centuries before, Rosie," he'd said. "A temporal art, left outside and ruined by the elements. Or drawn on hides. Biodegradable." Here, then, was the sad canvas of Mrs. Abernathy's face, going the way of all art. Rosemary felt an unnatural guilt in seeing Mrs. Abernathy being so mercilessly sluiced through the floodgates of time. She scooted past the old woman and into the parlor, which was bulging with porcelain birds, hand-painted by Mr. Roger Tory Peterson, Master Birder. These were birds unsusceptible to disease, these shiny sculptures newly flown from the Franklin Mint nesting grounds. These were birds who were oblivious to the gruesome wintry statistics.

"Are you okay, Mrs. Abernathy?" Rosemary ran a finger down the back of a hand-painted indigo bunting. An oily film of dust came away, soft as peach fuzz, gray as the tiny mustache above Mrs. Abernathy's thin upper lip. It was most unlike Mrs. Clara Abernathy to live in harmony with dust and its ilk. Rosemary could not ever recall, since childhood, seeing Mrs. Abernathy's front yard look so anxious to be put in order. Long grassy weeds had pushed viciously up from around the planted flowers, and the fake grass was scattered with dead leaves. An assortment of lilac bush droppings, those small, lavender bouquets, lay next to crumpled candy bar wrappers that had blown in from the street. Mrs. Abernathy would never have stood for such a flagrant disregard of orderliness just days ago. "She vacuums her goddamn grass, Rosie," Uncle Bishop had chanted many times. Now here was the parlor, as well, looking as if someone no longer cared that it was being painted over by the thin layer of forgetfulness that besets the elderly.

Mrs. Abernathy moved several pages of the *Bixley Times* from off the sofa so that Rosemary could sit upon it. Rosemary noticed that the pages were all her weekly columns, perhaps from the past month, with her usual trademark of a black-capped chickadee, Maine's state bird, adorning the upper right-hand side of the column. It had wrapped its wiry feet around an apple tree branch and was staring, with literariness, out at the reader.

"How have you been doing?" Rosemary asked, noticing this time how strained Mrs. Abernathy's movements had become, like a wind-up toy nearing the end of its strut. Her old bones seemed to be locking up all their joints and tossing out the keys.

"I'm well as can be expected," Mrs. Abernathy answered.

Rosemary recognized this as the ultimate truth. She was, this old woman approaching her octogenarian years, *as well as could be expected.* Her feet had taken almost all of the steps they were destined to take when they first arrived upon the planet. Her footfalls, quite simply, were about to run out.

"The old ticker only has so many beats in it and then kaput!" said Mrs. Abernathy. "At least that's what Mr. Abernathy was fond of saying." Rosemary looked at the fake mantelpiece where sat the picture of Horace Abernathy, taken under the Abernathys' cherry tree, probably the last time a camera's eye had ever closed to capture Horace's own dark orbs. Rosemary sat quietly in the dustiness of Mrs. Abernathy's bird-filled, cagelike parlor and heard the old woman whisper a second time, "As well, I guess, as can be expected." All the porcelain birds perched stiffly and listened.

Rosemary made a silent promise that she would look in on Mrs. Abernathy often. And she would call the county nurse the next day to inquire about the Bixley group designed to visit and care for the elderly who were too fragile for the heavy demands of everyday living.

"Your column last week about predator birds that come to feeders was, in my opinion, your very best," Rosemary said.

"Yes, well, thank you," said Mrs. Abernathy. "They're a nasty bunch." She clicked her teeth, but Rosemary was only half listening. She was remembering those sweet days of youth, those oppressive August days when Mrs. Abernathy would lure the neighborhood children into the parlor with Kool-Aid and a plate of fudge brownies. One day stood out most, a day more than twenty years earlier, when the rain had come like bullets pelting down the street at her heels, and Mrs. Abernathy had waved her in from the storm, wrapped her in a fat bath towel, and toweled her dry. There had been a cup of cocoa, hadn't there? And something red. An apple maybe. And the incessant rain, that eternal dripping. What was it William had told her? "When the earth's crust first cooled down, Rosie, it rained for sixty thousand years without stopping." So what was a childhood rain against the wash of time?

"Speaking of predators," Mrs. Abernathy said suddenly. She folded her last column into a paper handkerchief on her lap and then nodded toward Uncle Bishop's little beige-and-chocolate house. "Where is that awful uncle of yours?"

Outside in Mrs. Abernathy's front yard, Rosemary waited until the old lady locked herself safely inside the house before she pointed her bike at the street. It was well past dusk but Mrs. Abernathy's porch light was on, and Rosemary could see a large dark shape moving across the backyard. She slipped in closer for a better view and saw that it was Ralph, now lying flat on his stomach and sleek as a kamikaze, two round beady eyes under the rose of Sharon. Why was he even up there on Mrs. Abernathy's little hilltop? She watched as Ralph strolled up to a standing feeder, examined it closely, turned his back on it, and raised his tail. Then he pedaled his hind legs, as though he were on a unicycle, and urinated squarely on the feeder. He turned around and examined his signature proudly. "Mine," Ralph was saying. "All mine." Rosemary surmised what Ralph's mission might be. When dawn finally came with its rosiness, he would be there at his station while the feathery and unsuspicious munched upon chunks of apple, apricot, millet, and cracked corn. And then, when they dared think of it, an idea so abstract they had only dreamed vaguely of it at night as they twitched and scratched in their nests, waiting for daylight: the ephemeral Toll-House cookie.

When she got home the baby robin was dead, its eye frozen open like a black drop of blood, its head bent forward upon its chest, in the middle of its last dream of flying.

# The
# Cut-Out Stars

LIZZIE AND COMPANY were gone when Rosemary awoke. Downstairs she discovered that someone, most probably Lizzie, had given Mother a breakfast of cereal, toast, and orange juice. Mother was drawing on her magic slate. Someone had written a note, pinned by a strawberry magnet to the refrigerator. It said, *Back this evening. Will have dinner in Thomasville, if anyone has the stomach to eat. Lizzie.* So they were going to approach this like adults, after all, over bread breaking.

Rosemary gave Mother a quick kiss. In between munching on her toast, which was now cold and crusted with stiff pats of butter, Mother was creating an assortment of lighthouses on her magic slate. Some were tall and skinny, others short and bulging, all casting out radiating black lines of light to warn of the needlelike rocks and sullen, sunken reefs.

"They're very nice," Rosemary praised the lopsided structures as she peered over Mother's shoulder. Mother glanced up in terror, as though she'd just been caught breaking and entering into lighthouses that did not belong to her, the private property of the sane world. In an instant she reached out her bony little hand and flipped up the overlay sheet, erasing the artwork, as if a huge thick wave had just rushed in and swept all the lighthouses out to sea. No evidence left, in case the police were called.

"What a shame," Rosemary said, and patted Mother's shoulder.

"More Rorschach pictures?" Miriam asked from the kitchen doorway. She'd let herself in again, without knocking. "Lighthouses, right? Out in the middle of the ocean?" Rosemary nodded.

"Uncle Bishop says she perceives us all as sharks," said Rosemary. Miriam was supposed to come by at one o'clock to baby-sit Mother during her nap and allow Rosemary to escape for a few errands she needed to run. But here she was. Early. Rosemary watched as the car with BIXLEY CAB COMPANY on its door disappeared back down the gravel road. She could almost hear Uncle Bishop. "How do you explain taking a cab to Presto Pizza as a business deduction, Miriam?" Miriam was searching out a cigarette in her bottomless purse. Her face seemed a bit stretched on its bones and she wore no makeup. It was well known among family members that on the day of Miriam's now mythical car accident—when she rammed the ice cream truck—she had sat up in the speeding Bixley ambulance and applied a fresh layer of pink lipstick to her trembling lips. "L.O.A.," Uncle Bishop liked to remember the incident. "Lipstick on arrival."

"Is everything all right?" Rosemary passed her a book of matches, a tome with which Miriam was well read.

"Why do you ask?" Miriam lighted the Virginia Slim, her personal and slender statement to the world that she had, by Christ, *come a damn long way*. The usual thick swab of green eye shadow was missing from her upper lids. Someone had decided long ago that red hair was best exhibited and enhanced by shades of *vert,* and Miriam readily endorsed this philosophy. She had even tried to get the Bixley furrier to dye her mink coat green, but he had refused. "You've missed the point," he told her. "Mink are not green by nature."

Miriam was also wearing no lipstick, that cosmetic paste without which she had refused to go off into death. Rosemary imagined her beseeching Charon to hold his ferry steady in the fast-moving waters of the Styx until she could set her lips in cosmic order. And Charon himself, getting his fingers all gooey with lipstick as he fetched his well-earned coin from out of her painted mouth.

"I ask because you don't look yourself," Rosemary said. Miriam had been bemoaning her fortieth birthday, two days away, so Rosemary had suggested a dinner party to Uncle Bishop, hoping it might cheer Miriam up. "No thanks," Uncle Bishop had declined. "I don't look upon the occasion of Miriam's birth as cause to celebrate."

"I don't think I've seen you without mascara since grammar school," Rosemary said. "I wondered if it meant anything."

"Well, it *doesn't,*" Miriam snapped. She drew a long smoky breath down into her lungs. "I just didn't have time." Rosemary was incredulous of this statement from a woman who had found the seconds needed to apply lipstick in a shrieking, careening ambulance, a woman with a broken arm and, worse yet, *with that very arm!*

"Where's Raymond?" she asked.

"I'm here to baby-sit *your* mother," said Miriam, "and not to answer questions about my private life." Aha! Things were amiss in her current wedded bliss, albeit the fourth bliss. There was definitely trouble in condo heaven.

"Don't forget to bring my ladder back," Mother warned. She shook her finger at Miriam, peering at her with squinty eyes.

"Jesus," said Miriam. "What ladder? I didn't *take* your ladder."

"Yes you did," said Mother.

"No I didn't," said Miriam. "You're batty, is your problem."

"I don't want any bats in this house!" Mother shouted, her curls soggy on her forehead.

"Don't tease her," Rosemary warned. She was a bit reluctant to leave Mother, but she did have those errands.

"Did you bring me any chocolates, sweetie?" Mother asked Miriam, who made a sour face and then looked with disinterest out at the dining birds.

"I'll be back soon," Rosemary told her sister. She carried the picnic basket she'd packed earlier with sandwiches, pickles, soda, and a blanket to spread on the grass. She'd fasten it safely on the rear carrier of her bike, strap it down with stretch cords.

The road to the airport was alive with June. Devil's darning needles darted in and out of the sloping fields of hay like little black helicopters. Evening grosbeaks munched on seeds near the sides of the road and a telltale *caw caw* from off in the distance told Rosemary some crow was keeping good watch for the entire flock. The sky was an old blue, faded from so many mornings and afternoons and evenings. An occasional shoelace of cloud moved aimlessly across the measureless expanse. A groundhog slipped cautiously out from under a hay rake that had been left behind to rot and rust, its workdays over, the iron of its tusks useless against modern equipment. The groundhog stood on its hind legs to catch an excited glimpse of the mounted creature that was gliding down the road, part human, part chrome, before it dived into the dark damp earth of its home and disappeared into temporary safety.

It used to be that Rosemary and William hated the swirling dust that rose up behind each car as it passed on Old Airport Road. But two years ago, when the new highway brought potential fliers to the airport from the north side, most of the traffic on the road had died away. But there were still the rare travelers who preferred Old Airport Road, which was a shortcut, and it was because of these strangers and their mindless speeding that Rosemary had been obliged to erect Mugs's now famous CAT CROSSING sign. A reporter and a photographer from Bixley had even come out one sunny afternoon, perfect for a picture, and immortalized Mugs and the sign, at least for the Sunday that the picture appeared. Rosemary had brushed Mugs until he snapped with static electricity, and he moved with long, slow steps, sporting a *natural* fur coat, as he crossed the road for the camera.

At the airport Rosemary pushed her bike inside the gate and left it leaning on its kickstand. She looked across the small concrete runway, scanned the puny planes. There was no sign of the ultralight, no bright flash of red and yellow, so she went in through the main door of the tiny building. A coffee machine and a machine half-filled with crusty, stale sandwiches was as close as the Bixley airport came to a restaurant. She dug down into her cutoff jeans for two quarters, dropped them into the slot, and pushed EXTRA LIGHT. The coffee tasted moldy. A woman was busy behind the one and only departure counter, which also handled arrivals. A few men drifted in and out of doors. One seemed to be in complete charge of the others, an unmistakable top dog.

"Can I help you?" he asked, as Rosemary approached.

"I'm interested in ultralights," she explained. "I've seen one several times in the past few days soaring over my house and I think it looks like fun. I'd like to take some lessons." *Oh, what tangled webs,* she thought.

"Sweetheart, take my advice. When it comes to an ultralight, keep both of your pretty little feet on the ground. Those things are like riding on the backs of mosquitoes. You'll kill yourself." He wiped his hands on a towel, then tossed it behind the counter. So, the ultralight man *was* a daring young man.

"My name is Rosemary O'Neal," Rosemary said. He could take his *sweetheart* and shove it. "I live just three miles down on Old Airport Road. I'm interested in at least taking a look at the machine to see how it operates."

"Honey," the man said. *There he went again.* "I think your best bet is to take regular flying lessons. That little Cessna sitting out there would be a good place to start. We don't even have any ultralights here." He took a cigarette out of his shirt pocket and lighted it. Rosemary noticed the large gut that protruded slowly as he exhaled. She imagined this arrogant man alone someday, above the whispery clouds, slumped over the controls of a plane while his bowels emptied slowly into his shoes and his heart sent him a two-word message: *No more. No more.*

"Rosemary," she said.

"Rosemary, I'd be happy to have someone talk to you about the Cessna."

"But who owns the ultralight?" She had suddenly felt a chill that even the dull-tasting coffee could not shake. Had she imagined the daring young man? "Pterodactyl," she had said, immediately upon seeing him for the first time, a primitive fear rising up in her chest at the unusual combination of man and bird. "The Greeks could not accept man-on-horseback as a literal concept, so they invented the centaur," she remembered telling her literature class. Had she invented her own concept of man-as-bird?

"That's some joker from out of state who won't live to see any gray hairs," Top Dog stated factually. Rosemary would not be surprised if he suddenly barked. "You just missed him," he added.

"I finished the check, Jake," one of his puppies came inside to tell him. Jake shook ashes from his cigarette onto the shiny tiles of the airport floor. "Let some little woman clean that up," Rosemary could almost hear Jake thinking, in the uncomplicated coils of his mind.

"He's staying at one of Fraser's Sporting Camps," Jake said. "But as far as I know he don't give lessons. It's a hobby. But you take my advice, honey, and try the Cessna." A chimpanzee would have learned to say the word *Rosemary* by this time.

"It's Rosemary," she said, as Jake dropped his lit cigarette into an ashtray and went back outside. "Bastard," she mumbled, but all that was left of Jake was a faint curl of smoke rising up from the cigarette butt.

On the cool ride back home Rosemary watched the sky for a sign of *him* coming back. Religiously, she scoured the sleek lines of horizons, looked among the taller trees, kept a watch behind her shoulder. It *was* a kind of religious thing, this peering anxiously into the heavens for a glimpse of a man, whether it was one from *out of state,* or one who'd been dead for two thousand years. But there was no ultralight man to be seen anywhere in the skies over Bixley. She passed her own house on Old Airport Road and kept on toward the heart of town. She thought about her car sitting idle in the garage since William's death. She wasn't sure what it was about the car that kept her away from it. William had picked it out because Rosemary was uninterested as to the touted exploits of various makes. "As long as it's blue and makes that noise when I turn the key," she told William, who went off to the car dealer in Caribou and came back with a new blue car that did, indeed, *make that noise.* But the car was certainly no more representative of William than the polished cherry bed, or the painting of *The Chinese Horse,* or the big old house itself, and Rosemary had embraced these other things since his disappearance. She had not banished them as she seemed to have done the car. Perhaps it was because of the very *noise* she mentioned to William the day he bought the car. The quiet bicycle fit more keenly into her new notion of life. She would let the car sit until it was a colossal ball of dust lolling beneath a network of spider webs. Maybe she would drive it into the creek and let it rust there on its haunches. Maybe she would give it to the mailman. *No, no reason. I just wanted you to have it.*

The elm trees along the road shimmered in the wind and turned their silvery leaves bottoms up, like minnows flapping. The bike was a wonderful freedom, faster than running, like some sleek, sweaty, futuristic horse. A rabbit raced across the road in front of Rosemary and disappeared into the field of hay, its long ears like periscopes separating the grasses.

Rosemary left her bike on the sidewalk in front of Max's Camera and Supply Shop. There was no need to chain-lock it. No one stole bicycles in Bixley. Inside, Max was busy over the ancient body of an old Brownie camera someone had brought in to be resurrected.

"It's wonderful to still see one of these," he told Rosemary. "They took marvelous pictures. John Deardorf is trying to bring the Deardorf back, you know. Superb pictures. What a quality."

"Don't keep me dangling, Max," Rosemary said, and flipped through the scrapbook he left lying on the counter to subtly teach his customers the proper way to take a photograph. Rosemary stopped at a photo of a small girl with her arms around the neck of a graceful collie. The light *was* perfect. The composition correct. The child and her dog were sweetly frozen in time. Max was wise to choose this photo for his crash-course scrapbook. Now if his customers could only find such a blond child and such an ingratiating dog. To hell with natural light. You could *buy* light at Max's Camera and Supply Shop, if you had the money.

"Come on, Max," said Rosemary.

"This is a goner," Max said, and put the old Brownie back into its box where it could, finally, settle down to sleep, to dream of flappers, and Model T's, and small children who had already grown old and died. The camera was a graveyard, full of ghostly angles, and lines, and compositions of people and houses and landscapes that have disappeared.

"Max, I'm waiting," said Rosemary, trying to ignore the dead, worn-out body of the Brownie.

"Well." Max looked at her finally. "In that case, guess what? It's here."

"Oh, Max, is it?"

"Just last night, before I closed, the UPS truck brought it," said Max. "I called to leave a message for you a few minutes ago but your sister said you'd be by." He made his way to a large box in the corner of the room. It said MEADE 6-INCH REFLECTING TELESCOPE on the outside.

"I'll get Uncle Bishop to come get it in his pickup," Rosemary said. She ran one hand over the cardboard box, imagining the round tubular wonder within, suspecting what William would have said of this day, remembering how many times they had rocked well past midnight on the porch swing, with glasses of wine, and stared at the numberless pinpoints flickering like small, faraway campfires. And they had wondered aloud about the stellar secrets that had exploded and collapsed, the news of which had not yet reached the earth. They imagined the galaxies that had spiraled and swirled millions of years before William met Rosemary, before the small planet Earth and its one meager moon had taken its place in the universe of time.

"No, no," Max was saying. Rosemary had almost forgotten him there beside her, so strong was the sensation of William. Sweet William. She could almost smell his wonderful body sweat after an afternoon of painting, sweat and acrylics and the faint bouquet of the wild apple trees, or the small creek breeze if he had opened the window slightly to a spring day. All smell and color and all sound, this William, who had exploded one rainy night in London, a supernova of pure emotion. "When a star collapses, Rosie," he had said to her, one night on the swing, as they sat staring at the heavens, "it's like a great balloon deflating. It crushes itself at the center."

"No," she heard Max say again. "My boy is going to deliver it for you. It's no problem. He likes to drive the new truck. And he's young, remember, with nothing better to do." Could she spy upon the innocent stars without William there beside her, on the springy night lawn, all the windows of the old house black as insect eyes? Could she, like some solo space pioneer, get closer to Andromeda galaxy, that vaginal spiral they had found so many times with the naked eye? A birthing place, this heavenly slit. Maybe the very birth canal of the gods. Did she dare see it more clearly? "Remember," William would say, his arm aloft, silhouetted, as he pointed at some speck. "The stars are so far away that if you had Mount Palomar in your backyard it wouldn't make them bigger." Perhaps this was the major secret of the stars, that—telescope or not—they would remain sparkling secrets. Mere stardust.

"Are you sure you're okay?" she heard Max ask.

Rosemary and Max had already agreed upon a monthly payment, so she left him looking out at her, with concern, from his storefront window. She would cancel her little picnic alone, that long-planned outing to find the childhood spring, to look for Father's mossy, fossilized footsteps. The stunning realization of having lost one man overwhelmed her. She would deal with Father's disappearance at another time, when the smell and touch of William faded slightly, like the trapped, dead images in the old Brownie. And now here was the telescope to throw things off kilter. *Teleskopos.* Greek for *seeing at a distance.* What was William's artistic word for such? Pointillism, those little luminescent dots of painty stars best observed at a distance. Someday, she knew, the meaning of William's ghosthood, of the relationship that was obviously foundering long before he left for London, would be revealed to her. At some time in the future. *Teleskopos.* At some distance from the pain, she would study the two of them the way historians study wars. In the meantime, the telescope gave her none of the excitement and comfort she imagined it would. This was new territory, this *telescopio* notion of Galileo's. She would be treading down alchemical highways alone. She would be going ahead without William.

On the jolting ride back up Old Airport Road to home, the picnic basket bounced and made clinking noises with its bottles, the diet Coke and the pickles talking. She would eat the special lunch on the patio with Mother, later, when she felt like food again. Food was for the sustenance of the body.

Now Rosemary needed a sustenance for the soul. She remembered a passage of *Romeo and Juliet* she had recited many times for William, many times in bed, many times beneath the icy stars.

" 'And when he shall die,' " she whispered, " 'take him and cut him out in little stars, and he will make the face of heaven so fine that all the world will be in love with night.' " She felt the pressure of tears, watery balls, pushing up out of their ducts, as she pedaled her noiseless bike on home.

Unable to face Miriam right away, Rosemary biked on past the house, allowing herself a few more minutes to vent this sudden sadness. She had thought that the telescope would bring only peace and a sense of beginning anew. But she had been wrong.

At the old hay rake, where she turned her bicycle around, the groundhog was quite dead, a cold layer of blood crusting its exposed teeth. She surmised that Jan Ferguson's German shepherd, with its sharp canines, had stumbled upon the groundhog. She reached a finger down and touched the tip of one paw, already stiffening. It had come out of the safety of its hole only to bask in a pleasant June day, and now it was on its short trip back to Mother Earth. A panic overcame her, and she felt a warm sweat surfacing on her forehead, the palms of her hands. She stared down the road, to where the big mushroom of a house rose up from among the apple trees, her own safety.

"I must be careful," she reminded herself, and wondered if she'd ever see the ultralight again.

# The Human Things

AT THE URGING of a full bladder, Rosemary pulled herself out of bed at six-thirty. Miriam's birthday was opening with a red sky above the horizon. *Sailors take warning*. Rosemary had dozed fitfully throughout the night, unable to shake the notion of William's soft presence in the old cherry bed, an ache brought on by yesterday's lonely purchase of the telescope. So she stayed up to watch the first ground feeders darting about, their bills like fat needles poking the stiff grass for seeds. It was a strange dream this time that had rippled through her sleep. A *stranger* dream than other times. The muscles in her stomach were drawn up into balls from the anxiety of it. She watched the sky, the same sky as forty years ago, when Mother had borne her first child and set about on the short path of life with Father. It was crimson now, filtering to light pinks as it left the line of the treed horizon and moved out toward its middle. "It was raining, a terrible downpour," Mother used to tell them, when they asked as children, about the weather conditions on the special day each was born. "It was all cats and dogs and thundering when Miriam was born, but you, Rosemary, came in on the sunniest, brightest January day I can ever remember. So cold everything was snapping. So sky blue it hurt your eyes." And only as an adult did Rosemary wonder if these weather conditions had helped to shape their lives, to mark their personalities. "You're too gloomy, Miriam. Why don't you have more of Rosemary's sunny disposition?"

William had come home from London in this dream, so real Rosemary could still feel the crushed beads of sweat that wet her pajama top, leaving it cold and limp. She had heard his footfalls in the kitchen first, then on all fifteen steps as they creaked beneath his trail boots. William on the stairs, come home from London, come back from death. "How many steps, William?" Yes, it was so like him to know. "Fifteen steps, Rosie." And then he had come to the side of her bed, their bed, and sat on it. She was awake, or so she believed, and she was not afraid. She realized now that it had been at the back of her mind all along that some grisly mistake had been made. She had never seen the body. It was days before the coffin arrived from London. Now, in the heart of the night, in the midst of her subconscious reckonings, Rosemary knew she'd been waiting all along for an apologetic letter, a brief phone call that would set things in proper order. Young men should not kill themselves.

In the dream, she had tried to say his name, but couldn't. Her tongue had swollen inside its red mouth, was heavy as an old shoe's tongue. And she couldn't reach out a hand to touch again the smooth skin, almost girlish it was so soft. This was skin she hadn't touched since that January day, when she had stood by the kitchen door and watched him loading his luggage and boxes of books and treasures into the back of Uncle Bishop's pickup for a lift to the airport. A January day, much like her own *birth day,* blue with cold, the icicles hanging from the eaves like glassy fangs, prehistoric tusks. And she had wrapped the Christmas scarf tightly about his neck, had bit the bottom of his lip gently as they kissed good-bye. And then he was gone, with his pale January skin sinking beneath the plaid lining of his best jacket. A cold, deathly skin that Rosemary, awake, refused to remember, for remembering it would cause her to ponder William's condition three weeks into his death, a month, two months. Here were hideous images that her brain tried to block out. How many weeks before the eyes rolled like gum balls out of their sockets? Before the tight leg muscles turned jellyish, the stomach muscles forgot the countless sit-ups, and the facial skin peeled back to reveal that Halloween leer of the skull? In the dream her arms were small trees placed on each side of her body. They weren't a part of her and, without them, she had no means to reach out and touch the pale face, tousle the brownish hair still in need of a trim, as it was the last time she'd seen it disappearing beneath his jacket collar. "Dear William." That's what she tried to say to the lover who'd returned triumphant from the ultimate battle and was now sitting on the side of her bed. "William." Rosemary thought this. She could not say it. The two-syllable song remained unspoken. It was lodged like batting in her closed mouth. It pounded like a toothache. Instead, William spoke, as though he were Hamlet's father come home for a bit of explaining. "Hello, Rosie." Precious William, still the vision of the artist in pursuit of the dream. Still full lipped, with his perfect nose, and eyes the color of copper beneath the shank of cedar-brown hair that hung above them. "I've missed you. I've missed the human things." Rosemary had looked at her arms with deep curiosity. Had they been amputated? Something had rendered them useless. She *was* awake. She was sure of it. And this was really the resurrected William. Then he said things she had never wanted to hear, awake or asleep. "It was over, Rosie. We were over."

Rosemary let the sky go back to its bleaching process, to losing its magnificent pinks and reds to the approaching day, and went off to the kitchen to make coffee. Waiting for the percolator, she filled the cat's dish with the familiar rattle of brown stars, which bounced out of the box in a meteoric shower. Supernovas for Mugs. She leaned against the sink to watch him dine, and to wait for the first glorious cup.

"Thank you, Mr. Coffee," she said, as she added some Sweet 'n Low, skim milk, and then went into the den to view what was left of the morning sky. Mother was still asleep. At least she was still in her room, soundless. Rosemary imagined her lying like a baby on its back, her arms and legs flailing gently as her eyes glued themselves to the ceiling overhead. Maybe she should make Mother a mobile. She could glue pictures of important family events to it, instead of geometric shapes or cuddly animals. Maybe it would prompt Mother to take part in reality again: her fragile wedding picture, each of the children's baby photos, the first school pictures minus the front teeth, the high school graduation pictures.

Gazing out the patio window, Rosemary saw Winston, the outdoor cat, stretched lazily on the backyard pile of firewood, a line of sunlight ricocheting off his name tag. Rosemary thought wistfully of the baby robin. What if she had kept the bell on Winston's collar? The baby was too little to recognize the siren of the bell as a deathly knell, too small to fly even if it had. And what about death knells? What was the subconscious meaning of last night's dream? What had she blinded herself against for months? Maybe years? The pain of the dream that most remained was the terrible sensation of seeing him again, so lifelike, so near, and being unable to touch him. Or even speak to him. "It was over, Rosie. We were over." He had been wearing his great-grandfather's Civil War sword on his side! She just that moment remembered this fashion item. She drank her coffee and tried to recall more of the ghastly dream. The sword going with him on this last trip had caused discomfort to her, but she had never really looked at the heart of the action. And he had taken all those heavy art books, that photo album of their eight years together. Now she suddenly understood what it meant, what the dream was trying to tell her.

"My God," Rosemary said softly, and put her coffee cup down. "My God," she said again, and all the little symbols, all the tiny hints that had been given her over a period of months bumped into each other for the last time. She bounded up the cursed fifteen steps and into William's favorite painting room, a place she'd avoided greatly since his death. The best easel, gone. The most-used paints, missing. All the precious things, vanished. Behind, he'd left only discards, really, things he'd accumulated but no longer needed. And in their bedroom closet Rosemary fingered all the shirts on their hangers, old ones worn thin, buttonless ones, outdated ones, all Salvation Army goodies. It was the same all over the house. It was the god-awful truth. He'd taken all the items he could not do without. He'd done an excellent job of spring cleaning right under her very nose and she had missed it. It was loud as a cat's bell and she hadn't even heard it!

Now the pain hit her, in the stomach, around the heart,

pain deep as a cat's claws. He had never meant to come back. "William was a gentleman," she remembered thinking, those long shadowy nights on the swing, after his death, when the old moon with its same Mongoloid face had mocked her through the frozen branches of the cherry tree. A round, full moon rising up out of January, February, March evenings as she sat bundled in warm sweaters and a jacket, wearing gloves in the spring months to hold her glass of wine, but hardly feeling the cold at all. She had fooled herself because she wanted to be fooled. She wanted the security of his clothes still hanging in the closet, his useless socks with the swiss-cheese holes that lay piled in the dresser drawer, all the dried-up tubes of paint, the rotting canvases, the mismated shoes on the closet floor, books he'd never read. He'd left behind his goddamn junk and had gone off like a thief with his treasures, out into the wide, open places of the world.

Rosemary went back into his painting room, with its long narrow church windows that enabled the best sunlight to come in and play a role on William's canvases, to become a part of his art. "Levels of consciousness depend upon the light, Rosemary," he'd told her. Well, her consciousness was wide awake now that she'd *seen* the goddamn light. Sitting down upon the shiny hardwood floor, she picked up a half-dried tube of red acrylic from amidst the leftovers of William's eight years with her. She squeezed the tube until a small tear appeared in its side and a slight ooze of paint leaked out into her palm. She looked down at the crushed aluminum and red stickiness, a heart smashed and bleeding. He never meant to come back. He would've told her, when the time was right. He would have used the same satellite that brought her his death news, mincing and biting off its hateful words, delayed, for the pain to settle in. Or perhaps he would've sent one of his childish postcards.

*I dreamed of Goya last night and how he lay in the Sierra Morena to fix the axle on the duchess of Alba's carriage. Oh, by the way, it's over.*

"Funny," Rosemary thought. "William dreamed of Goya and I dream of William." Christ, but she had hated those postcards! All revolutionary and Romantic in notion. As foolish as Byron going off to die for the glory of Greece and, instead, having all those unwritten poems bled out of him by leeches. She had hated William's idealism for years, hadn't she? Yet she'd never been able to tell him. Never been able to insist that he take some responsibility for the relationship. She had covered his idle tracks, offered weak excuses for his *independent studies*.

Rosemary cried her heart out, cried out all the blasphemous red. But instead of anger at William, what she felt was anger at Father for *the other woman,* for dying when she was still so young and malleable. It was anger at Mother for going wickedly, softly crazy and leaving her orphaned. Anger at Miriam for not being a loving big sister. Anger came into her body as quickly as some people claim to receive the Holy Ghost. Anger at Uncle Bishop, at Lizzie. *Rosemary and her sunny disposition.* She should have been born in the midst of Miriam's thunder and lightning and black swelling clouds and thick downpour. Those had been the weather conditions going on *inside* her all these years. Yet, there in the softness of the big room of light he had so willingly left behind, Rosemary could not feel anger at William. She felt only the intense longing for someone she had dearly loved. When she heard Mother stirring about in the hallway, bewildered as a street person, she tossed the tube of paint into the trash and then closed the door to William's favorite room.

After a slow afternoon run, Rosemary deposited Mother in front of the television for her daily soap opera. Mother followed the story of "One Life to Live" with an intensity, according to Aunt Rachel. "Just as she knows when the cuckoo clock is going to sound, she knows when that show is on." So Rosemary left her rocking happily and clutching Betsy Kathleen to her flappy bosom. She decided that a cake mix was elegant enough for Miriam's birthday party, a chocolate with white frosting. She was in the midst of adding frost-hard pink roses and the candy *Happy Birthday* letters when Lizzie, who'd been gone when Rosemary got back from her run, drove into the driveway with Charles. She came into the kitchen while Charles stomped up the fifteen steps and slammed his bedroom door.

"Did you send him to his room?" Rosemary asked, as she offered Lizzie the last lick of the frosting spoon before she rinsed it and filed it away in the dishwasher.

"How old is Miriam, anyway?" Lizzie wondered.

"In which life?" asked Rosemary. Mugs insisted on viewing the cake, so Rosemary lifted him up within a foot of it. He stretched his neck and one paw out toward it, before she put him back down on all four sturdy paws. "Forty," she answered Lizzie.

"That'll be us soon," Lizzie said, and took a diet 7-Up out of the refrigerator.

"I don't even care anymore," said Rosemary. She pushed the cake far back against the wall and covered it with the glass cover of her cake dish in case Mugs decided to celebrate early and by himself.

"Is something bothering you?" Lizzie asked. "One would expect *me* to be uptight, what with the Smothers Brothers escorting me everywhere I go. But you're the one who seems upset." She fidgeted in the refrigerator for a carrot stick.

"Don't spoil your dinner tonight," Rosemary warned, and dreaded the thought of a family get-together, downright rued Miriam's fortieth birthday. And she was tired of all three of her downstate guests.

"By the way, have you seen Philip?" Lizzie's carrot was loud and crunchy. "He's been punishing himself in his room all day."

"Well," Rosemary said. "I guess that means you've made a decision."

"No I haven't," said Lizzie. "I'm making light of it, but the truth is that I'm about to crack. One minute I'm ready to start this foolish game all over again with Philip. On the other hand, Charles and I haven't talked this much since before the babies were born."

"As a wiser person than either you or I once said, *que sera sera.*"

"Doris Day?" asked Lizzie.

"The same," said Rosemary.

The dinner was spaghetti again. It was the most convenient way to feed a large group of people and even Miriam had to admit that Uncle Bishop's sauce was exquisite. It was his own version of spaghetti sauce Bolognese, but he called it *spaghetti sauce Bishop.*

Uncle Bishop liked Philip immediately, more for his taste buds than for his legal sensibilities.

"Try this," Uncle Bishop insisted, as he thrust a saucy spoon into Philip's mouth. Philip rolled the sauce on his tongue as though it were a rare old wine. He sucked in his cheeks to further savor it. "An expert!" Uncle Bishop exclaimed to the others. He gave Philip a second spoonful. "Thank you, Lord," he added.

"That's an incredible sauce," Philip said intensely, and Uncle Bishop glanced about to see if any sauce laymen had heard.

"It depends greatly on how much sweet butter and olive oil," Uncle Bishop whispered. "And good prosciutto, although Rosemary won't eat it."

"This is a *remarkable* sauce," Philip said again, seemingly surprised to find culinary delights as far north as Bixley. He returned the empty spoon to Uncle Bishop.

"And I soak the mushrooms in white wine for an hour," Uncle Bishop whispered loudly. "I'm tempted to give you the recipe, but you understand, don't you, Philip? It's a matter of tradition."

"Most of northern Maine has that recipe," Miriam said. She had tromped into the kitchen to pour herself a glass of cabernet and now she was giving Philip a quick up-and-down scrutiny with eyes that lolled suggestively beneath heavily shaded green lids. Uncle Bishop sighed heavily.

"Have you met Medusa?" he asked Philip, who shook his head.

"A word to the wise," Miriam warned Philip. "Keep your shoes tied tight." She opened a bottle of Bacardi, poured a shot, then emptied it into the glass of wine, mixing it well.

"Shoes?" asked Philip.

"Now here," said Uncle Bishop, pointing at Miriam's glass with disgust, "you witness taste buds that have been sprayed with Pledge. This woman's tongue has an epithelium thicker than shag carpet." Miriam slugged the entire glass of wine-rum down and mixed up another.

"Shoes?" Philip asked again. Drink in hand, Miriam spun

on her heel, flicked a finger under Philip's chin, and then puckered her lips to give him a pretend, noisy kiss. She swished past in her silky green pantsuit and into the dining room with her "mixed drink."

"Nail your pants to your bones," Uncle Bishop said sadly to Philip. "Her pheromones have kicked in."

The big rectangular table in Rosemary's dining room sat ten comfortably, so space wasn't a problem. But she had no idea how to arrange this strange assortment of relatives and bedfellows about its edges without causing some sort of Armageddon, Bolognese style or otherwise. Raymond and Miriam were ignoring each other. This was what Rosemary had guessed earlier in the week when Miriam had chosen to babysit Mother without makeup. With tension smoldering in the air like heat lightning, the eight diners gravitated toward the dining room and found themselves standing at random behind empty chairs. Lizzie wound up in the captain's chair at one end, opposite Rosemary, who, as hostess, always claimed the end position closest the kitchen. Philip and Charles had both entered the dining room on Lizzie's right and suffered a slight, tacit altercation when both tried to claim the empty chair next to her. Charles was victorious and sank into it even as Philip tried to slide it away. Rosemary noticed that none of these three seemed to be speaking to each other as well. She caught Lizzie's eye.

"Assholes," Lizzie formed the word on her lips, then rolled her eyes at Philip and Charles. Philip plunked into the chair next to Charles, mid-table and two whole chairs away from Lizzie. He gazed up at the ceiling fan so as to avoid Miriam's wild and passionate glances. Rosemary seated Mother at Philip's right, at the place setting closest to her own. That way she could see to Mother's whimsical needs. Uncle

Bishop had scuttled to Rosemary's right, on the other side of the table. To his great disappointment, Miriam ended up in the empty chair next to him, mid-table on that side, and directly across from the brooding Philip. The faint smell of a very long Virginia Slim was still lingering about her head, a craziness in her eyes. Rosemary was worried about this. This was Miriam at her lowest stance. And, judging by the looks of Raymond, who had managed to get the chair to Miriam's right but *Lizzie's* left, the stance might get even lower. He was totally absorbed in Lizzie's slanty-green eyes, mirrored in them. Lizzie appeared uncomfortable that Raymond had headquartered himself at her left elbow. But then, Charles was at her right elbow, and she didn't seem too thrilled by that either. Rosemary glanced around the table at her guests. They sat stiffly, an austere gathering, looking very much like the characters in some Clue game. Lizzie. Charles. Philip. Mother. Rosemary. Uncle Bishop. Miriam. Raymond. *Mr. Green, in the Ballroom, with the Lead Pipe.* It was not a Kodak moment. Uncle Bishop had loaded plates with spaghetti and sauce for Lizzie and Rosemary to carry to the table, and now the diners sat staring down at them. All except for Mother, who was ogling *The Chinese Horse.*

"Where's Robbie?" asked Lizzie.

"Too busy for his sister's fortieth birthday party," Miriam answered angrily.

"He's gone camping downstate with friends," Rosemary told Lizzie. "They made plans months ago."

"I was lucky to get a card," Miriam announced.

"You were lucky the card wasn't ticking," Uncle Bishop muttered.

"So, let's eat," said Rosemary. She cut Mother's spaghetti into short pieces. Charles poured wine from one of the two open bottles on the table. The gathering looked like a drinking crowd straight out of some battered USO club during the worst moments of the war. Miriam hiccupped, and then there was more awkward silence before everyone found themselves eating, enjoying the garlic bread, the salad, praising the sauce. Rosemary had remembered to get several bottles of wine at Laker's. It would take many, she knew, to get them all past Miriam's fortieth birthday. Most of Miriam's birthdays had been dramatic showcases, the sixteenth, the twenty-first, the thirtieth coming quickly to Rosemary's mind. Now here was the big four-zero.

"The world is generally mistaken about the origins of spaghetti," Uncle Bishop lectured, pleased that tonight his crowd was larger, more cosmopolitan.

"Doesn't he sound like a whale spouting?" Miriam asked the visitors sitting across from her. Uncle Bishop smiled cordially. Miriam *was,* after all, the guest of honor.

"Another metaphor, Miriam," he said sweetly. "How many does that make now, in these forty years? Two? Three?"

"What about the origins of spaghetti?" asked Philip, and Uncle Bishop smiled a triumphant smile.

"Welllll," he drawled, "the Indians and the Arabians had noodles fifty years before Marco Polo came back from China with his little bundle of goodies."

"Really?" asked Lizzie.

"The Arabians had a different word for it than the Indians did, but both words meant *thread.*" Uncle Bishop beamed at Lizzie.

"How interesting," said Lizzie.

"Yes, isn't it?" said Rosemary.

"It sure is," said Charles.

"Yes," said Philip, not wanting to be left out, especially if Charles had been included. Mother merely stared at Miriam, who was returning from the kitchen with the bottle of Bacardi.

"To hell with decorum," Miriam said. "It *is* my birthday." She plunked the bottle down on the table.

"Then the Italians, those big thinkers of the Mediterranean, those early Perry Comos and Frank Sinatras, come along and call it spaghetti," Uncle Bishop pushed on. "Which comes from a word that means *string.*" He was very pleased with his culinary classroom. He paused—Rosemary knew these pauses—just in case there were questions.

"Why don't you take some of that *string* and sew up your big fat lips?" Miriam asked him suddenly. She filled her wineglass with straight Bacardi. Uncle Bishop turned white with anger. This was not the kind of question he had anticipated from his class. And anticipate he did, for he had all the colorful answers ready. The Indians called it *sevika,* and the Arabians called it *rishta.* And the Italians derived it from *spago,* or *string.* Rosemary had heard it all, many times, at spaghetti dinners in the past.

"When is Father getting here?" Mother asked gingerly.

"Any minute now," Rosemary assured her. Uncle Bishop sat staring with round and furious eyes. Rosemary gave him a sad little look.

"Please don't," she begged.

"Okay," Uncle Bishop agreed, nodding his head dramatically. "But if she continues to waft upon our ears, I promise you nothing."

"I'll waft all I want," Miriam declared. "It's my birthday."

"You actually *rant,*" Uncle Bishop corrected.

"Lizzie, would you pass me the salt, please?" Rosemary asked. She didn't use much salt, but Uncle Bishop craved it. He called it poor man's cocaine. Rosemary would get him salt, quickly, and encourage him to cover his food with it. It might not be healthy, but it would distract him. The Salt Proposal, however, only served to further embroil the situation by bringing out into the open exactly *who* was furious with *whom.* Lizzie picked up the shaker, looked to her right at Charles, fairly snorted, then passed it to her left, to Raymond, who accepted it as though it were a lover's glove tossed idly down. But all too soon he realized the trap. It was only salt and he would have to pass it on. The logical choice was Miriam, not necessarily because she was his life's partner, someone to share the very burden of salt with, but because she sat to his immediate left.

"Shit," Raymond muttered, and quickly shoved the shaker of salt across the table to Charles. Charles took it and, without even considering Philip, at his right, passed it back across the table to Miriam. In Miriam's hands it became a sexual talisman. She rolled it sensuously about her fingers, her eyelashes fluttering at Philip like butterflies gone berserk.

"Pheromone alert!" Uncle Bishop announced loudly. Miriam had no intention of relinquishing this shaker to *him,* the bulging homo who crowded her on the left. Instead, it went fondly back across the table, little love songs caught up in every grain, to Philip, who was forced to take it while avoiding Miriam's caresses on his knuckles.

"Here, for crying out loud," said Philip, as he slid the shaker in front of Mother, quickly, as though it were a hot potato.

"He'd better not forget my chocolates," Mother said, looking down at the salt shaker as if to suggest that Father was playing some dastardly joke on her.

"He won't," Rosemary said, and took the salt from Mother's wrinkly hand. She plopped it loudly in front of Uncle Bishop's plate.

"Salt your damn *thread,*" Rosemary said. She could not believe the spectacle that had unraveled itself around her big cherry table. "It's a good thing you people weren't trying to salt a bird's tail." She imagined this same angry crew at an old-fashioned bucket brigade, while behind them a house full of screaming occupants burned to the ground.

"Shouldn't we toast the birthday girl?" asked Lizzie.

"I think that's an excellent idea," Miriam giggled, and raised her glass. Rosemary, Charles, and Philip hoisted theirs as well, but on Miriam's side of the table things were not so mirthful. Uncle Bishop and Raymond seemed incapable of toasting the woman who slouched between them. This left Miriam's arm stuck out, solo.

" 'Happy birthday to you,' " Rosemary began, but the song was more awkward than the toast since Uncle Bishop and Raymond were quiet as loons in winter. And even Miriam would be too embarrassed to sing "Happy Birthday" to herself. Her half of the table lay silent and melancholy while the other half sang as gladsomely as it could muster. Rosemary kept her eyes on *The Chinese Horse* as it flexed its ancient muscles in the light that flickered up from the candles, an old campfire's light of broken branches gathered twenty thousand years ago by prehistoric hands. The artwork seemed terribly appropriate to her. They were no more than Cro-Magnons sitting around a shank of mammoth. And she wondered if this was what William was longing for in the dream. "I miss the human things," he had said. Well, here she was. Alive. Still plugging. Surrounded by human things.

"You're not missing much, William," Rosemary thought. "Maybe you're better off where you are."

"Do you see now-ow-ow what I me-me-mean?" Miriam was sobbing drunkenly. "My oh-oh-own husband won't sing 'Happy Bir-ir-irthday' to me." Raymond looked sheepish. Miriam wiped her eyes and nose and felt, mistakenly, that she had regained her composure. She had always possessed an uncanny ability to control the fluid in her tear ducts.

"Ladies and gentlemen," Uncle Bishop noted, "we've just heard from the Human Faucet."

"Well, I suppose you might as well be told," Miriam said, ignoring him. She blew her nose dramatically. Raymond winced in anticipation. "Ray and I are splitting up." Miriam said this as though she expected shock to ripple through her listeners.

"You must have ring burn," Uncle Bishop said, and grappled at Miriam's left hand for a look.

"Let go of me!" she screamed, and jerked her arm from Uncle Bishop's grasp. "It's bad enough that we leave ourselves open to AIDS every time we eat your sauce."

"French-kiss me, Miriam, *please,*" Uncle Bishop pleaded, pursing his lips. "Here. Want a blood transfusion?" He pretended to insert the prongs of a fork into his arm.

"Uncle Bishop!" Rosemary snapped, and he let Miriam be.

"A divorce is the only answer," Miriam said sadly.

"You *both* have to work to keep a marriage together," said Charles, prophetically.

"Can it, Charles," Lizzie snapped. This pleased Philip. He put his napkin on the table beside his plate, crossed his arms, and sat back to listen to the case. Not even in night court had he come across such loonies.

"Let me tell you what my dear husband, Raymond, is planning this time." Miriam uncapped her Bacardi bottle and filled the glass again. "He's leaving real estate and going into the Port-O-Let business. Shit houses on wheels! Is that or is that not reason to move to Japan?"

"You'll like Japan," Uncle Bishop said. He was still eating his spaghetti. So was Mother. The others seemed to have had enough. "In Japan, Miriam, you can take rickshaws instead of cabs."

"I could have gone into selling vibrators." Raymond was quickly indignant. "I've had enough experience with Miriam's own personal collection to be familiar with the line."

"How dare you?" Miriam demanded, and turned red as her hair. "How absolutely dare you?"

"Tell me the truth," Uncle Bishop begged. "Was Miriam the cause of that blackout Bixley had last fall? Maybe she should have her own generator."

"Come on, you two!" Rosemary said to the warring couple. Again, she sounded like the perpetual high school teacher, and she hated it. "We're in the middle of a birthday celebration."

"Rosie, read the tea leaves," Uncle Bishop stopped eating to say. "Celebrating Miriam's birth is like observing Salman Rushdie Day in Iran."

"I'm sorry," said Raymond. "But all she does is lay around the house smoking those long straws. And when 'Wheel of Fortune' comes on you should hear the awful stuff she says about Vanna White."

"Vanna White! Vanna White!" Miriam was mimicking Raymond. Uncle Bishop continued to eat. Mother dabbed at her own short spaghetti while making small, grunting noises. Lizzie excused herself and, therefore, so did Charles and Philip, simultaneously. They rose from their chairs like three paper dolls, cut out and hooked miserably together.

"Maybe there will be cake later," Rosemary said vaguely.

"This is the last time I give my heart to a man," Miriam was lamenting.

"Try to visualize the tattered shape of that heart," Uncle Bishop remarked. "It's probably even gone through Christian Barnard's hands." He made another large stab at his spaghetti, rolled it around his fork until it formed a nice ball.

"Let's give it to Mikey," said Mother. "He'll eat anything." Miriam continued to caterwaul.

"This celebration is officially over," Rosemary said, and stood up. Uncle Bishop sighed.

"But I was just beginning to like Raymond," he said. "And you know how I never like her husbands." Raymond grinned appreciatively.

"I never liked you before, either," he admitted.

Mother's attention had gone back to *The Chinese Horse,* and now her little eyes ran up and down its back as though she were grooming it, brushing it until it shone.

"Where's Mr. Ed?" Mother asked.

"On a farm in Michigan," Uncle Bishop whispered, and Mother smiled, willing to accept any fact from the bizarre world of reality.

"Take her down to the den and give her the toy xylophone," Rosemary told him. "I'll bring her some cake in a minute." She was ready to have them *all* committed, and that included old college friends.

"Can I stay for a few days, Rosie, until I'm back on my feet?" Miriam's eyes were moist and ingratiating. *Rosie.* Even as children it was *Rosie* only if she wanted something.

"I don't know, Miriam," Rosemary stalled. "As you can see, I have a full house as it is."

"She's not coming home with *me,*" Raymond assured the group. "And someone better come get that goddamn Chihuahua before it ends up in a casserole." Uncle Bishop made a face at this gourmet suggestion. Raymond poured himself more wine, as if the party were still going on.

"So who wants to go home with you and your limp little thingy?" Miriam hissed.

"It ain't limp when I watch Vanna White," Raymond boasted, and raised his glass to Uncle Bishop, his new confederate. It was then that Miriam grabbed the wine bottle, Robbie's favorite brand, Partager, meaning *to share,* and shared it with Raymond by knocking him out of his chair, and out cold. His glass stayed in his hand. Some things you *can* take with you.

It was Uncle Bishop who helped Rosemary put the cold pack on Raymond's swelling head. Miriam sat at the table and wept things into the leftover spaghetti sauce Bishop about her life being over, and making bawdy references to what she called *the herd* of insensitive men who had stampeded through her life. Raymond had enough alcohol in his system that the pain was minimal, something he referred to laughingly as *a little headache.*

"Wait till morning," Uncle Bishop predicted, as he regarded the blue, hairy tepee on Raymond's head.

"Talk to him to keep him rational while I do something about Miriam," Rosemary said.

"You expect a man who is married to Miriam to be rational?" Uncle Bishop asked incredulously. "Bump or no bump, that's a long shot." Raymond guffawed loudly.

Rosemary led Miriam out of the dining room and toward the stairs, all fifteen of them. One. Two. Three. Miriam sank to her knees.

"I hate my life," she wailed. The stench of rum swept out of her mouth and Rosemary moved back from it.

"Come on," she coaxed. "The situation will look different

tomorrow." She remembered words such as these from Miriam herself, and the whole blasted family, not so very long ago. "Try to look at it this way," Miriam said to Rosemary, about why William had committed suicide. "Shit happens." Now here was the opportunity for Miriam to take her own shitty advice.

"And I hate Raymond," Miriam added drunkenly. "I *really* hate Raymond."

"Let's go up to the spare bedroom and I'll tuck you in," said Rosemary. She wondered if she had a spare bedroom left. "You'll get a good night's sleep and we can talk about it tomorrow." Four. Five steps.

"Do you want to know something?" Miriam cried. She fought off Rosemary's arms.

"Shit happens, Miriam," said Rosemary. "I know that much. Now don't slap like that." She was trying to catch hold of one of the pudgy wrists, but couldn't. Miriam was heavy when sober but now, full drunk, she was waterlogged and sluggish as an old tree. Rosemary feared she would tumble down the stairs.

"Listen," Miriam whispered, and Rosemary leaned forward. "Do you know how much I hate my life?" Rosemary was perplexed as her mind raced for the answer that would most please Miriam and get her upstairs and into bed. She decided to feign interest.

"How much do you hate your life?" she finally asked.

"Watch!" screamed Miriam. She tossed off Rosemary's grasp and bounded down the five steps. Stumbling on the last, then regaining her footing, she was in the den in an instant. Before Rosemary could catch up to her she had thrown Mother's xylophone up against the wall in a tinkling, crashing, musical sound, all the pitches running together. And then she grabbed Mother's little doll face roughly between her hands.

"Father's dead!" Miriam was shouting over and over

again, above Mother's own screams, as Rosemary pulled her away. "The son of a bitch is dead!"

When Rosemary settled into bed herself, an hour after Miriam had finally passed out, after Raymond's taillights had disappeared down Old Airport Road, just behind his good friend who was driving the Datsun, an hour after Mother finally stopped her hysterical sobbing and fell asleep assured that Father's annoying tire had simply gone flat again, Rosemary was no longer weary of the onslaught of nightmares. Let them come and take her off, a ride through terror, the manes of all the demon mares stinging her face. It would be a welcomed relief from the *daymares* of Miriam turning forty, of Mother crazy, of Uncle Bishop and the shoe fairy. She drifted off, almost wishing to meet up with William again, out there in the subconscious darkness, when the ringing sounded. At first Rosemary thought it was a fire alarm, until she realized it was the telephone. One-thirty. Uncle Bishop. "The Children's Hour."

"Rosie, do you have any idea how Hollywood treated all those little Munchkins in *The Wizard of Oz?*" Uncle Bishop asked sadly.

"Come on, nightmares," Rosemary thought. "Come unbridled and frothing at the mouth. Come with your evil nostrils flaring. Anything is better than this." She placed the phone beside the clock on the bedside table. Let Uncle Bishop, like a puppy on its first night away from home, hear the continual ticking, the reassurance of a mother's heartbeat. Let him talk on and on into the night while the luminous numbers on the clock's face listened, happily as a friend, to what he had to say. Rosemary's own face turned itself away from the clock, away from the tinny voice seeping out of the receiver, and went off to sleep.

# The Jaunty Skeleton

WHEN ROSEMARY AWOKE the next morning she thought at first she had dreamed the gothic birthday party of the previous evening. It had all the macabre dimensions of dream. But she knew she hadn't. Lately, there was more reality filtering into her in the deep dreams of night than there was in the waking moments she shared with her bizarre family. "I used to think of you as that normal girl on 'The Munsters,' " Lizzie had said.

She twisted in her bed to catch a glimpse of the numbers on the clock. Nine-thirty. She had slept in an old T-shirt, instead of pajamas, and now she slipped it off and reached for her bathrobe. She peered out of her doorway to see if the bathroom was occupied. Mugs followed her into the hallway, grabbing at the hem of the terry cloth bathrobe and wondering why his eight-thirty outing had been postponed. Time was suddenly going crazy.

Downstairs, coffee had been made by one of the household denizens and Rosemary tasted a cup quickly to test its freshness. It had begun to turn stale but it was not so stale as to prompt her to make a fresh pot. Mother and Miriam were out on the swing, swinging together in harmony. Mother had undoubtedly misplaced the facts of what had happened the night before. She seemed rested, peaceful. Miriam, on the other hand, had eyes that were swollen as old fruit, the lids bluish as grapes. Her countenance told Rosemary much, especially after years of dealing with Miriam: hung over and overly apologetic. Hoping they hadn't noticed her movement, Rosemary inched her way back from the window, stepping on the tip of Mugs's tail. He caterwauled fiercely, causing her to slosh hot coffee on her wrist.

"Sorry," she whispered, and leaned down to pat the furry head. Then she opened the front door and Mugs quickly slipped around her shins—as well as around the stumpy legs standing on the front steps—and was gone beneath the lilac bushes. Rosemary glanced up in surprise. Uncle Bishop was lounging on the porch steps, a suitcase clutched in one of his fat hands. She recognized it immediately. It was Miriam green.

"Raymond dropped this off at my house," Uncle Bishop stated. "He said we might as well take it so Miriam will have something green to wear until he gets the rest of her shit packed. He's not as naive as the others. The house is in his name." Uncle Bishop thumped Miriam's suitcase onto the floor of the foyer before Rosemary could protest.

"Uncle Bishop, I can't take in any more boarders, especially Miriam," Rosemary insisted.

"Well, you'll have to tell Raymond that."

"Where the hell *is* Raymond?" Rosemary pushed the suitcase to one side with her foot.

"He must be home. I suppose he didn't come himself because he doesn't want to be subjected to another one of Miriam's Gregorian chants." Uncle Bishop was fidgeting with something outside on the steps. He suddenly fetched it into the foyer and Rosemary saw that it was another suitcase, this one brown and masculine, certainly not of the same set as Miriam's olive green.

"Besides," Uncle Bishop said, positioning a large leg in front of the brown suitcase, as if to hide it. "He says he feels like he's just had brain surgery."

"What's that?" Rosemary asked.

"That's surgery on the brain."

"That!" Rosemary said again, and pointed.

"What?"

"That brown suitcase which has a decal of the Arc de Triomphe pasted to its side."

"That's my suitcase," said Uncle Bishop.

"Why is it sitting on my steps rather than at some French airport?" She wrapped her robe tighter.

"I'd like to join all of you for a couple of days," Uncle Bishop said airily.

"Join us?" Rosemary was incredulous. "What do you think this is? A club? A junket? At first Lizzie acts like it's a sorority house where she's sneaked in two guys. Then it became a mental institution when Mother arrived. Now Miriam is convalescing on my swing right this minute as if it's some kind of halfway house for emotionally battered, forty-year-old wives. I know my front yard resembles a used-car lot, but to me this is my home. Now, what would *you* like this place to be, Uncle Bishop?"

"A home away from home, I guess," he said, and looked over his shoulder at the mailbox to avoid her piercing stare.

"And why do you suddenly need a home away from home?"

"Well, let me rephrase that," Uncle Bishop said, and adjusted the crotch of a pair of baby-blue shorts that were covered with small pink teddy bears. "Let's just say I need a home away from Mrs. Abernathy's home."

"Uncle Bishop, I told you to leave that old woman alone." Rosemary was not pleased with him, and he knew it. He fidgeted openly in his teddy bear shorts and looked miserably uncomfortable.

"She's having me arrested," he said finally. "Or so she claims." Rosemary gasped.

"What for?"

"For trespassing and mental cruelty," Uncle Bishop told her. He peered at her intently. "Doesn't one have to be married before one can be sued for mental cruelty? I need to talk to Philip about that."

"What did you do to her, Uncle Bishop?" Rosemary could not remember being so angry at him.

"I put something in her yard," he said boyishly, his eyes staring at his brown sandals with the red toes painted on their tips.

"What did you put in her yard?" She pronounced each word evenly so that he would not miss her displeasure. It was her schoolteacher's voice. He winced.

"Well, I put it on the top of her hedge, to be exact," he said. "Overlooking her tray feeders."

"What was it?" Rosemary waited. Uncle Bishop sighed a large sigh, befitting the body that bore it, a great sigh, and then he knelt on one knee to turn the big brown suitcase over on its side. He zippered it open and dug beneath a mammoth pair of shorts with classic cars emblazoned on them.

"This," he said, holding up a large stuffed bird, which she

immediately recognized as a great horned owl, its ear tufts reaching heavenward, its blank eyes peering out of its flattened face. Rosemary gasped.

"Where did you get that thing?" she asked. It would frighten the daylights out of Mrs. Abernathy's readers. What was it she had said in her column, just that Sunday, about such birds? *Even God makes mistakes, Dear Birders, and the bird of prey is a fine example of this.*

"At the flea market," Uncle Bishop said gleefully. "Just yesterday. It was a toss-up between this and a stuffed lynx. But the lynx cost too much." Uncle Bishop put the large bird in Rosemary's outstretched arms. *Pterodactyl.* Imagining it perched on Mrs. Abernathy's hedge, she tried not to think of what commotion it caused inside the old woman's aging heart. What was it Mr. Abernathy himself had said? "The old ticker has only so many beats in it and then kaput."

"It was only twenty-five dollars," Uncle Bishop continued happily. "That's because it's got just one leg. See?" Rosemary tipped the magnificent bird on its side. It was true. The poor creature was, indeed, one-legged. A gaping hole remained where there had once been a leg, a hooked claw, a feathered foot. Some human being had paid a taxidermist good money, one fine day, to have this animal mounted. Someone who couldn't exist without a *stuffed owl.* Sad creatures, these humans. Sadder than one-legged owls.

"I ran over and took it down after she phoned to say that the cops had been alerted," Uncle Bishop said. "Most cops don't have a sense of humor." He was having a good little laugh. Rosemary stared at the bird's splendidly hooked bill and thought about the flight of those glorious creatures, noiseless, mothlike, swooping down upon their dinner with just a slight swoosh of wind, a little woodsy breeze.

"Can you imagine the scare it gave the old bat?" Uncle

Bishop wanted to know, and Rosemary was suddenly reminded of another of Mrs. Abernathy's columns that spring. *For the more discerning birder,* it had cautioned, *bats are the only mammal capable of true flight. But the bat is not a bird, I repeat, it is not! Bats carry bubonic plague, typhoid fever, and, nowadays, the dreaded disease AIDS. This is also true of the common household cat.*

"She's not an old bat," Rosemary said flatly.

"The lynx wouldn't have worked anyway," Uncle Bishop went on. "It looked too much like Ralphie."

"She's a fragile old woman."

"She'll think twice before she puts another bell on *my* cat." He thumped the owl's rump. Its yellow eyes stared unblinking, maybe remembering the forests around Hudson Bay, where it made its nest in January and laid eggs while the ground was still blanketed with snow. Or perhaps the slap of summer waters around Tierra del Fuego, before it sat on a shelf in someone's den, next to the gun rack, next to a copy of *TV Guide.*

"You disappoint me," Rosemary said softly. "Miriam is one thing, but Mrs. Abernathy is another." She put the dead owl back in his hands. Was she imagining it, or could she smell the thick noxious odor of rotting flesh?

"Oh, Rosie, come on." Uncle Bishop was chagrined. "This'll keep the blood pumping in her old veins, keep them from clogging up. Think of this as a kind of cardiovascular Drãno."

"If you go near her again, Uncle Bishop, so help me," Rosemary threatened, "I'll turn you in myself."

"She's not why I've come," he said. "I'm not afraid of her threats. I have exhibit A right here." He bobbed the owl at her and then knelt to rebury it, beneath the exotic clothing in his suitcase, a little brown grave.

"Why *are* you here?"

"I'm going crazy alone," he said unhappily, and Rosemary reluctantly stepped back to let him drag the big brown suitcase past her.

She spent the rest of the afternoon in the bedroom next to her own, the one that Mother had been occupying for the week. Now Mother's little visit was almost over. Aunt Rachel would arrive later in the day to retrieve her, and the room would go to Uncle Bishop. "For a couple of days," or so he said. The large brown suitcase sat happily in the corner, waiting to be unpacked. Rosemary had come up to the room to spend Mother's last afternoon with her. She found her seated in a big chair by the window, with a coloring book. Years earlier, Mother had enjoyed coloring with her children, patiently encouraging Rosemary and Robbie to stay within the dark heavy lines. Now here Mother was, outside the heavy lines society had laid down, outside all the proper rules. But she had taken to her hobby with gusto and was already on her third picture, one of children in galoshes stomping about in mud puddles, beneath April showers, beneath mushroomlike umbrellas, which Mother chose to color green and orange. It was a relief to watch this activity in lieu of reading about the vicissitudes of Hester Prynne and the increasingly unlikable Arthur Dimmesdale, Puritanical jerk. Rosemary had long ago decided that the Puritans were all a miserable lot. "Keep in mind," she had told her students, "that the Puritans were not hanging witches. They were hanging other Puritans." Did any of her past students, she wondered now, ever keep that in mind? Did they keep *anything* in mind that she had taught them?

As Mother began a new picture, Rosemary heard car doors slam and engines come to life. She peered out the big window over Mother's head to see Lizzie roar off, with Charles and Philip following behind in Philip's little blue Mercedes.

Charles and Philip in union against Lizzie. Charles riding in a non–General Motors car. What would this bizarre threesome do next? Better yet, when would they do it in their own homes? Philip had been in residence for over a week. Charles had been in Bixley for four days. Lizzie had been in Rosemary's spare bedroom for almost three weeks.

"If something isn't done soon," Rosemary promised herself, "I'm taking action."

At three o'clock Mother abandoned her coloring book and crayons, rubbed her small eyes, and fell asleep on the bed. Rosemary carefully inched an arm in under the yellow head, pulled her in close, cradled her, as though she were a child. She'd been aching to hold Mother for years, but only asleep would Mother allow such a display of emotions with this stranger. The next two hours, which passed so slowly, were the best between mother and daughter that Rosemary could remember since childhood. Those were the days, long summery afternoons, when she fell asleep to the melodic lilt of Mother's voice as she read some storybook story. In those days, days yellow from the sun, she would drift off in the very heart of the story and Mother would leave her alone for her tiny nap. When she woke, there would be questions: What happened to the prince? Did they ever find the glass slipper? Did the Wicked Witch get Dorothy? And with the questions there would be a homemade buttermilk doughnut sitting next to a tall glass of milk and the reddest, most delicious apple you could imagine, all waiting on her headboard like the participants in a still life. And there would be a perfumy smell where Mother had been, where she had come and gone, Mother, whose breasts back then were still firm and accommodating to a little girl's head. Whose silk blouse rustled like autumn leaves, and who wore fake pearl hair combs in her lustrous hair. She was all smell and touch, this Mother of the happy answer: the prince is no longer a frog, Cinderella is dancing in her little glass slippers, and Dorothy is safe and sound back in dusty Kansas.

"Where are your perfect answers for me now?" Rosemary wondered, as she held Mother's tiny body in her arms. "When I come full awake with such fright, in the heart of the night, where are the answers?" But she knew there would be no one there to offer her endings. No one to say, "William is alive and well. He's painting in Kansas these days." Rosemary stroked the Goldilocks hair, traced the laugh lines and crow's feet and other road signs nature had left during its trek across Mother's face. She held Mother, who was tired from coloring, tired as a dirty child from the long day, and watched as the small red mouth opened and closed, bringing Mother air as she slept, bringing her the dream of life. "Oh, Mother," Rosemary wished she could say, as she had struggled to say William's name in the terror of the last dream. She shooed a small mosquito away from the wrinkled forehead, a buzzing little ultralight. The truth was that their relationship had turned rotten suddenly, when Father died. He was their focal point. He was what they had in common. They had dearly loved the same man and, in dying, he had jilted them, as though they were foolish girlfriends. Now Mother was waiting for chocolates, for the candy of apology, for some long-overdue sweetness in her life. And Rosemary was watching the sky like a religious zealot, hoping for a crack, a fissure, so that the men who had disappeared would have a crawl space back into her life.

She stayed with Mother until five o'clock, until she heard Aunt Rachel's little Volvo rattle up into the yard. Aunt Rachel had the eyes of the dead, round and listless, uninterested in life's tiny schemes. She seemed to gather new strength in seeing Mother again and caught her up in a swift hug. Mother was ecstatic. She had finally been rescued from the House of Crazies by her trusted guardian and protector. She held on to Aunt Rachel's hand as Rosemary packed the broken xylophone, the books, and Betsy Kathleen into the tired Volvo. Uncle Bishop would drive the rocking chair home.

"Are you sure you don't want me to keep her another week so that you can rest a bit more?" Rosemary asked.

"No," Aunt Rachel said, and patted Rosemary's arm. "It's better to take her home with me now. I garner energy from her in some strange way."

Rosemary watched them swoop off in the rattling Volvo down the swell of Old Airport Road, Mother's ringlets bouncing happily, as though she were a child on the way to a drive-in movie. *Good-bye, Mother.*

She went back upstairs to find Uncle Bishop happily arranging knickknacks and framed photographs on the tiny mahogany table by the bed. The owl sat stiffly in Mother's rocker.

"What's this?" Rosemary asked sternly, her teacher's voice again. She was still very unhappy with him. He flinched.

"It's a photograph," he said, taking the picture of a dark, petite man out of her hand and placing it back on the bedside table.

"Do you always take your photographs with you when you visit for a couple of days?" Rosemary challenged him.

"Sometimes," Uncle Bishop said sadly. "And sometimes I even take them on short trips to Thomasville to run a quick errand."

"Why?" Rosemary took the photograph up again. The face in the picture was a man haunted, a sadness in his eyes.

"So that I can be close to the people who are important to me," Uncle Bishop mumbled.

"Is this who I think it is?" she asked.

He nodded.

"Jason?" A second nod.

"Is he still with his wife?" A third nod.

"Can't you do better than nod?" A fourth nod.

"Come on, Uncle Bish. Where is Jason these days?"

"Still with her, I guess," Uncle Bishop said. "I gave him three or four days. Seven at the most. It's been three weeks, Rosie, and still nothing." Rosemary took the white flabby hands up into her own, stopped the nervous game of the fingers, the frantic twiddling.

"Could this be why you've been so particularly hard on Mrs. Abernathy?" she asked him.

"I suppose it could have added to my stress in some small way, when dealing with the old bat." He took Jason's sad face out of Rosemary's hands and peered at it himself. Rosemary thought of Horace Abernathy's last picture, back on Mrs. Abernathy's mantel, the one she must have snapped before the cancer jumped poor Horace in the canyon of his life. Ambushed him. Cut him off at the pass.

"Can't you also, then, try to imagine what that old lady is going through right next door to you?" Rosemary asked. "Mr. Abernathy's dead. She has no children. She certainly doesn't have the luxury of packing a suitcase and visiting loved ones for a couple of days, as you're doing."

"Do you think we should get her a cat?" Uncle Bishop asked, and nervously rubbed his bald spot. It shone like a small planet amidst a universe of thinning hair. Rosemary took a spare blanket out of the closet and tossed it onto the bed.

"I'd appreciate it if you would be kind enough to act as my emissary," she told him. "Please let these people know, including yourself, that I want my privacy back very soon." With that, she went out and closed the door roughly.

"Tell them yourself," she heard him say loudly. "I personally don't associate with the hoi polloi."

When Rosemary found her in the den, Miriam was enduring a headache, although probably nothing at all like the conductorless symphony going on inside poor Raymond's head. She had even, she informed Rosemary, given up her Virginia Slims for an hour or so in a valiant attempt to dissuade the headache.

"I should never mix wine and hard stuff," Miriam lamented, as though this were a suggestion proffered by *Bon Appétit.*

"Miriam, what's your problem?" Rosemary asked.

"What do you mean?"

"I mean, why are you in my house instead of your own?"

"Well," said Miriam, and fidgeted a bit on the sofa. Rosemary could see her sister's mind working, the thoughts forming. *What's come over passive little Rosemary?* Miriam was no doubt wondering. *What's got little Shirley Temple up in arms?*

"Do you plan to straighten things out with Raymond soon?" Rosemary picked up an orange crayon that must have fallen from Mother's giant box of colors. She placed it on the coffee table. She would drop it off at Aunt Rachel's later in the week. Mother might want to color Sally's hair with it. Or perhaps Spot, a small orange dog peeing up against a purple tree.

"What do you mean by *soon,* Rosie?" Miriam squinted her eyes as though she were, indeed, still smoking. Rosemary sighed.

"There you go again," she said. "It was always *Rosie,* can I borrow your bicycle? *Rosie,* can I wear your new sweater? Will you do my homework, *Rosie?* Well, let me tell you something, Miriam. Shit happens. It just goddamn happens. I have my own problems. I'll listen to yours, preferably over the telephone, and only if I must."

"Some sister you've turned out to be," Miriam hooted.

Breaking her new health regimen, she reached for a slender Virginia Slim and set it on fire. Smoke came out of her nose.

"Doesn't she look like an old Plymouth with no exhaust pipe?" Uncle Bishop asked from the doorway. He disappeared into the kitchen and Rosemary heard the refrigerator door open and close.

"I want my privacy back, especially after Lizzie leaves," Rosemary continued. Miriam began to weep.

"No one cares about *me,*" she cried. "Raymond even treats people he doesn't like better than he treats me."

"Not my problem," Rosemary told her.

"He gave that awful daughter of his money for a boob job," Miriam sobbed. "Two thousand bucks because Janie swore she'd die without new tits."

"In one ear and out the other," Rosemary warned. She picked up *The Scarlet Letter* and opened to her marker.

"Now Janie wants to have her nose straightened," Miriam went on. "And guess who's gonna pay for it."

"I can't hear a single word," said Rosemary. Hester Prynne was waiting, and the Puritans suddenly seemed so much more sensible, forgiving even, than her own family.

"You don't have to put up with an ex-wife and alimony payments either," Miriam persisted.

" 'Hester Prynne went one day to the mansion of Governor Bellingham,' " Rosemary read aloud, " 'with a pair of gloves.' "

"Oh, fuck Hester Prynne," Miriam cried. "Just fuck her. Hester Prynne doesn't know the half of it."

" 'Which she had fringed and embroidered to his order.' "

"Do you think I should have a baby?" Miriam suddenly asked. This got Rosemary's attention. She put Hester and Arthur down on the coffee table. Hester had had a baby, too. Hester had been the ultimate single working mother. Miriam accepted a large cloud of smoke into her lungs, but it resurfaced shortly through her nose.

"You couldn't burp Tupperware, Miriam," Uncle Bishop said, appearing again in the doorway with a glass of lemonade. "What would a nullipara like you do with a baby?" Rosemary felt saved by the bell.

"Thank you, Uncle Bishop," she thought, then, *"Nullipara?"*

At seven o'clock Lizzie knocked on Rosemary's door and came inside her bedroom to sit on the bed.

"I think every woman should have a husband *and* a lover," Lizzie said, when Rosemary inquired as to the state of affairs. "It's cleared up my face."

"Where are Philip and Charles?" asked Rosemary.

"I finally gave them the slip in that sharp turn just as you come into Bixley. Then I drove to Thomasville and went to a movie alone."

"Sounds like your life is more entertaining than a movie."

"It's funny, Rosemary, but I'm curious as to whether I'm getting this sudden attention from Charles just because there's a Philip."

"Could be."

"And I'm suddenly wondering if there is a Philip just because I want some attention from Charles."

"It's certainly possible."

"At least I'm trying to be levelheaded," Lizzie said, and bit at a nail. "I sometimes also think that what's going on between Philip and Charles is a male kind of competition and that it's more important than me. It's the fight and not the prize." She appeared even more tired than the previous day, when she had looked exhausted. "And by the way, we'll be out of your hair soon," she promised.

"Tell me," said Rosemary. "Are Charles and Philip forming a lasting relationship these days?"

"Oh no," said Lizzie. "They hate each other."

"I saw them driving away together."

"Well, I stormed off in my car," Lizzie explained. "So Philip decided to follow me. I guess he had one final legal point to make. Charles was obliged to go, too, if Philip was going because he wouldn't want us to sneak away to some motel."

"All right." Rosemary nodded. "I think I have that so far."

"When Charles discovered that Uncle Bishop's Datsun had him blocked in, he ran over and jumped in with Philip rather than miss a ride altogether. And Philip was so afraid that if he stopped to insist Charles get out, I'd have time to make a clean getaway." Lizzie was finished.

"It's a good thing you've had all that experience raising your kids, Lizzie. It seems to be paying off for you now."

"When was this taken?" Lizzie asked. She was holding a picture that Rosemary kept on the headboard of her bed. It was of her and William and Mugs. They were in a canoe on Madawaska Lake, on a magnificent autumn day of blue sky and the first signs of color coming to the leaves. "Scientists understand the life and death process of a leaf, Rosie," William had told her that day. "But no one knows what causes them to burst into such incredible colors." Rosemary's hair was much longer in the picture, waist length, and a strong wind had caught it up in an autumn-blond swirl about her head. William sat on the bottom of the canoe, leaning back between Rosemary's legs. Rosemary was tilting forward, her arms folded on William's head. He wore a T-shirt that said BOSTON RED SOX, their favorites since it was the major league team nearest Maine. William's camera had been set up at the bow of the canoe with its time release mechanism ready to go, just like the pressure valve that would soon blow in William himself. Mugs sat on William's lap, and was just coming into the fatness of tomcathood. There they all were, the little family, frozen onto a frame of time.

"Three or four years ago," Rosemary answered Lizzie, and she was struck suddenly with how amusing it would have been on that autumny, crackling afternoon if someone from shore had rowed out toward them, slow motioned, deathly, to tell them William had three years, three months, and twelve days to live? Would they have killed the messenger? "He slit his wrists," Michael had said. "A razor blade. Jesus, Rosemary, he had to go out to a store to buy the goddamn thing." Rosemary could even see William, moving idly up and down the aisles of some British store, reading all the fine print. Knowing him, he would have chosen the most functional razor for the best price. Would they have even *believed* the messenger? Rosemary took the photo from Lizzie and looked down at a segment of her own existence, an eternity away now, this *three or four years*.

"We would have laughed ourselves silly," she thought. And it was the truth.

But as she gazed down at the picture, she didn't see the leafy fire coming to Black Fly Hill, or the corduroy of waves wafting in to rock the canoe as though it were a large cradle. And Rosemary didn't see Mugs craning his fat neck away from the camera. She didn't see herself with skin a bit younger, her head canted to one side, her left cheekbone lit up with a spray of October sunlight. What she saw instead was a young man with three years, three months, and twelve days of life left ahead of him. She saw her precious William, his hair wet from a lake-cold dip, his open smile like a slice of apple on a cidery fall day. She saw his bone-white skeleton reclining jauntily between her legs as though she had given it birth.

# The Inland Murmur

*But there's a tree, of many, one,*
*a single field which I have looked upon,*
*Both of them speak of something that is gone . . .*

—William Wordsworth,
"Intimations of Immortality"

For two days the tenants of the house on Old Airport Road came and went without causing any commotion, like the intermixing parts of a tightly wound clock. The house itself had become a kind of Lourdes, attracting the emotionally handicapped from all walks of life. Uncle Bishop seemed content simply to be around people, especially Rosemary. Miriam appeared to be in no great hurry to reconcile with Raymond. She spent much time instead on the back swing, smoking an endless trail of Virginia Slims and even taking an interest in the birds, occasionally asking Rosemary to identify a sparrow or designate the sexes of the goldfinches. "She's just doing that to get on your good side," Uncle Bishop told Rosemary. "She probably had hummingbird tongues for breakfast." Lizzie's children would finish their camping in a week and she would be compelled to leave. In the meantime, if Lizzie walked to the mailbox, Philip and Charles went hither. "Don't those two men work?" Uncle Bishop asked condescendingly. This was the same perennial question Miriam loved to ask of *him*. "Where does Bishop get his money, will someone please tell me?" Rosemary avoided them as much as she could, spending a few hours each day at the library. She could at least read in peace there, except for when the heavy, watchful eyes of Mrs. Waddell were pressing themselves hotly on her shoulder. She kept up the running, reminding herself each time a foot hit the pavement that her burgeoning household would soon be gone. Like a litter of noisy puppies, they would all be in their own homes one day. "Soon," she told herself, as she stretched before each distance, increasing the run to four miles.

In between avoiding her guests, Rosemary spent some time thinking about Father's spring. Her spring. The childhood fountain. Was it still there? Could she find it? She had not been east of Bixley since the house burning. Not even with William could she make the descent down that cobwebby tunnel leading to her past. "Let's go together and find it," William had urged. "Someday," Rosemary would tell him. "When the magic is right, we'll go." Now William himself had disappeared into that tunnel of old memories, that Bermuda Triangle of dreams and wishes and plans, a tunnel smelling like the entrails of good intentions. "Someday, William, when the magic is right, I'll untangle the old webs."

The morning had begun cloudy, but by two o'clock the sky was clear, as though someone had dusted away those clouds. The birds sang in their different notes from the grasses, and trees, and telephone wires. Bluebells bent their necks, turning their mouths downward. If the magic wasn't *right,* it was certainly *workable.* Rosemary, wearing her tight-legged jeans that wouldn't catch in the chain, and tying her denim shirttails up into a hard knot, backed the bicycle out of its resting place and then glided down the driveway and out onto the bumpy surface of Old Airport Road.

A pickup truck came toward her, pulling behind it a light brown parachute of dust. The driver tooted his horn. It was Jan Ferguson, who lived beyond Rosemary's own house. Rosemary waved back, then lowered her head, her eyes on the ground and squinting until the filmy shield had passed over. Old Airport Road's only pollution, this occasional flare-up from the tires of passersby.

Sharon Masefield, Rosemary's old school chum, now Sharon Masefield Greene, whipped by in a shiny blue Ford Escort that would no longer be shiny when it reached its destination near the end of Old Airport Road, the home Sharon had bought and renovated with her husband, Bill. People pairing up. Two small children floated like balloons on the backseat of the Escort, suspended inside the moving car as though they were helium filled. Sharon honked her horn and waved frantically. Rosemary couldn't help but wonder if Sharon looked into her rearview mirror, back into the wake of wavy dust, over the unruly heads of her children, and wished that all she had to do on such a glorious June day was to pedal a bicycle up and down the road. She remembered Sharon's high school hurry, sporting her newly styled shag hairdo, Sharon rushing in the halls, in the corridors, late for class, late for ball practice, or just missing the Bixley bus. The Escort went on inside its ball of dust, went on with its hurrying.

As the car and its occupants disappeared over a rise in the road, Rosemary felt an intense loneliness, an old anxiety that crept in occasionally. Sharon had been someone to share a rattail comb with in the girl's bathroom but not a close friend. This was true of all the old high school classmates. And even the college classmates, except for Lizzie, were not much more than faces in old yearbooks.

She braked for the incline into Bixley, which had its share of shoppers bustling in and out of the two dozen or so stores and businesses. It also had the *little town* architecture: two small banks, an insurance agency, Gary's hardware store, two drugstores, Max's Camera and Supply Shop, an IGA grocery, Bixley's Economat grocery, Ron's Chevrolet, Miller's Ford, J.C. Penney's, Nora's Clothing, two restaurants, a cafe, the post office, the library, Joy's Magazines and Books, Larry's Sunoco, the town office, the police station, the firehouse, Radio Shack, and the newly acquired McDonald's. Human ideas, structured and architectural, arranged in a scheme, caught up in a design, nailed, sawed, plastered, and framed into a single thought: the small New England town.

Betty Gleason, another old high school classmate, smiled at Rosemary and waved from behind the naked mannequin she was dressing in the window of Betty's Boutique. Marvin Casey leaned out of the United States post office and shouted hello. Rosemary waved back over her shoulder and left him smiling in her wake. As she rolled past the IGA, Bixley fell behind her, growing and groaning and swelling at its seams as much and as fast as a small town possibly can. Already on her right she saw the staked signs declaring the future site of Bixley's new shopping mall.

Rosemary had not been to the Bixley Drive-In—which sat on the outskirts of town—for years. She was surprised to see that it was closed, no longer functioning, a dinosaur looming over the modern trappings of electronic sundries. It saddened her to think of the big old screen dying a slow death out among the elements and uninterested passersby. She was also shocked at the numerous upcroppings of new homes, a long line of subdivisions—*baby factories*, Uncle Bishop called them—covering the hillsides on each side of the road like colorful gardens planted by real estate sowers. Miriam's ilk. The Manifest Destiny crowd of Bixley, Maine. How had Bixley grown so without her noticing it?

The truth was that she had driven like a rat in a maze, for years, to her teaching job in Thomasville by means of New Airport Road, and the new interstate that had finally inched its way north, up the state of Maine, to Bixley. She had come home, kicked off her shoes and the long day of brain-muddled high school students, and she had stayed within or near her big old house. Daily, she had seen the subdivisions mushroom to life along New Airport Road, all the way out northward to the new highway. It made sense that the same development was occurring along the peaceful edges of Norris Road, which also ran northeasterly to meet the new highway. But that was the childhood road. The bicycle's path. The trail of magic that led, once, to a house now turned to ashes, to a man now gone to dust. It was inconceivable for Rosemary to admit that progress had come to the delicate elms, the teetering pines, the soft layer of duff that stretched like shag carpet beneath a child's bare feet. But here progress was, towering above what used to be open fields of hay, now houses of people trying desperately to plant different flowers in their front yards, struggling for individuality. Aside from the color of paint, aside from the pansies and zinnias, they were crackerjack boxes all in a row. *Baby factories.* Here and there a convenience store broke the monotony.

"Where are these people coming from?" Rosemary wondered. "Are they extraterrestrials?"

A half mile past the drive-in Rosemary braked and stared ahead to the spot where the family homestead had once stood, the house where she had been given birth on a cracking winter's day by a woman destined to go demurely crazy. The road leading off Norris Road, which was once gravel, was now tarred and became, after five hundred yards or so, a cul-de-sac. Houses clung to it, the modern crouching paranoid kind, none of those rambling two- and three-story giants that spoke of the many children families used to have. New life, new blood had crept into the population of Bixley. But Rosemary was not ready for the disappearance of the only magic she had ever known in her life: childhood.

She pedaled to the end of the cul-de-sac and left the bike leaning on its kickstand. Making her way past the marigolds in someone's front yard, she walked past the marigolds in their backyard with that boldness and familiarity that comes from having once owned a house and its land, as though, through some kind of divine right, it still belongs to you. What judge in the country would convict her if she tearfully took the stand and explained about that bluish January birthday *so cold everything was snapping. So sky blue it hurt your eyes.* And then would come the fluid tales of father smelling of Old Spice, of Rosemary sailing the clipper ship on the bottle as she lay near his sleeping body. Of the tiny Canada warbler and the Ponce de León spring out in the woods off Norris Road, where people rarely visited, let alone moved en masse. She would go scot-free, she mused, as she padded across this stranger's backyard, where Mother had once leaned far out in her summer's dress to check on the children's whereabouts. The yard had been leveled and now it sprouted bright green grass, the store-bought kind that one seeds and waters and clips. The original backyard had welcomed the dandelion, the occasional stray mustard, the sneaking crabgrass. And poles had risen out of the earth there to hold the clothesline where Mother moved like a slow, wind-up doll, hanging wet things for the old sun to dry, pushing the basket along with her foot. Mother humming her summer tunes. Rosemary's eyes watered with memory. *He would fly through the air with the greatest of ease.*

A few feet past the backyard, she stopped in amazement. The entire hill and field of trees that had once housed a forest of animals, that had once been the old battleground for make-believe cowboys and Indians, was not as it used to be. Instead of scraggly pines, silvery willows, instead of clover clumps in the open meadow, there grew even rows of fir trees and spruce trees, all four feet to six feet in height. Everywhere, a well-trained army of trees swelling with appropriate fullness for their destiny. A large sign was posted at the entrance to the dirt road that led around this field. COLBY BROTHERS CHRISTMAS TREE FARM, it announced. Off in one of the rows three men were squatting at the base of a tree, probably discussing some aspect of its holiday nature. The Colby brothers, no doubt, greedy elves gone astray. And the trees themselves stood, like the subdivision houses, without expression, without individuality, with a single function, like chickens squatting in a hatchery. True, the Christmas tree farm might save other trees from city dwellers who sometimes drove to the country in order to stomp around on private property in search of the ideal spruce. But why did her little piece of land and the tiny spring have to go the way of all progress? She knew that the spring was probably being pumped now, to water these trees during the dry months, the dog days. And these trees would go to apartments and homes in New York City, in Boston, in Hartford, all grown out of the magic of the countryside, bottled magic now, pumped, packaged, shipped. Rosemary felt a lightness wash over her, as though something ephemeral was passing through her, Father's ghost maybe, lost and confused among the even, well-trained spruce, thirsty for a drink from the fragile spring.

She turned back to her bicycle before the Colby brothers

spotted her and inquired as to her business on their land. It was not the most appropriate setting. It was not the best magic, but Rosemary said good-bye to Father, walking again past the old yard, the old house site where the mailbox was now shiny and said THE NAYLORS. If she let Father go, William would be next in line. That's how the ghost of memory disappears, like some drifting scent of wild berries that hits your nostrils on a summer's day and then is gone. Just sensations. Moments. That's what these two men had been. "But what are a couple men, William, when pitted against the wash of time?"

She bicycled sadly out of the cul-de-sac and paused up on Norris Road to look back for a minute. With the sun beginning its ascent into the west, the subdivision found itself beneath a golden sheath of light. All the Christmas trees were sheeny with it, as if they had been sprayed a magnificent yellow. Artificial sunlight, instead of artificial snow. *It's all canned nowadays, Lizzie.* The cramped house, the Naylors' statement of their lives, lurched up out of the earth to meet the filtering tint of the sun, and for a second Rosemary saw the old house again, now new, with BOX 81 printed boldly on the mailbox, boldly enough to last a lifetime. And in the window were the same lace curtains with the diamond pattern, and lights in all the rooms warming the house, stating that everyone was home, not gone off into the world, or away from the world, but safe, here and now. Rosemary saw this, and behind the house she heard the ripple of the elm leaves, silver as dimes, and the rattling of the cones on all the bedraggled pines. She heard this. "Levels of consciousness," William always said, "depend upon the light." And the light shifted quickly, as it must have done for the little match girl, it shifted and moved and grew dimmer. It could not hold its instant forever, Rosemary knew. It could not hold this instant on a June afternoon forever.

"You can't depend on the light, William," Rosemary whispered, and the light shimmered, as if a little wind had flown through it, that ephemeral thing that had gone through Rosemary minutes earlier. It shifted and dimmed and now the houses returned with their bleak statements about modern living, and the Christmas trees went back to simple green, without the eerie spray of sunlight, went back to snowy dreams of the big city. Rosemary pedaled away, gliding down what was left of Norris Road, toward Bixley. Not as foolish as Lot's nosy little wife, she did not turn around. Her pride was too great to acknowledge once more the strip mining that had been done to her fondest memories. She pedaled away. *Good-bye, Father.*

Putting the bicycle into its corner of the garage, she could hear the upraised voices in the kitchen, which meant Miriam and Uncle Bishop were in another interlocking of personalities. Having finally buried Father, Rosemary was in no mood for the mortal goings-on in the kitchen. But before she could escape, the kitchen door was flung open. Mugs rushed out into the garage and disappeared into the backyard. It was too much for him, too. Uncle Bishop saw Rosemary hovering over her bicycle and threw both his hands up into the air.

"Listen to this, Rosie," Uncle Bishop implored. "Miriam is thinking of opening a whorehouse in Bixley."

"A massage parlor," Miriam corrected.

"This entire family will be laughed out of town," Uncle Bishop prophesied.

Rosemary was paying them no mind. If the family hadn't been laughed out of Bixley by now, she knew they probably never would be. Instead, she went on digging past boxes of articles and items until she found what she was looking for: William's pup tent. The shelter tent. Just what she needed: *shelter*. She dragged the two sections of it out into the backyard and then up the hill to where the wild cherry trees were fluttering. As she tramped down the tall grass to make a site for the tent, Miriam and Uncle Bishop stood in the garage doorway to watch what looked like a military maneuver unfolding.

It took her more than a half hour to get the tent up good and sturdy. Then she brushed past Miriam and Uncle Bishop, still framed in the doorway, and went down to where her small office lay cluttered with papers and books. Taking her small desk lamp, she plodded past the two again. They scooted obediently aside, as if in fear. But Rosemary knew—as did Mother, the night she broke up the silly row between Philip and Charles—there was power in being crazy.

She found the long orange extension cord she used for plugging in the block heater of her car on those sky-blue, ice-cold January mornings, and plugged it into the outdoor outlet. Then she unrolled the coil all the way up the hill until she reached the tent. Electricity for the lamp. Now she marched back down past the spectators, who by now had amassed to include Lizzie and Philip and Charles. Weeds springing up. Uncle Bishop had no doubt summoned them to add to the list of witnesses. Who would believe just two people, especially if one of them was Miriam? Rosemary picked up *The Scarlet Letter* and her old college paperback volume of Romantic poetry. She found her binoculars and strapped them around her neck. She took a pad of paper and a pen, in case she might need to communicate with the enemy. She also took with her the BB gun that William had had as a boy and kept as an adult to shoot the heads from dying dandelions. "Euthanasia," he told Rosemary. She shook the gun. It rattled with a full load. She laid it crosswise on her folded sleeping bag. With Mugs at her heels, she trudged up the hill with her load and crawled into the pup tent. Then she zippered herself in, leaving out the gaping mouths in the moonish faces at the bottom of the hill.

What struck her at first, as Mugs curled up kittenish beside her, was the tranquillity of it all. She could hear a song sparrow off somewhere in the grass with its four crisp notes, *sweet sweet sweet sweet.* And then its call note, the blunt *tchep.* Then she heard another sparrow, the wonderful little chipping sparrow that had frequented her tray feeders with its succinct, blunt *chip.* Overhead she heard a small wind still in the cherry tree leaves, and she heard the thin shimmer of the elms, and the firs bending along the fields, the pines leaning with their long weight. She tried to imagine what all the insects, millions of them, were doing in their societies around her. *Society.* Perhaps they would invite her, the large, shell-like newcomer, to a welcome tea. *Welcome to nature. We are all parts of a great whole,* the invitation would read.

She opened her old copy of the Romantic poets, ink marked and well beaten, and read, " 'Again I hear these waters, rolling from their mountain springs with a soft inland murmur.' " Rosemary knew about springs. She knew about murmurs. She had felt one rush through her being, back at the Christmas tree farm, a tingle of electricity. She reached a hand down to tickle Mugs. He opened his red mouth, showing his teeth, and brought his hind paws up to kick at her hands. Then he began to purr, another kind of inland murmur. They were both happy in the tent, with the poems and the bird songs and the contented leaves. She flipped over to "Intimations of Immortality."

" 'Nothing can bring back the hour,' " she read to Mugs, " 'of splendor in the grass, of glory in the flower.' "

"Natalie Wood," Miriam's voice announced from outside the tent. Rosemary and Mugs both jumped at the intrusion. "I saw *Splendor in the Grass* four times," Miriam added. "That's when Natalie had that affair with Warren Beatty." Rosemary pulled back the flap. Miriam was standing at the edge of the lawn, where the neatly mown grass ended. Uncle

Bishop was with her. Rosemary shook the BBs in the gun and they rattled like the moving artillery of a small, angry army. She jacked it. She wasn't too afraid of them coming closer. Miriam was frightened of snakes and Uncle Bishop was terrified of grass. She pointed the gun at the intruders.

"Stay back, Miriam, unless you want your kneecaps to look like pin cushions," Rosemary warned. She took aim at Miriam's pudgy knees. "I needn't tell you how this can sting."

Miriam and Uncle Bishop put hands up to their mouths to hide their words and spoke quietly for a minute. This was something new. Uncle Bishop conferring with Miriam. Rosemary kept the BB gun trained on them.

"This is aberrant behavior, Rosie," Uncle Bishop finally shouted from the safety of the short grass. Rosemary thought about this statement, uttered by a large man who believed his dollhouses were real residences and who lived, not long ago, with another man who wore his wife's shoes. Aberrant behavior.

"I'm warning you," Rosemary said again. "I will find privacy at any cost."

"Please," Uncle Bishop pleaded. He moved forward, but the junglelike quality of the tall hay discouraged him and he stepped back from it. "I've unplugged your electricity. Any self-respecting general would know better than to look for a food or water source in enemy territory." Rosemary let fly a few gold BBs and smiled as Uncle Bishop and Miriam jumped like carnival ducks.

"Rosemary, for crying out loud!" Miriam shouted. "Even Mother isn't this crazy!" She put one foot into the deep grass, then grimaced, perhaps at the thought of an enraged Maine boa slithering around her beefy calf only to crush it. But what caused her to withdraw the leg promptly, however, was the crisp *plop plop* of two more BBs slicing into the grass by her foot. She and Uncle Bishop retreated. Rosemary watched them cautiously as they weaved in and around the tray feeders.

"Who does she think she is?" Uncle Bishop was plaintively asking Miriam. "Patty Hearst?"

"Is this or is this not," Miriam wanted to know, "reason to move bag and baggage to Greenland?"

"You'd *like* Greenland, Miriam," Uncle Bishop noted. "There are no snakes there."

Rosemary threw the BB gun on the floor of the tent. Mugs lay back again, curled like a large O, and soon went to sleep. Rosemary, too, dozed until five-thirty, when Uncle Bishop appeared near the edge of the grass with a tray of food and left it there.

"Soup's on, Joan of Arc!" he shouted. "I trust your voices will tell you to eat." But Rosemary ignored him. Instead, she tore a sheet of paper from her pad and drew a huge house on it, the chimney laced up as though it were a shoe, with a firm knot on top and plenty of stick figures in the windows. Beneath it she scribbled, *She had so many houseguests, she didn't know what to do.* Then she shaped the artwork into an airplane and sent it off over the tops of the hay and mustard. Uncle Bishop scooped it up. Rosemary heard him guffaw as he retreated down the hill.

At eight o'clock she had finished her run. She tromped in through the kitchen and up the stairs to the bathroom, avoiding the curious faces that stared at her from the den. They were all gathered, Lizzie, Philip, Charles, Miriam, and Uncle Bishop, looking like the confused members of a family that has lost one of its own to the Moonies. Rosemary went on upstairs, where she showered and brushed her teeth. She took an extra blanket from her bedroom closet. Now she would not have to come back inside until her morning shower. During the night she could pee into the tall grass beyond the tent. After all, where did all those first pioneers pee? That original prairie grass wasn't green by accident.

In the kitchen she got a carrot from the fridge and put Mugs's box of Cat Chow under her arm.

"This shows she still has a sense of humor," Lizzie could be heard saying of the cartoon.

"You know, when you think of it, she was always a bit of a loner," Miriam offered. "I don't think many people realize that about Rosemary."

"Thank you, Joyce Brothers," said Uncle Bishop. Laughter floated up from the den. So they thought it was humorous, did they? Well, it might get even funnier. Rosemary wondered if she should have the Bixley police issue a warrant declaring that they vacate at the owner's request. Or a bomb scare. Yes! That might do it. She could write them a letter back in her tent and put it in the mailbox: *This is to inform you that a bomb is concealed in one of the many rooms with the tall windows to let in all the light. It is bigger than a bread box. Beware the ides of June. Shit happens.*

Out in the garage, she saw the big orange extension cord lying where Uncle Bishop had unplugged it. Since he would probably continue to do so, Rosemary came up with plan B: William's Coleman lantern. She found it hanging on a nail behind a large straw gardening hat and fetched it down. There was still fuel in it—she could hear it sloshing about—so she wiped the dust away and hiked back up to the tent. She suddenly liked the idea that when darkness came, the Coleman lantern would hiss and flicker.

Back in her new home, Rosemary lay with her head outside the tent for a while, taking in the celestial sights. From off in the woods came the night cry of the whippoorwill. Again and again the *whip-poor-weel* drifted over to her, and occasionally a *purple-rib, purple-rib.* Rosemary listened, delighted.

"How does that bird do it?" she wondered. "How does it never grow tired?" But she was thankful that it didn't. As her ears became receptive to other night sounds, she sensed an electricity in the air, a commotion most house dwellers missed out on. Crickets. The occasional owl. The soft buzz of traffic wending its way over on New Airport Road. And the ceaseless *purple-rib, purple-rib, whip-poor-weel.* She watched Cassiopeia and Cepheus and Cygnus begin their slow, timeless trek across the heavens. She found the Great Square of Pegasus and counted five stars, from Andromeda's head to her knee and out to where the Andromeda galaxy lay, the most distant object seen with the naked eye. Here was a world 2.7 million light-years away, small and hazy at Andromeda's bent knee. A universe. Rosemary focused her binoculars and found it, spiral and cloudy, *vaginal.* She wondered if someone was staring back, all the way across those light-years to earth. William maybe. Father. Men she had loved, sharing binoculars. She smiled at the thought, and then slid back inside the tent, pulled the warm and purring cat in closer to her stomach.

"Night, Muggser," she said softly, and fell asleep to the whippoorwill, to the old starlight that began its journey millions of years ago, to the faint and ghostly hum of inland murmurs. For the first time in her life she felt acutely alive.

# The Ultra-Light Man

*And then the lover, shining like furnace, with a woeful ballad made to his mistress' eyebrow.*

—William Shakespeare,
"THE SEVEN AGES OF MAN"

THE FIRST SOUNDS Rosemary heard were of the birds of dawn, a rhapsody of *chirps, cleers, peets, smacks, chiks,* and *chups.* She was rarely awake in time to catch the show, but now here she was sacked out in the midst of it, the best seat in the house. Mugs was still asleep, at her feet now. Rosemary snuggled beneath the blankets, enthralled to be the sole guest at such a grand performance. She was about to drift off when a small filtering sound from over in the trees rose gently above the feeding sounds. A staccato outpouring of *chips,* and *swee-ditcheties.* She listened vaguely until recognition settled in: *the Canada warbler,* the little ghost bird that had led her and Father to the spring in *caverns measureless to man.* She smiled, her eyes still closed, her ears alive with sounds beating out of nature's heart. *Chip. Chupety. Swee-ditchety.* She imagined its bold yellow blouse, bright as sun among the shady undergrowth and thickets, its black stripes arranged neat as a necklace on the throat. She drifted back to sleep, listening to the shy, delicate warbling, the trills and quavers of an old tune she'd heard before, light-years ago, on a whispery spring day. *Listen, Father, they're playing our song.*

When Uncle Bishop shouted from the safety of the short grass at ten o'clock that he was leaving a cup of coffee there for her, Rosemary had been sleeping soundly. Mugs had already slipped through the flap, probably right on the nose of eight-thirty, and was off somewhere. When she heard Uncle Bishop slam the kitchen door she crawled out of the tent, stretched her arms, and then found the coffee he had left at the edge of the grass, a delightful and aromatic brew.

The morning was cool. A breeze came in, most likely from the direction of the creek since it carried with it a vigorous scent of fresh water and pine. There was something more vibrant in this morning than had existed on those times she and William had camped out at Madawaska Lake. Perhaps it was an overlay from yesterday's experience of her pending mortality. But there remained a strength in that revelation, that out of the mortality would spring a poetic immortality, something transient as perfume, but clinging nevertheless. There was an excitement now in the mystery of the grave.

"I will crumble like wood," Rosemary thought, as she sat on her hill and sipped her coffee. "I will drop like a leaf, one day, and rot." But now this knowledge didn't frighten or repulse her. She could even consider the muscles of her legs, as once she couldn't consider William's, the muscles of all those long strenuous miles run, leaving their bones and withering back, the fingernails falling off like little turtle shells, the eyeballs exploding softly and quietly, scattering cells like seed. She could now accept this decomposition, this soundless work of bacteria and fungi, *consummate work,* as that which went into Uncle Bishop's dollhouse. Work too small for human hands. Work too small, even, for spiders, this unraveling, unbraiding, unlacing of sinews and tendons and tissues. It no longer even saddened her, because out of the rot would come wild cherries, and the grasses and twigs to build nests. Christmas trees would sprout out of her heart and her fingers would become roots for the blossoming lilac. From her eye sockets wild mustard would careen sunward, and the wildest of hay. Over her bones houses would spurt to life, their foundations chalky white with her sacrificial marrow. This was her own *intimation of immortality* and it seemed to her now, with Uncle Bishop's earthly coffee thickening on her tongue, that it was a statement she'd been struggling to make all her life. So why, then, was she lingering on earth in such a mortal body?

Rosemary took her mortal body down the hill, into the house, and up the stairs to her bedroom. She selected fresh jeans and a clean sweatshirt and then sneaked into the bathroom without any human confrontation. After a cool shower, she dressed and then slipped quietly back into the hallway, where she ran into Lizzie.

"What are you up to?" Lizzie asked. Rosemary considered telling her the truth: *I'm making a clean getaway from you humanoids so that I can go back to the insect and animal world beneath the sun and other stars.*

"Taking a shower," she answered.

"I told them all that they should just let you be," Lizzie whispered. It was what Rosemary had suspected all along: each of her guests assumed it was one of the others who had put her over the edge. Uncle Bishop was sure it was Miriam. Lizzie was sure it was Uncle Bishop and Miriam. Miriam was sure of God knows what.

"Thanks." Rosemary smiled faintly.

"Philip is leaving tomorrow," Lizzie went on, "and so is Charles. Do you mind if I wait it out until the weekend? That way I can stop and pick up the kids on my way back to Portland."

"Of course not." Rosemary tucked her T-shirt inside her jeans and gave Lizzie a hug. "I'm just not used to being confined for more than a few hours with Uncle Bishop and Miriam." Let Lizzie think she was right about the situation.

"I figured as much," Lizzie said, nodding sympathetically.

Out in the garage the bike's seat needed no dusting. It was getting its share of usage lately. Rosemary pointed its face toward the airport and pushed off. Despite the shadowy threat of rain on the horizon, it was a mild day full of insect sounds and small breezes. A car roared past, one that she didn't recognize as being indigenous to Old Airport Road.

"Slow down!" Rosemary screamed, shaking a fist in front of her, hoping its implications were noted by the driver via the rearview mirror. No wonder she was forever finding the rabbit spilling its guts, the grosbeak motionless except for the wind riffling its feathers. "Asshole!" she added. The dust settled back down and so did she.

At the airport, there was no sign of the ultralight. Had she just missed him again, or would he come swooping in over the tops of the trees, bouncing to a halt on the warm concrete like some giant dragonfly? Rosemary walked up to a chubby woman behind the ticket desk who looked vaguely familiar—one out of the carnival of Bixley faces—and asked about the man who flies the ultralight.

"He's gone, hon," the woman said. Was everyone in the airport in the habit of condescending, regardless of sex?

"Gone where?" Rosemary was curtly polite.

"Home, I guess," she said, and snapped a pop of gum.

"Don't tell me," said Rosemary. "You're Jake's wife."

"How'd you know that?" The woman smiled in surprise, revealing a front tooth with a black round cavity, as if a worm had eaten its way into the red apple of her mouth.

"Just a guess," Rosemary told her. "Thanks anyway."

Out on the bumpiness of the road again she cursed herself for not asking his address. She could have dropped him a short note, couldn't she? *Dear Ultralight Man: You don't know me but we sat across a bar from each other and, once, we waved, sky and earth meeting with a flick of the wrist. Shit happened.* Maybe Mrs. Jake wouldn't have given her his address, but instead would have reported to her husband that a ponytailed spy was lurking about the airport, asking ultralight questions. Jake would love this bulletin. He was a man longing to fly into action, airplane or no.

"The sporting camp!" Rosemary said, and pedaled faster. Maybe he was still there. Mrs. Jake hadn't said when he left. Not all of the goddamn men on earth worth knowing could slip out of the flimsy dimension of her life and leave her stranded.

A mile south of the airport she cut a sharp turn onto a well-used dirt road that led westward toward Bixley's sprawling woods, thousands of acres of forested land that enclasped the lakes that lay like blue beads among the shadowy green. At least they would be blue beads from up on high, an aerial view. She was seeing things at a distance these days. "Pointillism," she could hear William whispering in his thick voice.

"Number seven," Fraser Paul said, as he flipped through the numerous silver keys on his enormous ring. They flapped like fish until he came to the right one and slipped it into the knob's slot. "He was from Boston, but he left here for a few days in Quebec City." Rosemary had known Fraser for years. She knew his children, had graduated from high school with Loreen, his oldest daughter.

"I want to write about ultralights for the Bixley newspaper," Rosemary had reluctantly lied to Fraser. "That's why I need to see if he left a copy of *The Modern Ultralight.* Jake's wife said he was always reading it. The Bixley library hasn't even heard of it." It made sense to her that ultralight folks would have their own magazine. Fraser wasn't surprised at any of this, or even doubtful.

"How is Mrs. Waddell these days?" he asked Rosemary. "She's getting up there, you know."

"As well as can be expected," Rosemary told him, remembering Mrs. Abernathy's fateful response.

"Well, you look to your heart's content. It's just as he left it until Loreen's girls come to clean up. They make their summer money out here doing the cabins."

"Thanks, Fraser." Rosemary took the key. Jesus, did Loreen have kids that old? What's a couple of kids in the wash of time, anyway?

"He was the quiet type," Fraser added to the mystery. "You look to your heart's content. No harm in looking."

"Tell Loreen I said hello," Rosemary said, and watched Fraser slump off in the direction of the one cabin that said OFFICE above the door. She noticed a slight limp, a stiffness in Fraser's gait, more of that consummate work, that work too small to be done by spiders. Age had already grabbed poor Fraser by the ankle and was slowly pulling him down.

The door let in a bit of fresh air, but the room smelled too piney for comfortable breathing, a thick accent of varnish against wood. The bunk was neatly made. Pans were stacked near the sink, waiting to be used by the next stranger with an urge to cook something. The small bathroom crouched to one side and was only big enough to hold the commode and a slender shower stall. Rosemary sat on the bed and breathed the smell of varnish and veneer more deeply into her lungs. Now the aroma was almost as pleasant as a cake baking. The scent brought back pictures to her mind of the childhood home with its varnished floors, floors she loved to stretch out upon, to press her nose against their boards and breathe as though the wood were still alive, as though it still had roots.

Three magazines did indeed lie on the table, as if Rosemary had created them with her fibbing, had caused them to drop out of some crazy black hole and flop themselves down on the barren table, living things.

"If one of these is called *The Modern Ultralight* I'm checking myself into the nearest mental health clinic," she promised and picked up the magazines. *Soldier of Fortune, The Outdoor Sportsman,* and a special issue of *Hustler's Beaver Hunt,* which sported amateur vulvae from Portsmouth, New Hampshire, to Great Falls, Montana. Rosemary flipped through a few pages. The participants seemed to be secretaries and Hot Stop clerks and bored housewives setting themselves free in one wild, crazy moment of abandon. *The Beaver Hunt.* It was all in the usual day of a sportsman. She imagined the flashbulbs on uncountable Kodak Instamatics from around the country snapping and popping, flashing like gunpowder. Rosemary might have forgiven the ultralight man for taking part in the Beaver Hunt. A dangerously anorectic girl from Hoboken, with a pinched face and widely spread legs—her vagina was smiling more widely than she—had won the distinctive honor, photographed by her boyfriend, Tony. But how could she forgive him, her future lover, for buying *Soldier of Fortune* and *The Outdoor Sportsman?* Heaven help the real-life beaver that wandered into one of those scenarios. Rosemary's disappointment was physical enough to be felt in her stomach, like a quick, sharp menstrual cramp grabbing up muscle. The trash can proved to be even more upsetting. It held an empty can of chewing tobacco!

"He actually puts that manure into his mouth?" she wondered. She sniffed the inside of the can. The empty bottles of four white-wine coolers lay intertwined in the trash can, little glass logs.

"A connoisseur," Rosemary said, tossing one of the bottles back into the rubble. How could he have seemed so debonair, so seemingly intelligent from across the bar, from up above the tree line? "Pointillism," she could hear William's taunt rise up from the varnished heat of the cabin. "When you get close enough, Rosie, the dots are really wine coolers and snuff cans and pale-haired beavers."

"I nearly followed him out into BJ's parking lot," Rosemary thought, and felt instant relief. What would he have done? Licked the tobacco trickle from the corner of his mouth, a little brown dirt road, and asked, "Can I help you, sweetheart?" But with relief came a vague sadness, that sense of having counted on something, having filmed it a certain way in one's mind, only to have the movie unfold much differently. The romance of speculation was gone.

"A real Hemingway boy," Rosemary thought, "with his dangerous machine and his pressing need to finger a trigger, maybe shoot a beaver, would 'twere from Hoboken."

Three crumpled-up messages on Fraser Paul's scratch paper added the final blow. *Call Davie O'Hara about the October deer hunt. Re: supplies.* The second, *Vickie has arrived in Quebec City. Call Chateau Frontenac.* The last note, which was not even crumpled, as if not one ounce of emotion or thought was given it, said simply, *Call your wife. Important.* Bless her heart, maybe she wanted a divorce. So there, then, was the ultralight man unveiled. Rosemary took the soft leaf of the wife's message, *important,* and crushed it, like things left behind are meant to be crushed. *Good-bye, Ultralight Man.*

Outside the cabin again, she waved to Fraser Paul.

"Tell Loreen I can't believe her girls are already in high school," Rosemary said, to Fraser's nod. Then she biked away, left the little log camp with all its clues and hints about the tenant idly behind her, as if it were a Parker Brothers game she had grown too old to play, a box of Tinker Toys.

Rosemary slid the bike inside the garage doors and left it leaning like an old fence on its kickstand. Uncle Bishop's truck was gone. He and Miriam must have left with it since there seemed to be no territorial disputes going on inside the house. Charles was asleep on the sofa in the den, and through the glass doors leading to the patio Rosemary could see Philip swinging back and forth. Here were two men both dissatisfied with their emotional lives. And there was a woman upstairs—she could hear Lizzie running water in the tub—distraught with *her* life. Uncle Bishop and Miriam were both off somewhere, taking *distraught* to new heights of meaning. Mother was crazily distraught. Aunt Rachel was distraught with cancer. William had been so distraught that he chose to go feet first into the Big Mystery. And, oh yes, Raymond, distraught and now partially maimed. Even Mugs was distraught. Mrs. Abernathy was distraught with Ralph the cat and Ralph the cat was born distraught. The birds were distraught: 80 percent mortality rates, after all. Mrs. Waddell was most distraught, especially when people came into her library with their mouths full of loud words waiting to pop like pistols. The whole goddamn world was distraught and Rosemary had had enough of it.

⋙ ⋙ ⋙

At seven o'clock Rosemary left the tent and found Lizzie upstairs, in her own bedroom, still attempting to finish the same paperback she'd brought with her three weeks earlier.

"Can I borrow the New Yorker for a couple of hours?" Rosemary asked. "I don't think my poor car has any gas in it." She had a strange urge to see Mother and Aunt Rachel again, but her legs were sore from bicycling to the airport.

"I'll be holding court in the den this evening," Lizzie said. "So help yourself."

Rosemary drove—for the second time in months—down the dusty road toward Bixley. There was freedom behind the wheel. Now that her mode of transportation was mainly biking, she could sense the power of the machine, so smooth and quiet that one mistakenly imagined that it was one's own power.

Aunt Rachel was haggard and bony. Mother was still crazy. Rosemary declined the offer of a sandwich and iced tea, and opted instead to sit out on the wide front porch with Mother. She had no reason for this need. It was an unexplainable urge. She was reminded of the eels that swim back across a rugged, hostile ocean to return to the spot of their parents' breeding grounds. Was she back on Aunt Rachel's front porch, the original home where Mother had been born and raised, because of some inexplicable genetic longing? Was this the spawning grounds of her parents? Had Father pressed Mother back against the swing, where the hollyhocks leaned in with blossoms hovering like hummingbirds, and had he lifted the flared skirt, pushed up the little silk blouse as if it were nothing more than tissue? Had all the genetic coding that would make Rosemary a human being happened that night on the drafty porch, the cells lining up like small universes while nuclei spun inside them, planets inside their membrane orbits?

"Good evening, America, and all the ships at sea,"

Mother announced. Rosemary smiled, thinking of the wonderful museum that was housed in Mother's head. And Mother was the sole curator. Who could but envy her for that? They sat in rocking chairs, rocking out of sync, two genetically linked women. They were old tongues in a pair of mismatched shoes, with nothing more to wag about. And then, it suddenly occurred to Rosemary that there was nothing left of her mother. Her old memory of those summer mornings in the kitchen had gone far away. Mother was as dead as father.

"You got any candy?" Mother asked. Rosemary leaned over and kissed the warm little forehead, touched the yellow curls. She shouted a goodnight in to Aunt Rachel. But instead of sending a reply out through the screens of the house, Aunt Rachel turned the classical music down on her radio, put a sweater around her shoulders, and came out to the front porch.

"I wanted to give you this," she said, and put a small sack rattling with bottles of homemade mustard pickles in Rosemary's arms. "I'll walk you out to the car." Rosemary took the sack and held the bottles tightly against her side to silence them. There was a solemnity in Aunt Rachel's tone that deserved this. Mother stopped her rocking suddenly.

"You bring the car back before midnight!" she warned. Instinctively, Rosemary responded. She had even turned to face Mother with a promise.

"Looks like she got you," Aunt Rachel laughed.

"For a second there," Rosemary admitted, "I was at the Bixley Drive-In with Cole McPherson and it was past midnight."

"I remember Cole McPherson," said Aunt Rachel. "He was a dark, handsome boy."

"If he hadn't been drafted, I probably would have married him," Rosemary said, and opened her door.

"I'm worried about you, dear," Aunt Rachel said, her voice soft as petals, her voice sotto voce to Mother's shrillness.

"I'm worried about *you,*" Rosemary confessed, too quickly to retract, and then she was glad that she said it. She *was* worried. Cancer was a dastardly trick.

"I'm a nurse," Aunt Rachel reminded her. "I know what's going to happen to *me.* What I want to know is, what about you?" Rosemary stalled. What does one say to a woman who is quietly dying?

"Thank you for the pickles," she said. There was nothing else she need say, not to Aunt Rachel. After Father's death, Aunt Rachel had been the nurturing element. Rosemary's bicycle was always in her yard after school. There was a safety in her aunt's house, not to mention the mustard pickles. And there had been a camaraderie between them. They had been Girl Scouts, determining together how to tie up the loose ends of their lives, and what knot would best do it. Aunt Rachel always listened to the problems that Rosemary had at school, why she was upset about a test grade, a spat with a girlfriend. Then Cole McPherson came into the picture for a few months during her senior year, and Rosemary never asked Aunt Rachel about anything again. Now she was embarrassed about that. Youth had misguided her. Cole had grown inward as a mole in the grease pits of Bixley's largest garage, turning flabby around his middle, turning gray young, thin black smiles of grease beneath his fingernails. Cole McPherson, her first love, disappeared into a body she barely recognized.

Aunt Rachel stood like a ghost in her driveway and watched as Rosemary backed slowly toward the street. She waved feebly, one white hand cutting an arc in the blue-black night, like the vigorous hand of a drowning soul. The headlights swept like the yellow strands of a lighthouse across Mother's doll face. What was she doing there in the dark of the porch?

Singing, her red lips moving like small tropical fish. *Once I was happy but now I'm forlorn. Like an old coat that's tattered and torn. His movements were graceful, all the girls he could please.*

In the kitchen, Rosemary ate a light snack. Miriam and Uncle Bishop were talking in raised voices in the den. No one else was about. She uncorked a bottle of Louis Jadot and selected one of her most expensive wineglasses. Then she hurried back outside, not wanting interaction with her houseguests, although she already surmised that they had come out of their powwow with the collective decision to leave her alone. *Until she gets over this little conniption,* she could almost hear Miriam saying.

With the aid of her pocket flashlight, she found her way back up the hill to her tent. She balanced the flashlight between her knees while she struck a match, then held its quick flare to the Coleman. The match caught the turned-up filament and it hissed into a blue-white light. Rosemary poured a glass of red wine. It was purple in the strange light of the Coleman, as purple as the mother grape. She swirled the wine, gently. The glass trapped the ruby red color as it cascaded down its side, violet as a bruise. She let the bouquet fill her nostrils. Here was more pure nature. Here were tannins and acids dissipating even as they breathed their first breaths, as they loosed old memories of the French countryside, of the mother vine, of the warm womb of the bottle. Here were memories of the ocean they crossed, like slaves, in the holds of ships. The sacrifice of the wine was warm to the palate and all the tiny taste buds saluted, fully satisfied. This was a wonderful moment, this sitting in a tent, with wine, with the magic of lantern light, and the beginning song of the whippoorwill. Rosemary raised her glass.

"Here's to you, Vickie," she said. "I hope Quebec City

agrees with you." Mugs meowed at the flap and Rosemary let him in. Then she left the flap open, allowing some of that old, slow starlight to take part in this ceremony, in this cave above ground, in this modern alchemy. She slid a hand over Mugs's dewy back as he flopped down happily onto the sleeping bag. Lights had come on in the house below. From her spot on the hill the house appeared as a large dark ship suspended on the crest of a frozen wave. The *Titanic,* perhaps, with orchestra music wafting over the rails and the occasional interlocked couple strolling on deck for a long, sweet breath of ocean air. Rosemary saw people moving past the windows, but they were not Uncle Bishop, or Miriam, or Lizzie, these moving figures, not hazy pointillistic dots but sharply cut waiters and deck-hands, and some millionaire's thin daughter who had grown pale and bored in Philadelphia. And up ahead, unbeknownst to everyone on board, the looming, lurking iceberg.

"Shit happens," Rosemary thought, and poured another glass of wine. "But we're safe up here, Muggser," she said to the sleeping cat.

# The Deadly Storm

*Late, late yestereen, I saw the new moon*
*with the old moon in her arms*
*and I fear, I fear my Master dear!*
*We shall have a deadly storm.*

—Anonymous,
"Ballad of Sir Patrick Spence"

At dawn Rosemary woke slowly, the Louis Jadot bottle on the floor of the tent holding only a half inch of unconsumed wine.

"Two of them are leaving today, Muggser," she said as she peered down upon the gaggle of cars in her yard. The house lay like a beached whale, the lights not yet on, turning grayish as spoiled meat, big and wide and tall to the light that finally came and identified it: *a house.* Rosemary saw this take place, this early naming of parts. She watched as licks of sunlight crept in and lit up heretofore shadowy, undefined objects. Lilac bushes ceased to be billowing parachutes. The soldier, stiff and solid by the road, grew into the mailbox and turned silver in the light. The old house flopped and spouted mist from its chimney—or was it the wind that suddenly shook it?—and then lay back on its foundations, all the angles precise, the windows sharp, the chimney rising out of the rest of the architecture like a periscope. It was just a house again, the house Rosemary bought fresh out of college, a year before she met William, that day he substituted at Bixley High School. To the big house she had brought wallpaper with roses small as puffs of breath, little red hearts on all the walls. And feathery lilacs grew on the paper along the staircase and throughout the wide long hallways. In the kitchen small daisies lined up neatly and, outside the house, the river roses straggled the banks of the creek and burned up the hillside, their petals turning hot and red as fire in the sun. Wishlike daisies ran mad in all the fields, scattering themselves among the hawkweed and wild violets. In the front yard, cascading along the porch and up to the three front steps, were the massive lilacs that sometimes ended their blossoming careers in antique pitchers that sat on tables in both the upstairs and downstairs hallways. Rosemary looked down on the house of flowers and imagined all the humans asleep in their soft beds, heavy-eyed as the dolls in Uncle Bishop's dollhouse, their joints stiff and locked in sleep, the corners of their mouths crusted with the white residue of dreams.

It was almost noon before she felt Mugs stomping on her legs, stropping, trying to make himself a bed between them. Half-asleep, Rosemary reached out a hand for her running watch. It announced the time in large digits, the seconds blinking in urgency. Time could pester and blink all it wanted. Rosemary was learning to be timeless. *Shit happens anyway.*

The yard wasn't bulging with cars as it had been the evening before. Philip's Mercedes and Charles's General Motors special—whatever it was—were both gone. Rosemary had missed the departure, but she had no doubt that one man would not leave before the other. They had probably tailgated each other all the way back to Portland. Uncle Bishop was still around. The Datsun seemed serene, almost dazed, sunning itself like a sleek blue lizard in the overhead sun of a hot day. Rosemary walked past Lizzie's New Yorker, which dominated the yard. The back window was scattered with items—a belt, some letters, a fingernail file reflecting the sun, and a *Newsweek* already faded and probably dated weeks ago. Winston meowed at her from the garage doorway and then went off, his tail jerking in stiff wags, to find a square of shade.

Inside the house Uncle Bishop's coffee seemed still fresh in the percolator, so Rosemary poured herself a cup. She closed cupboard and refrigerator doors softly, hoping to avoid detection.

"Is that you, Squeaky Fromme?" Uncle Bishop bellowed from the den. "And if so, are you armed?" Rosemary grimaced and let the spoon fall in the sink with a heavy thud. No need to soft-shoe it now. A covered pot simmered on the stove and spices hung in the air. Uncle Bishop appeared in the doorway. He was wearing a T-shirt Rosemary had not seen before, the material stretched to its outer limits. The letters were large and black, the kind of block letters that are pressed on quickly in mall shops and then come off during the second machine washing. Rosemary strained forward to read the walking billboard. PLEASE FREE SACCO AND VANZETTI, it read. Sacco and Vanzetti!

"Uncle Bishop, where on earth did you get that T-shirt?" she asked him.

"I got it last week," he answered. "At Jeans and Things."

"Why do I believe that no one at Jeans and Things has even remotely heard of either Sacco or Vanzetti?"

"They haven't."

"Then this is indeed custom made?" He nodded.

"At first it read 'Taco and Vanzetti' until I had the tub of lard redo it." Rosemary smiled. Uncle Bishop referring to another as a *tub of lard* was surely a case of pots maligning kettles. Uncle Bishop's huge belly, beneath the stretched cloth of the T-shirt, rolled like a pail of water looking for some way out.

"Is there a reason, Uncle Bishop, that these two men just happened to surface last week on your T-shirt?"

"They were framed," he said. "Wrongly executed."

"Agreed, but may I assume that this month's selection from your Strange But True Book Club has arrived?"

"No, there's no book. Can't you give me enough credit to care about social ills long past without some stupid book?"

"What's the name of it?"

"*Our Country's Silent Martyrs,*" he said sadly. "You got a second T-shirt done free for the price of one," he added, as if to prove that there are *some* social justices in a world of unfairness.

"What does the second one say?" Rosemary asked.

" 'Let the Rosenbergs Go,' " Uncle Bishop said. He was idly fingering the *V* in *Vanzetti,* which was already coming loose in the mild heat of June, in the gray steam of the soup, under the tremendous social pressure.

Rosemary uncovered the pot and sniffed the rising vapor. Very spicy.

"It's only minestrone," Uncle Bishop harped. "So stop acting like one of the witches in *Macbeth.*" She put the cover back. Could she stand the indoor humans long enough to suffer through a delicious bowl of minestrone?

"Is this ready to eat?" she asked.

"So, you've left your weaponry on the hill, have you?" Uncle Bishop made a face at the way in which Rosemary replaced the lid. He dabbed at it with a pot holder until it sank securely onto its pot. He shook a warning finger. "Now leave this stuff alone. It has no beans yet, or ditali."

"Ditali? Where did you find ditali in my cupboards? In Bixley, for that matter?" This reminded Rosemary of Miriam's suspicions of Uncle Bishop's warlock capacity to conjure things up. "Where does he get that white sand that's always on the floor of the Datsun?" Miriam wanted to know. "This is northern Maine!"

"When I need ditali, I *think* ditali." Uncle Bishop waved a spoon over his head as though it were some kind of wand. "I picture all of Bixley swarming with ditali and, voilà!" He pointed to a sack on the counter. "Ditali."

"You're crazy," Rosemary told him.

"Speaking of crazy." Uncle Bishop had a small dash of spit on his bottom lip. "Did you lay down your arms or are you simply out of bullets? Is that it? Are you making an ammo run to Bixley?"

"Please can it," Rosemary suggested. She took an apple from the wicker basket she kept in the refrigerator to hold fruit. Someone had piled it high with fresh apples. A nectarine, a pear, and a banana had been added to the larder. Someone guilty, no doubt, for their large imposition on her privacy. Let the great war generals think in terms of cannons, soldiers, and attacks at dawn. When it came to capturing the enemy's attention, Uncle Bishop believed in attacks at *breakfast, lunch,* and *dinner.* The minestrone, Rosemary's favorite soup, was not simmering on her kitchen stove for naught. The spiced smell of bribery abounded.

"The Brothers Grimm are gone," Uncle Bishop said into a glass of lemonade.

"Now, what about Uncle Grimm?" Rosemary asked, and let the refrigerator door close on its own accord. The basket of fruit went back into darkness, an unappreciated still life.

"An artist should study each pear, each apple, like it's a human face," William had preached, "and if he does, his still life comes alive." Rosemary imagined all the faces in the trapped basket inside getting colder and colder, like children sliding in winter. Apple cheeks. Wicker sleds.

"Tell me something," Uncle Bishop prodded. "Do you intend to come off your hill soon? It wouldn't hurt for you to get your life in order. Do you intend to go back teaching this fall, for instance?" Rosemary thought about that. In fact, she had been thinking a great deal about what her future vocation would be. Would she go back to teaching, back to the blackboard of her old classroom to turn chalky with age, crusty with anger, until a fine layer of grayish limestone covered her? "Do you know what chalk is made of, class?" is how she started each new school term, thinking it poetic enough to capture those blank-slate minds. "It's made of fossilized sea creatures." Perhaps, if she went back, she would become fossilized herself, the roar and the pressure of some old primordial sea rushing through her bones. And then one day, just before retirement, just before they gave her a gold-plated letter opener and shoved her out the gymnasium door, maybe she would go berserk. "Here before you I hold small pulverized seashells!" she would scream, waving the chalk above her head. Or she would hold it to her ear and whisper, "Listen, you little bastards! There is some of the sea in this!" She could visualize their blank eyes as they watched her. In those eyes she would see the reflections of fire whispering across cave walls, the heavy outlines of bison billowing their muscles, memories of the days when chalk was already asleep and tired in its bed, waiting for the blackboard, the *chalk talk,* as it gathered up the little sea creatures and sucked them out of their homes forever.

"What's this spice I'm smelling?" Rosemary asked Uncle Bishop.

"You forget," Uncle Bishop said, "that Miriam perceives herself as single again. She's emitting enough pheromones to beckon unmated men as far away as Bangor. And that's not to mention the confusion she's causing among the neighborhood dogs." Rosemary refused to smile. She did not want Uncle Bishop to read this as a positive sign in regard to his eviction notice. After all her efforts, she would hate to find herself entrapped by the earthly aroma of minestrone soup and what Miriam referred to as *homosexual humor*.

Uncle Bishop unlidded the pot and the aroma rose again in a little misty puff to join the rest of the spice-filled kitchen. A house with something cooking in it. There was nothing better.

"Maybe Miriam isn't looking for a new husband this time," said Rosemary. "Maybe she'll end up back with Raymond." All through Miriam's third wedding—and for each one she had a large ceremony because she vowed it was the last, the very last—Uncle Bishop had referred to the wedding car as *the hearse*.

"I tell you, the woman is leaving a wide stream of pheromones in her wake," Uncle Bishop warned. "I expect the moths tonight."

Rosemary went up and changed into her running clothes, laced her Nikes, stretched her leg muscles. Lizzie was running shower water in the bathroom. Rosemary wondered if she was, at that moment, brushing her teeth. A twinge of guilt for avoiding Lizzie came over her, then left immediately.

"My problems are as large as Lizzie's, if not larger," Rosemary thought. "At least Philip and Charles are still flesh and blood." Besides, she and Lizzie had spent many days together before Philip and Charles—Uncle Bishop had begun calling them Chang and Eng—had arrived.

She pushed the button that made her watch turn from a

time-of-the-day watch into a stopwatch. All the digits flashed to zeroes in the face. If only she could make the houseguests disappear so quietly and quickly. She threw her sweaty headband from the past few runs into her laundry basket and went down to the tiny laundry room for a clean one. In the den something stopped her, something looming. It was huge and metallic and said LIFE STYLER in large red letters across its side.

"Uncle Bishop, come here please!"

"Should someone cover me?" he asked, peering around the doorway. "I'm surprised you haven't found a way to Velcro that BB gun to your running shorts."

"What is that?"

"Miriam's treadmill."

"Why is it here?"

"That's what I've been telling you, Rosie. She's trying to walk off the unmarriageable flab. You can hear her *treading* all night long. She sounds like a hamster."

"How'd it get here?"

"It got here by means of my Datsun," Uncle Bishop said. "She pestered me to death. You know how she can be. Remember how the chief of police, that Conrad person, finally had a heart attack over Miriam's UFO report?"

"I have a headache," Rosemary said, and pressed two fingers against her left temple. It had begun to throb, a small pressure valve, such as the lid on Uncle Bishop's pot, waiting to blow.

"At least we can be thankful that Helene Cantor is going to baby-sit the Chihuahua," Uncle Bishop said helpfully. "Miriam doesn't trust your cats. What is it she calls that little pink-eyed weasel. Broderick Crawford?"

"Miriam doesn't trust my cats with Oddkins Bodkins!" Rosemary felt her other temple flare up. "You mean, that's the only reason I don't have her dog, too!" But Uncle Bishop wasn't listening.

"Remember how upset she was the night of her big UFO sighting?" he asked. "She thought aliens were going to kidnap her and that animated rat. If *I* were the chief of police, I'd sue. But I wouldn't leave Ralphie with Helene Cantor, that's for sure. I just went by to check up on him. Mrs. Abernathy was out inspecting her flowers with a magnifying glass. We're lucky she hasn't burned Bixley to the ground, considering how sunny it's been lately. She's so old, Rosie, she's got brontosaurus bites on her ankles." Uncle Bishop was doing what Rosemary had always called his *stream-of-unctuousness* technique, unwilling to stop talking for fear the opposition would begin. Rosemary looked at the zeroes on her watch. Time was frozen. Time was zero.

"You need to move home soon, Uncle Bishop," she said.

Rosemary stood on the front porch and breathed a few deep breaths to loosen the muscles in her stomach. Tension grew there daily now. Tension lived in her stomach. Like lichen, it had adapted easily to the membranous walls. It had a neat little nest in her gut. Miriam and Uncle Bishop. They were both up to no good in the big house. Rosemary walked to the road, looked an even eye down the straight stretch she planned to run, and set off. She snapped a button on her watch. Time was going again. Time was reeling. And here she was, running down the dusty road to Bixley, dreamlike, running *with* time, speeding it up, heaving it forward. Miriam on her treadmill. Uncle Bishop in the kitchen. All's wrong with the world. When would the information she was sending these people, like old starlight, finally reach them?

The run released some of the tension. Concentration on

the soft footfalls, light as raindrops, that pattered out beneath her feet kept her mind off her real problems. The home sprint left her heart pumping fast enough that her thoughts were riveted on her physicalities, not on Miriam and Uncle Bishop. She pressed fingers to her jugular vein. William had taught her how to take her pulse rate before her heart slowed down. Checking her watch, she counted the heartbeats for six seconds. Fifteen of them. She added a zero. One hundred fifty. Not bad for a quick run. *Fifteen heartbeats, William. One for every step in the dangerous stairway. Fifteen little drums, dearest, drumming.* Her heart might be broken but it was still doing its job. Her nylon top was limp with perspiration. She pushed her sweatband up to wipe the sweat on her brow, then clicked the watch and looked at her time. Thirty-three minutes, forty seconds for the four-mile run. Not bad for hobby running.

Uncle Bishop was on the desk phone when Rosemary came in to pour a glass of water, then lean against the sink to drink it.

"And what did she do then?" he was asking the party on the other end of the line. "Well, you keep up the good work, Mrs. Stoneman. I'll see that you're rewarded for this trouble. You're a fine neighbor." He flung the receiver back onto its cradle. "You old goat," he said.

In the kitchen, he found Rosemary on a second glass of water.

"That was Mrs. Stoneman, my neighbor on the other side." Uncle Bishop was hoping to be most cordial. "She doesn't get along with Mrs. Abernathy either. She says if it weren't for Mrs. Abernathy's bird feeders there wouldn't be birdshit all over her patio." Rosemary ignored him. She put the glass back into the sink and turned to lean against the fridge, to stretch out good, unknot all the leg muscles.

"Mrs. Stoneman says that if things *have* to fly around she prefers butterflies," Uncle Bishop rambled on. He put Rosemary's glass in the dishwasher. "Butterfly shit is tiny, like grains of sand."

"I'm not interested in the texture, if you don't mind," said Rosemary, and thrust her left leg up behind her and grasped it with her right hand. She applied a bit of steady pressure.

"Did you know," Uncle Bishop asked, "that when I was a kid I hated to lie on the beach when your grandma took us to southern Maine because I thought the beach was made up entirely of butterfly droppings?" He cocked his head to one side, like a large condor, and watched Rosemary, waited for a reply. But she said nothing. She might have. She could have said, "Is that where the sand in your Datsun comes from, then? Do thousands of butterflies migrate in through an open window at night, while all of Bixley is sleeping, and press downward on their itsy colons until they empty? Do butterflies have colons?" She could have said a lot of things.

Later, thinking back on ways how she might have prevented the next terrifying minutes, she realized anything might have been spoken. Words were nothing anymore. They were empty, armless, wingless, and featherless, accumulating, after thirty-three years, to nothing, with not even enough consistency to pile up, over the sentences of seasons, as softly and delicately as butterfly droppings. It was the sound of tires braking, of pebbles fluttering, of an anguished scream, not human, but humanlike, pained. Had she even heard the thud? She would never be sure. It may have been the thump of her own heart against its rib cage, a final kick to signify the end of a long run. She said it—she was positive later—she said it loudly: "Mugs!" And her insides rose up like a wave of spoiled water, sloshing, the two glasses wanting to come back up, as though her throat were a pump, pumping. "Oh, please," she thought, "if something has to die, if something must die, let it be something wild."

The run to the road was a marathon. "So this is what I've been training for," she thought, a foolish thought that flashed quickly through her mind. "This little sprint to the road, this little race with time." She hated herself for wishing, in a guilty instant, that it would be Winston, the outdoor cat. But it was Mugs. She had known it would be Mugs. A car, stationwagonish and gray, still speeding, went on, taking the name and license plate number with it in an afternoon swirl of sun and dust. Mugs's stomach was split open, as though it had been sliced, and a part of the intestine protruded. He was half-sitting in the road, trying to pull his dead bottom along with his front paws. His mouth was opening and closing, as though he were hovering anxiously above his treasured little Cat Chow stars.

"Oh, Muggser," Rosemary whispered, kneeling beside him. "Uncle Bishop, get a towel, quick, and the Datsun," she said hoarsely, as he leaned over her shoulder to get a glimpse of the cat.

"Oh, no," she heard him say, the voice tinny, a Victrola's voice. In the years he was gone for the truck Rosemary scratched lightly under Mugs's chin, knowing he felt no pleasure, knowing his last memories of earth would be of bloodcrusted pain.

In the pickup she held the cat as best she could on her lap. Uncle Bishop flew down the road. He had taken Ralph on enough false emergency runs to know the exact location of the Bixley Veterinary Clinic. She shoved a bunching of the towel into Mugs's mouth and he bit on it gratefully as each painful spasm hit him, his back arching involuntarily, the terry cloth squeaking between the teeth, rending. His eyes were bright with pain.

"His spine is crushed," Rosemary mumbled to Uncle Bishop, but she wasn't sure if the words came out of her throat and aired themselves, or if she was merely thinking them. Words, she had come to realize in the kitchen, in that moment of calm foolishness before every tragedy, do nothing. Once, Mugs bit sharply when a cruel contortion shook him, and his bite went through the thickness of towel and grazed Rosemary's hand. It didn't hurt, but Mugs reached one paw up, gently, and placed it on her chest. An apology. Rosemary closed her eyes. Where was William now, the son of a bitch? Why was he always conveniently gone for the rough times? Maybe he could tell her some of the secrets he'd stumbled upon. Better yet, maybe he could tell her if it was all worth it. Maybe he could tell her—when the first slice split him open—if he was surprised at how warm and red the blood was, like the soft strings of yarn that go into the making of mittens. *Poor little kittens have lost their mittens.* Rosemary and Mugs rocked gently together in the pickup, as though they were a solid wave. Uncle Bishop was driving at his usual breakneck speed.

"They'll put him to sleep," Rosemary heard herself say. "Then the pain will be over."

"Hang on," was Uncle Bishop's only reply. Rosemary ran a hand over Mugs's thick smooth fur, now crumbly with blood. Was it just that William was too hopelessly injured? Beyond help, even hers? Had life become an ether-filled receptacle that he gladly dragged himself inside, doglike, to shut the door and die? "Tell me, you chicken son of a bitch," Rosemary thought. "Give me some answers."

"Rosemary, there isn't a chance," the vet said. "I'm sorry." This was Bruce Ashley, two years ahead of her in high school, pale and shy and dateless mostly. Bruce's was one of those sad faces forced to blend away from the in-crowd. He had asked her once to go to a movie. Was he getting back at her now? Had he waited all those years?

"There's nothing we can do," Bruce said. "I'm sure his lungs have collapsed." Rosemary looked at him vaguely. "I'll go out with you, Bruce," she thought. "We'll go to any movie you want to see. All these years we've been waiting, like cripples, to dance. So put on your old soft shoe. You can dump me at dawn along some farmer's back road, drenched and trembling and bruised, so don't tell me there's nothing we can do."

"Do it," Rosemary said. She and Mugs had locked eyes. Both pairs were glazed, sealed with different kinds of pain.

"Maybe it'd be better if you waited outside," said Bruce, still pale and shy and carrying the scars from those old, high school pimples.

"No," Rosemary said sharply. "I want to hold him." She looked at Bruce and raised her eyebrows, a pleading look. "I want to hold him," she said again. And she wanted to tell Bruce Ashley more. She wanted to tell Bruce Ashley that this was something William had denied her, this right, this need to be privy to the dying. He had denied her the honor of holding his winter-colored wrists while he went at them with a sickle. He hadn't given her even a tiny part to play in his bloody little harvest. The chicken-shit son of a bitch.

Uncle Bishop, large and pale, went out to the waiting room. Rosemary could hear his voice, high-pitched, shrill with emotion.

"Like one of the family," he was saying, among other things she quit listening to hear. Mugs had another spasm and then lay still, unable to respond any more to the pain. Dr. Ashley shaved a small square on the front leg, as though it were a little white garden patch.

"I love you, Muggser," Rosemary said. The needle missed the vein. Mugs tried to pull his paw away, then decided against it. Blood came out of the puncture. "It's warm at first, William, did you notice?" Rosemary thought. "Warm as socks. And blunt red, like paint that has dried in its tube but was meant, once, to brighten hearts and roses and apples. You're the worst kind of coward, William." The second stab hit a fat vein and went in easily enough. Mugs did not move. Instead his mouth opened and closed, visible only to those who loved him, the way the wind might open the petals of wild flowers on some hillside, then go away suddenly so that the petals collapse back in on themselves. The vein took the pentobarbital and grew large with it. "The vena amora, William, leads to the heart. But there are traffic jams, sometimes, and hideous crashes and pileups. Sometimes, William, the vena amora, like the spider's web, is an awful roadway." Rosemary put a trembling finger beneath Mugs's chin and stroked as best she could. It would upset him to hear her, in his last seconds, crying. Crying, like words, could wait. Crying was nothing. Rosemary noticed that she should have clipped Mugs's claws. They had grown long, longer than he would ever need them now. Mugs's round yellow eyes, the pupils dilated to full black, looked questioningly into Rosemary's own. There was a sudden quick burst of bowel movement, accompanied by its smell. And that was all. *"Good-bye, Mugs."*

Nobody bothered her back at the house. Even Miriam and Uncle Bishop sat across from each other and spoke little, and then softly, the even treble that honors the dead. Lizzie hugged her roughly and began to cry.

"This is the tragedy of loving something, Lizzie," Rosemary said, her words a monotone. "Unless we take it from ourselves first, it can one day be taken from us." William had taught her that.

"He was like your child, I know," said Lizzie, wringing her hands as though they were something she was trying to fold and put away. "First William, and now this." She waved a hand erratically. Rosemary looked up at her friend's pale face.

"Dying is nothing, Lizzie," she thought. "None of it, none of the worldly expectations—dying, crying, talking, eating, or loving—add up to one single ounce of butterfly droppings. Just ask our old friend William. Just ask the expert."

"I would simply perish," Miriam whispered, "if anything happened to Oddkins Bodkins, much less hold him while . . ." She shivered, unable to verbalize the act. Rosemary looked at her sister and smiled.

"Death is nothing, Miriam," she thought. "Death is not even one itsy-bitsy, teeny-weeny butterfly turd. Ask that son of a bitch William the next time you see him. He'll vouch for it."

Rosemary took two bottles of Louis Jadot and went out the back door. Outside in the garage Winston slid his warm fur across her shins. A wave of longing went through her.

"Oh, Mugs," she whispered. A sturdy brown box that said BOUNTY PAPER TOWELS sat quietly inside the garage door. It was the biggest box that Bruce Ashley had at his clinic. Nobody, not even Hallmark, makes Dead Cat boxes. Rosemary stroked Winston quickly. It wasn't his fault that the humans had let their machines get away from them. She remembered the brakes from earlier. Mugs's cries. Now there was only a straggling wind mustering up a few branches in an assortment of trees. And the usual far-off gossipy crickets. Pagan music. And a distant murmur, another inland one, of Bixley bustling with life, life mustering up a few emotions in an assortment of people. Rosemary imagined library books being returned, pizzas ordered and eaten, gas stations busy filling gas tanks, TV channels clicking, children's voices rising one against the other in argument. A few emotions in an assortment of people.

Back up on the hillside, she paused to look skyward. The stars had flicked themselves on already, busy at their job of night-lighting. "Even the constellations aren't real," William had told her. He hadn't left her much to believe in.

"You remember William, don't you, Mugs?" Rosemary asked the silence on the hilltop. "William says the constellations are fakes, Mugs. He says the constellations only appear to be hunters and lions and water bearers. It's from our little fixed position in the universe that we give them design and meaning. They've been tricking us for years, Muggser. Even the stars that seem to be neighbors in the sky are not neighbors in reality. This goes for streets as well as skies. Consider Uncle Bishop and Mrs. Abernathy. Consider Alcor and Mizar, in the Big Dipper's handle. They're known as horse-and-rider, but they aren't even close. And they sure as hell aren't riding, Mugs. They're a hundred twenty light-years apart. It's our line of vision here on earth that puts them together. Even the stars are phonies." And Rosemary knew this was true of people, too, the way they got together sometimes, as she and William had, as Miriam had with all her husbands, not seeing the light-years between them, only feeling some thick, unexplained pull.

The tent was warm, the flap having fallen back in place, trapping the day's heat inside. Rosemary fired up the Coleman and opened the wine. A mere two hours later the first bottle was gone, but in its place she had a plan. She opened the second bottle and took it with her down the hill. Uncle Bishop had brought a spade, as he'd promised on the sad ride home, and now it rested against the house. In the soft earth at the foot of the hill, where the dark line of willow trees began, Rosemary laid the flashlight on a rock and began to dig in its spray of light. Mugs's favorite toy had already gone into the box with him, a gray cloth mouse, full of catnip, with a bell on a string about its neck. When the hole was large enough, she lifted the cover of the box and shone her light inside. She gave Mugs's stiff body, the fur still sweetly soft and limp, a final stroke. Beautiful Mugs, going where William had gone, where Father had gone, where the groundhog and the robin had gone, into the earth, into the cherries, into the mind's museum of someone who had loved him dearly.

She fumbled in a kitchen drawer for a Magic Marker and found a black one. Her houseguests held themselves respectfully back from her, quiet as pallbearers. She left them in the lighted windows, peering out into the black night to see what she was up to. She selected a large rock from the pile near the grave site, rocks from the previous spring, which William promised would become an outdoor fireplace. More idle promises. Rosemary printed CAT CROSSING on the flattest rock she could find, then she threw the marker far off into the night, toward the field of grasses. It arched against the black sky like a small rocket and landed soundlessly somewhere in the grass. "No one knows why early man created cave art," William had once told her. "It may have occurred even earlier than twenty thousand years ago, because people created outside art, on animal hides and large rocks, but it was temporal and lost itself to exposure from the elements." Here, then, was Mugs's artistic statement, his greatest work, the rock that registered his life on the planet. "We're all temporal, William," Rosemary had replied, that night the two of them had lain before the fire, awash in its orange light. "We're all pebbles caught up in the stream." Rosemary fitted the rock snugly, a cobblestone effect, into the mound of earth, Mugs's own cave, and shining the light one final time to read the inscription, she left Mugs alone, on his first night's journey back to the mother ship.

On the road in front of the house, she put down the second

wine bottle, still nearly full. It was unlikely cars would pass this late at night, almost eleven, now that the tiny airport had buzzed to a halt. She shone the light steadily, back and forth across the road, studying, surveying. She took large sips from the wine bottle in between the mental architecture. A movement caught her eye and she looked quickly at the house. Three heads bobbed back from the window. And then the lights went out. She was not supposed to know that she was being watched.

She decided that, although the road's gravel was packed and solid, a spade, a chisel, and plenty of patience would suffice. She began with the spot of blood that had seeped like an oil spill into the gravel, taking her time, chiseling, spading, tossing the dirt aside, picking up the flashlight to inspect the job. Occasionally she came down on her haunches to drink from the bottle and peer heavenward as Boötes pushed high in the sky, Arcturus, its brightest star, hanging at the southern end of the formation. Corona Borealis was rising, and Coma Berenices was descending in the west. Old, faded cycles. Ursa Minor's light came from below Draco the Dragon, in the north. Rosemary found Serpens, its tail in the east, head as high in the southern sky as Arcturus. They were old friends, old house pets, these herdsmen and their flocks. In a few hours they would be gone and in their place would be Aquila the Eagle, setting tail-first into the west. And Pegasus, with his Great Square, where Andromeda is chained to her galaxy, nearly three million light-years away. Aquarius, Rosemary's birth sign, would be low in the southern sky. Cygnus and Lyra would be descending, come three o'clock, in the west, taking with them their greatest treasures, Deneb and Vega, those two stars that never set to Alaskans. Very old friends, acquaintances, compadres, these trusted, luminescent faces.

She might not, she suddenly decided, ever use the new telescope. Maybe she would sell it, would advertise for a buyer in Bixley's weekly newspaper. She would file the telescope away with the other idle notions she'd had in her life. The telescope would only remind her that she was earthbound, and she didn't enjoy that thought, not while William and Mugs were all weightlessness. "I want to go on the space shuttle, William," she had told him, once. She had told William a lot of things. Who would she tell things to now? "I want to go just so that I can look back. I want my chance, William, to dally among the constellations." William had been on another artistic binge, this time to New York, when the shuttle blew apart and came cascading down like money, like all the silver coins collected by NASA, falling. Space travel tickets, fluttering. "Were the astronauts afraid, William? Was Icarus afraid? Did the Great Wallenda cry out?" *I knew this would happen,* William wrote about the awful explosion in a letter. *It's just another feeble attempt of man's to marry the cosmos. The notion's been around forever.*

It was almost 2:00 A.M. when she finished. The wine was a swallow away from being gone. She drank the last mouthful and then shone her flashlight with pride at her job, a foot-wide trench, six inches deep. It spanned the road like a lurking gash, a sinister smile. Let the bastards hit that at sixty miles an hour. Let their axles weather the blow, and their necks grow limp with whiplash. A trench, all by herself.

"What do you think, Muggser?" Rosemary asked. She felt as though she had built a tunnel through a mountain, except this one was aboveground. The yellow canary could go in here and breathe from one end to the other and then wing its way back to tell of it.

Rosemary scattered handfuls of small pebbles into the ditch's bottom so that it would assume the same color as the rest of the road. She wanted no one to be forewarned. She wanted no one to have the opportunity to slow themselves down, much less stop. Mugs had been given no head starts.

By two-thirty she had collapsed inside the tent. She vaguely remembered Lizzie and Uncle Bishop pushing aside the flap to check on her.

"Leave me alone," she said. There would be no bathroom ritual at eight-thirty. Mugs had relieved himself for the last time back on the steel table of the Bixley Veterinary Clinic. "Mars was in Sagittarius, William, when old Muggser died, and Jupiter was in Pisces with all thirteen moons. Millions and millions of miles from the pain, William." Anger, which Rosemary had never suspected during the long, hurtful weeks since she'd received the fatal word, flared up inside her. Anger at William. His had been the most cruel, the worst kind of desertion.

"You chicken shit," Rosemary whispered.

From two-thirty until she fell asleep an hour later, sodden with excessive wine and physical exhaustion, Rosemary cursed the man with whom she had spent eight years of her life.

# The Ragged Dancer

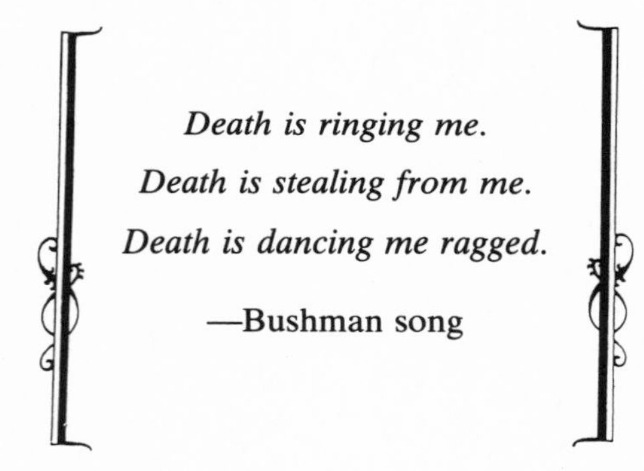

*Death is ringing me.*
*Death is stealing from me.*
*Death is dancing me ragged.*

—Bushman song

ROSEMARY HAD BEEN awake since eight-thirty. Her built-in clock, the same one that told her when the leaves were about to change color, had done its silent ringing to let her know that Mugs needed to pee. She hadn't bothered to open the flap and look out. Nothing out there interested her anymore.

"Maybe it's time for me to do it, too," she thought. "Maybe it's time for me to cash in all the chips." Perhaps that was the secret William had known. Should she take sleeping pills, hordes of them, enough to put an army out for the night? She would leave legions of suicide notes. Everyone would grieve for her endlessly.

At nine o'clock she heard the first speeder hit her trap,

the loud bouncing of the car on its frame, as though the whole contraption were really a trampoline and not a car. All this was followed by a car door slamming and a long trail of swear words. Or were they only *chips* and *chups* and *swee-ditchities,* these words? Language, as she perceived it now, was meaningless. Her eyes were plums, their lids swollen and salty from the tears. She touched them gently with an index finger and was amazed that they did not burst, purplish bubbles, to the touch. Her tongue was still thick with wine. And her temples buzzed with the effects of a hangover. She decided to lie there all day, on her hilltop, until she sorted out her fate. Perhaps she would drink herself to death, drown in Louis Jadot wine, a purple bloated corpse at the end. At ten-thirty she heard movement just outside the tent, and what sounded like a cup clinking on a saucer.

"Rosie? Yoo-hoo?" It was Uncle Bishop. She turned on her side, remembering the times Mugs had fitted himself into the curve of her stomach, like an embryo, and they had slept together, a bizarre Madonna and child. And she remembered how she and William had slept, snug as spoons.

"Rosie, four people have hit your trap already," Uncle Bishop said happily. She knew. She had heard the commotion. "Lizzie and Miriam are at the window cheering. Lizzie has a pad and she's keeping track for you. You'd swear she was at a hockey game." It must have been an uncomfortable walk for him, up through the frighteningly long grass. "I brought you some coffee," he said. She heard clinking again, this time just outside the flap. And then he went back down the hill.

Rosemary postponed her suicide in order to drink the coffee. She couldn't plan her final exit with a hangover, anyway. But perhaps, after a stimulating brew, she could visualize a rope being tied securely about a girder beneath the Bixley bridge, and then around her neck. She would drop, like Icarus, out of a blue sky and down into blue water. But as soon as she finished the cup, she felt a steady pressure on her bladder, a great need to urinate. She couldn't make definite plans with this kind of internal upheaval going on. Her hand shook so on the downhill walk that she expected the cup to bounce off the saucer. In the kitchen everyone said hello to her.

"Good morning," Rosemary answered, treating them as a single entity. They weren't to blame, after all. In the shower she soaked her hair, dusty from the road work, and shampooed it thoroughly. She dug dirt out from under her fingernails and then turned the shower head to massage and let the water beat at her aching muscles. This graveyard work, this shoveling, was strenuous.

"Rosie?" It was Lizzie tapping with her fingernails on the bathroom door. Rosemary slipped into her terry cloth robe. She wrapped her hair in a towel. Lizzie was pale and sad. That was okay.

"It's going around these days, Lizzie," Rosemary thought. Lizzie gave her a hug and Rosemary accepted it. With Mugs gone now, too, she had nothing to touch anymore. Nothing to touch her back when she ached for William.

"Honey, I'm planning on leaving tomorrow, but if you'd like for me to stay a little longer, just until you feel better . . ."

"No, Lizzie, please. It's okay." Rosemary unwrapped her hair and began toweling it dry.

"Charles can pick up the kids."

"Honestly, Lizzie, no. I'm not used to a lot of people anyway, and the way I feel now, I think I'd be much better off alone."

"Are you sure?" Lizzie bit at a nail. Her blue-green eyes were large with concern.

"In a few months, Lizzie, maybe when the leaves turn pretty, come back and visit me for a couple days."

"I'll worry about you," Lizzie said, and gave Rosemary a final hug. "And I'll come back when northern Maine has its autumn. I remember autumns up here, you know." She was trying to smile. Rosemary recalled the afternoon, at Madawaska Lake, with William, with autumn raging about their heads. "Scientists understand the life and death process of a leaf, Rosie," he had told her, "but no one knows what causes them to burst into such magnificent colors."

"Lizzie, this may sound rude, but could we say good-bye now? I'll probably go off on my bike, or read in the tent, and I'll still be half-asleep when you leave in the morning."

"Well, I sort of thought that, too," said Lizzie. "You know, that you'd want to be alone and I'd probably only spend another night with Miriam and Uncle Bishop and, well, really I could use the rest if I drive down to Bangor tonight, and pick the kids up tomorrow."

"I agree."

"You should never pick up kiddies without lots of rest, Rosie." Rosemary smiled at her. They hugged again. True, they would miss each other, but their lives had expanded since college, the way trees expand, branching and leafing and, in Lizzie's case, *acorning.*

Rosemary pedaled aimlessly up and down Old Airport Road. She took occasional excursions onto wide grassy tracks leading into the woods, tracks that were once wagon roads, before the automobile. *The auto-mobile,* that destroyer of pathways and, sometimes, pets. Now the woods were strung with magnificently spliced fences that had turned emerald with moss and rotted where they stood. The corpses of them wound in and around trees and marked the old wagon roads, which were themselves going back to nature, their surface padding thick and bouncy. Warblers of all kinds intertwined their songs in the branches, and bayberries grew in small orange clumps among the wild violets. *Pigeon berries,* they had called them as children. Rosemary picked a quick handful and popped them into her mouth. She followed a small brook a few yards down to where it joined the Bixley River. On the bank there she found a cluster of furbish louseworts, named for a Miss Louise Furbish, and once thought to be extinct until they were discovered in northern Maine. The fences, running like louseworts in among the spruce and pine, following a now extinct pathway, had not been so lucky. Rosemary did not want to think of things extinct, gone, vanished. It magnified the reason she was out carelessly biking. It reminded her that Father and William and Mugs, all, had gone the way of the old fences. What would she do without William and Mugs? A sadness swept over her, but there were no tears. She felt instead an anguish that Mugs's last moments on earth, what he took with him to meet the poison of the needle, was a remembrance of the gray car looming, the braking sounds, the gravel that stuck in his eye, and a searing pain he had never realized existed. All the old, happy moments had been for nothing.

Now Rosemary was forced to realize the same about the years she'd spent with William. What had he remembered in those last moments? The happy picnics, the Saturdays in bed with old movies on TV, the candlelight dinners for two beneath the painting of *The Chinese Horse?* Probably not. Maybe those eight years had been nothing to him, nothing at all. How could he think of her in those last minutes? She was only Rosemary O'Neal, after all, a high school teacher from northern Maine, competing with Death, the ultimate blind date. She sat by the old fence rails, near her leaning bike, near the surviving louseworts, and decided she would get some seeds for wild grasses next week in Bixley and sprinkle Mugs's grave with them, so that a bitter harvest could come of it. But, hard as she tried, there seemed to be no more tears for William.

The fast ride home was dizzying, her eyes sore and puffy in the wind. As she walked her bike into the driveway she noticed that the big New Yorker was gone. *Good-bye, Lizzie.*

Out of exhaustion Rosemary lay back on her sleeping bag to rest. Two hours later the rude sound of a horn woke her. She peeled back the flap and looked out to see the Datsun coming up the driveway in great jerking bounds, Uncle Bishop bouncing in the passenger's seat, Miriam's red hairdo loosening itself as she clung to the steering wheel in a panic. It looked as though Miriam was learning to drive again, with Uncle Bishop as instructor! What had brought this on? No one else to play with but each other, no doubt. No one there to hear their bitter barbs. "If Uncle Bishop insults Miriam in the forest," Rosemary wondered, "and there is no one there to hear it . . . " The passenger door flew open quickly and Uncle Bishop lurched out.

"Oh blessed, blessed earth," he cried. "Mea culpa." Then he knelt to kiss the gravel in Rosemary's driveway. Miriam slammed her own door, adjusted the pyramid of fiery hair, and put one hand on her hip. "Mea *maxima* culpa," Uncle Bishop added.

"What state had the audacity to give you a driver's license?" Miriam demanded of the now prostrate Uncle Bishop.

"Does the cry *brake!* have any meaning to you at all?" Uncle Bishop lamented. "Where is the logic in shooting ten feet past a stop sign, saying *oops,* and then backing up?"

"You're as adequate in teaching someone a skill as you are in being a well-adjusted human being," Miriam snarled, and stepped around Uncle Bishop's whale-back form.

"Monkeys—and trust me, Miriam, because I've read about them—could learn to drive more quickly than you."

"Aren't you ashamed of yourself?" she asked, as she disappeared into the house.

"Land," Uncle Bishop was saying softly, now supine, his pale spongy body sufficiently beached on the hard gravel. What if, like whales, he beckoned others to beach themselves? Rosemary imagined hundreds of large homosexuals lying in fleshy mounds, high and dry, emitting strange sonar sounds only they themselves understood. But after a few minutes of no further attention from Miriam, he pulled himself up, shook off the dust, and dragged into the house after her.

Rosemary was having a sandwich, eating it in small, tasteless bites. She needed something in her stomach. Already the absence of Mugs's personality was being felt. There was a loud bang in all the silences, the fridge door opening without a battery of meows, no under-the-table begging for her sandwich, the bowl of Cat Chow near the kitchen door holding the same amount as it had the previous day, the water bowl untouched. Uncle Bishop came up and gently put his arms, heavy as girders, around her. They felt wonderful and Rosemary sank back, lost herself in the immensity of them. Uncle Bishop's fatherly, motherly arms, big enough to hold a family. She collapsed within this circle of security and cried again for Mugs, for William, for Father, the whole shebang. When the crying subsided to small sobs, then was gone, Uncle Bishop turned her around so that he could look into her eyes.

"Do you still want Miriam and me to leave you alone?" he asked her. Rosemary nodded. "You'd feel better if we were gone?" She nodded a second time. "You're *positive?*" She sighed heavily. "Okay, okay," he said. "Move back into your house. But you have to promise me that I can check on you often." Rosemary nodded again. Uncle Bishop flipped the limp ponytail a couple of times and then gave her a hug. Miriam's head appeared from out of nowhere.

"I couldn't help hearing," she said.

"Of course not," said Uncle Bishop. "It's difficult when you're eavesdropping."

"The minute you want company, Rosemary," Miriam promised, "you call me at Helene Cantor's and I'll have her whisk me over here before you can say diddly-squat." She gave Uncle Bishop one of her piercing little stares. "I'll never ride in that space shuttle of yours again. There are dips in the road where one experiences weightlessness."

"You get a horse, lady." Uncle Bishop was shaking a furious finger. "You cheat the IRS and take a taxi because you've bummed your last ride with me."

"That's a relief," said Miriam. "Maybe I'll live to see my next birthday."

"Oh, please, Miriam," Rosemary thought. "Not another birthday."

Rosemary left them there in the kitchen. At the top of the stairs, she saw their suitcases already packed. This departure of theirs had been prediscussed, then. No difference, as long as they were leaving. She put on the same tired running shorts from yesterday, and nylon top, and laced her shoes slowly. She didn't want to run but it might help with the anxiety. It might shake her heart up and down enough to numb it. In the kitchen she let them both hug her again. She promised to be brave, and phone often, and get another cat, as Miriam would get another husband.

On the last mile home, running a soft, lazy pace, she saw the Datsun coming toward her, a small blue wave, the suitcases bouncing around in the back like well-trained dogs. Miriam's red hair was shaking the daylights out of itself as she bobbed in the front seat. Her face was scarlet, molten with anger. Rosemary could see their mouths going, Miriam's and Uncle Bishop's, behind the thick glass, as though they were trapped in a television set with the sound turned down. "The Miriam and Uncle Bishop Show." The Datsun whirled by in a blue flash. Miriam waved, the veins popping out on her neck. Uncle Bishop tooted. That was all. *Good-bye. Good-bye.*

Rosemary decided to stay in the tent. She wanted to be near the trees and grasses and bird sounds. She wanted to stay close to the sacred spot where Mugs was slowly becoming earth. She wanted firsthand information about the stars, without the safe glare of a windowpane between them. For two days she watched the snowy constellations pull themselves into patterns, listened to the rattling of the leaves, fed herself and the birds the way one does chores, and imagined Mugs sinking farther down, settling in. Maybe it wasn't so bad, this going back to nature. Maybe it *was* better to take one's destiny into one's own shaking hands. Perhaps she could start up the rickety, dusty car one bright morning, stoke up the old carbon monoxide. Taking the first step seemed to be the ticket. Maybe that's what William had learned. Maybe that's why he had shopped so diligently for razors.

On the third day Uncle Bishop came to visit and was quite surprised at the reception he got.

"You lied to me," he protested, as a BB zinged through the grass at his feet. In the afternoon, he returned with Miriam. Rosemary watched cautiously as the small band climbed the hill. She fired into the grass at Miriam's feet with a fierce *blep!* of the gun. She jacked it and aimed again. *Blep!*

"Jesus F. McGillicutty!" Miriam shouted. "You're not serious, are you, Rosemary?"

"I'm a survivalist now, Miriam. I'm unbelievably serious."

"You used to be a pacifist," shouted Uncle Bishop, in disappointment. The bottoms of his pants were rolled up for his trek up through the longer grass.

"And why don't you mow this lawn?" Miriam scolded. "It's nothing but a brothel for snakes."

"This is pure civil defense going on here," said Rosemary.

"You wouldn't shoot at a man's scrotum, would you, Rosie?" Uncle Bishop asked. He was poking at the grass with a stick he'd brought with him for protection from the societies that live and dwell beneath blades of grass and under rocks.

"I've just thought of something incredibly funny," Miriam squealed. She began to bleat, her own special brand of laughter.

"What?" asked Uncle Bishop, straightening up to swat at some blackflies that were circling his head.

"Well, it's just that I've never thought of you as *having* a scrotum," said Miriam. "I mean, what would you need one for?" Uncle Bishop swatted a hand extremely close to Miriam's own head.

"Careful," she said, adjusting her red curls. "You almost hit me. What are you swinging at, anyway?"

"Blackfly," Uncle Bishop said flatly.

"I'm warning you both for the last time," Rosemary shouted, and fired two more BBs, this time over their heads. She would need to pick up a new supply. She was averaging about ten per visitor. The interlopers finally retreated. Rosemary watched and listened as they pampered their way back down the little hill, reluctant to run into menacing potato bugs or log-sized caterpillars.

"She always did take after Mother a little," Miriam was pointing out.

"No," said Uncle Bishop. "I see this as the same thing that happened to Patty Hearst. Something just snaps." They went back to the Datsun and, like good cowboys, disappeared down the road and into the sunset.

On the fourth day, Robbie appeared in the Datsun. Uncle Bishop had obviously gone for reinforcements. Rosemary watched her brother climb the hill with his long, athletic stride, deerlike, youth at its best working form, its apex. Sweet Robbie. "I miss William, too, Rosie," he had told her, earlier that spring. "But it's time you came back to us." Well, now it was different. Now she was entitled to her own breakdown. Robbie handed her a sheet of paper.

"From Uncle Bishop," he said. Rosemary unfolded it and read: *The schizophrenic may resort to unusual habits, minimize his or her needs, resort sometimes to a single room. In this case, a tent.* She smiled. He must have phoned Arthur, the psychiatrist with whom he'd had a brief affair. Good. At least they were speaking again. She laid the gun against the tent and embraced Robbie. In just a month he appeared to have grown older, more confident.

"Does construction do that for you?" Rosemary asked.

"I'm done with construction," Robbie said. He handed her a cold beer, and then opened another for himself. "Even if Uncle Bishop hadn't called, I was coming home in a day or two."

"For good?" Rosemary fingered the gold hairs on his knuckles that she loved so, Rumpelstiltskin gold, those hairs.

"No, I'm going back to school," Robbie announced. "I'm going to find a room, or maybe a small apartment in Orono, and then go for the old master's."

"Oh, Robbie, good for you," Rosemary said. College, that old-memory place of the apartment she had shared with

Lizzie, where the wind chimes rattled so loudly, where the gangling notions of life were still new, where the campus sprawled like a large grassy womb. "Good for you, Robbie," she said, still tugging at the hairs. A master's in biology. "You'll put Mendel to shame."

"William was quite a guy, all right," Robbie said. Rosemary felt an emotional landslide in her gut.

"This is the terror of loving something, Robbie," she didn't say. "Unless you take it from yourself, it can be taken from you later, when giving it up is unthinkable." And she wanted to tell him, just as she'd wanted to tell the others, that she wasn't the only one to feel this way about the frailty of human beings. Even the Puritans had warned against parents loving their children, what with the early epidemics claiming so many young lives. Rosemary wasn't the only one who saw love as a weak link in the chain. But she said nothing to Robbie. Instead, she nodded.

"And Mugs was quite a cat," he added quickly. Rosemary smiled. "Do you want me around for a few days until I leave?" he asked.

"Come visit," she said. "But, no. I like the house at night with its lights off. I like to look down on it when it's totally quiet." She knew Robbie wouldn't question this, but would understand, somehow.

"I'll stay with Uncle Bishop, then. I think he was planning on it anyway. He's cooking." From far away the slurred *tee-yah, tee-yair* of the meadowlark came to them, melancholic and forlorn.

" 'Believe me, love, it was the nightingale, not the lark,' " said Rosemary.

"What?" Robbie asked her.

"Nothing," she replied. "Just something Juliet said, once, to Romeo." She threw her empty beer can onto the grass. "But she was only thirteen. What could she know?" A small wind rustled the aluminum can and it rolled away, down the hill. She could hear Uncle Bishop. "Jesus Christ, she's taken to littering." Surely another sign of the burgeoning schizophrenic.

Twenty minutes later, Robbie was only taillights going down Old Airport Road, and the purr of a tiny man-made engine, and the towering mushroom of dust he left behind him.

Rosemary stayed on in the tent, unable to take herself back into the big house, once made smaller by William and Mugs, a museum now, the house. When the evening's light washed in, it turned from beige to brown, like the thick hard shell of an old, weathered nut. She did go inside long enough to use the bathroom, to shower, to cook herself light, easy meals. She kept up the running, but she was back to drinking too much wine late into the cool nights. Sitting out on the hill, she was able to keep track of the old stars, battered as moth wings. She slept so late into the day that sometimes it was the mailman's truck at one or two in the afternoon that roused her. She felt, in the tiny tent, that she herself was slowly going back to nature.

Robbie came by for a few short visits. He left little advice with her. He knew she wanted none. And she gave little advice for him to take along to Orono and his master's degree. She knew he needed none. That was the lucky way she and Robbie were with each other. So she lolled away the long evenings camped out in the backyard, learned new bird sounds. "The single most important step man took was when he turned to an agricultural existence and gave up his nomadic wanderings," Uncle Bishop had said once, during one of his food lectures. So she became nomadic again, imagined herself pitching her little tent night after night on a different hilltop, lugging the wine along with her, covering mile after mile, but always with the same ragged stars straggling the ceiling overhead. Some things you cannot outrun. She gave a great deal of thought to suicide. It became familiar to her at the last. No longer terrifying, it became lighthearted, a sitcom, vaudeville. The ultimate slip on the old banana peel. She considered writing down her last thoughts, that perhaps they would be of interest to someone, someday. Maybe Uncle Bishop would cease fighting with Miriam long enough to read selected passages at her funeral, causing the multitude to weep. But, sadly for posterity, the only things she had to say were to Sacco and Vanzetti. And maybe she would leave a quick little note for the Rosenbergs. *Dear Sacco and Vanzetti. Dear Rosenbergs. Shit happens.*

Rosemary spent eight days on the hill, in the canvas dinghy, eight days swallowing the grisly news about Mugs, and the anger at William. She could have stayed in the existential tent forever, she was sure, pondering her fate, drinking her wine, had it not been for Aunt Rachel's frail appearance. She came out of the evening shadows at the corner of the house, out of the lilacs themselves. Rosemary had not even heard the sound of a car engine, or a slamming door, or even her footfalls. Yet there she was in her pale cotton dress, and beige cotton sweater, a ghost climbing the hill, clothes too big for the frame, clothes hanging on bones. Aunt Rachel was a clothes rack now, climbing.

"Rosemary, dear." Her voice was the wind that came out of the lilacs and rattled the grass ever so gently.

"Aunt Rachel," Rosemary whispered, as though they were identifying each other so that there could be no mistake. As though they hadn't seen each other in years. Rosemary had not noticed, just two weeks before, how physically abused Aunt Rachel had become from the cancer. Now she realized why. Aunt Rachel was being secretive about the dying. She was being greedy about the pain, keeping it to herself as though it were the last slice of bread.

"Rosemary?" A bird's voice, wind filled and downy, a feather rising in the wind and falling.

"Aunt Rachel, I'm here," Rosemary said, and stood up on the hillside. Now she could see Aunt Rachel's eyes in the uneven dusk, sunk back like walnuts into her face, large and dark and dying.

"Just that short climb and I'm exhausted," Aunt Rachel said. A hand resembling a hand fell against her chest, a hand *impersonating* a hand.

"I didn't realize," Rosemary said to her. "I didn't know it was like this."

"It's fast, Rosie, is all. Speeded up, like everything else nowadays." *It's all canned, Lizzie.* Aunt Rachel spread her cotton sweater on the grass, then carefully lowered herself to sit on it.

"Good heavens," she said. "There's a job in everything nowadays." Fireflies came out of the grass, their tiny beacons transmitting silent messages of urgency and love.

"I'm taking Mother," Rosemary said suddenly. "This is not fair to you."

"Oh, no." Aunt Rachel waved a mosquito away. "Your mother's not my problem. Your mother is, in many ways, my salvation."

"I've never understood that," Rosemary said, as she poured some wine. She handed Aunt Rachel the glass and, to her surprise, Aunt Rachel accepted it and took two small sips. Rosemary tipped the bottle up and took a large gulp for herself.

"It was never your job to understand," Aunt Rachel almost scolded.

"But she's my mother."

"She was my sister before that," Aunt Rachel reminded her. "She's caused you some embarrassment by being your mother, hasn't she?" Rosemary watched Winston's silhouette as it snaked through the tall dark grass, in pursuit of some evening prey.

"Yes," she finally said, what she could never say to Miriam. "Yes, she *has* embarrassed me." And she was relieved to offer this admission to Aunt Rachel.

"That's all right, dear," Aunt Rachel reassured her. "That's only human nature at work." Rosemary said nothing. More fireflies ignited among the elms and the cherry trees and the stiff Indian paintbrushes. She could hear the whispery action of small planes at the Bixley airport, and the occasional *whoosh* of a car on Old Airport Road. The highway department had, days ago, filled and packed the trench. They'd knocked on her door for an explanation. She had watched them with her binoculars from the safe distance of the tent and, finally, they went away. But four days of speeders had experienced a harsh reality in front of Rosemary's looming house.

"I've decided," Rosemary said carefully, "that Mother is dead." She stared off into the gray evening and saw Corona Borealis, the Northern Crown, the little tiara of the heavens, making its way across the beaten path. Hercules, large and dim, followed. She could faintly make out, thanks to northern Maine's unpolluted skies, what looked like a fragile, hazy star near the head. But she knew what it really was, the Great Cluster of Hercules, thousands of stars, and thousands of light-years away. There were tricks everywhere.

"She was a delightful, vibrant girl," Aunt Rachel said. "I'm sorry that you don't remember her that way. Do you know that in those first months of her illness, she always did her very best to maintain." *Maintenance.* A June bug tried out the deepening night, doing a series of plops into the black windows of the house, longing for the toasty lights again. Rosemary listened to the faint beating of its body, as the *plop plop* drifted up the brief hill to her ears. She tried not to cry. There had been so much of it lately, and now here was the long-awaited portion for Mother, *her* pound of tears.

"Do you think she chose this?" Aunt Rachel continued, and even the fireflies blinked *no, of course not,* and the June bug flew away from the question and into the billowing night. "You once felt people treated you differently because of William's death? Well, guess how they treat your mother. Guess how they treat you when you're dying yourself." Aunt Rachel touched the glass to her lips. Night had moved in around them. The moon now lighted the buildings, the landscapes, the way for the night animals that Rosemary knew must be moving in the fields, beneath the trees, along the weedy roadsides. Early evening in northern Maine, with a moon on the rise, with two women talking quietly on a small hill, their words passing between them like fireflies. Aunt Rachel ran a finger around the rim of her glass and the crystal cried out softly, a little funeral hymn being played on the hillside, near Mugs's resting place. Aunt Rachel sat still and listened to it, as though she were listening to the brittle music of her bones.

"Are you afraid to die?" Rosemary finally pushed the words past the lump in her throat. She felt she must say something, but Aunt Rachel started a bit at the question, almost surprised to hear that Rosemary was, indeed, sitting there in the young night, beside her. She threw her head back a bit. Her throat curved white in the moonlight, like a swan's neck, long and loving. Her cheekbones were radiant, sleek and mysterious, white as moonflowers. Gone were the black circles and ashen pallor. The moonlight had rejuvenated her. Or had it been a few helpful sips of wine? Rosemary took another long swallow from the bottle.

"I'm not *afraid* to die," Aunt Rachel answered finally. "I'm just *sad.*" Her words came to Rosemary, singing like the wing beats of the mute swan. The words, in a little **V** formation, came winging. Aunt Rachel's soft brown hair fell back, away from her face, exposing one white ear as though it were a delicate seashell. Rosemary knew that if she put her ear against Aunt Rachel's to listen, she would hear blood pulsing and not the beating sea. She would hear dilating and contracting, not ebbing and flowing.

"And I'm sad for those of you I'm leaving behind," Aunt Rachel continued. Rosemary could hear a common nighthawk, *pit-pit-pit, killy-kadick,* a night voice in the woods. Goatsuckers. Nightjars. The woods was a choir now, of animals and insects. The wild apple trees in the field across the road, black rounded shapes, moved in a little breeze from the river, one that was not received up on the hill. "I'm sad that the rest of you will have to listen to your mother ask where I am, every single day until the cows come home." Aunt Rachel laughed then, a full girlish laugh, and Rosemary, who had been paralyzed with the honesty of her aunt's revelations, found herself relaxed suddenly, peaceful.

"Aunt Rachel better bring me some chocolates," she mimicked, in Mother's shrill little voice. She heard Aunt Rachel's laughter rise again, a wonderful harmony to add to the night choir.

"Oh, Rosemary," Aunt Rachel said. "Life is such a sweet thing. Your father used to say that. 'Rachel, honey, life is all sugar,' he'd say." She stopped abruptly, her words still hovering in the air. Quickly, she said, "Isn't the moon lovely tonight?" But Rosemary had frozen next to her. Something was coming to the surface of her adult mind, something from her child's mind, facts that had been stored, piled up like toys in a chest, for the day when it would—could—all be explained.

The child she had been had remembered some important information, some whispers, some gestures, some nuances from the adults in her early life. Now she was an adult herself and could solve the years-long riddle. And she had spent a lot of years wondering about Father's *other woman.*

"Oh, my God," Rosemary said softly. It was like finding the last simple piece of puzzle, the final chunk that would finish the clown's face. And all these years she'd been looking for it.

"I'm so very sorry," Aunt Rachel whispered. A few more moments and fireflies passed between them before Rosemary spoke.

"Well, *I'm* not sorry," she said finally. Spika, the grain, the brightest star in the Virgin, hung in the southwest. Orange-colored Arcturus had begun its steep climb to overhead. Many lovers, legal and illegal, had been upon the earth and gone back to it since Arcturus, the star that began the festivities at the Chicago World's Fair in 1934 by shining through a photoelectric cell, began lighting them the way. So many answers flew in the night, like bugs. Why hadn't she realized before? Father and Aunt Rachel. It made perfect sense that they would appreciate the things about each other that Rosemary had loved so in them both.

"Did Mother find out?" Rosemary asked.

"Never," said Aunt Rachel. "She never did. It occurs to me now that I must have wanted you to know, or I wouldn't have been so careless." Aunt Rachel put the empty wineglass down beside Rosemary's bottle. Rosemary took it as a sign to pour more wine, but Aunt Rachel held up a chalky white hand and motioned *no.* "It isn't something I'm proud of, the part where your mother was concerned, and it seems almost vile to sit here now and discuss this with Jonathan's daughter. With Eleanor's daughter." *Eleanor.* How long had it been since

Rosemary had heard her mother's name spoken? "I guess I didn't want to take that secret with me when I go. Maybe I see you as the only person left that I can explain to. We humans don't always plan for things to happen. We don't always mean to hurt someone." Shit happens, Aunt Rachel was saying.

"And has all this caring for her—forgive me for being callous—but is it your way of paying Mother back?" Rosemary asked.

"Sometimes I wonder that myself," Aunt Rachel answered. She sighed heavily. "And then I hate myself for even wondering. I'd like to think the answer is no." The moon was now higher, fuller, brighter on her face. The swan neck was gone. That was only an old moonlighty memory, perhaps a memory of Father's. Aunt Rachel was deathly now, an emissary for Rosemary, as William and Mugs had been. Forerunners, all of them. Aunt Rachel reached a thin hand out in the moonlight. Rosemary found it, glowing white, thin and narrow as a trellis with skin growing on it. They clutched hands and Rosemary finally laid her head on Aunt Rachel's shoulder, a pillow of bone.

"Listen to me," Aunt Rachel whispered. Her voice was emollient in the darkness. It swept over Rosemary again, the way it did in grade school when her bicycle ended up in Aunt Rachel's yard. The same gravitational pull that had reeled in Father. "I didn't come here to confess, Rosemary. I came here to your silly tent to reprimand. I sit beside you, fifty-nine years old, in a body racked with cancer. I sit beside a healthy young woman with all her life ahead of her, and all I can think of saying is how dare you, Rosie? How the hell dare you?" Rosemary was crying suddenly. Aunt Rachel was crying. A family drowning in tears, this family. Miriam had even commented on it once. "The Kennedys have seen nothing compared to this," Miriam had wept.

"I had always thought of it as a lonely rendezvous in some motel room," Rosemary said. "But I know now he must have been happy, if he had you."

"Listen to me." Aunt Rachel's voice was cautionary. "Jonathan's been gone for more than twenty years, but don't you think he'd expect me to come here and talk some sense into the daughter he treasured so? Self-pity doesn't become you, Rosemary. William was weak, but you, you're the strong one. He was a wonderful boy in so many ways, but he was always without direction, always in search of some vague goal. William wasn't a very good soldier. You're the one who's tough, dear."

Rosemary spent that last night in the tent. Aquila, the magnificent eagle, was almost ready to roost when she finally drifted off to sleep, almost certain the wild cherry smell had turned to Old Spice, and that the extra pillow she liked to cradle in her arms was a large cat. All night long she dreamed of parachutes, tiny as mushrooms, cascading out of the sky, gods descending safely to earth, astronauts, maybe, safe this time, or ultralight men whose haggard wives had finally tossed them out.

The next day she packed her things carefully, the books, the lantern, and carried it all back down the hill. A fierce electrical storm broke in the evening, with thunder echoing down the chimney, with lightning lighting up the fields and road and yard. The electricity, competition for the storm, was zapped off. Rosemary let the blown fuse be, and sat in the dusky kitchen to watch the illuminating show that was being staged around her. She was safe again, in the house. "When the earth's crust first formed, Rosemary," William had said, "a heavy rain fell for sixty thousand years. And lightning snapped continually. This is nothing, this little shower. This is nothing at all."

An hour into the storm, and at its peak, she heard a scratching at the kitchen door. Her heart thumped. "A cat has nine lives, doesn't it, William? Mugs has eight to go." It was Winston, the outdoor cat, tortoiseshell and sleek, who frisked past her legs and padded down to the den to make himself a bed on the couch. "It was wonderful to see, William," Rosemary would've told him, had he been there, had he come back from his last trip to London alive. "It was like a royal succession. One king died and so another took over. Mars was in Sagittarius, William, when Winston ascended the throne." But William was not there. William would never be there again.

Rosemary put Mugs's dish back out and filled it. She filled the water bowl. But it would be weeks before she ventured back up the sloping hill to dismantle, as though it were a time bomb, as though it were a mission gone astray, the dangerous tent.

# The Tangled Braids

*Many a night I saw the Pleiads,*
*rising thro' the mellow shade,*
*Glitter like a swarm of fire-flies*
*tangled in a silver braid.*

—Alfred, Lord Tennyson,
"Locksley Hall"

AUTUMN HIT THE massive brown house on Old Airport Road in the form of strong winds laced with the first painted leaves of October. Already withered and gone were the lilacs, the violets, and the tiny strawberries that had dotted the hillside like round red buttons. Cherries had come out of the wild white blossoms and gone to the robins, and the orioles, and into mason jars in the basement. The sown seeds of wild grasses had thrived on Mugs's grave, and died, and now stood above their deadened roots, feeling the first tremor of cold shoot through the earth. Winter was coming to Bixley, Maine, population 23,160. The first snow would take away the final remnants of the things that had grown throughout the summer toward their own self-harvest, toward Nature's thrashing time. It had been a long season, even for Maine, with unusually stifling dog days curling in and out of July and August as Sirius, the dog star, the old scorcher, rose and set with the sun. Now it was over. Snow would soon turn the fields and roads and driveways white again. October was slowly inching into winter and soon icicles would hang from eaves, glassy stalactites. And storm windows would come out of the basements of the older houses, cobwebby and sleepy-eyed, to be Windexed back, shiny enough to stare out of for months. The migrating birds had gone, remembering their broken images of gulfs, and rain forests, and marshes, pictures slumbering in their heads from a previous year. Halloween came and went, like the pumpkin on its vine, like the witches of folklore, with only a handful of trick-or-treaters venturing out to goblin-ize Old Airport Road, to tap their chilled hands on Rosemary's front door, kids who lived along the road only, the town children preferring those sleek easy sidewalks of cement. Rambos and Terminators now, these trick-or-treaters carrying toy machine guns, rarely witches or ghosts.

The first heavy winds of snow struck the house just after the last Halloween pumpkin had finally sunk down into the juice of its own decay. A sadness engulfed the land, an expectancy, a hurriedness in all the animals. Would it be a harsh winter? Rosemary wasn't unnerved. She knew the migrating birds, like little clocks, would be back. And so would the cherries. And she knew that the old Bixley River would run again, free of ice, clear. She knew that the winter birds would do their best at the bulging feeders to avoid the mortality rates, so she kept the feeders filled. And she shoveled a path to the mailbox, a source of communication for her again, as it had been in those months following William's death. The first day that the weatherman threatened snow, she had backed her blue car out of the garage and drove it slowly down the road and into Bixley, where it could be serviced, and dressed with snow tires. She then covered the bicycle with a sheet of plastic and pushed it into a quiet corner of the garage. Winston settled easily into his role of indoor cat. Uncle Bishop came occasionally to visit, the Datsun's hind feet burdened with chains for Old Airport Road, not one of the best-plowed avenues in Bixley. Sometimes Miriam tagged along with him and talked incessantly of a current boyfriend, who would be, she claimed, the very last man in her life. Lizzie's cards still arrived once in a while. *Things are better with Charles and me. I think Philip is getting married. His secretary. Life is strange, isn't it, Rosie?* Rosemary wished Lizzie and Charles the best, but she would worry about them. Marriages, like cobwebs, were fragile things. Robbie studied hard, sent letters sparsely, called occasionally. Mrs. Abernathy's column ceased to appear in early September. Every day Rosemary planned to inch the car out of the big garage and take a spin over to check on her. Every day. But something kept getting in the way. Only the young, and Mrs. Abernathy probably knew this, have the pleasure of such delays. There would be a January opening now at Bixley High School, if Rosemary wanted it. Mary Templeton was taking a year's leave to have her first baby. Rosemary could teach Early American literature. She shuddered to think of Jonathan Edwards, the Mather boys, the Puritan writings. But she needed to give the school board a decision within the month. A month, now, seemed like an eternity to her.

Meals were simple affairs again, as they were in those days after losing William. She made large fires in her Schrader fireplace and sat sometimes late at night with a glass of wine, listening to the trees talking in snaps and pops and bursts, gossip of the old days when they were still standing in the mother forest. Her dreams were still around. They perched themselves in the long black corners of the night, curled beneath the handmade cherry bed, on those particularly long nights, those particularly cruel nights, when she could almost smell the sweet smell of William, and of Mugs. That's when the long finger of nightmare slid itself out from under the bed, crept up over the blankets, and poked her awake. Those nights.

A week before Thanksgiving she went with a handful of hothouse flowers, her own backyard flowers having long collapsed beneath the snow, to the white snowy mound of Aunt Rachel's grave. The snow was fluffy, being almost as new as the grave, and it spread evenly over the hillock like a beaten quilt brought over from the old country. Like Grandmother's quilt. A few headstones away, Father's grave, too, was snowy, one-half of his tombstone already sharing Mother's name, and the inscription 1924–blank. All snowy, these people, and dreamy now, some long gone, some newly gone. Rosemary imagined them, like the cast in *Our Town,* perching atop their tombstones, wishing she'd round up her foolishness and go away, go back to the living. She placed the deep red carnations on Father's grave, the irises on Aunt Rachel's. They sank into the snow, red as cardinals, blue as blue jays. Like William, they were all color on such a dreary, snowflaky day. Aunt Rachel and Father. "They should have a casket like Catherine and Heathcliff," Rosemary thought. But it was only a romantic notion. She knew that when one ceases to exist above the ground, one ceases to exist anywhere.

Nights were too cold to finally christen the telescope, so it sat in the den and collected dust. Instead, Rosemary watched the time-worn constellations from behind a paned glass. Sometimes, she didn't bother to make the long climb, the fifteen steps, up to the chilly, empty bedroom. Instead, she fell asleep on the sofa, listening to the dying snaps of the fire, cradling Winston against the curve of her stomach.

Two days before Thanksgiving a package arrived from Boston, from William's old friend and travel-mate, Michael. With it came a letter. It had taken its time in coming, considering Rosemary had sent Michael a letter in early July, in the middle of Lizzie's visit to Bixley. Over the months that followed since she mailed the letter, over the months that brought her past the warm summer, past the tent days, past Aunt Rachel's fast decline, she had come to realize Michael would have no answers either. There were none. Rosemary knew this weeks before the letter arrived. *I'm seeing a psychiatrist now,* Michael wrote. *I had given him up years ago, but after William's death I came back to him, the prodigal patient, and he scolded me, but took me in. He needs the money. I'm looking for answers myself, Rosemary. Dr. Wimmer tells me that sometimes there are no answers as to why people suddenly kill themselves. Not even he knows, sometimes. This is a good sign. Something positive has come out of William's death. I've never heard Dr. Wimmer admit such a thing before. Perhaps, with William's death, we will all turn a tad humble, not knowing.* The letter did not surprise her. It was true. William had his reasons, emotional, chemical, or both. And being *his* reasons, he took them greedily with him. Rosemary had long stopped reading books on suicide for an answer. In one book, she remembered, was a statement she read over and over again, and then underlined in black ink. It was something a Dr. Wilson had said about a certain type of suicidal person characterized by a *lack of constructive plans for the future, high chaotic energy levels, and general isolation.* Rosemary had underlined it, and then written *William* in the margin beside it, as though this were something she must remember for a future exam. At least it was a portion of the answer to a multiple-part question. Aunt Rachel had been right when she said that William lived without goals. William had always been running. Much of the blame had to lie in the nooks and corners of all those unhappy foster homes he'd been raised in. And some of it with Rosemary, too, for recognizing the distress signals of birds, instead of the people she loved. *No, Rosemary,* Michael's letter ended. *William and I were not lovers. You needn't apologize for asking. Dr. Wimmer will arrive at this thought himself one day, and when he finally asks me, I'll answer quickly. Time is, after all, money.*

The letter did not surprise her, but the painting did. It was of her, sitting on the sofa, with Mugs asleep near her leg. Rosemary's face was turned away from the cat, and she appeared about to speak to some person outside the perimeter of the picture. Some ghost, perhaps. She remembered the photograph William had used as his model, one that was in the album of pictures he had taken with him. It was of no particular event, no birthday, no holiday, no important gesture. Just Rosemary on the sofa, her profile, and Mugs sleeping in an embryonic ball, his throat thrust upward in pure submission. "The best action," William liked to say, "is the action you must imagine. There is glory, sometimes, in the things people do not do. Sometimes, Rosemary, there are even heroics." What surprised her most about the painting was that William was not in it. He had never done an oil of her or Mugs. Sketches with an intent to paint, yes, but they had never come to fruition. The only oil of Rosemary had William beside her in what he called a *Half Self-Portrait.* It hung in Uncle Bishop's den, a birthday gift.

William had had little personals for Michael to ship home. What he did have had arrived earlier in the summer. Rosemary had unpacked the heavy art books and replaced them on the library shelves, in the parking spaces reserved for them. His clothes she eventually gave to Goodwill, after Robbie had selected a few shirts, sweaters, and two jackets to take away to graduate school. William would like the idea of Robbie taking his clothes back to college. The Civil War sword she sent to William's sister, in Portland, since it was a family treasure. But she did not know of the existence of the painting until it arrived two days before Thanksgiving, snow piling up quietly on the brown wrapper as it leaned against the front door where the UPS driver had left it. *Oh, by the way, William began this in Amsterdam,* Michael added, in a postscript. *I wanted to keep it because it was his last work but really, Rosemary, it belongs to you.* She had stared at the painting a long time. No work of art this, taken from a photograph of a ponytailed woman, looking away from a sleeping cat. *Rosie and Mugs: Life as Usual* was the title he had written in pencil on the back.

Rosemary went up to William's room, with all the light, and the enviable consciousness, and found the photo album. There was the picture back in its plastic slot, but paint-smeared. "He wants to paint Goyas and El Grecos and Rembrandts," she had told others, as well as herself. "He wants to set his easel up before some masterpiece and share, stroke by stroke, the artist's genius." What was there to painting a woman in worn jeans and a flannel shirt—the woman you lived with—and a sleeping cat, if you were on an exodus to the land of the masters? "I told you Michelangelo would be all color," one postcard had said, "if they only wiped away the smoke." What was the sense of being in Amsterdam surrounded by Van Gogh's lifetime of works if William spent his time before an easel re-creating a thirty-five-millimeter photo processed by Kodak? What could he be thinking of to squander such valuable time in Europe?

She did, however, love the painting. It was large enough that Mugs was lifelike, the soft throat in need of a stroking, the eyes rolled back into sleep. And it was Rosemary all right, lackadaisical with the goings-on, staring off, about to say something, then preferring to think it instead. Oh, it was she! And it was Mugs, too, content with the humans, only dreaming now of the old terror of being stray. Rosemary was uncertain as to how she should feel about the painting. It saddened her as well as pleased her. So he was thinking of them, was he, in those final days? The last postcard had come from Brussels. *Today Brussels,* it read, *Tomorrow?* No cards had arrived from London, the last stop, the elephant's graveyard. *His last work,* Michael had said, and Michael would know. He was with him. So William had spent his time in Europe evaluating, stroke by stroke, his relationship with Rosemary. *Rosie and Mugs: Life as Usual.*

Rosemary took the painting upstairs and leaned it against the wall in William's room, his studio, his haven of light. Then she stood back to view it. Was there an answer in it somewhere? A goddamn *symbol?* It had been such an ordinary day in her life that she couldn't even remember when the picture was taken. Only that it was at least two years old. The blue sweater with the V neck had been gone that long. Had she said something, that very day, that made William realize their time together was fated?

"Oh, William," Rosemary said, after a time. "Do you want to hear about Life as Usual?" She could tell him lots, couldn't she, this man who had given life up, given it away? She had lived in a tent in the backyard. She had written imaginary letters to Sacco and Vanzetti, and the Rosenbergs, as though they were pen pals. William had not so much as written one lousy, crummy suicide note. Oh, she could tell William loads about Life as Usual. She had watched Uncle Bishop move a small plastic family into his dollhouse. She had bought a dress—twenty fucking dollars—for Mother's Cabbage Patch Kid. She had scanned the skies for an ultralight man. She had held Mugs down so that he could be killed, and the killing,

William, was only to spare him the pain of death. She had seen the best memories of Father sink back into the earth, where the pump was steadily pumping at the Christmas tree farm. She had talked to Father's other woman, and then she had buried Aunt Rachel, the same woman. Life had been pretty damn *unusual.*

Rosemary could not bring herself just yet to hang the painting, so she left it leaning against one of the stark white walls until she knew what to do with it. In the meantime, she had business to attend to with the still living.

After Aunt Rachel's death in September, Mother had drifted into a sharp decline, a long depression. Even the ringlets gave up, let loose the bounce, forgot the curls. With Aunt Rachel gone, Mother lost her remaining fragmental conceptions of the family, of the members in it. Now it was Uncle Bishop, her little brother, who gave her the greatest comfort, and Mrs. Fortney, a private nurse whom Uncle Bishop refused to let Rosemary help finance. "Where does he get his money?" Miriam was asking now, more than ever. "He's never lifted a homosexual finger to do a day's work in his life. He lifts them to read *Doll World* and to build those little houses." Where *did* Uncle Bishop get his money? An early lover of his, Rosemary knew, had died and left him all his personal belongings. She supposed that with the personal things there must have been a sizable life insurance. Maybe some stock. "I invest, Miriam," Uncle Bishop would rage. "Haven't you heard of Charles Schwabb? Weren't you even married to him once?" Regardless of where he got his money, Uncle Bishop's insistence on taking Mother into his home was a touching tribute to the sister he had once known. For the two months that Mother had been in his house, Rosemary tried to help as much as she could. But it was plain that Mother felt more comfortable with the nurse than she did with any of her children. So the nurse became like one of the family. The nurse became Aunt Rachel, and the cycle began again, this time in Uncle Bishop's little beige house with the chocolate-brown shutters. Mother was not long for the world. The family doctor had wasted his breath in telling them this because they knew simply by looking at her. She'd lost much weight and was now even smaller than Rosemary remembered her from childhood. Mother was shrinking. Mother, like so many other magic acts Rosemary had lived to see, was *disappearing*.

The day before Thanksgiving, Rosemary stopped by Uncle Bishop's house to say hello to Mother and to drop off a small roaster Uncle Bishop wished to borrow. Everyone was cooking their share for the holiday dinner and Uncle Bishop, who was in charge of the turkey and ham, needed the extra pan.

"Thanks for the roaster," he said. "Jason burned mine up this past summer. So I put it in the trash and the goddamn garbage men wouldn't take it. They said it didn't qualify as *garbage*."

"They're fussy," said Rosemary.

"Fussy?" Uncle Bishop snapped. "They're sanitation *engineers*. They're the PhD's of *gar-bazh*." How many times had Rosemary heard him screaming at the wheels of a departing truck about some item they refused to take, a blown tire, a Christmas tree, an old lamp. "If I don't *want* this goddamn shit, then it's garbage! Who do you people think you are? Archaeologists, for Chrissakes?"

Uncle Bishop arranged the holiday turkey in the pan she'd brought. Rosemary made a face of displeasure as he pried apart the unfortunate bird's goose-pimply legs, a culinary rape, and shoved it full of stuffing. Then he set about decorating a large ham with pineapple rings.

"Must *two* animals die this year?" Rosemary asked.

"I can't wait for Robbie to get home," Uncle Bishop said,

ignoring her question, as he did every year. He took a generous sip from his eggnog.

"I expect to see his car in the yard when I get home," Rosemary said. "I left a key for him under the mat. It'll be good to have some company for a few days." Was it she who had actually spoken these words? Wasn't it only four months earlier that she vowed no one would darken her guest room again? *Life is strange, isn't it, Rosie?* Lizzie had written. Even Lizzie could tell William some things about Life as Usual.

Rosemary stopped to check on Mother, who only pushed her away and went back to the television program that had engrossed her. Betsy Kathleen, the Cabbage Patch Kid, sat on Mother's bed in stiff denim jeans and a cute little sweater with a large *B* on the pocket.

"Your mother's a little cranky today," the nurse apologized. "She didn't sleep well last night, but she'll be just fine tomorrow. She'll have a nice sleeping pill at bedtime." The nurse patted Mother's hand and Mother sank back in comfort to finish out the drama of the show.

"I wish we didn't have to take her out but could have dinner here instead," Rosemary said. She reached over to touch Mother's arm, then decided against it. "But you can see how tiny Uncle Bishop's dining room and kitchen are."

"She'll be just fine," the nurse assured her. "I'll be with her." Then she went back to her crossword puzzle.

"Uncle Bishop," Rosemary said, "I was thinking that, since we'll have room, why don't we invite Mrs. Abernathy to dinner? My table sits ten and she must be so lonely on holidays."

Uncle Bishop was in a festive tizzy, banging pots and pans, tasting things, reading recipes. He was at his finest hour.

"You know," he said, "I haven't seen Mrs. Abernathy for

days. And from here it looks like no one has been shoveling her walk." He and Rosemary peered out of the kitchen window at Mrs. Abernathy's house. "She used to get Bradley Simon, two houses down, that little macho asshole, to come with his shovel." What surprised Rosemary most was not just the walk, brimming over with snow, but the feeders in the birdless backyard, some hanging, some standing, all empty. How many times had Mrs. Abernathy cautioned her readers, in her birder's column, to remember the birds each winter?

Rosemary waded in knee-deep snow up Mrs. Abernathy's walk and peeked through the glass of the front door. It was empty and quiet and forlorn, the house and its belongings. Had the relatives finally come for her? Was she so happily surrounded by human beings that she had forsaken the birds? Forgotten the mortality rates? Skipped town with the chimney swifts?

Back at Uncle Bishop's Rosemary called Senior Sunshine, the Bixley civic group that she had contacted earlier in the summer about looking after Mrs. Abernathy. An extension of the group that took meals around to shut-ins, Senior Sunshine also brought them companionship.

"A terrible stroke two weeks ago," Mildred Buchannon told Rosemary, over a roar of background noise at the tiny community center where the meals were being prepared and readied for delivery. A busy time, Thanksgiving. "She's at the Bixley Nursing Home."

Rosemary sat quietly next to Uncle Bishop as the Datsun spun its tires on the snow, caught, and shot off in the direction of Bixley's nursing home. A soft snow that had begun to fall was now accumulating on the windshield in not-one-alike snowflakes that were licked away by the wipers.

"I hope Robbie beats this home," Uncle Bishop said. He was leaning in close to the steering wheel, peering out at the white road ahead.

"I won't be long," Rosemary said, as Uncle Bishop put the truck in park and leaned back against the seat to wait. Seeing his wide face looming in over her bed might be too much for Mrs. Abernathy.

Rosemary followed the home's director down a hallway that reminded her of grammar school, an institutional green reeking of fresh paint.

"We haven't had her with us long," the director was saying, as Rosemary walked past the weathered faces that sat in doorways, or peered out at her from their beds, like cats in a humane society, all wanting a good home for Thanksgiving Day. The director left Rosemary in Mrs. Abernathy's room.

Rosemary was shocked, stunned to see Mrs. Clara Abernathy stretched out immobile and helpless, her eyes tightly shut. Across the hallway a television was tuned in to "Wheel of Fortune." Two nurses sat on desk corners, their backs to Rosemary, and watched in anticipation as one of the contestants bought a vowel, purchased a few seconds of time.

"Come on, you idiot," one nurse cheered the player on. "It's 'A stitch in time saves nine.' I wonder where they find some of these contestants." Her companion was smoking a cigarette and watching the squares being turned through squinted eyes.

"Does she speak any at all?" Rosemary asked them, and they both jumped. The smoking nurse quickly extinguished her cigarette in an ashtray on the desk, and crossed the hall to Mrs. Abernathy's room.

"No, honey, not a single word. But she's only been here

a short time," the nurse added as encouragement. "She may yet. She your grandmother?"

Rosemary looked down at Mrs. Abernathy's soft curls that lay in blue-gray lumps on her head, little waves, little rivulets.

"I'm one of her biggest fans," Rosemary told the nurse.

"Really? Who was she?" Who *was* she. The nurse, at least, had given poor Mrs. Abernathy up for dead.

"A columnist," Rosemary said. "She was very well known."

"Really?" asked the nurse. "That's nice. I've got to turn her." Rosemary stepped back as the nurse resituated Mrs. Abernathy's tiny form. The little round eyes had suddenly opened but they stared only at what lay before them, patterns on the ceiling, perhaps, that might stand out like a wedge of Canada geese on their way to a warmer clime.

"Chafing and pressure," said the nurse, "can cause real bad sores in a bedridden person. Unhealthy tissue breaks down if it's subjected to more than one and a half to two pounds per square inch for a period of time." Lovely facts! How Mrs. Abernathy had lived for facts. What a pity she would miss these last ones about her own body.

Out of Mrs. Abernathy's throat came a soft whimpering sound, an inland murmur. A smell of pee and death ran together in the room, a smell Mrs. Abernathy, in her heyday, would demand go elsewhere to hover. Her body structure had begun to arrange itself into a question mark.

"So near to all the answers," Rosemary thought. "Why a question now?" But Clara Abernathy's frame was twisting into a perfect quizzical form. The gown fell open in back as the nurse quickly turned the body, and Rosemary saw tiny sores running along the spine, the geese formation far off now, flying away, over the useless mountain of bones.

What kind of work was this? Was this Nature on the unemployment line? Was this Nature amusing herself until some real work could be found?

"Why linger?" Rosemary wondered, as she stared down upon the ravaging of what she knew was once a vivacious girl. She thought of the old pictures she had seen, in the *Pictorial History of Bixley,* and she imagined Clara Abernathy running through the dirt streets of town, hand in hand with Horace Abernathy, on the heels of the fire horses, maybe, during the great fire of 1929. But even Shakespeare had known what was in store for the girl that had been Mrs. Abernathy. What was it the Bard had predicted, in William's old college book, for that last terrible age? *Second childishness and mere oblivion, sans teeth, sans eyes, sans taste, sans everything.* Mrs. Abernathy gurgled again, like some kind of little bird. *Twi-do. Clep. Cher.* The nurse checked the intravenous tubing near the bed, with its seconds dripping down, one by one, with its silent ticking. Liquid oranges now, and liquid toast and tea, this food keeping her alive. Not the hearty breakfast Mrs. Abernathy would have eaten in her prime. Rosemary remembered remnants from Mrs. Abernathy's many columns. *Dear Birder: The shape of a bird's bill will indicate the kind of food it prefers, and do feed the birds. Winter is the cruelest season. The starling has brought down airplanes. The chickadee weighs as much as four pennies. The hummingbird's nest is the size of a fifty-cent piece. Birds cannot, I repeat, cannot smell. Dear Birder. Dear Birder. Dear Birder.* Mrs. Abernathy, Rosemary knew, was alive with bird facts. Her foggy dreams were full of beaks, and feathers, and wing bars, and other helpful information.

"Yes, well then," Rosemary mumbled to the nurse.

Outside, Uncle Bishop said nothing as he drove her over the glistening streets of town. Snow was still falling lightly. Rosemary imagined Orion somewhere overhead, unseen for the gray sheet of flakes that covered the night sky. She thought of Rigel, the glorious star which is his foot, a star born before Columbus was born, behind the snow, still there, still functioning. And Betelgeuse would be there, holding up Orion's tired shoulder, and the fuzzy nebulae in the sword, three hundred light-years away, a thin, hazy gas cloud ten thousand times greater than our sun. All this was there, beyond the gray snow falling, beyond the breakdown of Mrs. Abernathy's bones, falling, and the slow death of brain cells in all the earthlings. Beyond the mythology, beyond the suicidal lovers, beyond mothers and fathers and aunts, beyond the houses and the house pets, the stars were still weaving their patterns. And even they would one day burn out, tired from the script, sick of the job.

"Tell Robbie I said hello," Uncle Bishop reminded her.

"He's bringing his new girlfriend with him," said Rosemary. "Did I mention that? I think he's really serious this time." She kissed Uncle Bishop goodnight on the stubble of new growth across his cheek, which would, like the spring buds, soon sprout a beard.

Rosemary drove her own little car through the snow filtering down on Old Airport Road. At home, Robbie's truck was in the driveway, already asleep beneath a half inch of snow. She looked around her yard, and then down the white, shapeless road. How quickly snow covered the old mistakes, filled up the holes, whitened the oil spills, the blood spills, corrected the dips. A warm light was on in the kitchen and one in the den. There was nothing better than a house along a snowy, tree-lined road on a chilly, starless night, with a warm light in its kitchen. These images had been alive in Rosemary since she was a child, since she was a part of the big warm house of childhood.

A slow-moving car slid along Old Airport Road, inching its way home. It looked like the Fergusons. The falling snow quickly ate up the red taillights and soon the sound of the engine, too, fell away from Rosemary's ears and was gone. She pulled her jacket about herself and stood outside for a few minutes. Later, she would take a midnight walk, while Robbie and his new girlfriend were sound asleep in the guest room. There was now so much snow on the hill by the wild cherries that her tent would only be half-visible if it were still there. The willows beyond the cherries were barren now, but in the spring the catkins would burst to life before the leaves came, all velvety and furry, pussy willows all over the tree, Mugs on every branch. Now, Mugs's grave was lost in the white of the field, beneath a foot of snow.

Rosemary watched the smoke of her breath rising in the night, like signals. When they were children—she and Miriam and Robbie—they pretended to be smokers on nights this cold, and they stopped between slides down the hill to share an invisible cigarette, have a good puff. The snow snapped beneath her boots and the night sounds of it echoed in the large yard. Did she still want the same things, these months after William's death, as she had wanted in those early spring evenings? *I want to grow crazy as I grow old, William,* she had lain awake and told his ghost. *I want the gray to come to my hair slowly and the hair itself to go wild. I want time to come together at the last so that it seems like one long, lazy day that is passing and not my life.*

"Rosie?" There was a voice coming out of the garage doorway. A voice in the night could be any voice. William's. Aunt Rachel's. A voice that comes out of the snow itself could be Father's voice, or maybe even Mrs. Abernathy's own, on its way out.

"Rosie?" It was Robbie, and Rosemary felt a sudden surge of love rise up in her. She wanted to tell him what Father had told her, via Aunt Rachel. She wanted to say, "Oh, Robbie, life is such a sweet thing. Life is all sugar."

"Over here," she said, from her spot in the shadows, where she could better see the snow ricocheting off the porch light, and he came to her, shivering without his coat, so they could hug. Snowflakes flew like soft white moths around them. The trees and bushes and firewood, all usual landmarks, were buried beneath snow, and enchanted.

"Come inside. I'm freezing to death out here," Robbie said, rubbing his arms. "And yes. I have Carol with me."

"Carol?" Rosemary thought. "Oh, Robbie, life *is* all sugar. There are Carols at every turn in the road."

"What are you thinking?" he asked, and pulled her by the sleeve of her jacket closer to the garage door.

"I have eight white hairs now," Rosemary said, and swept the snow off her shoulders, arranged the ponytail in an orderly fashion for her first introduction to Carol. "Soon it will be all white," she added.

# The Receding Ice

*And in the winter*
*extra blankets for the cold,*
*fix the heater getting old*
*I am wiser now you know.*

—Janis Ian,
"In the Winter"

IT HAD BEEN almost a year since William's suicide. January would mark not just the new year, but the anniversary of his death. A cycle had spun its way through the spring, summer, and fall, and was now back again, full circle.

On Thanksgiving Day the gods bombarded the house with a foot of snow. Uncle Bishop brought Mother, her rocking chair, and the nurse easily up Old Airport Road in the Datsun, the chains biting into the snow each inch of the way. Miriam and her recent boyfriend, whom everyone had yet to meet, were not so lucky. Sliding and swerving precariously close to ditches, they came into Rosemary's house pounding snow from their boots, with Miriam relating in excited tones how death had pursued them at every turn in the road, in every branch that hung low with ice.

"This is it," Uncle Bishop said, unzipping the abnormally large parka and rubbing his plump hands together. "This is my last winter in Bixley. Mark my words. Humans beings are crazy to subject themselves to this torture." As every man in Miriam's life was the last, the very last, so was every winter Uncle Bishop suffered through in northern Maine.

Robbie took their coats and introduced them to Carol, a tall, thin girl, quiet and intelligent. Neither Robbie nor Rosemary had prepared her as to the phenomenon that would occur once the entire family got together. She would discover that on her own soon enough. Mother, it appeared, felt even more like she was in a room full of rowdy, partying strangers. But this pleased her more than struggling with remnants, montages in her brain of babies she had once birthed but couldn't quite recall. Better she think herself in a friendly little pub full of polite revelers for the holiday. Uncle Bishop convinced the nurse that a glass of wine, in honor of the festivity, would help Mother better accept her circumstances, and soon her little cheeks were blushed. She grasped Carol's long, slender hand.

"Good night, Mrs. Calabash," Mother said emphatically, "wherever you are."

Robbie built a boisterous fire in the Schrader fireplace and the den was soon full of the sound and the warmth of it. He and Rosemary made sure that everyone had a glass of wine. Everyone, that is, but Lloyd, the new man in Miriam's shambles of a life. To their surprise, he didn't drink. Miriam had introduced him—gaunt and fortyish—to the family, and now she was most intent on their liking him.

"Oh, Rosemary," she whispered, while Lloyd went to the

bathroom to wash his hands. "He even brings me flowers. The only time I got a rose from Raymond was when a Moonie shook one in his face at the carwash."

"And what do you do for a living?" Uncle Bishop asked Lloyd when he reappeared. He and Miriam exchanged warning glances.

"You might say I deal with the fragility of human souls," Lloyd said. He let loose a hearty, cryptic laugh. His eyebrows were bushy, and Rosemary had noticed a bald spot flowering on his head.

"Are you with the IRS?" asked Uncle Bishop. Rosemary could already tell he didn't like Lloyd, which was not surprising. Raymond had been the most bearable of the lot so far, but he had already moved from Bixley. Miriam was divorcing again and liked to tell her friends that *business divergences* had taken her future ex-husband from the area. The truth was that doors had opened to Raymond in the portable toilet business and he was busy closing them on Johnny-on-the-Spots all over New England.

"I'm a minister," said Lloyd. "A man of the cloth."

"What?" Robbie, and Uncle Bishop, and Rosemary all seemed to ask at once. Miriam with a minister!

"Is the cloth *green,* by any chance?" Uncle Bishop wondered aloud.

"Tell them, Lloyd honey," Miriam said, "what it is you want to do. Listen to this, Rosie," she said, and nudged the minister's arm.

"Well," said Lloyd. He cleaned teeth that looked to be false with a quick swipe of his tongue, something he'd done several times since he'd entered Rosemary's house. "Quite frankly, I'd like to put a capital *B* back in *Bible,*" he said reflectively. Miriam fairly swooned.

"Isn't that absolutely adorable?" she squealed. "I just *love* that." Rosemary was shocked. Where would Miriam go shopping next when it came to husbands? "Tell them what your hobby is, Lloyd," she prodded him further. "This will interest you, Rosie. You and Lloyd have a lot in common." Something in common with Lloyd. When would the universe stop playing its lowly tricks on her?

"I just happen to love old films," Lloyd conceded.

"Just like you do, Rosemary," Miriam reminded her. "And he knows the names of all those old stars." She sucked on her wine.

"I think of movie stars in an *evolutionary* way," Uncle Bishop began, in his best lecture voice. He scratched under his chin with the swizzle stick Miriam had discarded on the coffee table. "I've often wondered," he continued, "just how many muscled, pea-brained Stallones had to come and go over the millennium before one weakly Woody Allen, pinkish and unshelled, managed to crawl beneath some foliage and there to slowly evolve all the way to *Annie Hall.*"

"You have an unorthodox way of approaching film," Lloyd sniffed.

"It's the most *natural* way," Uncle Bishop sniffed back. "For instance, when I think of Stallone, I think of a large brontosaurus mowing down ferns and toppling trees. But Woody Allen I see as one of those soft furry creatures that clung to trees, hiding out in the branches by day, foraging by night, lemurs with big round eyes and small gentle digits that were slowly becoming fingers, thinking, all the time thinking." Lloyd was chagrined. Here was a kind of cinema verité that he had never encountered within the dark, popcorn-strewn confines of the Bixley Square Theater, an aleatory technique that would have caused even Bergman to run.

"Rosie," Miriam whined softly. Rosemary looked at her and shrugged.

"Shit happens, Miriam," she thought, "but life is sweet. Life is all sugar. Fight your own battles, kid." Without even her hostess as an ally, Miriam grew panicky.

"The Bible says that those whosoever shall lie down upon the ground with their own kind," she blurted out, "shall be made to stand up and take their punishment like men." She looked at Lloyd, who nodded his approval.

"Something like that," Lloyd said, and reached for Miriam's hand, but it had quickly engaged itself in the drama of lighting a Virginia Slim.

"For your information, Miss Mary Magdalene," said Uncle Bishop, "I have never lain upon the ground with my own kind, not since God invented beds. Unless you count the Quebec Winter Carnival. Is it still a sin if there's snow on the ground?"

"Just where *is* Aunt Mary?" Mother demanded to know. It was bad enough that Father was always late.

"I told you this would happen, Rosie," Uncle Bishop complained. "First it was Ayn Rand. Then Pyramid Power. Now it's Jesus because Miriam smells money with a capital *M*."

"That's an absolute lie," Miriam snapped back, embarrassed in front of her minister.

"And you remember her Kahlil Gibran stage, don't you?" Uncle Bishop implored. "You couldn't ask her to pass the steak sauce without hearing that cryptic language out of *The Prophet.*"

"Perhaps we should be going," Lloyd said, and Miriam looked piteously at Rosemary.

"No, of course not," said Rosemary. "Dinner's almost ready."

"Perhaps one of these days, Bishop," said Lloyd—and sounded professionally sorry—"you'll give yourself to Jesus, and your life will be on a more natural and heavenly course."

A more natural course? That was food for thought. And Miriam probably hadn't even told Lloyd yet about the shoe fights. "The Heavenly Father is a forgiving Father," the minister added.

"Just where *is* Father?" Mother cried.

"He'll be here soon, love," Rosemary assured her, and took the empty wineglass from her little hand.

"That's more like it," said Mother.

"I'll get her a glass of cranberry juice until dinner," Rosemary told the nurse. Miriam followed.

"Rosie, *please,*" she whined in the kitchen. "Make him stop." She had unscrewed a pint of rum from her bulging purse and was pouring some into her wine.

"I don't control Uncle Bishop's mouth, Miriam," was Rosemary's reply.

"This man is so different from Raymond," Miriam was saying as she stirred her drink.

"No shit," said Rosemary. She poured a small glass of cranberry juice and hoped that it would satisfy Mother. "Now that Raymond's left town, what news do you hear from his daughter?" Miriam waved a hand vaguely in the air.

"Well, Janie burned her wrist with a cigarette, took a bunch of pills, and then called everyone she knew to come save her. Half of Bixley was parked in her yard. They're starting to call them suicide parties."

"Sounds interesting," said Rosemary.

"No, it doesn't," said Miriam, a little light going on in her eyes that spoke of more than wine and rum. "You're just asking me this to get my mind off Bishop. Now, will you, or will you not, make him stop?" Rosemary looked at her big sister, at the glowing red hair, the abnormally green outfit.

"Not," Rosemary said.

"Then what must I do?" Miriam fussed. "Sit there mute?"

Rosemary examined again the kelly-green sweater, kelly-green headband, green earrings, dark green wool slacks. Unlike William, Miriam was not all color. Miriam was all one color: a guzzling green vegetable. Mute?

"What an excellent idea," Rosemary said.

The kitchen table was loaded with salads. Vegetables were in the pots they'd cooked in, on the stove. As this was an informal family dinner, everyone was advised to fix his or her own plate. A small breadline formed, except for Mother, who was waiting for Rosemary to bring her some food. Robbie and Carol were talking politics.

"To this day President Bush has no shame for bombing Iraq," Carol was saying. "And let's face it, that war was for *oil.*" Robbie nodded.

"Gibbon wrote that a large show of military force a long way from home is symptomatic of a sick society," he told her. "These days, I think it's symptomatic of the Republicans." College students, so wonderfully sharp, political. Rosemary felt a twinge of jealousy, a longing for the old schooldays, those days when every -ism and tenet seemed to matter. Then, it was Vietnam, something she hoped would never reoccur. But bombs were all the talk again, more things falling from the sky to earth like huge deadly stars exploding, this time over the very birthplace of civilization.

"That ham looks overcooked," said Miriam, poking with a fork. "I knew I should've offered to cook the ham. This happens every year." She slapped a spoonful of mashed potatoes onto her plate. Uncle Bishop turned as pale as the *pommes de terre.*

"All right, Miriam," thought Rosemary. "You're fair game now. Go for one of life's sugary battles."

"Miriam, please lower your voice." Uncle Bishop's own voice trembled with anger. "You're causing paint to flake and peel from the ceiling. I trust Lloyd isn't aware that you have this special, God-given talent?"

"You can trust your car to the man that wears the star!" Mother shouted loudly from the dining room. Uncle Bishop fidgeted with a shrimp salad the nurse had made and pretended not to notice Miriam, who had turned her flaming red head around in line and was staring back at him.

"Any news of Jason?" Rosemary asked.

"I still get his bills," Uncle Bishop answered, his finger now scooping up a little mound of potato salad to his mouth. "He owes the Wishing Well Stamp Company twenty-eight fifty, to name but one creditor, and I understand that's a substantial amount for their wares. He's made off with stamps from Zimbabwe, Ethiopia, and some other god-awful country that has no stable government but plenty of beautiful stamps."

"A regular Butch Cassidy," Rosemary mused. Uncle Bishop flopped a large serving of marshmellowed yams onto his plate just as Miriam sashayed past, Lloyd in tow. Uncle Bishop took note of the towering pinnacle of fiery hair, the French curls frozen into a bed of spray on the top of Miriam's head.

"Mount Stupid," he said to Rosemary, nodding his chin at Miriam's disappearing hairdo.

Arranged at the table, the diners looked carefully at one another, a small silence tugging at them, except for Mother, who had been given her second glass of wine to accompany dinner and was now slurping at it. The silence was only in deference to Lloyd, gentleman of the cloth, which appeared to be polyester from the way he dressed. More than likely Lloyd would want to deliver a grace before he glutted himself.

"Lloyd, I'm not a believer in God, or in giving thanks to one," Rosemary finally said. "And I know that Uncle Bishop and Robbie are not believers."

"Neither am I," said Carol.

"Nor me," said Mrs. Fortney, the nurse, in a confession that surprised Rosemary. She had always perceived Mrs. Fortney as one of those widows who run daily to their cookie jars at the request of a TV preacher. Fig Newtons for Jesus.

"Atheists, five," Uncle Bishop said gleefully. "Believers, two."

"Nor are Carol and Mrs. Fortney," Rosemary went on. "And I have no idea what Mother believes any longer, but if you would like to offer a blessing for the food, you are certainly welcome to do so." Uncle Bishop let loose a loud, impatient sigh. Miriam and Lloyd bowed their heads and sealed their hands together in prayer. Their eyes grew heavy with meditation and, in Miriam's case, green eye shadow.

"She looks just like a praying mantis, doesn't she?" Uncle Bishop whispered, and Miriam opened one eye to survey the blasphemous heathen.

"Please bless this food we have before us, dear Heavenly Father," Lloyd intoned.

"He'd better bring my chocolates!" Mother shouted, slamming her wineglass down on the table.

"Please try not to use the word *father,*" Miriam whispered softly to Lloyd, who looked confused at what appeared to be religious censorship, the very kind the pilgrims had sought to escape.

"Bless this food we have before us, Lord," he went on. "And thank you for the safe crossing of the Pilgrims, by which we mark this day."

"That was one bitch of a canoe trip," Uncle Bishop whispered too loudly, that old family trait. "Before they even got settled on shore, William Bradford's wife jumped off the ship and drowned herself."

"Your blessings abound here today, dear Heavenly Fath . . . ah, Person." Lloyd's voice vibrated with nervousness. "Just as they did for our forefath . . . ah . . . fore*people*."

"They fought like cats and dogs," Uncle Bishop added. "A real microcosm of what's wrong with humanity, that's what Plymouth Colony was. Not to mention the diseases God saw fit to give them so that fifty percent of them died the first winter."

"Rosie, are you going to read the true story of the Pilgrims again this year?" Robbie asked. "I told Carol how it's been a ritual for years now." That was true. It was a family ritual, each Thanksgiving, to gather before the fire with wine and listen as Rosemary read the true rendition of the Pilgrims and their hardships. That's where Uncle Bishop had gotten his information, from years of hearing it.

"Oh, that would be wonderful," said Carol. She was going to be just fine. Rosemary could see already how, like William, she'd settled into the rhythm of the family. "Tolstoy was right," William often noted. "All happy families are alike. You're lucky, Rosie, that your family is so unhappy." Carol would do wonderfully. Robbie had done well in picking a mate, in pairing up.

"Everybody, *shut up!*" Miriam shouted.

"And like the Pilgrims, dear Lord," said Lloyd, "we are gathered here meekly in your presence."

"Why do we always assume the woman is the salt?" Uncle Bishop asked suddenly, as he picked up Rosemary's little Pilgrim salt and pepper shakers from the table. "And that the man is the pepper?"

"And so, in ending, Dear Father, let me say—"

"He better not have a flat tire!" Mother screamed, angry

at Father's tardiness. "Hard chocolates hurt my gums," she confessed to Mrs. Fortney.

"Well, in that case," said Lloyd, "Amen." Miriam's face outshone her hair. She peered at Uncle Bishop with stony eyes, unblinking.

"Doesn't she remind you of Medusa when she does that?" he asked Carol. "Don't those curls look just like sleeping snakes?"

"Excuse me, please," Miriam said curtly, and disappeared with her glass into the kitchen. She returned with a drink that looked more like watery rosé than the cabernet it was. Dilution with rum was a tricky, alchemical art. She plopped the glass on the table.

"How long have you been cooking, Uncle Bishop?" Carol asked. "This ham is delicious." She would learn, even by the next Thanksgiving, not to ask such questions. This was the novice's question, this highway toward one of Uncle Bishop's food lectures.

"Cooking is a strange ritual," Uncle Bishop cleared his throat and began. Those who knew him ate their food, well aware that they would not need empty mouths to respond. "Now, Rosemary here won't eat meat. But you must consider what prompted man to be carnivorous in the first place." Miriam belched. She pushed her thrice-blessed plate of food aside and concentrated instead on her wine-rum.

"And what was that?" Carol asked, getting herself in deeper.

"He managed to survive the last Ice Age because he had fire in his possession," Uncle Bishop continued. "But when it retreated, ten thousand years ago, he was forced to view things differently."

"Ten thousand years ago," Rosemary thought, staring at *The Chinese Horse.* That had been a long, vicious lesson, that never-ending glaze. By the time the Ice Age curled backward, like an old tongue, man had been an artist already, for at least ten thousand long, white, Stone Age winters.

"He had learned a lesson by the time the ice retreated," Uncle Bishop went on. "He learned to depend less on plants and more on animals, to hunt *herds* of them, to follow the pack."

"Rosemary, are you just gonna sit there and let him go on and on?" Miriam whined. "Can't you even say something?"

Rosemary arched her shoulders into a nice little shrug. "I think Sacco and Vanzetti were framed," she said. Fight your own sugary battles, kid. Dig out all the ammo you can, while there's still time for such things. That's something Sacco and Vanzetti probably learned.

"No doubt about it," said Lloyd, "this has been an unusual Thanksgiving dinner." He rose over his barely touched plate, towered like Ichabod Crane above the strangest, the wildest, the most challenging flock that had ever hoofed itself past him.

"Do you have my flashlight?" Mother asked him, tugging at the pocket of his jacket.

"I've never even *seen* your flashlight," Lloyd answered politely. "Perhaps, Miriam, we can talk at another time." He put aside Mother's small bony hand as it searched for imaginary things in his pocket. Miriam barely noticed him, so angry was she at Uncle Bishop.

"You know, Lloyd," Uncle Bishop said. He was downright endearing. "Miriam has always been quietly religious. She's been turning red wine into white wine for years."

"Large gay blimp," Miriam noted. She turned to Carol. "And by *gay* I don't mean happy," she reported.

"With that in mind, then," said Lloyd, "I'll be on my way." Robbie went off to get his coat in an upstairs bedroom.

"Well, Miriam of Bath," said Uncle Bishop. "Now that

you've rebuked the Friar and entertained the company in doing so, is your tale finally over?"

"Do you think you can make it back down to Bixley?" Rosemary asked Lloyd. She wondered if even Jesus, albeit he had a reputation for doing wonderful things on water, could make his way over the tricky ice spots on such a snowy Thanksgiving Day. But Lloyd nodded, obviously willing to risk it rather than stay behind with a family that would frighten poor Tolstoy.

After dinner, Miriam dozed off on the sofa in the den.

"I see Miriam's knock-out drops are working," Uncle Bishop said, and Rosemary nodded. She was watching her sister's face. Miriam's mouth had fallen open, in the midst of dreams, or so Rosemary imagined. But what would Miriam dream of? It would be a dream of green clothing she'd yet to buy, or shamrocks, maybe, cool between the toes. Or money, green and crisp and spendable.

"Let's plant something in her mouth," Uncle Bishop suggested. "Mushrooms will grow in dark moist places."

"Poor Miriam," said Rosemary. "What will she do next?"

"I've been thinking," said Uncle Bishop. "With her penchant for men *and* for green, she might turn up one day with a leprechaun."

With the fire going well, and the food settling in their stomachs, the family gathered faithfully to listen to the ordeals of the Pilgrims, three and a half centuries old. Here were stories of other human beings, filtering down through the generations like slow starlight, wavering, curving, bending. Rosemary read slowly as the fire snapped and an occasional soft snore erupted from Miriam's open mouth.

" 'The gale persisted throughout the day and night, without any sign of letting up. Mary Allerton gave birth to a child at the height of the storm, but it was stillborn, probably because of the conditions aboard the restlessly pitching ship.' " The story struggled on, through the first dwellings, the first squabbles, the horrible spring plague.

"Here comes the part about the beer," she heard Uncle Bishop mumble.

" 'The shortage of beer seems to have been a prime problem,' " Rosemary read on, " 'although there was little they could do to remedy the deficiency in the immediate future.' "

"The Budweiser truck got stuck in Boston traffic," Uncle Bishop whispered, as he did every year, a part of the ritual now. "Have you ever driven in Boston?"

" 'During that dreadful spring, when so many had perished, they had still managed to sow some six acres of barley and peas, and twenty acres of Indian corn. The peas crop had failed, the barley was barely successful; but the Indian corn had done well.' "

"I *love* that 'barley was barely' part," Uncle Bishop said happily.

"Here comes the first Thanksgiving," Robbie whispered to Carol, who took his hand in hers and stared into the fire as she listened.

" 'Four men had been sent out by the governor on a fowling expedition and had brought back enough to last the community a whole week. The happy planters had amused themselves with ground sport and a little musket drill, and then, with the arrival of Massasoit and about ninety of his braves, who brought five deer with them, they held a joint feast.' " The reading was over for another year. Miriam snored loudly. The Pilgrims themselves had gone back to sleep.

While Miriam snoozed, Uncle Bishop watched a tape he'd brought with him of "The People's Court," a show he'd missed earlier in the week.

"It should be good," he told Rosemary and Robbie. "It's the one where the dog bites that awful Doug Llewelyn. It isn't a reenactment, you know. Those are actual idiots." He had, on a plate in his hands, a large wedge of pumpkin pie topped with whipped cream. Mrs. Fortney was before the fire, working out the last of her crossword puzzle, while Mother, in her rocking chair, drew lighthouses on her magic slate. Winston had rolled into a snug ball beneath Rosemary's telescope, safe from the snowy night.

While Carol went upstairs to shower, Robbie and Rosemary bundled up in heavy coats and mittens and went out into the snowy evening. The snow was falling in huge thick flakes, white moths everywhere, tiny angels, fluttering.

"Carol is really having her period," Robbie said, "and wants to lie down a bit. Menstrual cramps." Rosemary smiled. There were more cycles now in the old house, from menarche to menopause. And there was ovulation, too, with its little white eggs, those small children unborn and unbroken, tiny flawless pearls escaping from the ruptured graafian follicles. Escapes. Ruptures. Hair-raising journeys. Thrills. There were worlds within worlds. There were galaxies and nebulas and white gassy stars within them all, little universes waiting to explode.

"I wish the stars were out," Robbie said, his head craned back, his face skyward to the pelting snow.

"The stars are always out, silly," Rosemary answered, and then caught a snowflake on her tongue. "You just can't see them tonight." She looked up into the blackness of the Bixley night sky, looked toward the stars.

"Telescopio, William," she thought. "Pointillism. Seeing at a distance." She decided that on the first snowless night she would christen the telescope, chilling her fingers, sending galaxies of warm breath into cold little orbits. The telescope had been waiting to teach her, as Mrs. Waddell's library books were waiting, stellar sparks, all. "Having a wonderful time, William," Rosemary thought. "Wish you were here."

"Remember when we were children," Robbie asked, "how we used to throw ourselves backward on the snow, then spread our arms and legs to make snow angels?"

"I'd forgotten that," said Rosemary. "Let's make some."

They spent a chilly, snowy half hour, their laughter ringing and echoing about the forms and shapes that lay waiting for spring. When the time came that they were too cold to go on, the front yard was filled with life-size, flaky angels.

"Too bad Lloyd missed these," Rosemary said, as they stood, cold as snowmen, and surveyed their artwork. "This suggests a religious side to our natures he may have appreciated."

"Where *does* she find them?" Robbie asked, and pulled one mitten off with his teeth. His fingers beneath were brimming red.

"Let's go in," Rosemary offered. Even as children, she was the first one to end their play, noticing how red his cheeks had become, his eyes watering, a tiny cough.

"You're still mothering me," Robbie said. Rosemary smiled.

"Some of us who have never had children," she said, "have been mothering all our lives." She knew it was true. She knew that some women have risen vaguely for daylight feedings, have warmed bottles of milk that turn sour, never used. They have coddled and powdered and cooed. Their arms are curved, from the bundles they have never held. "There are worse things than mothering," Rosemary added.

When they came back inside to warm themselves by the fire, Miriam was awake.

"Let's play charades," Uncle Bishop begged, already past the unlucky circumstances of Doug Llewelyn's dog bite.

"Bishop, your entire life has been a charade," said Miriam. "What with your impersonating a man and all." She promptly lighted a cigarette. The nap had obviously rejuvenated her. She was back with a glass in her hand, another wine-rum. She was almost bubbly, perhaps even relieved to be rid of Lloyd. Sometimes even Miriam could see her own mistakes before they happened. And with Raymond now on the outs, she was in the midst of what Uncle Bishop referred to as her *auditioning period.* Between husbands, the family had seen many candidates worse than Lloyd. Uncle Bishop pulled Rosemary aside.

"I've composed a small poem about Miriam's husbands," he told her excitedly. "It's the same cadence as 'The Night Before Christmas,' when Santa calls out to Dasher, Dancer, and the guys. I was saving it for Christmas dinner, but I'll tell *you.*" His eyes were burning with glee, anticipating Christmas the way children await their presents.

"Let's hear it," Rosemary said. She leaned against the den wall and closed her eyes. Miriam and Uncle Bishop. Uncle Bishop and Miriam. They didn't need anyone else in their lives.

"There's Peter the salesman, and Maynard and Bill, and Raymond and God knows they all got their fill. To the preacher in spring, to the lawyer in fall, now divorce them, divorce them, divorce them all."

Christmas would be the next big family gathering. After that, they would probably assemble for Mother's funeral, the only difference being, perhaps, that no one present would demand chocolates, soft or otherwise.

"How is Ralph?" Robbie asked Uncle Bishop, who was stroking Winston. Winston, in turn, was happily kneading the rug and appreciating the rub. The humans had their good sides, he had grown to realize.

"Very healthy, knock on wood," Uncle Bishop said, knocking on the small measure of wood in the sofa's arm.

"Speaking of Ralph," said Miriam, and blew smoke skyward, so that it funneled up past her forehead. "Bishop bought him a baby seat and strapped it onto the seat of the Datsun. Is that or is that not reason to institutionalize?" More smoke issued from the holes of her nostrils, little escape valves.

"And with Moses gone, just how do you intend to part the snow long enough to get back to Bixley?" Uncle Bishop thundered. "You call a cab, miss, that's all I can say. And I'm *not* driving you and Broderick Crawford to the vet next week."

Carol had come back down from upstairs to join the group. She was pale but looked happy and contented to be where she was. A good sign. "Some of us are nomads, Rosie," said William, once. "We're at home anywhere."

"Broderick Crawford?" asked Carol. Miriam frowned.

"Don't be surprised if you get up one morning and discover that Ralph has lost his balls," Miriam warned. She made her fingers work like scissors, cutting the air. "Then there will be *two* eunuchs living in your house."

"I would've thought you already had your quota of male testicles," said Uncle Bishop. "But let me tell you this, Lucrezia Borgia. If anything happens to Ralph, little Broderick Crawford will pray it's only a spaceship chasing him."

"A spaceship chased Broderick Crawford?" Carol's eyes widened. Robbie gave her a glass of wine. Mother rocked in her chair, in frantic jerks, and stared into the fire. Not much had changed, Rosemary realized, with William gone. Some habits were hard to break.

"You've no idea," Miriam said to Carol, "how much money Mother spent dry-cleaning Daddy's suits until we gave them to Goodwill."

"Here's a toast," said Rosemary. She was feeling warm from the wine, from the splendid fire. Everyone raised their glasses and waited. Mother stopped rocking to peer at this stranger who was her daughter. The nurse poured a little of her own wine into Mother's glass.

"Here's to our family," Rosemary said.

"To the family," Uncle Bishop seconded. Rosemary caught his eye and winked at him, her uncle, her dear old, odd friend, her compatriot. They drank the toast down quickly.

"You know," Uncle Bishop said, sentimental now. "When I die I want to be cremated. Please remember that, Rosie. Rob. And I want you to take my ashes and scatter the bejesus out of me. I'm talking all over town."

"I doubt Bixley's large enough to receive your ashes," Miriam snorted. She patted a long cigarette out of its pack. "It'd be like one of those Oklahoma dust storms. Certain species may even die out, like what happened to the dinosaurs." She began fumbling in her purse for a book of matches. Rosemary smiled. It was true about the dinosaurs that, for whatever reason, they had vanished. They had been so huge, and so strong, and yet they had *disappeared.* She thought of them often these days, when she stood outside at night to look up at the Pleiades, the Seven Sisters, in the tip of Taurus's horn. Rosemary had read about how these massive stars had been born *after* the dinosaurs had already grown extinct. The stars were still babies, still surrounded by cosmic afterbirth, and destined to die young because they were so huge and magnificent. There were sacrifices in all things. And, destined to die young himself, maybe William knew that.

"Please, let's play charades," Uncle Bishop pleaded again. He was cheery, suddenly, with the warm Thanksgiving evolving around him in the form of fire, family, and potables.

"In a minute," Rosemary promised.

The road was still filling up with snow when she flicked the porch light on to let Winston outside. In a half hour she would coax him back in. She hated for him to be out on blustery nights, dark and snowy. It was decided, owing to the weather, everyone would take advantage once again of the numerous guest rooms and not venture out into the storm. Rosemary could find nightgowns and pajamas for everyone but Uncle Bishop, who would have to sleep in his enormous undies.

She left the boisterous group snug around the fire in the den. She told them she was rounding up sheets and blankets. That was not true. Instead, she went up the long steep stairs. *How many steps, William?* She ascended all fifteen steps, and then followed the small roses blooming on the wallpaper down the narrow hallway to William's room, the one with the big church windows that brought in all the light. "The level of light exemplifies a field of consciousness, Rosemary," he had said, so many times. "Yes, William," she had answered him since his death, so many times, "but you cannot trust the light. It wavers. Like starlight, it sometimes appears to be bigger, better, brighter than it is just because it's so close to us. Pointillism, William, remember? You should have just stood back a bit, old compadre, old friend, rather than lurching headfirst."

In William's room, Rosemary flicked on the small night lamp that still sat on his desk, sixty watts, dim and moody. No one downstairs heard the nail go into the wall. She pounded gently on it with the rock paperweight from the desk, and it quickly ate into the wood. Tomorrow, next week, she would do a more professional job. For now, this would suffice. On the nail she hung the painting, *Rosie and Mugs: Life as Usual,* and then straightened it. She stood back, her glass of wine in hand, to study it. Mugs was full, large, soft enough to touch. There he was, alive again on the wall. Rosemary thought about the magical powers that primitive hunters conjured up when they painted animals on cave walls. Did it really help them in the hunt, the kill, give them some kind of skill if they believed it would?

She put her glass of wine on William's desk and slid a folder that said CORRESPONDENCE out of the center drawer. In another drawer she found a wrinkled book of matches, half-full, that advertised RAPUNZEL'S HAIR SALON, another of William's quaint finds. In the gray metallic wastepaper basket she dropped his postcards, slowly, one by one, William's words, set afire. They fell like large, burning snowflakes, snow falling inside the house, not one card alike. *Amsterdam. Paris. Madrid. Cezannes. Van Goghs. Brueghels. Dear Rosemary. Hello, sweetie. Hi, honey. Today Brussels. Tomorrow?* They piled up as though they were letters from all of the world's greatest lovers. Letters from mothers who did their best, their very best, the very best they could. Letters from sisters with many husbands, from unusual uncles, from loving brothers, from dead fathers and aunts, from the old friends who get lost in the shuffle of life and dance off to the wayside. The postcards caught the fire and burst up red and orange, caught up all the words in a hot, destructive swoop, and took them off. It was as if those words had seen the light some people see when dying, the light of the brain going off somewhere, a small round beacon in the heart of the flames. The words curled in on themselves, broke apart into syllables and fragments, fell away from all syntax and semantics, and were gone. William's words, the words of every unfortunate soul who has come and gone upon the earth, unsettled. As Rosemary was most surely unsettled. "I don't know, Uncle Bishop," she'd told him earlier. "Maybe I'll join the Peace Corps." And she had answered Robbie, too, as best she could. "I don't know, Robbie, perhaps I'll ask the Fergusons to take care of Winston. The birds will find other food. Maybe I'll put the big old house up for sale.

Go to Europe myself and gaze firsthand upon masterpieces." Maybe she would go back to Bixley High School one day, if she had no place else to go. But, in the meantime, high school students would have to learn to hate Puritan literature without her. "I'll find a man when I'm ready, Miriam. Until then, I leave them all to you and, no, regardless of what I do, I'll probably never wear a bra, so please stop using them as stocking stuffers."

Rosemary stared, enchanted, at the dying flames in the gray metallic wastebasket. "Was Icarus afraid, William? The chickadee, Mrs. Abernathy, weighs one-third of an ounce." She watched as the fire settled down to become embers, small glowing dots, like orange campsites spread across the nighttime savanna, where the bones of old ancestors, millions of years old, still lie huddled.

Outside, the handmade angels had already disappeared. A long, steady wind buffeted the house, fiercely. The gods, angry and threatening, shook the house and it heaved on its foundation in the force of the gale, the force of the old myths born in caves, in winter-whipped nightmares, in the lightning flash itself. The gods were doing their jobs. The sharp clear voices of the mortals came up to her from below, little birds winging, filled with the treble of their ancestors' first guttural grunts. The humans were doing their jobs. Rosemary looked one more time at William's last work. *Rosie and Mugs: Life as Usual.*

"Bullshit," Rosemary said softly. What had she always told him? "You get to know people only so that you can paint them, William. The art transcends the human being." But did he think that with pig hairs and colors he could nail *her* to a piece of canvas? What was it that Aunt Rachel had said of William? *He wasn't a very good soldier, Rosemary.* And what was it Shakespeare had said of soldiers, in the very book that William had loved so, the book that he had left behind on her bookshelf? *Then the soldier, seeking the bubble reputation, even in the cannon's mouth.* Rosemary raised her glass to the painting.

"To you, dear heart," she toasted him, his last work. She had come out of the fire scathed but three-dimensional. She had avoided the cannon's cruel blast, and where was William? In what dimension did he hang his canvases these days?

"Good-bye, William," Rosemary said, and flicked out the light, closed the door, left William's *idea of her* hanging where it had always hung, in his mind, in the enveloping dark. She would continue to miss him dearly. But for whatever reason, no matter how just or unjust, there was a small round organ inside her, receiving blood from the veins and pumping it through the arteries. Dilating and contracting. And there was a mass of nerve tissue in her cranium receiving sensory impulses and transmitting motor impulses. She was alive.

At the top of the stairs she stood and looked down the sharp decline. Fifteen steps. Fifteen wicked places to hit and bounce and bruise. "Was the Great Wallenda afraid, William? Did the astronauts cry out?"

Wind and snow rocked the house. It was a house with something cooking in it, with warm yellow lights, and with human voices rising and falling like old water beating against cave walls. *Today Bixley. Tomorrow?* Her hand grasped the stair rail and for a moment she dreamed the old dream of falling, the cosmos tossing her back to earth in a melding of sea and sky.

"Bullshit," Rosemary said again, and took the dangerous steps two at a time.